Don't miss a single word of J.D. Barker's riveting trilogy!

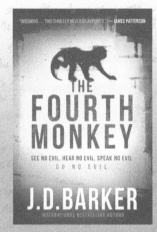
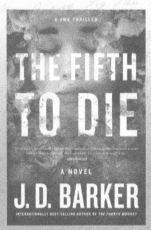

D1426298

The
Sixth Wicked Child

J. D. Barker

The Sixth Wicked Child

Published by:
Hampton Creek Press
P.O. Box 177
New Castle, NH 03854

Hampton Creek Press is a registered Trademark of Hampton Creek Publishing, LLC

Cover Design by Stuart Bache
Book design and formatting by Maureen Cutajar,
www.gopublished.com
Author photograph by Bill Peterson of Peterson Gallery

Hardcover ISBN-13: 978-0-9906949-7-7
eBook ISBN: 978-0-9906949-8-4
Paperback ISBN-13: 978-0-9906949-9-1

For Truth

Welcome to the final show.
Hope you're wearing your best clothes.

—*Sign of the Times,* HARRY STYLES

Daddy what else did you leave for me?
Daddy, what'd'ja leave behind for me?

—*Another Brick in the Wall,* PINK FLOYD

The
Sixth Wicked Child

1

Tray

Day 5 • 5:19 AM

"Hey, shithead, this look like a fucking bed-and-breakfast to you?"

The voice was gruff, gravelly. At this hour, it had to be a cop, security guard, or maybe just an angry homeowner. Whoever it was, Tray Stouffer didn't move within the folds of the musty quilt. Sometimes, when you're still enough, they go away. Sometimes, they get bored.

The boot came again—fast, hard. Direct hit to the stomach.

Tray wanted to shout out, to grab the leg and fight back. Didn't, though. Remained perfectly still.

"Goddamn it, I'm talking to you!"

Another kick, harder than the last, right in the ribs.

Tray grunted, couldn't help it. Pulled the quilt tighter.

"Do you have any idea what you and your friends do to resale value when you camp out here? You scare the kids half to death. The older folk won't leave the building. They shouldn't have to step over a piece of garbage like you just to run to the store."

Homeowner, then.

Tray had heard it all before.

"Do you know what *I'm* doing out here at five in the morning while you're taking a nap? While you're all snug on our front stoop? I just got off a ten-hour shift at Delphine's Bakery. Did twelve hours the night before in that devil's asshole of a kitchen. Gotta go back in another ten. I do that to pay for this place. I do that to contribute. You'll never catch me living on the streets like you lazy shits. Get a damn job! Make something of yourself!"

At fourteen, there was no work. Not the legal kind. Not without some kind of parental consent, and *that* was never going to happen.

Tray braced for another kick.

Instead, the man grabbed ahold of the quilt and yanked it away, tossed it to the side. The quilt landed in a slushy puddle of half-melted snow at the base of the steps.

Tray shivered, coiled up, ready for another kick.

"Hey, you're a chick. You're just a kid," the man said, the anger dropping from his voice. "I'm really sorry. What's your name?"

"Tracy," she said. "Most people call me Tray." She regretted the words the moment they left her lips. She knew what happened whenever she talked to one of them. Best to keep her mouth shut, stay invisible.

The man knelt down, a paper sack dangling from his left hand. He wasn't very old, maybe mid-twenties. Heavy coat. Brown hair tucked under a navy blue watch cap. Hazel eyes. Whatever was in the sack smelled delicious.

He caught her looking at it. "Tray, my name is Emmitt. Are you hungry?"

She nodded. Knowing this too was a mistake. But she *was* hungry. So hungry.

He reached into the paper sack and took out a small loaf of bread. Steam floated from the crusty surface through the icy Chicago air, and for a moment Tray forgot about the bitter wind coming off the lake, howling through the street each time it kicked up.

Her stomach gurgled, loud enough for both of them to hear.

Emmitt tore off a piece of bread and handed it to her. She devoured it in two bites, barely bothering to chew. Possibly the best bread she'd ever eaten.

"Do you want more?"

Tray nodded, although she knew she shouldn't.

Emmitt let out a breath. He reached out and stroked her cheek with the side of his pointer finger. Drifting from her face to her neck, slipping beneath the collar of her sweater. "Why don't you come inside with me? You can have all the bread you want. I've got more food, too. A warm shower. A comfortable bed. I'll—"

With both arms, Tray slammed the man in his shoulders. He had been precariously balanced, kneeling down on one knee like that, and he wasn't prepared for the blow. He rolled backward, the sack tumbled from his hands, and his head slammed into the metal railing of the building's staircase.

"You little bitch!" he shouted.

Before he could get up, Tray was on her feet. She grabbed the paper sack, scooped up her backpack, and raced down the five steps, snagged her quilt, and took off down Mercer. He wouldn't chase her; they rarely did, but sometimes—

"Stay the hell away from here! I catch you again, I'm calling the cops!"

When Tray did risk a glance back, Emmitt had stood, gathered up his things, and was pushing through the door into the building. Even from this distance, she imagined she could feel the warmth of that hallway.

She didn't slow until she reached the gates of Rose Hill Cemetery. At this hour, they were locked, but she was thin, and a moment later she had wriggled through the wrought iron bars to the other side, pulling her backpack and quilt behind her.

Chicago had its share of shelters, but she'd gone that route before. At this hour, they'd be locked tight. They all locked their doors somewhere between 7 p.m. and midnight, and none would admit you after hours. Even if they did, it wouldn't matter. They'd be full. Sometimes the lines started as early as noon, and there was never enough room. Besides, Tray felt safer on the streets. There were "Emmitts" everywhere, especially in the shelters, and the only thing worse than running into an Emmitt on the stoop of some building or in an alley shielded from the wind was being locked overnight in a shelter with one. Sometimes more than one. Emmitts tended to stick together and hunt in packs.

Tray wasn't afraid of the cemetery. After two years on the streets, she'd slept in them all at least once. Rose Hill was one of her favorites on account of the mausoleums. Unlike Oakwood or Graceland, Rose Hill didn't lock the mausoleums at night. And while there were several security guards, on a cold night like tonight, they'd be in the office playing cards, watching television, or even sleeping. She'd seen them enough through the windows.

She stomped up Tranquility Lane through the fresh snow. She wasn't too worried about the tracks behind her; she knew the wind would take care of those. There was no reason to take chances, though, so when she reached the top of the hill, rather than making the left at Bliss Road, she cut across Tranquility and ducked down into the small patch of woods running along the side of Bliss.

Although there were no lights, the moon was nearly full, and when the reflecting pond came into view, Tray couldn't help but stop and look at it. The icy surface glistened under the thin layer of fresh snow. Marble statues stood silently along the edge of the water, stone benches between them. This was such a peaceful place. So quiet.

Tray didn't see her at first, the girl kneeling at the water's edge, facing away. Long, blonde hair trailing down her back. She looked like one of the statues, unmoving, facing the pond like that. Her skin was so pale, nearly white, almost as colorless as her white dress. She wore no shoes on her bare feet, no coat, only the white dress made of a material so thin it was nearly translucent. Her hands were clasped together near her breasts as if lost in prayer, her head tilted to one side.

Tray didn't speak, but drew closer. Close enough to realize the thin layer of snow that covered everything else covered this girl, too. And when she circled around to her side, she realized it wasn't a girl at all but a woman. The stark whiteness of her, every inch of her, was broken by the thin line of red stretching from under her hair down the side of her face. There was another line from the side of her left eye, a stream of red tears, and yet a third from the corner of her mouth—this one painting her lips the brightest rose.

Something was written on her forehead.

Wait, not written.

At her knees, sitting in the snow, was a silver serving tray. The kind you might find at a fancy dinner party, a high-priced restaurant, the sort of place Tray already knew, even at fourteen, she'd never see in her lifetime outside of television or the movies.

On that tray were three small, white boxes. Each sealed tight with black string.

Behind the boxes, propped up against the woman's chest, was a cardboard sign not unlike the ones Tray had held to raise money for food. Only she had never used these three particular words before. The sign simply read:

FATHER, FORGIVE ME

Tray did the only thing she could do. She ran.

2

Poole

Hello Sam,

I imagine you're confused.

I imagine you have questions.

I know I did. I have. I do.

Questions are the foundation of knowledge, learning, discovery, and rediscovery. An inquisitive mind has no outer walls. An inquisitive mind is a warehouse with unlimited square footage, a memory palace of infinite rooms and floors and shiny pretty things. Sometimes, though, a mind suffers damage, a wall crumbles, the memory palace is in need of a renovation, rooms found in dire disrepair. Your mind, I'm afraid, falls into the latter category. The photographs around you, the diaries to your side, these are the keys that will aid you as you dig from the rubble, as you rebuild.

I'm here for you, Sam.

I'll be here for you as I always have been.

I've forgiven you, Sam. Perhaps others will, too. You're not that man anymore. You've become so much more.

—Anson

"What am I looking at?" Special Agent Frank Poole grumbled, setting the printout aside. He closed his eyes and pressed the heels of his palms against his temples. He had the worst headache. He tried to sleep on the jet back from New Orleans, but that proved impossible. The sat phone rang off the hook. There was the FBI's New Orleans field office, still crawling over Sarah Werner's law office and the apartment above—only nine hours ago, Poole had discovered the attorney's body staring up at him from her couch, watching him through milky eyes, the rotten remains of dinner across her lap, a small, black bullet hole in the center of her forehead. The medical examiner confirmed she had been dead for weeks, much longer than Poole initially thought. Positively identified as Sarah Werner, this meant the woman seen with Detective Sam Porter over the past several days, who claimed to be Sarah Werner, was not. She was some kind of imposter, a plant. Together, they broke a female prisoner out of the local jail and transported her across the country to Chicago.

Between calls with the New Orleans field office, Porter's partner lit up the sat phone line. They found Porter in the Guyon, an abandoned hotel in Chicago. The female prisoner he helped escape was in the lobby, shot dead. Porter sat nearly catatonic in a room on the fourth floor, surrounded by photos of himself with known serial killer Anson Bishop, the Four Monkey Killer, a stack of composition books at his side, and a laptop with the above message on the screen.

From what he had been told, Chicago Metro tied the laptop to a bizarre round of killings over the past several days—several young girls drowned and resuscitated until their bodies finally gave out, and adults murdered in a multitude of ways, all of them associated with the medical care of a man named Paul Upchurch, currently in surgery at Stroger Hospital.

When Poole wasn't on the sat phone with the New Orleans field office or Detective Nash, he was on with Detective Clair Norton, who was at the hospital, fielding some kind of outbreak. An outbreak triggered by Bishop, Upchurch, and possibly others.

The only person who hadn't called the sat phone was his immediate supervisor, SAIC Hurless, and Poole knew that that call would come soon enough and he damn well better have some answers before it did.

"Let me talk to him," Detective Nash said from somewhere behind him in the observation room.

Poole's head remained buried in his hands. "No way."

On the other side of the one-way observation window, Porter sat slumped in a metal chair, his body hunched over the matching metal table. He wasn't handcuffed. Poole was having second thoughts about that.

"He'll talk to me," Nash insisted.

Porter hadn't spoken to anyone. He hadn't uttered a word.

"No."

"Sam's not a bad guy. He's not part of this."

"He's knee deep in it."

"Not Sam."

"The woman he broke out of prison was found dead of a gunshot wound from the gun found with him. GSR all over his hand. He made no attempt to hide the weapon or run. He sat there waiting for you to arrest him."

"We don't know he killed her."

"He's not denying that he did," Poole countered.

"He wouldn't kill her unless it was self-defense."

Poole ignored him. "He called Detective Norton at Stroger Hospital and gave her information he simply could not possess unless he was involved. He knew Upchurch had glioblastoma. How did he even know Upchurch's name? He knew about both girls. Details he couldn't possibly know if he were straight."

"You heard Clair. She said Bishop told him."

"Bishop told him," Poole repeated with frustration. "Bishop told him that he injected the two missing girls with the SARS virus. Left them in that house with Upchurch like some kind of Trojan horse."

Poole was still trying to wrap his head around that part, too. Kati Quigley and Larissa Biel, both missing, both found in Upchurch's house. Porter claimed they had been injected with some variation of the SARS virus. The entire hospital was on lockdown while they ran blood work to determine whether or not the claim was true. At best, it was some kind of hoax. At worst...

"Bishop is playing him," Nash said. "That's what he does."

"He told Clair he fucked up. He told her he was sorry. An innocent man doesn't say those things."

"A guilty man runs. He doesn't sit in a room and wait for the cops to come and get him. He hides his tracks, he disappears."

Poole said, "He stole evidence. He defied orders. He ran off to New Orleans, broke one woman out of jail, and left a dead body behind. Another one here. This is precisely why you can't talk to him: You're too close to see it. Forget he's your partner, forget he's your friend. Look at the evidence, look at him as an unsub. Until you're able to do that, you can't be objective. And if you're not objective, you're part of the problem."

Poole picked up the printout and studied the text again. "Where's the laptop now?"

"Our IT department upstairs."

"Call up there and tell them to bag it. I don't want your people touching it. Your entire team is compromised. The FBI lab will take it apart and analyze the data," Poole said. "What about the photographs and composition books you found in the room with him?"

Nash said nothing.

"Don't make me ask again."

"The photographs are still at the Guyon Hotel, room 405. I had the room photographed and taped off. I've got a uniform watching the floor, two more outside the building," Nash said. "I brought the composition books back here and checked them into evidence myself."

"Leave everything as is. Your people touch nothing from here on out."

Nash didn't reply.

Poole stood, the motion causing his head to throb like a bowling ball was rolling from one side of his skull to the other and smacking the walls. He rubbed his temples again. "Look, I'm doing you a favor here. Whatever is going on with Sam, if this makes it to a courtroom, you and your team need to distance yourselves. Any attorney worth his or her salt will tear the case apart if you don't. They'll start with Sam, then you, Clair, Klozowski, anything you've touched. From here out, you're an observer. All of you. Anything else is professional suicide."

"I don't desert my friends."

"No, but sometimes they desert you."

Poole reached for the door to the interview room, pulled it open, and stepped inside. The metallic clink as that door closed was one of the loudest sounds he ever heard.

3

Clair

Day 5 • 5:36 AM

Clair sneezed.

"Fuck me," Klozowski muttered, watching her from across the room in their temporary office in an old exam room at John H. Stroger, Jr. Hospital.

"The proper response is 'bless you,'" Clair said before blowing her nose.

"My skin feels clammy. My throat's dry. I'm achy all over," Klozowski said. "You know what we have to look forward to? Diarrhea comes next. Nothing worse than the shits when you're not in the comfort of your own home. After that, all our internal organs will start to melt and turn into mush, our eyes too. We're both going to exit this world as a puddle of waste. That's not how I expected to go out. When I joined the police force, I always figured I'd die in some glorific gun battle, or a raid, or some kind of SWAT takedown. Not like this."

"*Glorific* isn't a word," Clair said. "And you're in the IT department. None of those things happen to members of the nerd herd. You're more likely to die from a paper cut or some horrible pocket-protector mishap." She wadded up her tissue and tossed it into the trash can under the table that still held all of Upchurch's medical records. "You've got the symptoms wrong, too. You're thinking of Ebola. SARS won't melt our organs."

"Well, yay for that, I guess."

Clair nodded at Klozowski's laptop. "Do you have a total for me?"

"You don't want to know."

"I need to."

"Twenty-three," he said.

Clair perked up at this. "That's not as many as I thought. This could be much worse."

Klozowski waved a finger. "We identified twenty-three potential victims from Upchurch's file and brought them here to the hospital, along with their families. If you include spouses and children, our total rises to eighty-seven."

"Oh, balls," Clair said.

Once they realized Upchurch and his partner were killing the people responsible for the perceived failure of his medical care, Clair had rounded them all up and brought them here to the hospital, thinking it was the only place they could keep such a large group of people safe. Upchurch and his partner had counted on this—they infected Upchurch's last two victims—Larissa Biel and Kati Quigley—with a contagious pathogen, knowing the girls would be brought here, too, as the closest hospital.

In just a few short hours, they exposed not only the rest of the people Upchurch wanted dead but also everyone else in the hospital. Which included Clair Norton and Edwin Klozowski.

Porter had called her to not only tell her this but also to tell her the pathogen was SARS and Upchurch's partner was Anson Bishop. The entire hospital immediately went under lockdown. Per protocol, the hospital notified the Center for Disease Control, and they immediately dispatched a response team from their local quarantine station at Chicago's O'Hare Airport. They arrived within twenty-seven minutes. Kloz timed them. He checked his own temperature four times while waiting.

Clair was still trying to make sense of that last conversation with Porter.

The man who called her didn't sound like the man she knew.

He sounded defeated, broken.

Sam knew things he shouldn't.

When Nash and SWAT raided Upchurch's house, they found Upchurch in a little girl's bedroom upstairs. There was no little girl, though; only a mannequin dressed in girl's clothing, surrounded by stuffed animals and drawings. The girl turned out to be nothing but a character in some failed comic book Upchurch had created. He willingly gave himself up. In the basement, they found Larissa Biel, drugged and unconscious. They later learned she swallowed glass. At first, they thought Upchurch had forced her to do this, but it turned out she had swallowed the glass herself in an attempt to prevent him from using her as he did the others. In a written statement, she explained that Upchurch had been drowning girls to the point of death, then bringing them back to life, all as part of some twisted attempt to learn if there was life after death. When she swallowed the glass, she was damaged, no longer a viable test subject.

Clair couldn't imagine making such a decision. The strength Larissa Biel demonstrated by taking her fate away from such a madman and back into her own hands was incredible. Biel was currently in recovery post-surgery to remove the glass and correct damage to her throat, vocal cords, and stomach. Although she was expected to recover from the injuries suffered in the Upchurch house, she had also begun to demonstrate symptoms of the virus that Anson Bishop had injected into her damaged body. Whether or not she would recover from that was yet to be seen.

In the kitchen of the Upchurch house, unconscious and lying on the table, they found the body of Kati Quigley. In her hand was a small white box tied with a black string, Anson Bishop's signature. Inside that box was a key for a locker in this hospital. Within that locker, they found Paul Upchurch's medical records and an apple with a syringe embedded in it. According to Porter, that syringe contained a pure sample of the pathogen. Bishop told him if Upchurch died, he would unleash the pathogen on a larger scale somewhere else in the city.

Snow White didn't know better, either, Porter had said.

Paul Upchurch, currently in surgery himself after collapsing in police custody, suffered from glioblastoma. Stage four brain cancer. Porter went on to tell Clair that she needed to track down someone named Dr. Ryan Beyer, a neurosurgeon at Johns Hopkins. She had tasked Klozowski with that—he found him in under ten minutes. At that point, Clair called Frank Poole with the FBI, and he made arrangements to transport Dr. Beyer from Baltimore to Chicago aboard one of the FBI's private jets. The flight left Washington International Thurgood Marshall Airport at shortly after midnight and arrived at O'Hare at 2:21 in the morning. From there, a police escort brought Dr. Beyer to Stroger Hospital, where he was routed around those who had been infected and rushed to a surgical suite on the third floor where Upchurch waited, prepped by a local team. Upchurch and Bishop had killed numerous people because they felt he didn't receive the care required to properly treat his illness. For better or worse, his actions bounced him to the top of a very long list—the predominant specialist in the field now poking around in his head.

Someone knocked at their door.

Sue Miflin, an orderly with the hospital, looked inside. "Detective? Dr. Beyer has stepped out of the OR. He'd like a word with you."

4

Poole

Detective Sam Porter of Chicago Metro didn't look up when Poole entered the interview room. He didn't acknowledge his presence at all. He remained still, oblivious to the events around him, his lips lost in some private conversation. His eyes watched his hands. His fingers twitched, but the motion didn't appear voluntary. Poole was reminded of the moments before someone drifted off to sleep, those sudden jerks and spasms the body did to work out the last bit of consciousness. Porter was far from sleep, though. His eyes held the sharpness of a tweaker, a meth-head, someone who just snorted their third line of coke. Hypersensitive, spastic, rabid yet calculating. A mind racing with complex thoughts that made sense to no one else.

Poole didn't know Sam Porter well, no better than he knew the rest of the original 4MK task force, but he knew people. Poole prided himself on his ability to size someone up with a glance, to understand a person's motivations and fears, their intellect and misgivings. When he first met Detective Porter, his instincts told him Porter was a good cop. Poole believed he truly wished to catch the Four Monkey Killer and put him behind bars. He recognized Porter as a sharp, seasoned member of law enforcement both respected and admired by his peers. The kind of man Poole himself strived to be every day he carried a badge. Although Porter had said very little during the brief time they knew each other, Poole was certain the man understood much. He didn't jump to conclusions; he followed the evidence. He cared for the victims and he fought for their memories. He sought justice for those left behind.

The Detective Sam Porter Frank Poole knew was a righteous man.

The man sitting in the interview room was not *that* Sam Porter. This person was a shell.

This man was broken.

His rumpled clothing smelled of sweat and dirt. He hadn't shaved in days. His spastic eyes, twitching this way and that, were bloodshot, looking out from above deep, dark, bags, heavy with lack of sleep.

Poole lowered himself into the chair opposite Porter and folded his hands on the table. "Sam?"

Porter continued to stare at his own hands, his lips still lost in a conversation only he could hear.

Poole snapped his fingers.

Nothing.

"Can you hear me, Sam?"

Nothing.

Poole raised his right hand and brought his open palm down on the top of the table with all the force he could muster.

It hurt like hell.

Porter looked up. His eyes narrowed. "Frank."

He said Poole's name not as a question, not as some sort of recognition, but merely as a statement of fact. The single word was uttered in one quiet breath, barely spoken at all.

"We need to talk, Sam."

Porter leaned back in the chair, his eyes dropping back to his hands. "I want to speak to Sarah Werner."

"She's dead."

Porter cocked his head. "What?"

"Killed with a single gunshot wound to the head, at least three weeks ago. I found her sitting on her couch in her apartment in New Orleans."

Porter shook his head. "Not her, the other one. The other Sarah Werner."

"Tell me where to find her, and I'll bring her in."

Porter said nothing.

"Were you aware she killed the real Sarah Werner?"

"We don't know that she did."

Based on the estimated time of death, they were certain Porter was still in Chicago when the real Sarah Werner was murdered. Porter was right about the other part. Aside from assuming her identity, they had no proof she killed the other woman.

Poole said, "*Your* Sarah Werner, the impostor, do you know who she really is?"

"Do you?"

"I know with your help she broke another woman out of prison in New Orleans. A woman believed to be the mother of Anson Bishop— 4MK. I know the two of you transported that fugitive across numerous state lines and brought her back to Chicago. I know that woman was then murdered last night at the Guyon Hotel with a gun that was found in your possession shortly after. I know she's in the wind, and you didn't have time or inclination to wash the gunshot residue from your hands before SWAT showed up." Poole let out a sigh. "I know enough. Now, why don't you tell me what I don't know."

"She's Bishop's mother," Porter said quietly.

"The dead woman? That's what I said."

"Not the dead woman, the one who was with me. The other Sarah Werner. The fake Sarah Werner. Right before she left with Bishop, after *he* shot the prisoner, they told me *she* was Bishop's mother."

"Do you believe them? After everything he's put you through?"

Porter's eyes dropped back to his fidgeting hands. "I need to read the diaries, all the diaries, everything he left in that room. It's all there. Everything we need. All the answers. All there. All there."

"Sam, you're rambling. You need rest."

Porter looked up, leaned in toward Poole. "I need to read those diaries."

Poole shook his head. "Not a chance."

"The answers are in those diaries."

"I think the diaries are bullshit," Poole said.

Porter quickly shook his head. "I found the lake. The house. You saw it all, right? You were there. I know you were there. They're real." His voice dropped low, conspiratorial. "There's a bloodstain in the basement, right where he said it would be. Right where Carter died."

"Let's talk about that, Sam. Is that the first time you've been to Simpsonville, South Carolina? To 12 Jenkins Crawl Road?"

Porter glared at him, puzzled. "What? Of course. Why?"

"When I arrived in Simpsonville, I reviewed the property records with the local sheriff. Your name is on the deed."

Porter didn't seem to hear him. He said, "Did you find Carter in the lake?"

"We pulled six bodies from the lake. Five full bodies, another chopped up, in trash bags."

"Carter," Porter said softly.

"The property records, Sam. Why are they in your name?"

Porter was staring at his hand again, his lips moving soundlessly.

"Sam?"

His head shot back up. "What?"

"Why is your name on the deed for 12 Jenkins Crawl Road?"

Porter waved a hand through the air. "That's just Bishop. Forged, faked, swapped…doesn't matter. He did it, and it doesn't matter." He sat back in his chair, a grin growing on his lips. "You found Carter. You…found…Carter. Holy shit, you found Carter."

Poole watched the other man's hands, still twitching on the table. Porter seemed unaware. "You're not well, Sam. You need to rest."

Porter slammed both hands down on the table and leaned forward. "I need to read those diaries!"

"Who are the other five bodies we pulled from that lake?"

"I have no idea."

"It's your property."

Porter opened his mouth as if to answer, then went quiet again. His eyes fell back to his hands. He weaved his fingers together, pulled them back apart. "This is Bishop. This is what he does. He fills the world with lies."

"If that's the case, why do you believe the diaries?" Poole asked. "If Bishop isn't to be believed, why do you care what's in those books?"

Porter looked back up, hopeful. "Where are they now? Still at the Guyon Hotel?"

"I asked you a question, Sam."

"Your other five bodies will be in those books."

"You don't know that."

Porter leaned in closer. A thin trail of spittle glistened on the corner of his mouth. "We know it's true because you found Carter, right where he said he put him. We know it's true because there's a bloodstain in the basement—there's a lock on the refrigerator. He wants us to know what happened. The rest—my name on some deed—that's your smoke and mirrors, that's your bullshit, *that's* what you have to see through."

Poole leaned back in his chair, his eyes never leaving the man sitting across from him. This time, Porter's gaze didn't falter, either.

Porter's voice dropped low. *"Her name was Rose Finicky, and she deserved to die, she deserved to die a hundred times over—hardly pure at all."*

"What?"

"That's what Bishop told me right after he shot her in the head."

"The woman we found in the lobby of the Guyon?"

Porter nodded. "The other woman, the woman I thought was Sarah Werner, she's Bishop's mother. He used me to get them both to Chicago. He said he had a bomb."

"You have GSR on your hand from that weapon."

"I got the gun away from him and fired a warning shot. I didn't shoot her. He did."

"If you had the gun, why did you let them both leave? Why not take them into custody?"

"You know why."

"Because of what you told Clair?"

Porter nodded. "He injected those girls with the SARS virus and left a sample at the hospital in an apple to prove he had the real thing. He told me he had more, and if I didn't let them walk, he made arrangements to spread the virus. I couldn't chance he was telling the truth. I had to let them go. He told me I had to make the call from room 405. He said I'd find more evidence there."

"You did what he told you?"

"What choice did I have?"

Poole wanted to tell him he had many choices. Porter had made many decisions from the first moment he took on this case until the present, and he continued to go through the wrong door. His vision had been so clouded he might as well be blind. The rabbit hole was deep, and he and Bishop appeared to be taking turns with the shovel.

"There's something else. Something you need to know." The light in Porter's eyes flickered, like a bulb caught in a power surge. He blinked. Focused on Poole. "Some parts of the diary are true—the houses, the lake, the Carters—I think all that is accurate, but others are not. I see that now. It's in the cadence of the writing, the word choice. He left clues. I think I can tell the difference. That Beaver Cleaver shimmer, I can see through it. You saw it too, right?"

Poole was growing frustrated. "Those diaries are a distraction."

"No!" The word came from Porter at a much louder volume than he must have intended, because he shrank back at the sound of it, settled himself deeper in the chair. "No, those diaries are key to it all. We just have to solve the puzzle."

"All I need to do is catch a killer."

"*Killers,*" Porter replied.

"What?"

"Right before they left me in that hotel, Bishop's mother said, "'Why would you tell this nice man your father was dead.' She was talking about the diary." Porter leaned forward again. "Don't you get it? I see it now. The words scream off the page at me. The falsities and the truth, it's like they're printed in different colors, I see them so clearly. You saw Libby McInley's body—I don't think Bishop killed her. I think he was trying to protect her. If it wasn't Bishop…" His fingers were twisting together again, weaving, kneading invisible dough. "They're all killers—his mother, his father, and Bishop, and I think all three of them are here in Chicago, right now. The three of them are finishing something that started years ago, something that began way back in Bishop's childhood. Something in those diaries. Something true hidden in the mess of lies." He started to nod, a grin rolling over his lips. "Something I can see now." He looked up at Poole. "You need to trust me."

Poole stared at him, and the seconds ticked by. "Some people believe you might be Anson Bishop's father."

The spittle fell from Porter's mouth, dropped to the metal table in a small puddle. He wiped at his lip and looked Poole dead in the eye. "What do you think?"

"I think we found compelling evidence in your room at the Guyon."

Porter snickered. "Photographs? Come on. You know how easily those can be faked."

"Some of those pictures date back more than twenty years," Poole replied. "Even if he wanted to fake them, where would Bishop get twenty-year-old images of you to work with? How long have you known him, Sam?"

"Less than half a year," Porter replied. "I met him the same day Nash did—with the bus accident, when he was pretending to work for Chicago Metro. Give me a polygraph if that will ease your mind, I don't care. I've got nothing to hide. The pictures are no different than the property deed—he's trying to distract you from the truth."

"The truth only you can see in his diaries."

Porter said nothing to this. His mind had gone elsewhere again.

Poole tried not to let the frustration show in his face. "Who is Rose Finicky?"

"You need to let me read the diaries. You know he wouldn't have left them if they weren't important. At the very least, you understand that."

"I'll have my people go through them."

"We don't have time. They don't know what to look for. They can't see through the bullshit to the truth. I know Bishop."

"Do you?" Poole countered. "How well?"

Someone knocked on the one-way window. A heavy fist. Two quick hits.

Poole remained still for a moment, his eyes fixed on Porter, Porter glaring back. He couldn't read him. He wanted to, but he couldn't. If Porter was lying, his body language didn't betray him. He believed everything he said.

That doesn't make it true, Poole reminded himself.

He stood, went to the door.

From behind him, Porter said, "You can't catch him without me. You can't catch any of them."

5

Clair

Day 5 • 5:43 AM

Clair looked up at the nurse standing in the doorway of their office. The woman had been on duty since they arrived and looked no better than the rest of them—bloodshot eyes, dark bags, slouched. She hadn't slowed down, though. Clair didn't think she had even taken a break.

"The doctor's on line four," she said, nodding at the phone on the wall.

Clair thanked her and got to her feet. Her body creaked more than the old metal chair she'd called home for the past several hours.

Her everything hurt.

Her bones were sore. Her throat. Even her eyes throbbed. Her nose had turned into a snot factory, and she couldn't get warm.

Kloz watched her wearily from his own corner of the room. He didn't appear to be in any better shape.

She crossed to the phone, picked up the receiver, and pressed the illuminated button. "This is Detective Norton."

"Detective? Dr. Beyer here."

Due to the quarantine, she had yet to meet the man in person. She told herself he probably looked like a cross between George Clooney, Patrick Dempsey, and that cute guy from *Scrubs* because that made her smile and she really needed something to smile about. His voice was low, gruff, filled with sand. The voice of a man who spent a lifetime choosing his words very carefully before speaking.

He cleared his throat and told her exactly what she didn't want to hear. "This is a hopeless case. You know that, right? There is no saving this man."

Clair glanced back at Kloz. He'd stopped doing whatever computer stuff he'd been doing and was watching her. She pressed the receiver against her ear and lowered her voice. "If that man dies, there's a good chance Anson Bishop will release the SARS virus somewhere in the city. Thousands of lives could be at risk."

"That doesn't change the facts, Detective. This man is at the end stage of glioblastoma. A large portion of his brain has been compromised by a very aggressive tumor. I removed what I could, but it's simply impossible to repair the damage left behind. I'm frankly surprised he is still alive. Aside from loss of memory and motor function, the cancer has invaded his posterior parietal cortex, primary motor cortex, and supplementary. Post-surgery, at the very least, he'll require a ventilator. We've noted abnormalities in his heart rhythm, and I believe his vision has been compromised. His quality of life..."

Clair closed her eyes as the doctor droned on. "We were told you could save him, that you had some kind of treatment—"

"My studies at Hopkins are in focused ultrasound therapy," Dr. Beyer interrupted. "A noninvasive treatment for glioblastoma, but we're in the very early stages of clinical trials. Had he been referred to me at the onset a few years ago, perhaps I would have been able to help him, but now? The disease has progressed too far. There is no known treatment or path to wellness from here. We're too late."

"What else can you do?"

"Nothing that hasn't already been done. Stabilize him, make him comfortable, wait for the inevitable. I'd be surprised if he lasted more than a day or two in his current condition."

Clair glanced over at Kloz. He had this hopeful look in his eyes. She turned away from him and spoke again. "I need you to tell the press Paul Upchurch came out of surgery better than expected. He's stable. And you plan to take him back to Hopkins to continue his treatment the moment he's able to travel. You need to convince them you're hopeful of his outcome."

Dr. Beyer didn't reply.

Clair glanced down at her watch. "Doctor, Anson Bishop is still out there somewhere. We need him to believe we're doing everything we can, that Upchurch is receiving the treatment he insisted on. You don't have to go into detail—blame privacy laws for lack of information—just leave them with that impression."

"Detective, I have a responsibility to my patient, a reputation—"

"Your actions could potentially save thousands of lives. That man, Paul Upchurch, kidnapped and murdered multiple girls. Two of his victims are here in this very hospital, fighting for their lives. When he dies, nobody will do a more elaborate happy dance than me, but as far as the public is concerned, *as far as Anson Bishop is concerned*, his prognosis needs to appear positive. At least for now."

He didn't say anything for a long time. "I'll need to think about that, Detective. Maybe speak to my attorney. What if Bishop has someone in the hospital watching this situation, reporting to him? I don't personally know any of the people who were in that operating room with me. My team is in Baltimore back at Hopkins."

Clair sighed and picked at her tangled hair. "I'm stuck in this room. I need you to talk to them, too. Explain what's at stake."

"You're asking a lot, Detective."

"Will you do it?"

"I'll get back to you."

He hung up before she could say anything else. Clair stood there for a few moments before replacing the receiver.

"Well, how is he?" Kloz asked.

"Peachy."

Before he could reply, someone else knocked on their door. Through the window, Clair recognized Jarred Maltby from the CDC. He didn't look happy.

6

Poole

The number of people in the observation room had grown by two since Poole stepped in with Porter. In addition to Nash, Captain Henry Dalton was there along with someone Poole didn't recognize.

Although Dalton was nearly a half foot shorter than Poole, he carried an air of authority with him that made him seem larger than he was. And even though it was only five something in the morning, he appeared neatly shaven, showered, and fresh. Poole would kill for a shower right now.

"You can't hold him," Dalton said, dispensing with pleasantries.

"The hell I can't."

"If the press gets wind that you have him in custody, they'll crucify him."

"I imagine you've been briefed, Captain. That man crucified himself. Not only is he a suspect in the murder at the Guyon, he's wanted for breaking the dead woman out of prison in New Orleans, transporting her across state lines. He defied your orders and left Chicago on some vigilante chase for Bishop. He's an obvious flight risk. He's not going anywhere. I don't care what the press says." Poole glared at the other man in the room. "Who are you?"

Dressed in a dark blue suit with neatly cropped white hair, the fiftyish man offered his hand. "I'm Anthony Warnick, with the mayor's office."

Poole didn't shake his hand. Instead, he turned back to Dalton. "I'll need to see all of Porter's employment records—background checks, psych screenings, evaluations—everything you have on him. I need to piece together his past."

"I think you need to take a step back and think about all this," Dalton said. "We all do."

Warnick stepped up. "Agent, it would be irresponsible to implicate a member of law enforcement in crimes as heinous as those committed by Anson Bishop without fully understanding all the facts. Members of the press are like hungry stray dogs. They'll take whatever scrap you throw at them and run with it, consequences be damned. Somebody captures an image of you doing some kind of perp walk with Detective Porter, and not only will *he* be victimized, but all of law enforcement will be, including your agency. They won't draw the line at him. They'll see all of you as corrupt. This city can't handle that, not now. With recent events, what's happening over at Stroger, everyone is on edge."

He lowered his voice and put a hand on Poole's shoulder. Poole shrugged it off. The man continued anyway. "If he is, in fact, involved, there will always be time for justice. There is no reason why we can't build a case privately, make sure we have all the facts straight, then go public. That's the responsible thing to do."

"That's not Sam."

This came from Nash. He stood at the observation window, looking inside. "Scatterbrained, disorganized...he doesn't look like he's slept in days. Even when his wife was murdered, he wasn't like this. You take this case away from him, it might break him."

"That man is already broken," Poole replied.

"He needs to see this through. He needs closure."

"What do you suggest?"

Nash shrugged. "You give him the books. The diaries."

"They're evidence, possibly evidence that might incriminate *him*. No way I can hand them over. I need to get them to the

Behavioral Analysis Unit back at Quantico. If there's something there, they'll find it."

Dalton exchanged a quick look with the guy from the mayor's office, then said, "We can digitize them here and your people will have the files in a few hours. Sam can review them, too. We tell Sam if he wants to read the diaries, he needs to do it here at Metro—not under arrest—he stays here on his own accord. He finds something, that's great. If not, at least he doesn't leave custody. He stays where we can watch him. That will give your people time to figure out what you found down in South Carolina, too."

In the interview room, Porter's hands were folded on the table again, his fingers knotted together. His lips moving in that silent conversation.

Nash's phone rang, and he stepped out into the hallway to take the call.

"Does that work for you, Agent?"

Warnick again.

Poole's phone began to ring, too. He fished it from his pocket and glanced at the display.

SAIC Hurless.

He held up a finger. "Excuse me, I need to take this."

Hurless didn't wait for him to say hello. "We've got another body fitting Bishop's MO. A woman in a cemetery here in Chicago. Rose Hill Cemetery. I've got a team en route. Is Porter secure?"

Poole glanced back through the window. "He is."

"I've got reports coming in from Granger in South Carolina, the prison in New Orleans, and the CDC from the hospital here in Chicago. We're consolidating everything at the field office. When you're done at the crime scene, I need you to report back here."

"Yes, sir."

Hurless hung up.

Nash stepped back into the room, his face pale. He glanced at Dalton, then to Poole. "We've got another body."

"I just heard. I'm heading there now."

Nash blew out a breath and turned back to his supervisor. "Sir, until we're able to move the victim from the tracks, the Red Line will be out of commission. We've got to get word out to commuters."

Poole frowned. "Red Line? The body is in a cemetery."

Nash's face somehow managed to grow whiter. "The call I got was for a body found on the subway tracks for the Red Line off Clark. A woman. She's posed. Three white boxes tied off with black string on the ground next to her."

7

Nash

Day 5 • 6:13 AM

Detective Brian Nash pulled his partially restored '72 Chevy Nova behind an ambulance double-parked on the curb at Lake Street off LaSalle, found his police placard in the wheel well of the passenger seat, and placed it on his dashboard. Clair had called him a few minutes ago to bring him up to speed. She was still on the line.

"They're sure?" he said into the phone before shifting into park. He held his free hand over the heater vent—the air was blowing but didn't feel much warmer than the wind off the lake.

"Maltby from CDC said they ran the tests twice before he came to see me," Clair told him. "The hypodermic we found in the apple with Upchurch's file contains a pure strain of the SARS virus, laboratory quality."

"Shit."

"Yeah, shit," Clair said. "They're doling out antibiotics here like they're candy, but aside from that, there's not much they can do. There's no preventative treatment. They've got this place locked down tighter than a Catholic schoolgirl's asshole."

Nash laughed, and it quickly devolved into a wet cough.

"Christ, you don't sound good."

"I'm coming down with a cold or something. No rest, shitty weather, my body can't handle it. It's all just catching up."

"Your diet of fast food and candy bars doesn't help. Your body is supposed to be a temple. You treat yours like a slum lord hoping to collect insurance after the fire."

Nash glanced down at the McDonald's wrappers on the floor of his car and changed the subject. "I heard Upchurch's doctor on the radio a few minutes ago—at least it sounds like we're in the clear there."

"That was all bullshit. The doctor's covering for us to buy time. Upchurch is on his way out. He's got forty-eight hours at most. I've got a tight leash on anyone who has contact with him to make sure his condition doesn't get out."

"If you called to cheer me up, Clair-bear, you're doing a lousy job."

From the mouth of the subway station, a uniformed officer ducked under the yellow crime-scene tape and started toward Nash's Nova. The wind kicked up loose snow around his feet, swirled it through the air. When the officer realized who the car belonged to, he gave Nash a half-hearted wave and turned right back around.

"Is the body one of Bishop's?"

"I'm still outside," Nash told her. "Sounds like it, though."

"Do you believe what Sam said about Bishop's parents?"

"I don't know what to believe right now."

"Because it could be one of them, too. Or it could be none of them. Might be some copycat."

Nash turned off the heat, turned it back on again. The fucking thing was definitely blowing out cold. His skin felt like ice—he couldn't get warm. "Sam would tell us to focus on the evidence, everything else is noise. That's what we'll do."

"...you saw him, right?" Clair asked.

"I'm not sure what I saw. I don't know if he can come back from this."

Clair went quiet for a moment. "Does that FBI agent know you're there?"

"Yeah, he knows. He set parameters."

"Parameters?"

Someone knocked on Nash's window, and his heart nearly leaped up his throat. "Jesus!"

"What?" Clair asked.

Nash turned to the side. Lizeth Loudon from Channel Seven News was standing next to his car. She shoved her hands deep into the pockets of her fur-lined jacket and danced from her left foot to her right in an effort to stay warm.

"I gotta go, Clair. I'll call you back."

He disconnected the call and switched off the engine. The motor sputtered, as if undecided about shutting down, then silenced. He climbed out of the car, slammed the door, and pushed past Loudon toward the subway entrance. "I'm not talking to you."

"You don't, and I'll just have to make something up," she replied, chasing after him.

"Where's your cameraman?"

She shot a thumb back toward her van, parked three spaces behind him. "Staying warm."

"Maybe you should join him."

"I know you have a body down there. A possible 4MK victim."

"There's no body."

She thrust her phone out. A FaceBook post was loaded on the screen. "That looks a lot like a body."

Nash made a mental note of the username. "Looks fake to me."

He ducked under the crime-scene tape. When she tried to follow, the uniformed officer reappeared and told her to step back.

"I'm with him," she said.

Nash shook his head and started down the steps. "No, she's not."

"Where's Detective Porter?" she called out after him. "Shouldn't he be here?"

Nash didn't answer her. He followed the steps to the platform, toward the hum of voices.

Although fluorescents glowed on the ceiling, the four large halogen lamps erected down on the tracks glowed brighter, a bubble of white light under the yellow cast down from above. A train had been stopped near the east end of the tunnel, and a Ford F150 outfitted with special rims sat on the track and blocked the west side. The headlights were on, pointing down the tracks. They petered out about fifty feet down, no match for the thick darkness.

At the edge of the subway platform, Nash was directed to a set of steps. He took them down to the tracks.

"The third rail is live. We can't shut it down without impacting the rest of the route," someone said behind him. "Careful where you step."

More yellow crime-scene tape created a large square around the section of track between the pickup truck and the train. The halogen lights had chased off every shadow. About half a dozen people stood outside the tape—several uniformed officers, two crime technicians from Chicago Metro, three more from the FBI. Nobody stood inside the tape. All eyes were on him. All conversations muffled and died away.

Nash ducked under the tape and walked to the center of the tracks. He knelt.

He took his phone back out and called Poole.

"Describe it to me," Poole said when he picked up. "Every detail. Take your time. Don't leave anything out."

Nash snuck a quick glance back at the three FBI agents behind the tape, the CSI agents from Metro beside them, all watching. None of them looked happy about standing on the sideline.

The moment they discovered there were two bodies and Poole tried to claim jurisdiction, Warwick called the mayor, the mayor called the FBI director, and the director called Poole's supervisor. Within five minutes, Poole was under orders to not only keep Chicago Metro in the loop, but to include them in his team. Apparently, the powers that be felt working together was the best way to save face publicly. Poole had objected and was immediately shot down. Nash was under no illusion as to why Poole's supervisor had so readily agreed—the FBI wanted to keep a scapegoat at arm's length. If this went sideways, they wanted someone to blame, someone *not* FBI. Our lovely government at work.

Nash cleared his throat. "She's, ah…I'm not sure on age. I'd guess thirties, maybe forties. It's difficult to gauge. She's wearing a white negligee. Thin material. Nothing else, from what I can tell. No shoes, no undergarments, no coat or anything else lying around the scene. Her skin is covered in some kind of white, powdery substance. Her hair, too."

"Is it on her clothes?"

"No."

"So she was dressed postmortem?"

"Looks that way."

"What else?"

Nash removed his black leather gloves and pulled a pair of latex from his pocket and tugged them on, pairing them with a surgical mask in case the white powder was some sort of contaminant. He leaned a little closer. "Her eyes are closed, but I think the right one has been removed. There's a little dried blood in the corner." With a slow hand, he pulled her hair back. "She's missing an ear. She's posed, positioned…looks like she's praying. She's on her knees."

He reached for her mouth, tried to open it. "She's stiff. I can't get her mouth open."

"Rigor?"

"Doesn't feel like rigor. Maybe it's the cold."

"Don't force it," Poole told him. "The medical examiner can confirm her tongue has been removed. Do you have three boxes? Tied with black string?"

"Yeah," Nash said. "But this isn't typically how we find them. Bishop usually mails the boxes, one at a time, over about a week. He doesn't leave all three like this."

"He did with the body you found in the tunnels with Porter. Talbot's CFO," Poole pointed out.

"Gunther Herbert," Nash said.

Bishop had told Porter he tortured Herbert for information about Arthur Talbot's finances. Information that incriminated the Chicago real estate mogul in a number of underground crimes.

"Same with Libby McInley," Poole added. "He left the three boxes on her coffee table."

"Our unsub wrote on her forehead with some kind of blade."

"What does it say?"

"I am evil."

Libby had also been cut. Thousands of tiny razor blade cuts, all over her body.

"Herbert and McInley were both tortured for information," Nash said softly. "Different from his other victims."

"What else?"

Nash leaned in closer. She looked more like a statue than a person. He'd never seen a body positioned like this.

Praying.

His eyes narrowed. "Her fingertips..."

"What about them?"

"They're...burned."

"Her prints have been removed?"

"I think so," Nash said, trying to get a better look without moving her hands. "He's never done that before."

"Is there a sign?"

"A sign?"

"A piece of cardboard, paper...anything written near her?"

Nash looked around her. "Nothing that I can see...oh, wait."

"What is it?"

Nash stood, walked toward the wall. He glanced up at the various members of law enforcement watching him. "Does anyone know if this is new?"

Nobody answered.

"What?" Poole said again.

Nash reached up and touched the paint. It was still wet.

FATHER, FORGIVE ME

Spray-painted on the wall of the tunnel, nearly lost in all the other graffiti.

8

Poole

Day 5 • 6:22 AM

Poole's eyes didn't leave the body as he spoke to Detective Nash. The woman knelt at the pond's edge—looked like she was praying. A silver serving tray in front of her held three white boxes tied with black string. *Father, forgive me* on a sign propped against her. *I am evil* carved into her forehead.

A team of bureau crime-scene techs watched him from a distance. Someone from the medical examiner's office, too. Like the scene at the subway station, they had all been told to hold back.

Poole knelt down in the snow and took a closer look at her fingertips. Although her hands were pressed together, he could see her prints had been burned away. A chemical burn of some kind, probably acid—sulfuric, maybe hydrochloric.

He reached for her mouth and tried to force it open, but it didn't budge. Just like Nash had said. Too stiff for rigor. Possibly frozen. The temperature was currently in the teens. Last night had hovered in the single digits with wind chill in the negatives.

There was the white powder, too. She was covered in snow, so it was difficult to see, but it was there. Some kind of thin film covering her body but not the gown she wore. She'd been dressed after it came into contact with her skin. It shimmered slightly, crystalline.

Salt?

With Bishop's help, Paul Upchurch had drowned his victims in a saltwater tank. Could this be some kind of residue from that tank?

Poole's phone rang. He fished it from his pocket and didn't recognize the number.

"This is Agent Poole."

"Hey, this is Sheriff Banister down in Simpsonville. I'm sorry to bother you so early. Are you still in New Orleans?"

"Back in Chicago," Poole replied. He rose to his feet and signaled for the investigators to begin documenting and cataloging the scene. "What can I do for you, Sheriff?"

"I've…I've got a body down here." She sounded rattled. Her voice was shaky. "Found it right on the courthouse steps about two hours ago. Just…just kneeling there. Praying, almost. That's what it looks like, anyway. There's three white boxes wrapped up with string. Someone wrote on the steps next to it, too."

"Father, forgive me," Poole muttered.

"Yeah. How did you know that?"

"Any idea who she is?"

"It's not a she, it's a he. I know exactly who he is."

9

Clair

Day 5 • 6:29 AM

Clair sneezed and plucked another tissue from the box on the table beside her.

"We're gonna need a bigger box," Kloz said in his best New England accent, which wasn't very good. He inhaled, sucking snot back up into his nose.

Clair glared at him. "I really don't want to die here with you."

Kloz leaned back in his chair. The old metal squeaked. "If you could die anywhere, with anyone, who would you pick?"

She thought about this for a second. "Matthew McConaughey. I always thought he was sexy for a white guy. Forty-something McConaughey, though, not the young one from *Dazed and Confused*. He didn't grow into that face until he got older."

"Where?"

"Maybe a beach in Barbados."

Kloz shook his head. "Oh, I don't know about that. The only way to die on a beach is from a shark. Nobody wants to get eaten by a shark."

"This is a stupid fucking game."

Kloz ignored her. "I'd go with Jennifer Lawrence, but only if she was wearing that leather outfit from *The Hunger Games*."

"And where exactly would you want to die?"

"Toledo, Ohio. No question."

"Why Toledo?"

He shrugged. "No sharks."

"Obviously."

"There's also nothing to do in Toledo, so if I'm trapped there with a leather-clad Jennifer Lawerence, locked in some seedy motel room with nothing but—"

Clair pinched her eyes shut and covered her ears. "Enough. I don't want to know what's in your head. Not now, not ever."

"I'm just trying to lighten the mood."

"I know."

"I don't want to die here."

"I know."

"We can't leave the building, and I'm getting stir-crazy."

"I know."

Using his right foot, Kloz pushed against the floor and started turning his chair in a slow counterclockwise circle. "The SARS virus has an incubation period as long as ten days. Our friend from the CDC hasn't come out and said it yet, but their protocol dictates this place remain on lockdown for no less than ten days from the last known case. If the virus doesn't kill us, there's a good chance we won't be allowed to leave for nearly two weeks."

"They won't hold us here that long."

"Why not?" Kloz replied. "We've got beds, food, access to all things medical, and we're isolated. Can you think of a better place to hold all of us? They won't risk the virus leaving this building."

"Bishop has the virus. He could be anywhere."

"And if he infects other people, the CDC will most likely bring them here for treatment for the same reasons they'll try to keep *all of us* here—beds, medical, food, isolation. They'll keep us here with the doors locked and let the virus work through us, burn itself out. Without treatment, nothing else makes sense. Nobody will risk an outbreak. Even if they catch Bishop today and shut him down, they won't let us out. Not until this runs its course."

Clair knew he was right, but she wasn't about to admit that. She wadded up her tissue and tossed it toward the trash can. It landed about a foot short.

Three quick knocks at their door.

They both looked up.

Jerome Stout pushed into the room before either of them had a chance to say anything.

As head of hospital security, he hadn't slowed down since they arrived, and he looked as beaten down as the rest of them. Stubble was beginning to show on his otherwise shaved head, and his uniform had sweat stains under the pits. She'd heard he'd taken the job at the hospital after retiring from Chicago Metro at fifty, five years ago. He hadn't signed on for this. He wore a white surgical mask over his mouth, and it muffled his tired voice. "Detective. I need you to come with me."

"Why?"

His nervous eyes glanced at Klozowski in the back corner, then back to her. "We've got a body. It's bad."

"Oh, hell," Kloz said in a low tone.

Clair stood and started toward the door.

"Wear that," Stout instructed, nodding toward the mask they'd given her.

She pulled it over her head and fitted the straps over her ears, hustling after him.

Clair didn't want to pass through the cafeteria, but before she could ask him if there was another route, he had started through the room. The moment everyone saw her, they erupted. When the police had brought Bishop's eighty-seven potential victims to the hospital, they were instructed to remain within this room and the two adjoining employee lounges. Aside from Klozowski, she was the only representative from Chicago Metro on-site, and they recognized her immediately. Some wore masks, others didn't, all were shouting. People stood, started toward her, their eyes angry. They wanted answers, no different than her, but she had nothing to tell them. She pushed through as quickly as she could, telling those around her to remain calm, it would all be over soon. They smelled bullshit, though. Many of them were doctors. They knew the score. Their children had been brought here, their spouses. Tables had been pushed aside, and many had begun constructing tents with hospital sheets, segregating themselves from the others. At least twenty or thirty people were missing. From what she had been told earlier, some families were given rooms, but there weren't enough for everyone. Since many were staff members, those who had them went to their offices, others took over the locker rooms. A few had even gone on rounds as if nothing were happening. They'd tried to gather them back up before they spread the virus, but most of the staff knew it was already too late for that. The building, not the cafeteria, would contain the virus now, just as Kloz had said.

Stout led her to a bank of elevators. She sighed as the doors closed, sealing out the angry mob.

When they were alone, Stout said, "A few of them tried to break through the glass doors in the lobby and get outside, but Metro has SWAT out there. They're in full riot gear. I'm trying not to think about what would happen if someone crossed that line."

Clair had been the one who suggested they position SWAT, but she wasn't about to tell him that. During her years with Chicago Metro, she found herself in the middle of three "escalated civil events" (the police didn't like to call them riots). With each, there had been something in the air first, a precursor. This hospital stunk of precursor, and she hadn't been the first to notice. The staff moved about their business in near silence, their eyes on each other and the crowd of strangers in their cafeteria. Parents coddled their children, and death stares were issued at the slightest cough or sneeze from someone nearby. There was talk of isolating the sick by the CDC. They'd been speaking to senior staff about cordoning off a wing on the second floor, but if the plan had gone further, they hadn't shared the details with her.

They rode the elevator to the fourth floor.

When the doors opened, Stout directed her down the hallway to the left. A sign on the wall said *Cardiovascular*. "A nurse found him about ten minutes ago."

"Found who?"

He didn't answer. Instead, he turned down another hallway, then a third, entering some type of administrative wing. Most of the doors were closed, blinds drawn. "Second one there on the left," Stout said, pointing.

Clair followed his finger. A placard on the closed door read: *Dr. Stanford Pentz*. Her hand dropped to the butt of her service weapon holstered on her hip.

"You won't need that."

Clair unsnapped the leather strap on the gun anyway and tightened her grip as she reached for the doorknob with her other hand. The door swung in on the office. There was a couch on her left and a mahogany desk on the right grouped with two plush leather chairs. Various degrees covered the wall, and a single family photo sat on top of the desk, three people—a man in his sixties, his wife, and a boy of around twelve—all smiling and dressed to the nines.

In the center of the room, turned away from Clair and facing the large window occupying the back wall of the office, a man kneeled. His head slumped forward, his chin on his chest. He wore no shoes. A pair of black loafers sat beside him.

Clair stepped closer.

At the door, Stout cleared his throat but otherwise said nothing.

Clair stepped around the man, got between him and the window, and that was when she saw the blood and the three small boxes lined up on the floor.

10

Nash

Day 5 • 8:31 AM

Nash shrugged out of his coat as the elevator doors opened on the basement level of Chicago Metro. Normally deserted, the hallway buzzed with activity. The moment the doors opened, some kid in his twenties stepped inside, wheeling a hand truck loaded with file boxes.

Boxes Nash recognized.

"Where are you taking those?"

"Roosevelt," the kid replied.

Nash noticed the FBI badge clipped to his belt. "On whose orders?"

The kid reached forward and pressed the button for the ground floor. He jerked a thumb back toward the hallway. "You have any questions, I suggest you speak to Agent Poole."

When the elevator doors started to close, Nash jammed his foot between them. As they reversed and opened again, he reached over to the elevator control panel and pressed the buttons for every floor before stepping out.

Another young agent stepped past him with a hand truck holding six more file boxes.

For several years now, the 4MK task force operated out of the basement in a space they dubbed the War Room. They found it easier to focus downstairs rather than up in the bull pen with all the other detectives. Too many questions, too many prying eyes, too many leaks to the press. The isolation put a stop to all of it. Well, most of it. Several months ago, when Anson Bishop was identified as the 4MK killer and escaped, the FBI took over the investigation. They also took over the space across the hall from the War Room. Porter had insisted it was temporary. Either Bishop would be caught or the FBI would return the case to local law enforcement once it fell off the front page of the papers, but that never happened. Instead, things escalated. Things grew worse.

Nash looked first in the FBI office—four agents, none he recognized. All were packing boxes and stacking them near the door.

Across the hall, in the War Room, he found Special Agent Frank Poole sitting in a chair at the front of the room, staring up at the three white evidence boards.

Nash felt his face burn red as he stepped inside. "What the hell, Frank?"

"SAIC Hurless wants everything consolidated at the FBI field office on Roosevelt. We've got details coming in from New Orleans and Simpsonville—the six bodies found in that lake…the house…everything Sam stumbled through from the moment he left Chicago to when we found him at the Guyon Hotel."

"Why can't we do that here?"

"It's not my call." Without taking his eyes from the boards, Poole said, "How well do you know the mayor?"

"Me? I've met him twice at city functions, shook his hand, took a photo. I don't think he has any clue who I am."

"What about Anthony Warnick from his office?"

"I just met him today," Nash replied. "Why?"

Poole still didn't look up. "Warwick called the mayor's office. The mayor called my supervisor's supervisor, and in less than five minutes I was under orders to include you in this investigation. Ten minutes prior to that and SAIC Hurless wanted me to lock you up with Sam. Somebody is holding something over someone's head. Nothing else explains a knee-jerk reaction like that."

Poole stood, went to the first board and pointed at three words written with the information on Arthur Talbot—*Friend with mayor.*

"Sam must have written that," Nash said. "We know Talbot played golf with him. Contributed to his campaign, too. His real estate projects were all large-scale. I can't imagine those things happen without the mayor involved somehow."

"Did you tie him to anything criminal?"

Nash shook his head. "Nothing came up. I don't know that anyone looked, either. Talbot was our focus, not the mayor."

"I think he's got you here as his eyes and ears," Poole stated flatly.

Nash smirked. "If that's the case, he picked the wrong guy. I'm not talking to him."

Poole fell silent for a moment, then said. "Does he have anything hanging over your head?"

This time, Nash laughed. "You think he's going to strong-arm me somehow?"

Poole shrugged.

"That won't happen," Nash insisted. "He's got nothing on me. I'm a Boy Scout."

Poole opened his mouth to reply to that but changed his mind. Instead, he cleared his throat. "Let's just focus on the case."

"Yeah, let's do that."

Poole rolled his fingers over the arm of the chair in several rhythmic taps, and then his eyes went back to the boards. "A few hours ago, I got a call from the sheriff down in Simpsonville, South Carolina. She found a male posed on the courthouse steps, identical to the two women we found up here. Eye, ear, and tongue removed and placed in white boxes tied with black string near the body. The words 'father, forgive me' written nearby. He's covered in a white powder, just like the two we found up here. I haven't heard back from the lab yet, but I think it might be salt."

"Shit. That means we have four bodies today," Nash replied.

"What?"

"Clair called me. She's got a man, a doctor named Stanford

Busting that woman out of prison...I keep telling myself he kept me out of all that to protect me, Clair and Kloz too, but it doesn't feel like that. It feels secretive, deceptive. If I were to write everything he did on one of those boards up there and not put his name up at the top, just look at the evidence, his actions, he'd be my number-one suspect. I'm having a hard time with that, but I know it's true. That said, we've got four new bodies and he's been in custody the entire time. There's no way he's responsible, but that doesn't mean he's clean, either. There's something he's not telling me, something big, and whatever that something is, it's been growing over the years we've worked this case. I'm scared to death of learning what that something is, but the cop in me won't stop until I do. For better or worse, that's how this works."

They both went quiet for a minute or so, then Poole said, "At the bureau, they believe the investigation is compromised. They think that's why 4MK has eluded capture for so long."

Nash was shaking his head before Poole finished his statement. "4MK eluded capture for so long because he's a crazy fuck whose motives make no sense to anyone but himself. If Sam is involved, and that's a *big* if, it never compromised his work. You saw his apartment, that wall. Those weren't the actions of someone trying to derail a case. That was a glimpse inside an obsessed mind. Someone who wanted to take down Bishop at any cost. The man sitting up in that interview room still does." Nash turned to Poole. "You need to let him read those diaries. Let him help. Whether you trust him or not, nobody is more qualified to pick through Bishop's ramblings. You know that, whether you're willing to admit it or not."

"The box went up to him ten minutes ago," Poole said.

Nash frowned. "So you made me say all that for nothing?"

"Say what?" Poole said. "I wasn't listening."

"Oh, so you've got jokes, too?"

"Only that one."

Poole stood and photographed the boards with his phone. "There's a briefing in thirty minutes at Roosevelt. The mayor will want you there."

Nash wasn't sure if that last statement was meant as a joke or not.

II

Porter

Day 5 • 8:36 AM

Porter was too wired for sleep. They allowed him out of the interview room only long enough to use the bathroom and get a drink of water from the fountain in the hall. When a uniformed officer led him out, those in the hallway went quiet. Detectives he'd known for years, staffers, all of them just watched without a word. He fought the urge to raise his hands above his head and shout out "Boo!" to get a rise out of them. When they put him back in the room, they left him in there alone. He expected to be charged with a crime, anything from the jailbreak to the murder at the Guyon Hotel, but that hadn't happened. Not yet, anyway. He supposed there was no hurry. He knew they weren't letting him out. He'd closed his eyes, tried to rest, but found himself listening to the screaming in his head—all the facts of this case shouted at once, a hundred voices debating in his mind.

When someone knocked on the door, his eyes snapped open, and he realized two hours had passed.

He wasn't sure why they bothered to knock—he certainly couldn't open the door. He'd fought the urge to try the doorknob for more than an hour before he finally gave it a twist, confirming the door was locked. When the knock came, he only looked up at the door and waited. He heard the click of the lock disengaging.

The door swung open a moment later. A woman in her twenties wearing an FBI ID and a Chicago Metro visitor's pass stepped inside with a white file box. She set it on the table. "This is from Agent Poole."

A moment later and she was gone. The door closed and locked behind her.

The room went still, the hum of the HVAC the only sound.

Porter found himself staring at the box. He knew what was inside. He could damn well feel the composition books through the thin cardboard waiting like a living, breathing animal at rest. When he placed his palm on the lid, he swore it was warm.

Sweat trickled down from his brow to his cheek. He felt it drop to his shoulder and made no attempt to wipe the side of his face.

"I'll need something to write with," he said without looking up. He knew someone was watching him from the other side of the one-way window. Probably multiple someones. "Maybe some coffee, too."

They brought these things a minute or so later—a whiteboard, marker, a mug, and coffee in a pot stained deep brown with duct tape on the handle.

Only when he was alone again did Porter remove the lid from the file box, extract the composition books one at a time, and spread them out on the table. They were numbered, digits written in the top right corner of each—one through eleven—in handwriting he knew well.

When Porter poured himself a cup of black coffee and settled back in his chair with the first of the books, he felt one of the someones on the other side of that one-way glass lean just a little bit closer. He fought the urge to read aloud.

12
Diary

The Finicky House for Wayward Children spoke at night. There was the creak of old bones and joints, riddled with arthritis living within the walls, floor, and ceiling. The house gasped for breath—a subtle wheeze and raspy exhale which always seemed to start on the floors below and exit from somewhere above. The interior rooms of this place served as nothing more than tired lungs, pocked with cancerous tumors and scar tissue, abused and forgotten by those who once called this place home.

Home.

I found that to be a funny word, because a year ago I could have told you what it meant to me. Without question, without doubt, I understood home and could have pointed to it on a map and told you the best way to find it. It had been a singular place at that point, the only one I remembered or had ever known. Home had been the comfort of a warm blanket. The moist dirt between my toes as I walked barefoot down the path to my lake. Home had been Mother's laugh and Father's smile and a gentle wave from the lovely Mrs. Carter as I cut across her yard, hoping to gain a whiff of perfume or a glimpse of the lines of her body as the sun caught her yellow flowered dress just right from behind.

When I closed my eyes, I could go back there, and I did—I went back there often. As time passed, each time I returned, something had changed. At first, those changes were subtle—a bare clothesline rather than one *covered with damp, flapping linens. A refrigerator, once stocked, now containing nothing but half a gallon of spoiled milk. Rooms that had once been warm and inviting now chilled with the icy touch of fall, layered in dust. And that place,* my home, *grew harder to find, as if placed in a box in my mind against the far back wall, and each day new boxes appeared, stacked in front, slowly burying that first box away.*

I woke today thinking about my cat, all alone on the shore of my lake, nobody to take care of her anymore.

I wondered if I'd ever see my home again.

Then I remembered the last time I had seen that home—the fire, those men, and I wondered if anything was left at all.

Paul snored.

Mr. Paul Upchurch, the drawer of worlds, the creator of The Misadventures of Maybelle Markel, *and resident of the top bunk in our shared room, snored each and every night with the rumble of a poorly-maintained generator. Because he had the top bunk, being so close to the ceiling, each wet inhale echoed that much louder. So much so, he sometimes woke himself up with zero recollection of the cause. He'd mumble incoherently to himself, then drift back off again only to repeat the process an hour or so later.*

I had no such luck.

For some reason, when his malfunctioning respiratory system snatched me from slumber, I'd find myself wide awake, staring at the bunk above me, the glow of our alarm clock across the room illuminating the space in thin red light. This always seemed to happen at two minutes after four.

Tonight was such a night, and when I closed my eyes, all else seemed amplified. I tried to tune it all out and listen only for her.

I had yet to meet Libby McInley, the girl in the room across the hall, but part of me felt I already knew her, and with each passing day I felt a pull. This invisible rope securing the two of us together growing shorter by the hour. It started while I was under the care of the illustrious Dr. Joseph Oglesby in the Camden Treatment Center. As it was now, her room was slightly down the hall from mine—far enough to be out-of-reach, close enough to give off heat. Her time there had been spent behind closed doors, crying mostly. I longed to hear her laugh, If I had money, I'd pay a hefty sum just to hear her sneeze, but she only ever cried and I didn't know why. Aside from Ms. Finicky, the other girls in the house took turns with her— slipping in and out of her room at all hours. I knew their names were Kristina Niven and Tegan Savala, fifteen and sixteen respectively, but aside from passing glances in the hallway and awkward hellos, I didn't really know them, either.

Upon my first night here, Paul was kind enough to tell me Tegan was quite spank-worthy and Kristina could be if she cleaned herself up—a solid eight and six on his Spankometer Scale—the two of them had been here at Finicky house longer than anyone—going on two years now.

Personally, I was still trying to figure out what a home for wayward children really was. I expected a parade of wannabe parents to come streaming through on the regular, but that had yet to happen, no adoptions or fostering here, very few visitors at all. And our precise location was still up for debate. The large house sat in the middle of a substantial plot of land without another house anywhere around. The only building within eyesight was a dilapidated barn, one we'd been told was horribly dangerous and off limits, which only made it more intriguing. Paul had a plan in the works.

"We'll get the girls to check it out with us. I bet there's hay in there and quiet stalls, maybe even a loft—I'll play hide-the-salami with Tegan and you can play Yahtzee or something with Kristina. Maybe you can be lookout. We'll need to bring a bottle for spinning."

"Before you start naming your children, you need to get the guts to talk to her."

"I do talk to her."

"You grunt at her," I told him. "I've heard you. She'll say something like 'good morning' and you reply with 'huh ug ya' or some other non-sense."

"I'm a man of few words, all strong and silent. She gets me. That's why she's always undressing me with her eyes."

"Is that what her eyes are doing?"

"That's why she calls me 'Paul Take-Me-To-Church.'"

"She doesn't call you that."

"Her eyes do."

"Could be she just needs glasses."

"She had stars and fireworks in those eyes," Paul replied. "She's always talking about me with the other girls."

"How would you know?"

"What else are they going to talk about? If she gets me alone in that barn, there's no telling what she might do."

"You'd better drink plenty of fluids."

Paul went quiet for a moment, then, "Have you ever seen a real girl naked?"

"No," I told him, perhaps a little too quickly. But I had seen a woman, and I fell back asleep that night wondering where Mrs. Carter was at that particular moment and how far from home she had strayed.

13

Nash

The Federal Bureau of Investigation Chicago field office was located at 2111 Roosevelt Road, about ten minutes from Chicago Metro. Nash drove his Chevy. One of the box-toting FBI agents had offered to give Nash a ride, but he couldn't bring himself to accept. Everything about this felt off.

On the ground floor, he checked in at the security desk, surrendered both his primary weapon and backup, and was issued a visitor's badge after being photographed and passing through a metal detector. Poole had told him to report to the conference room on the fourth floor.

Nash wasn't sure what he expected, but it wasn't what he found. Conference Room C was at least several thousand square feet with a dozen rows of stadium seating going up the back wall, all facing a raised platform and floor-to-ceiling video monitors. Each screen bore a three-dimensional floating image of the FBI seal, glistening in animated light. He was ten minutes early, and there was no sign of Poole or his supervisor. At least twenty agents were already in attendance, spaced around the room.

While Nash didn't recognize anyone, they must have recognized him. Most of the voices either dropped away entirely or fell into hushed conversations. They weren't shy about watching him, though. Nash fought the urge to wave and poured himself a cup of coffee from a refreshment table near the door, then he took a seat in the third row and waited as the room continued to fill.

At exactly nine o'clock, the overhead lights dimmed and the two doors closed automatically. Nash half expected movie previews to come up on the screens. Instead, SAIC Hurless came out of a side door, and the room went quiet.

"While I understand most of you are new to this case, we don't have time for a learning curve. As of this morning, we have four more victims—three here in Chicago, another in Simpsonville, South Carolina. Detective Sam Porter has been apprehended and is currently being held at Chicago Metro."

To Nash's surprise, several agents actually cheered this. A couple clapped.

Hurless ignored them. "Agent Poole will provide the details."

Poole stepped through the same opening Hurless had used. Somehow he had found the time to shave and change his suit. He held a clicker in his hand and when he pressed one of the buttons, the screens came alive behind him.

Four bodies.

"Each body was found in the same pose—on their knees with their hands joined at their front and head bowed as if in prayer. Left eye, left ear, and the tongue have been removed from each with surgical precision and placed in white boxes tied with black string and left at the victim's side. Aside from Gunther Herbert and Libby McInley, Bishop always mailed the boxes over the course of a week, Herbert and McInley being the exceptions. Within close proximity of each body, we also found a note reading 'father, forgive me.'"

Poole walked to the left side of the platform and gestured at the two women pictured behind him. "This first victim was found in Rose Hill Cemetery. The second sitting on the tracks of the Red Line at the Clark subway station. With both, their fingerprints have been removed chemically. We have no identification at this time."

He crossed over to the third victim. "This man has been identified as Tom Langlin, a former inspector with the Simpsonville fire department. Our unsub placed him on the courthouse steps, in full view. He wrote up the original report on the fire at the Bishop property."

"Don't you mean Porter's property?" someone shouted out from the back.

"We'll get to that," Poole replied.

He stepped to the far right and pointed up at the last body. "This is Dr. Stanford Pentz. He worked in Cardiovascular at Stroger Hospital. He was found in his office this morning, posed like the others. The hospital has been on lockdown since yesterday—we don't have time-of-death yet, but most likely he was killed before the hospital was sealed. It's unlikely our unsub managed to get through enhanced security with a body, and nobody has been permitted in or out of the hospital with the exception of a surgeon brought in to operate on Paul Upchurch. Information on that can be found in the case file."

An agent sitting halfway down the second row stood. "You keep saying 'unsub' rather than Bishop. Do you believe someone else is responsible?"

Poole glanced over at Hurless, who nodded, then turned back to the agent. "Because we have multiple victims in several states all appearing at relatively the same time, we don't want to rule out the idea that Bishop is working with a partner. We're certain he aided Paul Upchurch with the abductions of Ella Reynolds, Lili Davies, and Larissa Biel. It's possible someone else is working with both of them. Detective Porter claims Anson Bishop is here in Chicago along with a woman who may or may not be his mother."

"Is Detective Porter Bishop's father?"

This came from someone on the far end of the room. An Asian woman in a tan pantsuit.

Hurless jumped in. "At this point, we're not ruling anything out."

Poole said, "Both female victims had *I am evil* cut into their foreheads. The male victims did not. We don't know the relevance of this yet. None of this is to be shared with the press."

There were several murmurs in the crowd.

Poole turned back to the video monitors. "There is something else you all need to know about these victims. With each, their skin was covered in salt. Not their clothing. This suggests they were exposed and dressed later. The salt found on them is not a match for the saltwater found in the tank at Paul Upchurch's home. It appears to be a finely ground form of the salt used on the roads."

The Asian woman stood and spoke again. "In the bible, Genesis, Lot's wife is turned into a pillar of salt when she looks back on Sodom. If you consider that along with the messages found, 'father, forgive me,' this could be something biblical. Something very different from Bishop's history."

"Or this could be Bishop sending some kind of direct message to his father," Hurless interjected. "If he is still alive."

Poole didn't seem to hear Hurless. He turned to the Asian woman and quoted, "'Flee for your life. Do not stop anywhere in the plain; flee to the hills, lest you be swept away.' Genesis 19:17. Angels told this to Lot and his wife right before they destroyed the city."

The Asian woman nodded. "I'm curious—were all four bodies found facing the same geographical direction?"

Poole appeared to be thinking about this when Nash's phone rang. The room went quiet, and all eyes turned toward him. Nash offered those around him an apologetic smile. He reached down, fumbled with his phone, and swiped the answer button before bringing it to his ear. Although he knew the voice, he hadn't heard it in a number of months. That did nothing to stop the sensation of spiders crawling about his spine as Anson Bishop spoke.

"I know where you are, Nash, so don't say anything, only listen. In a moment, I'm going to text you an address and you're going to leave your little meeting and go to that address. You'll do this alone. If I see any vehicle in the street other than your junker of a Chevy, a lot of people will get sick. I have more of that virus than I know what to do with, and I'm getting tired of carrying it around. It's so tempting to share it with everyone down at the Revival Food

Hall or maybe Woodfield Mall. The Bears are playing tonight at home on Monday Night Football—can you imagine the fun we'd have if I brought it to the game? That one is tempting most of all, but honestly, I think I'd rather just see you right now. Catch up. I miss all my old friends. And we have so much to talk about. I'll give you thirty minutes. Don't be late. I get grumpy when I'm kept waiting."

The phone dinged, and an address appeared on the screen.

Bishop said, "Only you, Nash. Nobody else. Cough if you understand."

Nash cleared his throat.

"Atta boy."

The call disconnected, and when Nash looked up, he realized everyone was still watching him.

14
Diary

I woke at a little after six and had to pee. Not the roll-on-my-side-think-about-something-else-and-hold-it-for-another-hour kind of pee, but really *had to pee, like my bladder would burst with a pop loud enough to wake the house if I didn't do something about it fast.*

Somehow my sheets got tangled up around my legs, and that didn't help matters any. I nearly fell from the bottom bunk trying to get out of that mess in my rushed state. In the bunk above me, Paul snored, rattled, and rolled. He was on his back, and his right arm hung over the side. The first hint of morning sniffed around the window.

I crossed the room to the door, opened it, and got to the hall nearly jogging in place with both hands covering my private parts under my pajamas. Any boy will tell you, when mother nature calls at full volume, two things happen—a sudden and all-encompassing need to jog and morning wood. Neither of these things would go away until I spent a little time in the bathroom at the other end of the hall.

Here's the thing, though: The boards in the hallway squeaked, and Vince Weidner had made it very clear that he could hear them squeak from his room across the hall. He also made it very clear that anyone on the starting end of such wakeful squeaking would be severely punished, possibly maimed, or maybe disappeared. Vince was fond of sleep and not so fond of anything, or anybody, else. Except maybe hurting people. He seemed fond of that.

I knew which boards squeaked.

Paul had a map, one he helped me memorize on my first day here at Finicky House for the reasons stated above, and with that in mind, I placed my left foot on the board closest to the opposite wall and swung my right around to a board at the center of the hall about three feet closer to the bathroom. This maneuver took place in blissful silence, despite my body's continued insistence on jogging in place.

Libby's door was closed, and as I did every time I passed it, I paused long enough to listen.

She wasn't crying, and that was good. She still cried a lot, but not as much as she did at the Camden Treatment Center. While I didn't want to hear her cry, I did want to hear her. There was something oddly comforting about knowing she was in that room so close. I knew this was strange. I hadn't even met her. Never spoke to her. I barely knew what she looked like, as I'd only caught glimpses.

A toilet flushed at the far end of the hall, and the door to the girl's bathroom swung open.

Tegan came out with her arms stretching above her head, her eyes closed, and a big yawn on her mouth. She wore nothing but a skimpy pair of white panties, and I froze in place—even the jogging stopped. The morning wood went nowhere, though, and when her eyes opened they dropped right to it—my boy parts in full-on tent under my pj's. I tried to cover up, but I was a bit too slow for that. I'd be lying if I said I wasn't distracted by why she wore (or, more appropriately, by what she didn't).

"Geez, stare much?" Tegan said as she came down the hall on long legs, numerous boards creaking as she did. "Pervert."

She ducked back into her own room and closed the door with enough force to rattle the walls.

From his room, I heard Vince groan.

I crossed the remainder of that hallway, got to the bathroom, and closed the door with the speed of an elk. I twisted the lock, a feeble thing I could pick in my sleep, got to the toilet, and did my business wondering if I'd have to spend the next hour on the john in order to avoid Vince or if I could get back to my bed.

There was a narrow window behind the toilet, one that overlooked the driveway, and as I stood there, relishing the relief of that first morning pee, I looked out. There was a car in the driveway, a white Chevy Malibu that I recognized. I watched as Detective Welderman rounded the side and opened the back door. Kristina Niven got out, said something to him, then stomped off toward the front door of the house. She was wearing a short black dress and matching heels and clutching a small purse.

When I looked back at the detective, I realized he was glaring up at me.

15

Clair

Clair stood in the cramped office of Jerome Stout, head of hospital security. He sat in a rickety rolling chair behind the desk, his bulky phone centered on the desk between them. At the request of Stout, she had dialed her captain, Henry Dalton.

"Five? That's it?" Dalton's voice rattled from the speaker. "How do you keep a hospital of that size safe with only five security officers on duty?"

Stout scratched at the top of his head. "That's a conversation you need to have with our budgetary committee, not me. I make do with what they provide me. Frankly, I've got a buddy at Cleveland General, and he's only got three per shift. I'm grateful for what I've got."

Clair leaned forward. "Captain, he's in here with us. We need more support."

"The CDC won't allow us to send anyone *in* any more than they'll let one of you *out*," he replied. "And we can't be sure he's in there."

"I'm fairly certain that man didn't cut off his own ear and tongue and wrap them neatly in boxes. Probably didn't take out his own eyeball, either," she said.

"We've got two similar bodies found here in Chicago this morning and one more just like it found in Simpsonville, South Carolina. It's very doubtful your guy was killed by Bishop. More likely it was some kind of copycat."

"That supposed to make me feel better? Either way, we got a killer locked in the hospital with us!"

"You're a detective. Get your head around it and detect. How many uniformed officers do you have in there with you?"

"Four," Clair replied. "I've got one stationed with Darlene Biel and her daughter, Larissa. Another outside Katy Quigley's door, and two more down in the cafeteria. I'd planned to move them all down there to keep that mess from turning into a full-on riot. No way I can do that now. I've got to keep them under protection. We need additional support. We can't keep this up 24/7."

"Nobody on Upchurch?"

"He's comatose and not expected to regain consciousness. I don't have the resources to keep someone on him."

The captain sighed. "I wish I could give you some help, but I can't. I'm under orders, just like you."

"What about the feds?"

"I've already spoken to SAIC Hurless, and he's in the same boat. Until the CDC allows us to open the doors, nobody gets in or out. The focus right now is on containment. Where is the body now? Who else knows about this?"

Clair glanced at Stout, then back down at the phone. "I had it brought down to the morgue. There's a pathologist on duty, a woman named Amelia Webber."

"Good," Dalton said. "Put her in contact with Eisley down at the medical examiner's office. He's got the other two from this morning. He's in touch with Simpsonville, too. They all need to compare notes. You'll obviously want to keep all this as quiet as possible. If word spreads around the hospital, your situation could easily escalate."

Clair rolled her eyes.

Little late for that.

The nurse who discovered Pentz's body told the others at the nurses station in a manner loud enough to attract the attention of several other staffers nearby—three orderlies, another doctor, and two members of the cafeteria staff. Clair had tried to corner all of them and explain the importance of discretion only to learn they had all told others, and those people had also talked.

"That cat is already out, Captain," she said.

"Then you need to treat this as you would any other homicide and work to solve it as quickly as possible. If we didn't have the other bodies this morning, I'd suspect a copycat who might have had it in for your dead cardiologist. Somebody trying to use all the hype around 4MK to cover up their own reasons for wanting the man dead. That's still a viable theory, but you need to remain open to other possibilities. Did Klozowski run the name? Is he connected to Upchurch?"

"No direct contact with Upchurch or his case, but he was on the hospital board. Kloz is trying to determine if he controlled funding that might have indirectly impacted Upchurch and put him on Bishop's radar."

"Good, good," Dalton said. "Keep me posted on what you find. I'll pass everything on to the feds."

He hung up.

"Well, that wasn't the least bit helpful," Clair said.

The back of Stout's chair groaned as he leaned back. "Whether it's Bishop, some copycat, or someone else entirely, whoever killed Dr. Pentz is locked in this hospital with us. Between SWAT and my guys, we've got every entrance covered."

Clair remembered something then. "Are you connected to the tunnel system under the city?"

"Tunnel system?"

Clair nodded. "The old bootlegging tunnels. They run from the harbor to heaven knows how many points under Chicago. They were created during prohibition to keep the booze flowing. Later the utility companies took most of them over. They still use them today. When we were trying to track down Emory Connors, we learned Bishop used the tunnels to get around unseen. You can get from one end of the city to the other down there."

Stout frowned. "I never heard of them."

"We need to check the basement."

16

Nash

Day 5 • 9:15 AM

Nash rolled up tight on the curb and parked his Chevy about half a block from the address Bishop had sent him—423 McCormick on the eastside. Shifting into park, he looked up and down the block. There wasn't much to look at. Most Chicagoans had given up on this part of the city back in the nineties. Once the gangs got a good foothold, the businesses began to fold one after the other until all that remained were several pawn shops, a bail bondsman, and a corner convenience store which no longer permitted patrons inside. Instead, they offered a window made up of two-inch ballistic glass on the street side. You placed your order through the intercom system, and the items were retrieved by the owner. Once paid for, the purchased items were delivered via a large metal drawer. Over the past several years, as the neighborhood degraded, residents of the community (gang members included) created an unspoken rule of protection surrounding the little store, and it had yet to be robbed in twenty-three years of operation. That didn't mean the owner would open the door, though. Not for anybody. Even a cop.

This perplexed Nash because the address Bishop had given him, 423 McCormick, was the store. The lights were on—he most likely opened shop at nine—but no one stood on the corner, and Nash didn't see anyone moving around behind that thick glass.

Reaching over to the glovebox, Nash pressed the release button, spilling eight-track tapes out on the floor. "Shit." He meant to fix that. At the back of the glove box, secured to the plastic with heavy-duty screws, was a leather holster housing a snub nose .38. He took that out, checked the cylinder, then shoved it under his belt at the small of his back. He also had his regulation Beretta in his shoulder rig and a Kel-Tec P-3AT in a holster on his ankle. He had no idea what to expect of the coming minutes, and if there had been a Samurai sword on the back seat, he probably would have grabbed that, too. Under his bulky down coat, he wore a kevlar vest. He'd put that on back at the FBI building—didn't want anyone to see him do it here.

He placed his POLICE placard on the dashboard, thought better of it, and tossed it down on the floor with the eight-track tapes. This wasn't the kind of place you wanted to advertise your employment with the po-po. Somebody had probably pegged him as a cop by now, anyway. He still hadn't seen a living soul, but he felt eyes on him—from up above, down the block, and behind. He was certain he was being watched. Whether those eyes belonged to Bishop or a local looking out for their own interest or the interests of their associates would remain to be seen.

With a deep breath, Nash shut off the Chevy and climbed out onto the icy cracked sidewalk. He closed the car door but didn't bother to lock it. The passenger side door didn't lock at all, and in a neighborhood like this, it was best to provide easy access to the interior. Otherwise, you'd find yourself shopping for a replacement window.

While the plows kept the streets relatively free of snow, even here, the sidewalks were another story. In some places, black snow reached heights of three to four feet. Against some of the abandoned storefronts, the drifts went even higher. Nobody had salted the sidewalk so Nash trudged along carefully, avoiding the icy patches, as the wind kicked up around him with a grumbling howl.

When he reached the window for the convenience store, noting the building had no signage depicting the store's name, he knocked on the glass, pressed his face up close, and looked inside. He spotted a man who was presumably the owner in a folding lawn chair at a desk to the left of the window reading the *Chicago Examiner*. He glanced up at Nash, then went back to the paper.

"What the fuck." Nash grumbled, knocking again.

Without looking up, the owner pressed the button on a bulky microphone beside him. "You want service, you use intercom." He went back to the paper, turning the page.

Nash started to reply, realized it wouldn't matter, and searched around the window until he found the intercom button embedded in an aluminum speaker on the left. He pressed the button with his gloved finger and said, "I'm here…"

His voice trailed off because he wasn't exactly sure what to say.

I'm here to see Anson Bishop.

Is Anson home?

Can Anson come out and play?

The man seemed to know exactly why he was here, though, and Nash didn't need to say anything further. The metal drawer below the window slid open—a flashlight and two D-cell batteries inside. "He said you can keep all your guns, but you'll need light."

Reaching into the drawer, Nash took out the large flashlight and fumbled with the cap on the bottom, twisting it off to get the batteries inside, then replacing it. Not an LED light but an older bulb model. Still bright, though.

"Six fifty-eight," the store owner said.

"What?"

"For the light and batteries. Six fifty-eight."

"Where's Bishop?"

The man rattled the drawer. "Six fifty-eight."

Digging in his pocket, Nash fished out a ten and put it in the drawer.

The owner pulled the drawer back to his side, took out the ten and put the bill in his own pocket, then settled back into his chair with the newspaper.

"What about my change?"

"Neighborhood beautification tax," the man said without looking up.

Nash wasn't in the mood to argue. It was too damn cold out. "Just tell me where to find Bishop."

The owner sighed, lowered the paper, and extended a bony finger. "He in 426, across street. You not alone, I supposed to say 430."

"I am alone."

"That's why 426. You some kind of dummy? I see you alone. Go now. Five-oh bad for business."

This time when the store owner raised the newspaper, he used it to shield himself from Nash's gaze. An impenetrable wall of ink and pulp.

Nash turned, nearly fell on a patch of ice, but managed to remain upright by grabbing the brick wall with his free hand. 426 across the street wasn't much to look at. A three-story red brick tenement with heavy black bars on the first-floor windows, plywood on the rest. Somebody had painted an orange penis on the green front door along with the phrase *CaliCorn '16*, which meant absolutely nothing to Nash.

"426 McCormick," he said aloud, looking up at the building. "As good a place to die as any."

He took a moment to look both ways before jaywalking across the center of the block, but the only other car he spotted was the burned out husk of an old van half-buried in snow.

17
Diary

"Turn to the left and give me a little pout," Paul Upchurch said from behind the camera.

I stuck my tongue out at him instead.

Father had told me to avoid photographs at all costs. Photographs created a record—documentation, evidence, timelines. All of these things could resurface at any point and become problematic. "You travel this world as a ghost, champ. The less people see you, the freer you become. Only the dead know true freedom."

Yet here we were. Standing in the parlor of Finicky's home. Me with my back against the wall and Paul holding up a thirty-five-millimeter camera that looked more expensive than some cars.

"What is this for?"

"The wall of shame on the stairs." Paul adjusted something on the camera, then got down on one knee and looked back through the lens. "Finicky usually insists we take them on the first full day, and you've been here nearly a week."

The camera clicked. The bright flash left white dots floating around the room.

"I saw that police detective this morning. The one who brought me here." I didn't tell Paul what I had seen of Tegan. That would lead to a two-hour grilling, and I wasn't ready to dedicate that kind of time today. I had plans.

"Welderman?"

"Yes, Welderman."

"The correct response is 'yeah.' You sound like an old person some-times. I think you should commit to using the word 'ain't' at least three times today."

The camera clicked again. Another flash.

"Turn to the right."

I couldn't say 'ain't' any more than I could say 'yeah' without a con-scious effort. Father had explained the importance of blending in to me, and I supposed I could do it in an effort to do so, but it would be an effort. Poor grammar did not come easily to me.

Paul made another camera adjustment. "Welderman is a tool, but he's here a lot. Same with that partner of his, Stocks. They're friends with Finicky, and sometimes they give the girls rides into town. The boys too, but mostly the girls."

"He smells like old grapefruit, but it beats walking."

This came from Kristina.

When I looked up, I found her standing in the parlor's arched entry-way. She wore nothing but a skimpy white bikini with a brown towel draped over her shoulder.

"Grapefruit and Old Spice," Tegan said, stepping up behind her in a black two-piece. Both girls had their hair pulled back in ponytails.

My face flushed at the sight of them, and my eyes went to the ground.

When Paul turned, his mouth fell open. "I think I love you both." Without looking through the viewfinder, he clicked off several shots of the girls with the camera. The two of them quickly fell into model-mode, pressing their backs together and smiling just so at the camera. Tilting their heads this way and that. Old pros.

"That's how you do it," Paul told them. His thumb jerked back in my direction. "Captain Stick-Up-His-Butt is camera shy."

"Is he now." Tegan grinned. "He wasn't so shy this morning."

She crossed the room, pulling Kristina along by the hand.

When they reached me, Tegan dropped her towel on the floor and put her arm around my waist. She leaned in close and whispered at my ear. "You weren't shy at all, were you, Anson?"

Kristina edged in on my other side and pressed her half-naked body against me.

My arms hung awkwardly at my sides. I wasn't sure where to put them. When my fingers brushed against Kristina's thigh, I curled them away.

Paul took another picture.

The two of them smelled like fresh wildflowers and baby powder. They pressed in tighter against me. Both so warm.

"Your face looks like a ripe tomato," Paul was kind enough to point out, which only made my cheeks burn more.

Tegan giggled. She reached over, tapped Kristina on the shoulder, and pointed down toward my crotch.

"Well, that was easy," Kristina said with a soft laugh.

"I told you." Tegan beamed. She cocked her head back toward the parlor's entrance. "Libby, want to see Anson's hard-on? I think he wants you to see it!"

Both my hands went to the front of my jeans, and the girls giggled again, grinding against me.

"Libby, come in here! Hurry up!"

I saw her shadow then, just a hint of it, beyond the parlor on the hallway wall. But she didn't step into the room.

"I think I'm going to go back up to my room," a thin voice said. I'd never heard her speak before, but the pitch of her voice, the inflection, sounded like I'd known it my entire life.

Tegan rolled her eyes and stomped off toward the hallway. "The last place you need to be is locked in your room. You're going to go with us to get some sun. You're as pasty as a corpse."

If I felt awkward sandwiched between the two girls, it felt even weirder to be standing there with Kristina alone.

Paul didn't seem to care. He snapped another picture.

None of us heard Ms. Finicky enter the room from the formal dining room. She'd probably been in the kitchen. "Anson, you should take your shirt off. The two of you look unbalanced—Kristina there in a lovely bathing suit, showing off her curves, and you dressed for church." She turned to Paul. "You'll never learn to properly photograph if these things aren't apparent to you."

"Yes, ma'am," Paul said.

Ms. Finicky turned back to me. "Well?"

When I didn't move, Kristina started on the buttons of my shirt. "I'll get it." Her voice no longer sounded playful. For a moment, I thought she actually sounded frightened.

18

Nash

Nash nearly fell on his ass climbing the icy steps. When he reached the top, he found someone had kicked in the green door with the large orange penis painted on it. The wood along the frame was splintered, the dead bolt gone. Looked like it had been that way for a while. He gave it a gentle push, and it swung inward on a dark hallway covered in peeling floral wallpaper. He switched on the flashlight and scrolled the light over the interior. Several boards were missing from the scratched and faded hardwood floors, revealing open joists and holes to the basement. The yellow beam of the flashlight dipped down into those holes but revealed nothing beneath. He could only see about ten feet down the hallway before the light petered out.

"Bishop? I'm coming in."

He stepped forward tentatively, wondering just how sturdy that floor was. He wasn't exactly a small man. At last check, he weighed in at two-twenty, and that was before he strapped on his arsenal and enough winter gear to survive a walk in the Arctic. He took out the Baretta. "I'm armed, and I will shoot you if you do anything stupid."

The only reply came from the wind, howling through an open window somewhere in the building. A piece of loose wallpaper beside him rattled, reminding Nash of a moth stuck to the wall trying to break free. "Where the hell are you?"

"Are you alone?"

Bishop's voice startled him, something he'd never admit. Not to *anyone*. There was something in the timbre of it. He hadn't shouted, he hadn't spoken the words loud at all, yet his voice seemed to come from every direction. From up ahead as well as sneaking up from behind. Above and below. His voice inched up on you the same way a snake might. You look down at your feet and it's just there, coiled and ready to strike.

"You said alone, so I came alone. I don't need an army to put a bullet in your head." Nash stepped deeper into the hallway, checking each room as he went with the flashlight—an old sitting room, a dining room, a dilapidated bathroom. "Why couldn't we just meet at Starbucks or something?"

"Where's the fun in that?"

The floorboards creaked behind him and Nash spun around, leading with his gun and following close behind with the flashlight. Nobody was there.

"Jumpy, aren't you?"

"Where are you?"

"Take the steps to the second floor," Bishop replied, and surely this time, his voice had come from above.

Nash brought the beam of the flashlight to the ceiling, and he thought he saw someone watching him through one of the holes. "If I fall and break something, it's on you. I'm suing. Metro PD healthcare is shit."

"I remember," Bishop said, his voice more muffled this time. More distant. "Take the steps slowly and stay close to the wall. You'll be just fine."

Nash had stopped at the staircase. It ran against the wall on the left, wooden treads disappearing up into the dark. "Why am I here?" He eyed the banister, but with the gun in his right hand and the flashlight in his left, something would have to give if he wanted to hold on—that wasn't happening. He placed a foot on the first step and felt it sag under his weight. He inched closer to the side of the wall and brought his other foot up. It held. He took the next step.

"You're doing just fine, Nash."

"Fuck you."

"So hostile."

The next step crunched underfoot, and Nash thought for sure he'd bust through, but the wood held. He took the final four a little faster and found himself standing on a landing at the foot of a hallway. Three doors were closed, two more open, another missing altogether.

"Where am I going, shithead?" He ran the beam up and down the hallway, toward each open door, but didn't see anything.

"We'll never be friends if you treat me like that. Friends respect each other."

"Step out in the open," Nash replied. "Give me a clean shot. I'd hate to just wing you. Best if I put you out of your misery quick. I catch you in your gut or something, and you could be up here bleeding out for days. That would be just terrible."

"I'm sure you would be wrought with worry and remorse. Last room, the one without the door."

Nash followed Bishop's voice, stepped forward. He pointed his gun toward that last room while also scanning the others with the flashlight as he passed. "Why don't you just come out into the open?"

"I don't want to give you your clean shot. I'm fairly certain you'd take it."

"You got that right," Nash replied under his breath.

He considered opening the closed doors but thought better of it. He knew where Bishop was; the strange echo downstairs was gone. Whenever Bishop spoke, his voice clearly came from that final room at the end of the hall. As he approached the opening, his grip tightened on the gun. "I'm coming in, Bishop. Don't try anything stupid."

"I wouldn't dream of it."

That final room was a large unfurnished bedroom with a boarded window on the far wall and a closet behind double louvered doors on the left. Like the rest of the house, wallpaper curled away from the cracked plasterboard, the lattice visible beneath. An old ceiling fan hung from nothing but a single wire at the center of the room, ready to fall with the slightest provocation.

Near the boarded window, kneeling on the floor with his back to the door, his hands clasped together and head bowed as if in prayer, was Anson Bishop.

Nash pointed his gun at the back of the man's head. "Don't move, you piece of shit."

19

Clair

Day 5 • 9:23 AM

The basement of John H. Stroger, Jr. Hospital was enormous. Aside from that, it was a cluttered mess. Years of discarded medical equipment filled nearly every available space—gurneys, beds, IV stands, wheelchairs—then there were boxes. It was obvious at some point someone had tried to keep it all organized, but it was also obvious that had been years ago. Although rooms were labeled, at this point those tags were no more than polite suggestions. If the staff needed to rid themselves of something, it went wherever it fit and was forgotten. The only space they found in relatively neat condition was the hospital's HVAC room, and that was where Clair had found Ernest Skow. A black man in his sixties, sitting on a milk crate wearing filthy overalls, and attempting to eat a breakfast sandwich when she, Stout, and the three other security guards Stout had ordered to help in the search had exited the elevator.

"Ernest, call me Ernest," he insisted, finishing off the sandwich and brushing the crumbs from his lips. "Now what's this about tunnels?"

Clair said, "Bootlegging tunnels. They run under most of the city. A lot of these older buildings, and even some of the new ones have access."

Ernest scratched at the stubble on his chin. "I've been working down here the better part of two decades, and I ain't ever noticed tunnels."

"How well do you know this basement?" Stout asked.

The man cocked his head. "I know the equipment, the hardware I maintain. As for the rest, I don't go out there. That's not my business."

"Do you know where the phone lines come into the building? The phone company leases some of the tunnels for equipment," Clair said.

His eyes rolled toward the ceiling, and he scratched his chin again. "I believe they come in on the west wall. There's another bank of elevators over there, and I hear the tech guys plodding around that part of the basement every once in a while. They don't venture over to this side much. Must be over there."

"Show us."

As Ernest led them through the maze of discarded equipment, Clair's eyes kept landing on the gurneys—some stood alone, others had been used to transport old equipment and boxes and still rested under their charge. Several were broken and scattered about. There were many of them, though, and Clair wondered if this was where Bishop found the ones he used for Emory and Guther Herbert. Both had been handcuffed to gurneys, and you couldn't exactly pick them up at the local Walmart.

Ernest pointed up at the ceiling. "Those are phone lines, the gray ones. The blue cables are Internet."

Dozens of thick cables, all bound together with zip ties and fastened to the concrete ceiling with brackets. All eyes were on the ceiling as they followed the bundle of wires deeper into the basement. When they finally reached the outer wall, the cables disappeared through a four-inch round hole in the concrete foundation sealed up tight with a rubber gasket.

No tunnel. No visible openings.

"Shit," Clair muttered, her eyes drifting up and down the wall. "I thought for sure..."

Stout had turned left at the wall and was following it, inching along with one hand pressing on the concrete as if some secret passage might reveal itself if he tripped a hidden lever.

Clair stared at the smooth concrete wall. "What year was this place built?"

Ernest didn't hesitate. "1912. That I do know."

"The tunnels were started around 1899," Clair replied. "Makes sense they would have used them here. This concrete looks more recent. I wonder if they covered them up."

"The foundation was reinforced back in the eighties. None of this is original construction. I suppose they could have sealed them up in the process."

Clair's phone rang—Kloz.

She answered and pressed it to her ear. "Yeah?"

"Paul Upchurch is awake."

Her brow furrowed. "What? They said he wouldn't—"

"He's talking," Klozowski interrupted. "You need to get up there."

20

Diary

"Keep your voice down!" Paul told me, even though I hadn't said anything and the volume of his own voice was loud enough to carry.

We were crawling through the tall grass behind the house, about half-way to the barn.

"I think I see them," he said, raising his head just enough to see out over the field. "About fifty feet before the barn."

I raised my own head, and he grabbed me by the shoulder and tugged me back down. "They'll see you!"

I frowned at him. "Did they see you?"

"No, but I'm stealthy. I'm like a ghost ninja. Practically invisible. No-body sees me unless I want them to."

The girls had left the parlor the moment Ms. Finicky turned her back—rushing down the hallway and out the back door. Libby hadn't stepped into the room at all, but I watched her shadow shrink away with the other two. I heard the patter of three pairs of feet leave the house. Finicky had taken the camera from Paul and ushered both of us out of the room, too. When we got to the foot of the stairs, he grabbed my arm and nodded toward the front door.

A moment later, we were outside, rounding the house.

"We'll give them a twenty count, then go after them. We don't want to be too close behind."

"Too close behind for what?"

Paul rolled his eyes. "To watch them. They clearly want us to watch them. Why else would they stop by the parlor dressed like that?"

"Maybe because it was on the way out?" I offered.

"God, you're naive when it comes to the ways of the modern woman."

I think I wanted you to see.

Ms. Carter's words echoed into my head from nowhere.

"Kristina was clearly flirting with you, and Tegan could barely keep her hands off me," Paul said. "You need to learn to read the signals."

"The signals?"

"All girls send signals. Like a homing beacon, or a siren's song. Do you really think they wanted to sunbathe?" He shook his head. "No way. They're lying around in the grass half-naked because they want us to watch."

Somewhere nearby, a girl giggled.

Paul pulled me closer to the ground. "Shit!"

Neither of us said anything for a minute or two, then he slowly raised his head again, just enough to see through the grass.

"Do you see them?"

"Uh huh," he said softly. "It's glorious."

He crawled on his belly about ten more feet, and I followed. When we stopped, I could hear the girls talking, but I couldn't make out the words. I pushed myself up on my elbows. I saw them then. Tegan was closest, lying on her towel on her belly, facing away from us. Kristina was beside her, also on her belly. She had her knees bent, her bare legs curled up behind her, absentmindedly swaying around. Libby was there, too, on the opposite side of both girls. I could barely see her, just a hint of a foot.

"I want to go around to the other side." I said.

"Why? Tegan is right there and—oh, shit—"

Tegan had reached around to her back and untied the string of her top. "Can you put lotion on me?"

We had edged close enough to hear her.

Kristina sat up with a bottle of lotion in her hand and squirted a little on Tegan's back and began to rub it in. "Just a little," Kristina said. "They said they wanted us to lose the tan lines."

"I don't want to burn."

"We won't stay out long," Kristina replied. "You should lose these, too." She tugged at the string on Tegan's bottoms, and they fell away. Just like that.

Beside me, Paul gasped. I might have, too.

"No more than thirty minutes," Tegan said. "I can't look like a lobster."

Kristina turned around, faced Libby. "I'm not sure if lotion is good for bruises or bad."

"I don't think it can hurt," Tegan said. "They'll fade. They're already going away. I think we can hide them with a little cover-up if we need to."

"Maybe a little lotion."

This voice was neither Tegan or Kristina. It had come from Libby.

"Just be careful with the spot on my back. That one still hurts pretty bad."

21

Nash

Day 5 • 9:25 AM

Kneeling, facing away from Nash and toward the boarded window, was Anson Bishop. He didn't turn as Nash entered the room, he didn't move at all. His body remained as still as a corpse, posed in much the same way as the bodies found earlier today.

"Please tell me there are three white boxes holding your various bits on the ground in front of you," Nash said as stepped closer, the barrel of his gun trained on the other man.

Bishop didn't reply.

The beam from Nash's flashlight caused Bishop's shadow to stretch across the room and rise up on the far wall, a creature of long sharp lines.

The floor groaned under Nash's weight. He cautiously stepped around Bishop.

Bishop's eyes were closed. "How's Sam? I worry about him."

"Do you have any weapons on you?"

"I do not."

Bishop wore only a gray sweatshirt, jeans, and hiking boots. A heavy jacket, scarf, and hat were balled up on the floor in the far corner of the room. There was no furniture.

Using the toe of his shoe, Nash lifted the back of Bishop's sweatshirt. No gun. "Put your hands behind your head."

Bishop did as he was told.

"Clasp your fingers together."

Bishop did.

That's when Nash noticed the sign.

Propped against Bishop's chest, identical to the one found on the body in the cemetery, was a cardboard sign. Only, this one didn't say, "Father, forgive me," this sign said, "I Surrender."

"Where's the rest of the virus?" Nash said.

Bishop's eyes remained closed. "What virus?"

Nash pressed the barrel of his gun into Bishop's temple, ground the metal into his skin. "Sam's the patient one, not me. I've got zero problem ending you right here and telling everyone I found you that way. Do you think anyone would care? The city would probably throw a parade. I've got a hospital full of sick people. I'm going to ask you one last time, where is the rest of the virus?"

Bishop licked his lips. "Aren't hospitals usually filled with sick people?"

Nash kicked him.

His foot hauled back and slammed into Bishop's chest before he even realized he did it. And it felt damn good. "Do you think the families of those two women this morning would care if I threw you through that fucking window? Where the hell is the rest of the virus?"

With the kick, Bishop had doubled over, but somehow he managed to keep his fingers interlaced on the back of his head, and after several coughs, he caught his breath and straightened back up. "I've clearly surrendered to a member of Chicago Metro. I've made no attempt at hostility. No aggressive moves. Yet this detective feels it is necessary to use force against me, threaten my life. This is why I invited you here, to witness this. To document the way I knew he would treat me. The way I *have been* treated from the beginning. Chicago Metro wants me as a scapegoat. All they're trying to do is protect their own. This man, Detective Brian Nash, is Sam Porter's partner. They've been friends for many years. I don't know how deep into it this detective is, but he's clearly dirty, maybe as dirty as Porter. I am innocent of everything these people have accused me of."

Nash's face burned red as he stared down at him. "Who the hell are you talking to?"

The wind kicked up outside, and the house groaned.

Bishop opened his eyes for the first time and nodded toward the corner of the room. Sitting in the dust and filth of the neglected hardwood floor, surrounded by cobwebs and grime, was a small GoPro camera. The tiny lens faced out into the room, faced the two of them.

With the heel of his shoe, Nash crushed it with a satisfying crunch. Stomped on it again, several more times, until it was nothing but a mangled mess.

This didn't seem to bother Bishop in the slightest. A smile grew on his lips. "I didn't trust you to bring me in clean, so I called Channel Seven before I called you. Your friend Lizeth Loudon. They placed the camera. They're recording the live feed from next door. You asked me why this building," Bishop looked up at him. "That's why."

Nash looked from Bishop to the smashed camera under his foot, then back again. His heart felt like it might burst through his rib cage. He took a step back and cupped his hand over the small microphone attached to the collar of his jacket. "Poole, can you hear me? Get your team in here, now."

22

Clair

Day 5 • 9:26 AM

After surgery, Paul Upchurch was moved to an isolation room at the far end of ICU on the fifth floor. Clair rode the elevator up from the basement, and Dr. Beyer met her in the hallway. His hair was slightly disheveled, and his eyes appeared a little weary, but beyond that, he looked better than she expected for a man plucked from his life and dropped into the center of this mess.

"The hospital tells me they have nearly a dozen people experiencing flu-like symptoms right now associated with the SARS virus."

"Uh huh," Clair said from behind her mask. Her eyes itched, and she fought the urge to sneeze again. She wasn't about to discuss the happenings of her stomach and gastrointestinal tract—she'd had more pleasant experiences after a night of binge-eating Mexican.

Beyer wore a mask, too, but he didn't look sick. "Are you…" The words trailed off, because he already knew the answer. "You were exposed earlier than most."

"I'm fine."

"You don't look fine. You should have someone administer a saline drip. You're dehydrated."

"I'm just tired. We haven't caught a break in this case in days. Things are just getting worse."

He took her by the wrist and pinched the skin on the back of her hand. "See how your skin tents and doesn't immediately go back? You're losing elasticity, a sure sign of dehydration." He released her hand. "Are they treating you at all?"

Clair shrugged. "They gave me a shot of something earlier to boost my immune system. Aside from that, there's not much they can do. I'll ask about the saline." She nodded toward the hall. "Look, I appreciate your concern, but I've got a job to do here—what did Upchurch tell you?"

Dr. Beyer looked back down the hallway. "We removed the ventilator tube as a standard postoperative test to see whether or not he was capable of involuntary actions such as breathing and swallowing on his own. I fully expected to replace the tube immediately, but he coughed, then he grabbed my arm." The doctor paused for a moment to consider this. He rubbed at his forearm. "I don't understand it. The parts of his brain that control speech and reasoning have been decimated. He shouldn't comprehend what a word is anymore, let alone have the ability to construct a sentence."

"Doctor, *what did he say?*"

Dr. Beyer started walking again, back toward ICU. "A name. I couldn't make it out at first. He struggled to get it out, then he repeated the name several times—Sarah...Sarah Werner. Does that mean anything to you?"

At this point, Clair knew the name well, but she still had no idea who Sarah Werner really was. Sam had called her from Werner's phone. They had learned that Sam had spent the last two days bouncing around the country with a woman he believed to be Sarah Werner. They also knew the real Sarah Werner, a New Orleans attorney, was dead and had been for several weeks now, her body left to rot in her apartment. A prison guard in New Orleans, a man named Vincent Weidner, had also asked for Sarah Werner when he was taken into custody. He, along with the woman pretending to be Werner, the one with Sam, had broken another woman out of that same prison. That woman had been found dead here in Chicago in the lobby of the Guyon Hotel. Sam was apparently the shooter. Something she knew in her heart couldn't possibly be true. Sam had told Poole the woman he knew as Sarah Werner was actually Bishop's mother. So, was Upchurch asking for her or the dead attorney?

"Through here," Dr. Beyer said, ushering her through a series of doors into a small antechamber. He handed her a sealed package containing clothing. "You'll need to put this on. He'd never survive contact with the virus. We can't risk contamination."

"You sure know how to make a girl feel welcome." Clair tore open the package and tugged on the disposable yellow plastic suit. He handed her a pair of matching boots and a large mask that covered her entire head and fastened to the rest of the suit with some kind of sticky seam on contact. He fastened a belt around her waist which held a small air tank. The hose snapped into the back of her suit. The moment it clicked into place, she felt the rush of cool air all around her.

When he finished helping her, Dr. Beyer put on a similar suit with practiced speed. "The air tank will last for fifteen minutes. I doubt we'll need more time than that." His voice came through some kind of built-in comm system. "Ready?"

Clair nodded.

She followed him through another door and into Paul Upchurch's room.

Clair hadn't gotten a good look at him when they brought him in. He had collapsed into police custody and was immediately ushered into the ICU and prepped for surgery. The man lying in the bed before her was the stuff of nightmares. His skin was pasty gray and shimmered with a thin layer of sweat. She expected his head to be wrapped in layers of bandages, but that wasn't the case at all. Instead, the surgical incision was clearly visible under a transparent bandage. Meant to expand, the bandage was filled with some kind of liquid. She didn't know if it was medicinal, placed there to help with the healing process, or some kind of pus, but the sight of it nearly made her gag. His hair and both eyebrows were gone. Either the hair had fallen out with treatment or had been shaved in preparation for surgery. He looked alien, not human at all, and he was staring directly at her.

Upchurch had blue eyes according to his file, but to look at them, you'd never know. The eyes that fixed on her were a milky gray, bloodshot and yellow where they should have been white.

Dr. Beyer crossed the room to the rack of machines beside the bed and studied the various graphs and numbers on the colorful readout. His back was to her. She couldn't see his face.

Clair edged closer to the bed. Upchurch's gaze followed her. His tongue came out and licked at his dry, chapped lips. Like his eyes and skin, his tongue wasn't pink but the same gray, lifeless color. She knew she was looking at a dead man. Something in his gaze told her that he knew the truth, too.

Upchurch's right hand twitched and lifted about an inch off the bed before falling back down. The handcuffs clattered against the metal. It seemed absurd they were there at all; this man wasn't going anywhere. When his lips moved, they didn't bring words but a dull smack, a labored gasp at the air.

Through all this, Upchurch's gaze remained on her. If he blinked, she hadn't seen it.

Clair took another step closer. "My name is Detective Clair Norton with Chicago Metro. Do you know where you are?"

With effort, his head moved in a slight nod. His eyes did close then.

"He's heavily medicated, but I imagine even the slightest move-ment would be painful right now. It would take immense concentration," Dr. Beyer told her.

She hadn't seen him turn around, but he was facing her now from the opposite side of Upchurch's bed.

"You asked for Sarah Werner," Clair told Upchurch. "She's dead."

If he understood what she said, his face didn't betray him. His lips smacked again, and Clair willed her feet to stay put while the rest of her wanted to run from the room.

Again, his lips moved, and this time she was certain he *was* try-ing to speak. There was a voice there, albeit feeble. She leaned in close enough to make out what he was saying, then frowned at him. "You see? You see what?"

A thin trail of blood began to seep out from the corner of his mouth, from one of the cracks, and it was almost too much for her to bear. "I finally see," he told her, his voice just a little stronger.

"See what?"

He tried to raise his head, to get closer to her, but the motion was too much. He fell back into his pillow.

Clair leaned in instead, as close as she could get, ready to tear off her mask if that's what she needed to do in order to hear him.

When Upchurch spoke again, the next four words fell from his dying mouth, the whispers of a ghost—Clair wished she could unhear them. She took a step back, her mouth falling open. "Oh, hell no."

Clair nearly tore off the containment suit as she backed out of Upchurch's room, Dr. Beyer and the others staring at her.

23

Clair

Day 5 • 9:31 AM

Ten minutes later, in the small office with Kloz, Clair had her head buried in her hands. She sat on the floor in the corner against the wall, rocking slowly back and forth.

At first, Klozowski had hovered over her, tried to comfort her, but he'd backed off and returned to his chair, settled back into the safety of his laptop's glow. He looked as uncomfortable as she felt.

This couldn't be happening.

"He's delirious, Clair. What he said, it's meaningless."

Clair continued to rock. "He said it. I'm a cop. I have to report it. There will be a record. Christ, when the papers get ahold of this…"

"Are you sure you heard him correctly? Maybe you misunderstood."

"I never heard something so clear in my life."

"You said you were in some kind of hazmat suit. How could you hear through that?"

Clair rocked even faster. "He said '*Sam Porter is 4MK.*' It was plain as day. I didn't misunderstand nothing. The doctor was right there, too. I'm sure he heard it. God, there was a nurse. She probably heard him. Who knows who else…"

"You need to get a statement from him," Kloz said softly. "Before he dies."

She stopped rocking. "I'm not going back in there."

"We need to understand what he knows."

"He's lying," she said defiantly. "Anson Bishop is 4MK."

"What if he's not?"

She glared at him. "Whose side are you on?"

Kloz held up both his hands. "I'm not on anybody's side, but we're in here alone and when this gets out—and you know it will—if we don't get some kind of statement out of him, how will that look? They'll accuse us of protecting Sam."

"We know Upchurch killed Ella Reynolds and Lili Davies…he tried to kill Larissa Biel and Katy Quigley. Probably the parents. He killed that boy, Wesley. He says something like this, who is going to believe him?"

Even as Clair said the words, she knew people would.

"You're not considering *not* reporting it, right?" Kloz asked. "That's not an option on the table right now. Is it?"

Clair looked up at him but said nothing.

Klozowski's mouth fell open. "Then why did you tell me?"

"Maybe we should just keep it quiet until we know what it means."

Kloz shook his head. "I'm calling Nash."

"I tried already. He's going to voice mail."

"Poole, then," Kloz said. "We should tell Poole."

"He's going straight to voice mail, too."

The phone on the wall began to ring, and the two of them looked up at the little flashing light. Neither moved. It wasn't until the fourth ring that Klozowski stood and answered.

Clair listened to his side of the conversation, watched as he nodded his head several times, then finally hung up. She knew exactly what that call was before he said a word. He said it anyway.

"Upchurch is dead."

24
Diary

Detective Welderman returned that night. He didn't come into the house. Instead, he sat out in the driveway, behind the wheel of his car, the engine rumbling, window down, a cigarette slipping out every minute or so as he tapped away the ashes. He sat out there for about five minutes before Tegan and Kristina left the house and climbed into his back seat. I watched as they drove off, his taillights turning into tiny red pinpricks before disappearing completely. It was just a little after nine.

"Do you know where they go?" I asked.

Paul was up on his bunk working on his comic, The Misadventures of Maybelle Markel. *He'd stolen one of Tegan's sweaters from her room the night before, and he raised it to his nose and gave it a good sniff. "Quiet. I'm trying to get inspiration."*

"By smelling Tegan's sweater?"

"Smelling her panties would be creepy."

I was fairly certain Paul had a wide assortment of Tegan's clothing hidden away somewhere, but I had yet to find it.

"He takes them somewhere nearly every night. Where do they go?"

Paul set the sweater aside and began drawing again. "I think you should focus on the positive—it's not you in the back of a police detective's car right now. That's no way to spend an evening."

"Do you know where he takes them?"

Paul shuffled through his markers, picked the red one, and began coloring in his sketch. "You, my friend, are asking the wrong questions."

"I am?"

"What you should be asking is how do you get Kristina to rub her hot little body up against you again like she did down in the parlor."

My face blushed again. "She was just messing around."

Paul snorted. "She was messing around, with you. For those of us well versed in the ways of the woman, this was her subtle way of saying you're tall enough to ride this ride, all you need to do is buy a ticket and climb aboard."

"I'm pretty sure that's not what she meant."

He ignored me. "She gave you an easy-pass. Wants you to smell her flower. A bit of bam-bam in the ham. Some aggressive cuddling. Boffing. Boinking. Dinky-tickling. Hide...the bishop...with Bishop. If you had half a brain, you'd be across the hall climbing under her sheets and waiting for your Maid Marian to come home all riled up after her girls' night out."

"A girls' night out? With the police detective?"

"Where do you think they went?" Paul capped the red marker and started in with the green one. "What were they wearing? Our two lovely housemates?"

I told him Tegan had been wearing a black dress and high heels. I think Kristina's dress was dark blue, but it was hard to tell in the light.

"They don't dress up like that for us," Paul pointed out. "We get jam-jams and frumpy sweats most of the time. Today was a special treat."

Down the hall, I heard a door slam. Then Weasel shouted at someone. Probably his roommate, The Kid. They were both a little younger than the rest of us and mostly kept to themselves. Weasel was probably around twelve. I had no idea what his real name was—Weasel suited him just fine. He had beady eyes, and he crinkled his nose whenever he got upset, which was most of the time. I had no idea why they called The Kid 'The Kid,' but they did, so I did too.

Paul held up his drawing.

Tegan, naked, lying on her towel with her eyes closed. Kristina hovering above her with the bottle of suntan lotion upside down, a single drop about to land on Tegan's back. Tegan's red sweater was bunched up near her head. It was quite good.

"Where's Libby?"

Paul glanced at the drawing and pointed to a foot in the far corner, barely visible. "Right there."

"No, I mean, why didn't she go with them?"

Paul rolled his eyes and went back to work on the drawing. "You've got a hottie like Kristina fawning all over you, and you're wondering about someone like Libby?" He shook his head. "She's broken, man. Let her go. A girl like that will never be right. She'll be here for a few weeks, and someone will cart her off to wherever they send girls like that. She's not long for our world. Best not to get too attached. Finicky didn't even bother to get a picture of her for the wall."

I still hadn't seen her, not really. Glimpses here and there. The flutter of blonde hair. Her shadow on the wall. Even today, outside in the open, she managed to stay invisible—shrinking into her surroundings until she was nothing but a ghost of a girl, a wispy afterthought.

I went to the door and pressed my ear against the wood. "What do you think Ms. Finicky is doing right now?"

Paul shrugged. "Practicing witchcraft, would be my guess. Boiling small children in a cauldron down in the basement. Gotta simmer for thirty, then add the paprika with just a pinch of salt."

When I opened the door and peered out into the hallway, I didn't see anyone. Weasel's door was closed. Kristina and Tegan had left their door open. Vince's door was open—I hadn't seen him all day. I wasn't sad about that. Libby's door wasn't open or closed, but cracked. Nothing but darkness on the other side.

Paul tossed a Snickers bar at me. It struck me in my side and fell to the ground. "Kristina likes chocolate—can't hurt to bring a bribe."

I picked up the candy bar, but I wasn't going to Kristina's room.

25

Nash

Day 5 • 9:37 AM

"Go! Go! Go!"

The voices came through Nash's earbud, and a moment later he heard them enter the building. The crash of the front door, boots on the stairs. They cleared each room as they went, calling out as they found each space empty, as they grew closer.

As the flurry of voices approached, Nash remained still. His eyes didn't leave Bishop. It took every ounce of his willpower to keep from pulling the trigger and ending him. Bishop didn't move, either. When two members of SWAT rushed into the room, followed swiftly by three more, he still didn't move. They shouted. They grabbed at his hands and arms and pulled them to his back before securing them with handcuffs. Then there was a foot in the center of Bishop's back, pushing him down—the officer leaned down over him, his full weight and the weight of his gear grinding Bishop's face into the filthy floor.

Bishop didn't make a sound.

Through all of this, Nash remained frozen.

They bound Bishop's feet together with zip ties.

They patted him down, turned all his pockets inside out. They found nothing.

Nash felt a hand on his shoulder.

Poole.

He didn't say anything. There was no need.

Nash finally holstered his gun, then knelt next to Bishop, cleared his throat. "You have the right to remain silent..." He rattled off the rest as the others watched, the room growing oddly quiet. When he finished, he told them to take Bishop outside.

Four of them lifted him from the ground, this inanimate thing, and carried him from the room.

"The press is already here," Poole said.

"I know."

"Get out there and make a statement before my supervisor calls and tells me to do it."

"This is Sam's bust. It should be him."

"Nobody is putting Sam in front of a camera. Not right now."

Nash ran his hand through his hair, smoothed it down as best he could. "Everything about this is fucked."

Poole said nothing to this, looking down at the remains of the camera.

Nash left the room before he could ask him about that, scooping up Bishop's cardboard sign on his way out.

He followed the men carrying Bishop through the hallway, down the steps, and out the front door onto the stoop of the building and froze.

The block, which had been completely deserted less than twenty minutes ago, was somehow teeming with people. Nearly a dozen law enforcement vehicles—vans, cars, SWAT—filled the street. He'd expected those. As per the instructions he'd worked out with Poole, they had followed about a half-mile behind him and positioned about two blocks over, just far enough to remain out of sight. The locals had crawled out, too, filled the icy sidewalks. Two news vans, another attempting to get past a Metro road block.

The four men carried Bishop down the steps and into the waiting mouth of a black SWAT van where two more helped get him inside and close the doors. All of this played out in a matter of minutes, and to Nash, none of it seemed real. Several of the reporters yelled out the same question that was running through his head—why would Bishop turn himself in?

Cameras clicked away all around and he realized their focus had shifted from Bishop being loaded into the van to him standing on the stoop of 426 McCormick, the green door busted and hanging at an odd angle on two of the three remaining hinges. *Half-cocked*, Nash thought as he looked at the orange penis spray-painted on the front. This made him smile, if only for a second. Several more camera clicks brought him back.

"Can you hold up the sign?"

This came from one of the photographers. He was wearing a navy blue jacket with *Chicago Examiner* emblazoned on the front.

Nash remembered Bishop's cardboard sign in his hand and turned it around backward so the writing was no longer visible. The photographer took the picture anyway.

Lizeth Loudon, the reporter from Channel Seven, stood at the bottom facing her own cameraman, but Nash couldn't hear what she was saying. A moment later, she turned to him and said, "You're live, Detective. Is it true Anson Bishop turned himself in?"

Nash opened his mouth to speak, then realized he wasn't sure what he should say. He hadn't given it a second of thought. Sam always made it look so easy—some off-the-cuff remark.

Loudon stood there, her microphone thrust at his face, for what was probably only a second or two but seemed to stretch on for minutes. Nash cleared his throat. "Earlier this morning, Anson Bishop contacted Chicago Metro and made..." He couldn't tell them about the threats. If he said Bishop threatened to release more of the virus if he didn't come to this meeting alone, it would just cause panic. He needed to say something comforting, something to set everyone at ease. That's what Sam would do. "We knew he'd be here, and through a joint effort with the FBI, Chicago Metro utilized the opportunity to capture Bishop and take him into custody."

Loudon's brow furrowed. She brought the microphone back to her mouth. "What about the victims found this morning? Has the virus been recovered? Will the people in Stroger Hospital be permitted to leave now?"

Nash didn't answer any of these things. Instead, he said, "Chicago can finally rest easy knowing the monster who has been terrorizing our city is behind bars."

He pushed past her, through the crowd, and made his way back to his Chevy.

Both his front tires were flat.

From the corner of his eye, he caught the convenience store owner watching him from the window of the corner market. When he turned to him, the man pulled down the blinds.

26

Clair

Day 5 • 10:02 AM

"Oh, this is messed up."

Clair didn't really need Klozowski to say it out loud, but the man felt the need to state the obvious anyway. She was ready to cross the room, slam his laptop shut, and beat him over the head with it. Not the first time she had such an urge, but maybe the first time she was ready to act on it. If she wasn't feeling so damn tired, achy, and sniffly, that was.

When she called Captain Dalton to tell him Upchurch was dead he didn't seem surprised by the news, and she supposed there was no reason to be, but when she told him what Upchurch said to her, that didn't seem to shock him either, and that *was* wrong. He knew Sam well enough to know it wasn't true, yet he'd taken the news as if she had just reiterated the latest weather report, then he told her not to tell anyone—not the press, not the feds, not anyone.

Her phone buzzed, and she glanced down at the screen—

Bishop in custody

The message was from Nash.

"Nash caught Bishop." Clair said this so quietly she wasn't sure Kloz even heard her.

He leaned in closer to his laptop screen. "I know. I said, it's messed up. Come here, you gotta see this."

She'd been sitting on the floor, her back against the wall, just inside the door, and when she stood, her various joints cracked in protest. He turned the laptop screen to face her. At the top of the screen was a still shot of Nash standing outside somewhere holding a cardboard sign that said *I Surrender*. Below that was another box with a video playing on a loop—Anson Bishop was crouched on the floor in some room, and Nash was kicking him. Each time his foot made contact with Bishop's stomach, the video looped and repeated. Below both images, in large block letters, was the caption—*Chicago's finest at work*.

"This is all over social media right now," Kloz said.

"Oh no."

"It gets worse." Kloz clicked on a link below the images, and another video came up. It started with Nash's foot catching Bishop in the gut—clearly where the other shot had come from—then Bishop recovered, coughed several times, and said, "I've clearly surrendered to a member of Chicago Metro. I've made no attempt at hostility. No aggressive moves. Yet this detective feels it is necessary to use force against me, threaten my life. This is why I invited you here, to witness this. To document the way I knew he would treat me. The way I *have been* treated from the beginning. Chicago Metro wants me as a scapegoat. All they're trying to do is protect their own. This man, Detective Brian Nash, is Sam Porter's partner. They've been friends for many years. I don't know how deep into it this detective is, but he's clearly dirty, maybe as dirty as Porter. I am innocent of everything these people have accused me of."

"Nash destroyed the camera right after that. Channel Seven has tape of all of it, and they've licensed the footage to everyone. All the major networks are running with it," Kloz said, his fingers clicking away furiously at the keys. "They're demanding access to Bishop and full transparency while he's in custody. They want to talk to Sam, too. They want to know Sam's whereabouts at the times of the murders this morning. All the other ones, too. This is a mess."

Sam Porter is 4MK.

"Bishop coordinated this with Upchurch," Clair said flatly. "Somehow, they worked this out in advance."

Clair's phone started to ring.

"Fuck, now what?" She dug it out and answered.

It was Stout. "We need both of you in the cafeteria right now. We've got a serious—"

The call dropped.

#

They heard the crowd the moment they pushed through the door out into the hallway, a churning mess of angry voices all trying to be heard above one another. Stout and three of his men were standing between the mob—there was no other way to describe it—and the glass doors leading out of the cafeteria into the hospital's main corridor, lobby, and ultimately the exits. One of the men in the crowd held a chair above his head, another had a metal coatrack; he was swinging it at Stout. The two officers Clair had stationed down here were nowhere to be seen.

She pushed through everyone and made her way to the front. She stood between Stout and Coatrack Man with one hand on the butt of her gun.

"You gonna start shooting us now?" Coatrack Man said.

"Everyone, calm down!" Clair tried to shout this, but her voice broke and she found herself coughing instead.

"She's no better than those other monsters with Metro!" A woman in a blue floral dress yelled out. She had her phone out, the camera pointed at Clair. "They'd rather keep us all locked away in here and wait for us to drop off one at a time. They're not trying to protect us, they're trying to *contain* us. I'm not staying in a cage anymore! I'm going home!"

Several others shouted in agreement and Clair fought the urge to step back.

Coatrack Man took a swing at her. The tip of the rack buzzed past her head with a whoosh of air. The crowd got quiet for just a second, then erupted even louder.

Clair was ready to draw her gun when a loud whistle cut through all of it. She turned to find Klozowski standing behind her with two fingers in his mouth.

"Enough!" Kloz shouted out.

This time, the room went quiet, and all eyes fell on him.

"We don't want to be here any more than all of you. We're stuck, too."

"We were told we had to stay here because 4MK was trying to kill us. They caught him, so why can't we leave?"

This came from an older man standing on the far left. He was wearing a tweed jacket and dark slacks. He must have noticed Clair trying to place him because he told her who he was before she could ask the question. "I'm Dr. Barrington with Oncology. Several of these fine folks work for me, and I think we'd all like to get back to our lives."

"It's not that simple," Clair said.

"Because of the virus?"

She didn't answer.

Barrington raised a hand. "It's okay, Detective. Most of us are medical professionals. We understand the protocols surrounding a quarantine. We also understand precisely how viruses spread and confining the bulk of us to this singular space is counterproductive. The sick should be isolated from those of us who are not. Safety precautions such as masks should be enforced at all times."

Clair realized she wasn't wearing her own mask. She'd left it on the floor back in their office. Only about half the people in the cafeteria had them on.

Barrington went on. "The CDC has been diligent about issuing antibiotics and other countermeasures, we're all grateful for that, but aside from removing the handful of people showing outright symptoms of SARS, they've treated us as a singular group by confining us to this cafeteria and surrounding rooms. We're at the height of cold and flu season—many of the people here were sick before they came into the hospital. We don't know who has contracted SARS, who has the common cold, who has the flu…the power of suggestion can bring on these symptoms, too—I can guarantee you there are people in this crowd who think they are sick and are not. It's human nature. When we're near someone who is ill, our bodies become defensive. Those defenses can manufacture symptoms that mimic the perceived illness, and our minds are trained to fear those symptoms which perpetuates the problem."

"What do you suggest?"

"SARS symptoms are difficult to distinguish until they fully present. In the early stages, an infected person appears 'flu-like,' some only have minor aches and pains, maybe the sniffles. If someone presents with these symptoms, there is no way to know if they've caught a cold, the flu, or heaven forbid, SARS. The problem is, a carrier of any of these illnesses is most contagious at the onset. We need to consider the use of subgroups for further isolation. Those with aches and pains should be held together. Sore throats held together. Sneezing and other respiratory ailments held together. Anyone with a fever should be removed entirely and quarantined from all others. Most of this is standard procedure—the CDC is aware, but they're not doing it. They feel keeping us all here is good enough. That may be the case when it comes to protecting the general public from an outbreak, but it does little good when it comes to protecting those of us who are not sick…yet. If nothing changes, we all will be very soon."

A sneeze crawled across the interior of Clair's nose and she willed it away. If she sneezed right now, these people looked like they might carry her to the incinerator.

Barrington took a step toward her and lowered his voice so only she could hear. "I understand you have another body—Stanford Pentz from Cardiology. That obviously caused a bit of a panic all on its own earlier today, but now that Bishop is in custody, it's subsided. I can tell you if you don't get this crowd under control, things here have the potential to get very ugly, very fast. Right now, we have an 'us vs. them' mentality brewing. I'm offering to help you fix that while we still can. I can help you if you let me."

Clair knew he was right, and she could tell these people trusted him just by the way they watched him, how quiet they had gotten when he started to speak. "Tell your friend to put the coatrack down, and I'll pretend he didn't just assault an officer. Let's start there."

Barrington turned to his left, keeping his eyes on Clair. "Put that down, Harry. Nobody here would be sad if she shot you. Probably best you don't give her a reason."

Coatrack Man glared at him for a moment, then grunted and set the coatrack down at his side. Stout stepped over and took it away. "Should I arrest him?"

Clair shook her head. "We all just need to calm down."

"If you can put me in touch with the proper person at the CDC, I can help," Barrington told her. He lowered his voice again. "Give these people a purpose so they're not just standing around, and I think you'll find they become more docile."

Clair knew he was right, and frankly, she didn't have time for crowd control. "You'll want to speak to Jarred Maltby. He's working upstairs. Let me see your phone."

He retrieved his phone from his back pocket, started to hand it to her, then pulled back as he got a closer look at her eyes, which were no doubt as red, itchy, and puffy, as they felt. "Perhaps you should just read me the number."

Someone screamed then, a woman.

27
Diary

Out in the hall, I pressed my ear against Libby's partially open door. I couldn't see anything through the crack, and I couldn't hear anything, either. Her name rolled out of my mouth before I could stop it.

"Libby?"

She didn't answer, not a sound.

I considered going in, and then I imagined her waking and scream-ing—this strange boy from across the hall hovering over her holding a Snickers bar. Not the best way to make proper introductions.

I went downstairs instead and found the first floor as quiet and deserted as the second. Several lights had been left burning in this corner or that, but the shadows were winning the battle for territory in the land of Finicky.

In the kitchen, I went straight to the silverware drawer. I found no knives inside, only forks and spoons. Ms. Finicky kept the nefarious utensils hidden away somewhere and only doled them out when needed, collecting them again when finished. She wasn't the trusting sort.

I missed my knife. I made a mental note to retrieve it the next time I ran into Dr. Oglesby. He said he didn't have it, but I knew he did. I wasn't fond of liars. Not in the least.

I went through every other drawer and cabinet in the kitchen, not sure what I was looking for or what I might find. Turns out, I didn't find much of anything. Kitchen stuff, nothing I hadn't seen before. Nothing useful.

The refrigerator hummed.

I found it odd that Ms. Finicky didn't keep the refrigerator locked. Aside from mealtimes, Mother always locked our refrigerator—that had been the case my entire life—I assumed all refrigerators came with a lock as standard fare. I opened the door, peered inside at what amounted to nothing as tasty as the Snickers bar already in my possession, and closed it again. The list of our daily chores fluttered, held in place with a heavy magnet, a calendar featuring kittens beside it. A small, red star marked today's date. Previous days had been crossed out. Many of the other days had red stars, too. I didn't find any writing to speak of, but the twenty-ninth of August was circled, also in red ink.

Through the kitchen window, far across the field, the barn loomed. This dark stain on the night sky. The moon looking down on it through a veil of black clouds.

A moment later, I was out the door and walking toward the barn with no memory of leaving the kitchen.

28

Nash

"What the fuck were you thinking?" Captain Dalton's face burned so red that Nash felt the heat from across the room.

He didn't need this, not now.

With two flat tires, he had to leave his car parked back on McCormick. If it wasn't already picked clean and up on blocks, it would be soon. Poole gave him a ride back to Metro in his Jeep—they followed behind the SWAT van holding Bishop, a trail of reporters following them. They found more reporters waiting at the front of Metro; he radioed the van and told them to go around back. More reporters were there, too. Not as many as in front, but enough to block their path, cameras everywhere. They'd draped a black jacket over Bishop's head as they shuffled him through the crowd and into the building. Dalton had cornered him the moment the door closed at their backs.

"You kicked a suspect!"

"You wouldn't?"

Oh, that wouldn't help.

Dalton somehow grew a shade redder. "The moment Bishop is secured, I want you up in my office!"

He stomped off before Nash could respond with one of the many arguments that popped into his head—

He resisted. He taunted me. He threatened the people of our fair city.

He wouldn't give up the virus. He's Anson Goddamned Bishop—if you put him on the sidewalk, half the city would line up to take a shot. He—

The truth was, he had no legitimate reason for kicking Bishop, and he knew it. He wished he could take it back, but he couldn't. Camera or not, it shouldn't have happened. He'd answer for it, he deserved to, but not right now.

"Where do you want him?"

This came from Espinosa, the SWAT agent on Bishop's right.

Nash turned to Poole behind him. "You sure about this?"

Poole nodded.

Nash eyed him for a moment, then turned back to Espinosa. "Interview Room Two. Across the hall from Porter."

Poole waited for them to disappear down the hall, then pulled out his phone and handed it to Nash. "I'm going to get a call from my supervisor wondering why we're here instead of down at Roosevelt. He may insist we bring Bishop down there. I need you to run some interference and buy time."

Nash took the phone. "You don't seem like the kind of guy who disobeys your boss."

"As long as he doesn't give me a direct order, I'm not disobeying anything," Poole said matter-of-factly. "We've only got one chance at questioning these two like this. If Porter is officially arrested, if Bishop is taken into federal custody, it's over. Outside these walls are a million moving parts all ready to pull this case in different directions. If we want the truth, it's now or never."

Nash knew he was right. They'd discussed it in the car, but that didn't change the fact that it felt like they were sitting in the middle of several ticking bombs all ready to blow.

Crowds had started to form in the halls. Law enforcement and staffers all trying to catch a glimpse of Bishop as he passed. Nash and Poole made their way through. They arrived at the interview room as Espinosa was stepping back out. He closed the door behind him and looked at Nash. "He's secured, in full restraints, not going anywhere, but I'm perfectly happy stationing one or more of my men outside the door here."

"Leave two," Nash told him. "And maybe clear everyone from this hall?"

"You got it."

Poole told Nash, "You know you can't go in with me, right?"

"I figured as much. I'll be in observation. If I get called out, I'll leave your phone with one of the SWAT guys."

"Keep it on you," Poole said. "If I can't find my phone for the next few hours, all the better."

With that, Poole opened the door, stepped into the interview room, and closed the door behind him.

Nash stepped into the observation room.

He found Anthony Warnick from the mayor's office already in there standing over the officer operating the recording equipment. They didn't exchange words. The glance that passed between them was enough.

Espinosa from SWAT stepped in a moment later and leaned in close to Nash so Warnick couldn't hear. "Hey, how are you feeling?"

"Numb right now. I don't think I've processed all this yet."

"That's not what I mean. Brogan called in sick with a 103 fever. His wife said if it goes any higher, she's taking him to the ER. He came into contact with both those girls at Upchurch's house before we knew what we were dealing with. I can't get Tibideaux on the phone at all—that's not like him—he was one of the first guys through the door there. Do you feel sick?"

Nash shook his head. The motion only reminded him of the achy feeling in all his bones and joints and the chill he couldn't shake.

In the interview room, Poole sat down at the aluminum table with Bishop opposite him. Nobody would move for the next two hours.

29

Clair

The scream came from down the hall on the far side of the cafeteria. Clair ran toward the sound—Stout, Klozowski, and Dr. Barrington on her heels. More people behind them. In the hallway, they found a woman in her twenties with her hands over her mouth and her eyes glued to the restroom door. A cart with cleaning supplies stood beside her. When she saw Clair, she pointed at the door. "In there."

Clair took out her gun. "All of you wait here."

Stepping past the woman, she pushed through the door, gun first. "Police! Nobody move!"

Turning quickly, she scanned the room. Her words echoed off the tile, but she saw no one. Clair dropped to one knee and looked under the stall doors. She spotted a pair of feet in the second to last stall, the door only partially closed. "Out! Now!"

The feet didn't move.

Scrambling back up, Clair took several steps across the bathroom, toward the stall.

She knew something was wrong even before she pushed open the door. White powder covered the floor around the feet and the toilet. Glistening in the harsh fluorescent light.

Salt.

There was a partial footprint in the salt. Large, probably male.

The woman was sitting on the toilet, fully dressed, her head slumped to the left. Her eyes were open, but only her right eye stared blankly. The left was a dark, black hole, with a trickle of blood running down her cheek. There was blood where her left ear used to be, too. Clair didn't need to see into her mouth to know her tongue was gone. The woman's hands were clasped together in her lap in prayer. Possibly glued—Clair could think of no other way to keep them in such a position. Three white boxes tied off with black string sat on the stainless steel toilet paper dispenser. On the wall, written in black marker, was the phrase, *Father, forgive me.*

Clair recognized her as one of the women from the cafeteria, but she didn't know her name. She'd seen her less than a few hours ago getting coffee.

"That's Christie Albee, she works in administration."

Dr. Barrington was standing behind her in the bathroom, now wearing a pair of glasses.

"I told you to wait outside."

He ignored her, took several steps forward, and placed two fingers on the side of the woman's neck. "No pulse. And she's cool to the touch. I'd guess she's been dead at least an hour."

"Christ, get back!" Clair tugged at his belt and pulled him out of the stall. He'd been standing in the salt. There were two new footprints now, and the original was smudged. "Shit. That was evidence. I need you to get out of here. You're contaminating my scene."

Barrington frowned at her. "I only meant to—"

"Please, Doctor. Step outside. Don't tell anyone what you've seen in here."

Klozowski and Stout came in then. Clair quickly told Stout, "Please keep everyone out of here."

He looked over her shoulder to the woman's body, grew pale, then turned right back around, ushering Barrington out the door.

Klozowski came up beside Clair, a puzzled look on his face. "Bishop's in custody. How..."

"Her name was Christie Albee. She's on your list, right?"

He nodded. "Admin office. She processed a bunch of Upchurch's claims. She was a liaison between the hospital and the insurance company. Clair, if Bishop is in custody and Sam's locked up, who's doing this?"

"Don't say Sam's name in the same breath as that guy."

"You know what I mean." He pointed at the boxes. "Those have starred in enough of my nightmares for me to say without a doubt, they're the same ones Bishop used."

Clair's mind was racing. "We need to get in front of this. I'll get pictures and document the scene, and then we need to seal off this bathroom. I want her body brought to the morgue to the same pathologist working on Stanford Pentz, our other body. We need to get her in touch with Eisley at the city morgue. Somehow, we've got to look for differences between these two bodies and Bishop's original victims. We need to compare them to the ones found in Chicago and South Carolina. I can't believe I'm saying this, but it can't be Bishop. It sure as shit can't be Sam. There's somebody else out there. Maybe multiple somebodies."

30
Diary

I found the door to the barn open. It was a large door—wide enough for a tractor—mounted to a railing at the top. It hadn't been opened enough for a tractor, but instead, someone had only slid it about two feet to the side. I stared at that open door for about a minute or so, trying to decide if the person who had left it open had been entering the barn or exiting.

Over the past months, there were several times when my hand involuntarily dipped into my pocket and searched for the comforting cool steel of my knife and each of those times, my fingers came away disappointed. Now was such a moment. To enter the barn without knowing whether or not someone was inside was foolhardy, I knew Father would not recommend doing so, nor would he be pleased if he learned that I did, but Father was not here and something compelled me to step inside that barn. I don't want to say some unseen force enticed me, I didn't believe in such things, yet that is what it felt like. Like a part of me was inside that barn, and I had no choice but to retrieve it.

Silently, I stepped through the opening and into the black maw. And knowing I was silhouetted with that opening at my back, I also shuffled quickly to the left—just enough for the blanket of black to take me into its folds. I was comfortable in the dark, but that wasn't always the case. When I was a little boy, I feared the dark. I feared the dark so much Mother took to leaving a lamp on in my room with an old scarf draped over it to mute the light. Father laughed at this, teased me for it, but I didn't care. I needed that light as much as I needed to breathe. I think that is why he took it from me.

When I entered my room, on that particular night, the bulb had been removed. I asked Mother about it, and she only put a finger to her lips and nodded back in the direction of our living room. I asked why Father would take my light, and those simple words were enough to make her go pale. It wasn't the fact that I spoke them. It was the volume at which I said them, for I was loud enough to draw Father to my door.

"Come with me," he had said.

And although I could tell Mother wished to protest, she did not, as Father led me to the basement door and down the steps. He removed each bulb on his way back out, taking the one at the top of the stairs moments before locking the door. From the other side of that door, he told me, "Forget your eyes—sight is a deceitful mistress—it's only when you trust your other senses equally that you truly learn to see."

He didn't give me a blanket until the second night, and three nights passed before I was granted a pillow. I spent more than a week down there, nearly two. It wasn't until I learned to embrace the dark that Father allowed me back upstairs. And he had been right, there were many ways to see without your eyes. The human mind adapted quickly, found a way.

There were sounds in that basement.

Sounds I heard here in the barn.

The patter of tiny feet running this way and that. The whispers of spiders crossing their webs. In a world as black as this, a world in which I was blind, there were a million eyes that could still see me, and I felt every one of them inching closer.

The air was cooler in the barn, motionless, yet I knew instantly I wasn't alone.

"I know you're in here."

My voice sounded much louder than I hoped. I didn't want to frighten her. I knew it was Libby. I'm not sure how I knew, but I did. I think I realized she was here the moment I pressed my ear to her door back in the house. I knew she was here as surely as I knew she was gone from the Camden Treatment Center on that day that seemed so long ago but wasn't really.

"Libby, it's me, Anson."

Silence again, then—

"Is anyone else with you?"

Her voice came from above me and to the left. A sweet, angelic voice as beautiful as music. A voice as pure as a mountain stream. A voice that could read the telephone book and make it sound as if it were the greatest story ever told.

"Only me," I told her. "Where are you?"

She said nothing at first, but I heard her shuffle. Something rained down from above, soft against my skin, powder or dust.

"There's a ladder to your left. I'm in the hayloft."

A light bloomed above. The ghostlike flutter of a flame spread over the interior of the barn.

"Hurry, before someone sees the light."

I spotted the ladder to the loft a dozen paces from where I stood. It didn't look very strong, but was sturdy enough. I climbed the ten feet to the top and crawled out onto the platform, dry straw crunching under my hands and knees. The ground looked impossibly far below.

Perched on an old wooden crate, a small, tarnished oil lamp burned in the far corner. Libby huddled to the side of them, her back against the wall, her head turned just enough to watch me. I couldn't really make her out; the shadows clung to her like a thick blanket, backlit by the lamp. But oh, how I wanted to see her. My skin tingled with a need to see her.

"Hurry, I'm killing the light."

I got to my feet and started toward her. I was about halfway when she extinguished the lamp. Even in the resulting darkness, I could hear her breathing, and I followed the sound. I settled near enough to feel the warmth of her body.

Too close, I thought. She'll move away.

She didn't though.

I fought the urge to edge closer.

"You were at Camden," she said quietly. "I saw you there."

"You were there, too." Which was a dumb thing to say, but it just came out. I was nervous, stupid because I never got nervous—not around Mother or Father or Mrs. Carter, or anyone—yet I was certainly nervous

now. And part of me was glad Father wasn't here to see me. I'm not sure what he would do to someone who made me nervous. I had several ideas, and they made me shiver.

"You're cold?"

"A little," I said, even though I wasn't.

There was a blanket draped over her legs, and she stretched the corner over me. The blanket was musty and old and probably dirty from years in the loft, but I didn't really care. Something about Libby next to me made all of that all right.

My eyes began to adjust to the dark, fed on the moonlight, and the muddle of black beside me turned into the shape of her, a rough outline at first, then a little clearer. She had a black eye. Another bruise on her temple. A third around her neck, like someone choked her. Several more on her right arm, another on her—

She looked away from me, lowering her head.

"I'm sorry. I didn't mean to make you uncomfortable."

"It's okay. I'd probably stare, too."

"Does it hurt?"

"It did. It hurt something awful, but it's getting better."

Libby wore a locket that glistened in the dim light on a gold chain around her neck.

"Were you in some kind of accident or did someone do that to you?" This was none of my business, and I probably shouldn't have asked, but I wanted to know. I wanted her to say it was an accident, because the idea of someone doing that to her was horrible, something I didn't want to think about.

"Can we maybe not talk about it? It's behind me now. I'd rather focus on where I'm going, not where I've been."

"Okay." I could do that. I wanted to do that.

I remembered the Snickers bar then, and I fished it from my pocket and held it out to her. "Are you hungry?"

She nodded, took it, and peeled off the wrapper. "Wanna split it?"

Before I could answer, she broke the bar down the middle, popped half in her mouth, and brought the other to my lips. It was gone in an instant and might have been the greatest candy bar I had ever eaten. She licked a *bit of chocolate from her fingertips and smiled. Her smile made me forget about the candy bar.*

She settled back against the wall. "The nurses at Camden were scared of you, you know."

"Why would they be scared of me?"

"Dr. Oglesby told them you were dangerous. He said you might have killed your parents. He said there were bodies in your house when they found you. Three of them."

I wondered when he told them that. I imagine it was the day Nurse Gilman stopped smiling at me.

"I didn't kill my parents."

"What about the other people they found in your house? Did you kill them?"

She asked this so matter-of-factly, no fear at all, as if asking what I had for dinner or what my favorite color might be. What did this say about her? This girl I hardly knew, yet felt I did, sitting beside me. What brings a girl to not fear the boy who has bodies in his basement?

"Those men had no business being inside," I told her. "All actions have consequences."

Under the blanket, her hand found mine. Her fingers laced into mine perfectly. "That they do."

31

Poole

Day 5 • 12:06 PM

Poole rarely touched alcohol. He couldn't remember the last time he'd even had a beer, let alone something stronger. Yet, when he stepped out of the interview room with Bishop several hours after entering, he needed a drink. A double, maybe a bottle. The idea of forgetting all about this case, even for a little while, had never been so enticing.

Nash met him in the hallway and quickly whispered in his ear. "Watch what you say around that guy, Warnick. He's been on his phone this entire time giving the play-by-play to someone. I'm not sure who he's talking to—he's been careful about not saying anyone's name. He asked the communications office for a copy of the interview, and I told him he'd have to get it from you—federal case and all that. I'm not sure how much time that bought, though."

"Did Hurless call?"

Nash rolled his eyes. "Only about a dozen times. I told him you were behind closed doors with Bishop. He wanted you to call him the minute you got out."

Nash tried to hand him his phone back, but Poole didn't take it. Poole told him "Not yet. You didn't give me that message yet, either."

When he started past the detective into the observation room,

Nash put a hand on his chest, stopping him. "You know everything that guy just said is bullshit, right?"

Poole didn't know what to believe, not anymore.

The moment he entered the observation room, Warnick was on him. "You need to call your supervisor, SAIC Hurless. You're under orders to provide a copy of that interview to me."

"Under whose authority?"

"That's not your concern," Warnick said. "There's a warrant on your boss's desk, and you're under orders to execute it immediately."

Nash glowered at the man. "The mayor's office doesn't have the authority to issue a warrant in a federal investigation."

"Nobody said the warrant originated with the mayor's office. And considering you're teetering on the edge of suspension, Detective, I'm not sure you should be running interference right now," Warnick told him.

Nash sneezed.

He didn't cover his nose or his mouth, in fact, Poole was fairly certain he had taken a step closer to Warnick before he let rip. He sneezed a second time.

Warnick shuffled back into the corner. "What the hell, Detective?!?"

"Sorry about that," Nash told him, wiping his nose on the sleeve of his jacket. "I think I"m coming down with a nasty bug. I might have picked something up at Upchurch's house."

Warnick's eyes went wide. "You should be in quarantine!"

"I'll get checked out as soon as we finish up here," Nash told him. "Hmm. Maybe you should, too. Better to be safe than sorry and all that."

Warnick's head spun back around to Poole, his face red. "Copy of the interview, now."

Poole let out a sigh and turned to the communications officer who had sat quietly through all of this. "Can you make me a copy, please?"

He reached over to the CPU from his computer and hit the eject button on the CD-ROM drive, then plucked the disk from the tray and handed it to Poole. "Already done."

"You can't give him that," Nash said.

"I will if I'm ordered to do so," Poole told him. "But as of this moment, I haven't received any such order." He started back for the door with the disc. "Right now, I need to discuss this with Detective Porter."

Warnick stepped up and tried to block him at the door. "Are you crazy? You can't share that with Porter! Not before we run it past the proper authorities. At the very least, we need to check the tapes at the lab, whatever else we can use to corroborate. We need to question Porter and—"

Poole interrupted—pointed first at himself, then at Warnick. "You and I aren't in a 'we' situation. I'm still not sure why you're even here. Step aside, or I'll charge you with impeding a federal investigation."

Warnick didn't move at first. Then he shook his head, stepped to the left, and dialed his phone again.

Back out in the hallway, Nash grabbed him by the shoulder. "Let me go in there with you. He'll talk to me."

"No way." Poole shook his head. "What I said earlier still stands. As long as your team is viewed as compromised, we need to keep you at a distance. Especially now, with that video circulating."

"You let me investigate a crime scene," Nash pointed out.

"With federal agents on site and me on the phone guiding you. That's different. My team documented and collected all evidence, not Metro. You were only there as an expert to confirm similarities with past cases. I've got some room to maneuver there, but not much. Frankly, you're more useful to me if you just observe right now. Until we get a handle on what's going on. At some point, I may need you to come in, but not yet."

Nash reluctantly nodded and stepped into the observation room on the opposite side of the hall.

Poole took a deep breath, then opened the door to the interview room.

Porter's face was buried in one of the diaries, and he didn't look up. Not at first. Under the table, his right knee bounced. The whiteboard they had brought in earlier was covered in writing, several sketches too, the layout of a house. The coffee pot was empty, as was his mug.

Poole settled into a chair opposite him, the same one he had sat in earlier. "Do you need more coffee, Sam?"

His eyes still lost in one of the diaries, Porter said, "He knew Libby McInley. Barbara McInley's sister. Did you know that? He was placed in some kind of foster home after the events at his house."

"The Finicky House for Wayward Children," Poole said.

This time, Porter did look up. "You know it?"

"It's written on your evidence board."

Porter nodded. "Vincent Weidner was there. Paul Upchurch—" He stood and went over to the board. "—these two girls, too— Kristina Niven and Tegan Savala. You need to run their names. They may be connected. There were several boys there, too. I'm still trying to identify them. Before going to this home, Bishop was held at someplace called the Camden Treatment Center. You'll want to pull whatever records they have on him from there. That's medical, so you'll need to get a warrant, but I can't imagine a judge denying you."

"Sam, what can you tell me about Montehugh Labs?"

Porter frowned for a second, then looked up at the board. "You're right. That should be up here." He found a blank spot in the top right corner and scribbled in the name under the heading: *Other Locations of Concern*.

"What do you know about it?"

"That's where Bishop said he got the virus. Have you confirmed that? If not, we need to. At the very least, they can tell us how much he has."

"Bishop is in custody."

It took a moment for the words to wash over Porter. When they did, he returned to the table and collapsed into his chair. "When?"

"About nine-thirty this morning, he turned himself in to Nash at some abandoned building downtown."

"He turned himself in? Was his mother with him? What building?"

"Why does it matter?"

"Was it the Guyon Hotel?"

Poole shook his head. "No, not the Guyon. 426 McCormick. No sign of the woman who called herself Sarah Werner."

Porter rose, wrote the address under Montehugh. "I don't know if the location means anything, but best to keep it up there just in case. We need to find her, too. She can't be far." His eyes went wide, and he asked his next question as if his brain were working on a slight delay. "Did he give you the rest of the virus? Did he tell you where it is?"

Poole didn't answer him, not at first, because he wasn't sure just what to say to that. He decided on the truth. "Bishop said *you* have it."

If this somehow shocked Porter, his face didn't betray him. "What?"

"He said you broke into Montehugh and stole the virus, not him."

Porter smiled, looked like he was about to laugh. "That's crazy. Why would I steal the virus?" The smile left his face, and he stood. "*Is he here?* In the building? Where did you bring him?"

"Sit down, Sam. I need to show you something." This time, it was Poole who got up. He went to the television in the corner of the room and placed the disc in the DVD player. Using the remote, he turned on the television.

Sam hadn't moved.

"Sit, Sam."

Bishop's face filled the screen, and Porter did sit.

32

Clair

Day 5 • 12:06 PM

"We've got two bodies outside the hospital and two inside. That means he's somehow getting in and out unnoticed. He's got to be using the tunnels," Clair said, glaring at Stout.

They were in his cramped office along with two of his security guards, Klozowski, and one Metro officer. She'd left another uniformed officer to guard Larissa Biel and Kati Quigley; two others were still missing.

"My guys have covered every inch of the basement, and there's no tunnel," Stout told her.

"There's a tunnel," she insisted.

"We've got some kind of copycat locked here in the hospital with us."

"That doesn't explain the bodies found *outside* the hospital."

"Do you have time-of-death on them? Maybe they were killed and positioned before the lockdown here at Stroger," Stout suggested. "Or maybe there's two of them—Bishop killed the ones outside before turning himself in, and someone else killed the ones in here."

Clair was getting frustrated. "Then who killed the one in South Carolina? Can't forget him. We've got a body down there, too."

Stout ran his hand over his shaved head, appearing annoyed at the growing stubble. "I was a beat cop with Metro. I never worked Homicide, but we were always told to keep an open mind, never jump to conclusions. What if the murders here in the hospital have nothing to do with Bishop or the 4MK killings? What if someone in the hospital, maybe even a member of the staff, is using the current circumstances as cover smoke? They killed these two people to settle some kind of score or agenda and just made them look like 4MK murders to cover their tracks. Your captain said as much. What if he's right?"

Clair pressed her palms against her temples and lowered her head. "Kloz, you said you linked both victims to Bishop, didn't you?"

Klozowski had brought his laptop with him and was busy tapping away at God-knows-what. He looked up at her. "Huh?"

"Nice of you to join us." She repeated her initial question.

Kloz shook his head. "I linked Christie Albee to Upchurch's insurance forms, but I haven't found anything to tie in Sandford Pentz from Cardiology. I'm still looking."

There was a chalkboard on the wall in Stout's office covered with scheduling information. Clair went over to it, erased everything, and wrote down the names of all the victims discovered today:

Jane Doe – Rose Hill Cemetery
Jane Doe – Red Line tracks / Clark Station
Tom Langlin – Simpsonville courthouse steps
Stanford Pentz – Stroger Hospital
Christie Albee – Stroger Hospital

Above them, she wrote the phrase *Father, forgive me* and circled it. She stared at the text for several moments, then turned back to Stout. "Any connection between Pentz and Christie Albee?"

"What, like were they sleeping together?"

Clair shrugged.

Stout thought about this. "Not that I know of, but that kind of thing happens a lot around here. I think it's the long shifts, all the time together and not with their families. The stress of the job. It's possible, I suppose."

"Can you poke around a little bit? See what you can find out?"

He didn't answer her. Instead, he let out a sigh.

Clair's eyes narrowed. "What, not a fan of homework?"

"It's not that," he said. "We're spread thin already, and my focus needs to be on keeping the peace in that cafeteria. Those people are ready to explode. It's not a question of *if* anymore, it's *when*. You saw them—they're ready to turn on each other, on us, whoever. That happens, we don't have the manpower to stop them."

She knew he was right, she needed to worry about that, too. She needed to worry about a lot of things right now. "What can you tell me about that doctor who offered to help? The one who tripped up my crime scene. Barrington?"

Stout said, "Nice enough guy. The staff seems to like him. He's been here at Stroger about a decade or so. I think he was up in New Hampshire before that."

"He graduated from Stanford," Kloz chimed in. "Then completed his residency in a small hospital outside Dartmouth, New Hampshire. Looks like he went to high school nearby, so he probably grew up in that area. Spent a good chunk of his career there. Started here at Stroger in 2007. He's focused on oncology his entire career. He was a consulting physician on Upchurch's case. That got Barrington on the list and locked up here with the rest of us. I'll keep digging in case he's got a skeleton out there, but I don't see anything."

Clair processed this and turned back to Stout. "I don't trust anyone right now, but we do need the help. I suggest we take it and keep him close. Maybe he can be our eyes and ears in that group. He's been working with the CDC. I got a text from Maltby about an hour ago." She nodded at the computer on Stout's desk. "We'll need all the video footage for the hallways around Pentz's office and anything you have near the bathroom where Christie Albee was found."

He exchanged a look with one of his security officers, the younger of the two.

Clair's eyes narrowed. "You have video, right? I've seen cameras all over this hospital."

"We do have cameras," Stout said hesitantly, "but they're not recording properly."

"What do you mean?"

"Our IT guy says the system got infected with some kind of virus or malware. Everything is recording, but the time stamps are all off. He's been working on it for over a week. He tried reformatting the drives, reinstalled the operating system. He even swapped out the recording hardware. Everything works well for a few hours, then the problem comes back. The more time that passes, the worse it gets. He said whatever it is, it doesn't just rewrite the date and time once, it keeps rewriting and speeds up over time."

"Progressive displacement," Klozowski said. "First it rewrites the original time stamp across the board with a bad one, then runs back through and rewrites the bad one with a worse one, and keeps going. I've seen this before. It's just a repetitive pattern. The real smart ones keep some of the footage in order so it appears the sequences are correct. The really smart ones use facial recognition and link footage with the same people together."

They were all just staring at him.

Kloz rolled his eyes. "You've got two people walking down a hallway together today. Let's say those same two people walked down the same hallway together two weeks ago. A smart virus will swap the two but keep all the surrounding footage in chronological order."

Clair groaned. "What's the point of that?"

Kloz shrugged his shoulders. "Hackers like to fuck with people in new and interesting ways. I'm sure someone saw it as a challenge and wrote the virus to see if they could pull it off. Once a virus like that is written, it goes up on the Darknet, gets copied, and becomes a tool in the box of other hackers. Circle of life, e-edition."

"Can it be fixed?" Clair asked.

"Probably. Maybe. I don't know, I'll have to look. If your IT guy has gone through all those steps and it's still happening, that means the virus is living somewhere else on your network. It monitors the hardware, and if something is swapped out or fixed, the virus installs again on the clean equipment. That's fairly easy to do. You can hide something like that anywhere—it could be in a router, one of the cameras, a switch, or any computer attached to the network."

"I need you on this right away," Clair told him.

Klozowski's face went blank, and his mouth dropped open.

"Kloz?"

His hands started to dart around him. He quickly found his mask and fumbled it over his face, then sneezed into it. Not once, but four times. When it was over, he lowered the mask and looked inside. "Oh, that's gross."

"I need you on this right away," Clair repeated, ignoring the sneezing fit.

He nodded. "Yes, in my weakened state of being, as I crawl down the hallway toward Death's Door ravaged by sickness, I will work for you until the bitter end."

"The people of Chicago thank you for your service."

Clair turned back to Stout. "How many guys do you have looking for the tunnels?"

"Two."

"Okay, keep them on it." Before he could protest, she looked over at his other two security guards. Neither had said a word since arriving. "I want the two of you in that cafeteria. Stay as visible as possible but not threatening—I mean, don't stand in front of the doors with your arms crossed and scowls on your faces—wander the crowd, get to know the people who don't work here, talk to the ones who do. Try to find some way to calm whatever is brewing in there. You hear anything—anything at all—pertaining to our two dead bodies, I want to know about it, understand?"

The two of them nodded.

To her lone Metro officer, a lanky kid with close-cropped

brown hair who still had that new-academy smell, she said, "Think you can organize interviews?"

"Yes, ma'am."

"Treat this like you would a house-to-house. Talk to each person. Find out if they have a connection to either of our two victims, if they know Upchurch. If they saw anything at all. Try to put together the movements of Pentz and Albee. Who saw them last…whatever you can learn."

"Yes, ma'am."

"What's your name?"

"Officer Dale Sutter, ma'am."

"When was the last time you saw Henricks and Childs?" Her two missing officers.

"About an hour before Albee was found in the bathroom. Henricks said he felt like he was catching a cold. He was pale, and his eyes were all red. He looked like…" His voice trailed off.

"Like the rest of us?" Clair finished for him.

He nodded. "Childs didn't look good, either." Sutter hesitated for a moment, then added, "Henricks said something about finding a bed somewhere where he could lay down for a minute. Childs might have went, too."

Clair would have killed for a bed right now. If she found one of her officers taking a nap, she knew exactly *who* she'd kill.

Raising her phone, she tried calling them both again—both went straight to voice mail. "Still no answer."

Stout picked up the phone on his desk. "I'll have them paged. Cell service is horrible in the building."

Stout's page came out over the speaker in the corner of his office. She heard it echoing out in the hallway. A moment later, his phone rang. He picked up the receiver and listened to someone on the other end of the call, his eyes on Clair. When he hung up, he said, "That was Dr. Webber in Pathology. She's got a cause of death on Pentz and asked if you could come down."

33

Poole

Day 5 • 12:07 PM

As Bishop's face filled the television monitor, Poole raised the remote for the DVD player and hit play. The video ticked forward. Porter's eyes locked on the screen.

"Why did you turn yourself in today?" Poole heard himself say from the television's thin speakers. Aside from the corner of his head and a little bit of his shoulder, he wasn't visible on screen. His back was to the camera. The camera was pointed at Bishop, over Poole's shoulder.

Bishop glanced down at his hands for a second, then forward. "I've been in contact with Detective Porter for months. I wanted to turn myself in sooner, but he told me not to. He said it would jeopardize his search for the real 4MK killer. He needed the public to think I was 4MK and still out there somewhere while he hunted for the person who was really responsible."

"That's complete and utter bullshit," Porter said. "Why would I tell him that? You saw my apartment. I've been trying to track him down from the moment we lost him."

Poole raised a hand, silencing him, and pointed back at the screen.

"I was stupid," Bishop went on. "Naive. I shouldn't have believed him. I should have gone to someone else, but he had me convinced.

He kept saying he was close and it wouldn't be much longer, kept telling me that, stringing me along. A day turned into a week, a week turned into a month, then several months. When I finally confronted him, he shot that woman, then tried to shoot me. I had to run again. I didn't have a choice."

"At the Guyon Hotel?"

"Yeah, at the Guyon."

"Why would he kill her?"

"He said she knew him, from his time in Charleston as a rookie. He said she was one of the last people alive who knew the truth about him." Bishop looked down at the table for a moment, rolled his thumb and index finger together, then turned back to Poole. "He said, 'she was there, she saw me do it, and she has to go,' those were his exact words. Then he looked up for a second, at nothing in particular, whispered 'father, forgive me,' and pulled the trigger."

Bishop's eyes got teary. He tried to wipe them with the back of his hand and had to bend down due to the restraints. "He shot her at point blank, right in the head, right in front of me! I was in shock, but somehow I snapped out of it when he turned the gun on me and shot again. He barely missed. I managed to get away."

Sitting across from Bishop at the table on the television, Poole took a moment to consider this, then leaned forward a bit, his head blocking Bishop's face for a moment before he settled back. "What about the woman who was with him? Sarah Werner."

Bishop's face grew puzzled. "There wasn't anyone with him. Unless she was outside or somewhere else in the hotel. I didn't see anyone with him."

"Porter said she was your mother."

Bishop's eyes closed and he let out a deep sigh. "My mother died years ago in a fire at our old house. My father, too. I'm sure it's all in my DCS file somewhere. There was a lake on our property, and I used to go out there a lot to skip rocks. If I hadn't been at the lake that particular day, I probably would have died too. I'd been gone a few hours, and when I came back, the house was burning completely out of control. The fire department was there, but I could tell they had given up. One of the firemen spotted me and asked if it was my house, and I told him it was. Then he asked me where my parents were, and I knew they were inside, I just knew, but I couldn't bring myself to say it aloud. I don't remember much after that. I was just a kid. They brought me to someplace called the Camden Treatment Center for a few weeks to recover while they tried to find a relative who could take me in. When they couldn't find anyone, I went into the foster care system."

"At someplace called the Finicky House for Wayward Children, right?"

This seemed to puzzle Bishop. "I...I don't know what that is. After Camden, I went to live with the Watsons about an hour and a half outside the city—Woodstock, Illinois—with David and Cindy Watson."

"Watson? Like the alias you used when you joined CSI for Metro?"

Bishop sighed again and tried to raise his hands. The chains clinked through the metal ring on the table. "That was stupid, I know. But I was worried that if I used my real name with Metro, someone would read about the fire and the way my parents died...I didn't want anyone to feel sorry for me or give me some kind of preferential treatment, so I figured it was best if I used a different name. Back when I was a kid, when the Watsons first adopted me, a few reporters sniffed around. They wanted to write about the fire. They enrolled me in school as 'Paul Watson' to throw them off." He waved a hand through the air. "Paul was David's middle name. I guess it worked, they left me alone, and the name stuck. As far as I know, they never legally changed my name. I suppose I should have done it at some point. I just never got around to it, and it felt less and less important as time went on."

Poole said, "You never stayed at someplace called the Finicky House for Wayward Children?"

Bishop shook his head.

"It's mentioned in your diaries."

Bishop leaned forward so fast the chains went tight and yanked him back. "Sorry, I...I don't know how much time we have. Please tell me Paul Upchurch is still alive. He might be the only person who knows the truth."

"Why? How do you know him?"

Bishop settled back in his chair. "I don't, not really. He's the guy Porter hired to write those things."

34
Diary

Dr. Oglesby had replaced my usual chair with a new one, a giant orange monstrosity that was all cushion and no support, and I kept sinking down into it. If I leaned back, I might disappear altogether, so I was forced to sit right on the edge. I'd grown a lot over the past year, but my legs were still a little short and barely touched the ground. I suppose I could sit on the floor, but—

"I see your mind is still prone to wandering, Anson. How about you face forward and do your best to remain in the moment."

I looked up at Dr. Oglesby. If an argyle sweater could eat a man, this one was hard at work. Green and yellow and white and possibly one of the most hideous garments I had ever laid eyes on, the sweater was at least two sizes too large for the good doctor, and he was swimming in it.

I smiled up at him. "I wouldn't dream of missing a second of our time together, Doctor."

"I'm glad to hear it. I look forward to our sessions together as well."

I thought to myself—he'll reach for them in three, two, one—

And there he went. He took the glasses hanging around his neck and placed them on his nose, then looked down at the notepad in his lap. "How are you enjoying your time with Ms. Finicky?"

"How are you enjoying my knife?" In previous sessions, he fell into the habit of leaving my knife on the corner of his desk, displaying it just out of

my reach—a not-so-subtle taunt, some kind of power play, a technique I'm sure he stole from someone else because he wasn't creative enough to come up with the idea on his own. My knife wasn't there today. The last time I saw him, as Detectives Welderman and Stocks were loading me into their car to take me to Finicky's, I had asked him if he had my knife, and the smug bastard had replied, "What knife?" As if it never existed at all.

"We're not here to talk about a knife, Anson, we're here to discuss your well-being, and we're on a limited timetable so I suggest we remain on task."

"Why am I here? Why are we talking at all? You don't have me locked up in one of your rooms anymore."

Dr. Oglesby smiled. "You may have left the Camden facility, but until the court says otherwise, you are still my patient. I have a vested interest in making sure you receive the treatment needed to become well."

"I am well, Doctor. I couldn't be better."

"Traumatic experiences tend to leave scars. Sometimes they're buried for a while and surface when we least expect them. So, although you may feel well today, tomorrow or the next day you may not, and it's up to me to help you get through that."

Father had once told me the health insurance industry loved to find ways to line the pockets of others within the health insurance industry—a general practitioner would recommend you see a specialist, and that specialist would send you off to a therapist, and that therapist might check your blood pressure so he can bill your insurance company for a "wellness visit" in addition to the prescribed therapy...he might prescribe one or more medications which required regular visits in order to monitor the effects of said medication...on and on, and even though the health issue could have probably been resolved by the first doctor, he involved two others—all this unnecessary time and billing—then the three of them would run off on Saturday to play golf together and spend a little of that hard-earned insurance money. If Dr. Oglesby had any interest in me, I doubted it went beyond my impact on his bottom line. The medical industry was a scam, and I didn't need anyone poking around in my head.

"We really do need to do something about your drifting off during conversations," the good doctor said.

"I'm not drifting, I'm contemplating."

"Contemplating what?"

"Your worth on this planet."

This seemed to amuse him. "And you feel you're sufficiently qualified to make such a determination?"

"The homeless man who roots around in the trash behind the community college is close enough to the academic world to see your intellect is a sham. I imagine you don't work for someplace like Camden out of choice but because you're unable to sustain yourself in private practice. You're nothing more than a mall security guard who failed to get into the police academy. You display your degrees because you're supposed to, but I bet you secretly hope nobody looks too closely. How many times has someone read the name of the school you went to and said, 'Huh, where is that, exactly?'"

That did it. The glasses came off, and Oglesby settled back in his chair. The smile didn't leave his face, though. "Perhaps I'm not the one who is acting. What happened to the quiet, polite boy from our previous sessions?"

"He's waiting for you to return his knife. The picture, too."

The doctor frowned. "Picture?"

"You know what picture."

The photograph I had of Mother and Mrs. Carter had been in my pocket when the knife was taken from me. I knew he had it, too. I hadn't brought it up until now.

He looked me dead in the eye. "I'm not aware of any photograph. If you cooperate, though, I can take another look through the items that came in with you. Perhaps something was misplaced, mislabeled, or misfiled. Those things do happen on occasion."

This time it was my turn to offer a blatantly disingenuous smile. "I'd appreciate that."

Back on went the glasses. He glanced at his notepad. "Tell me about Libby McInley. You seemed so concerned for her while staying with us. If you don't want to talk about how you're adjusting at Finicky's, why don't we discuss how she is coping?"

I'd been talking too much. I'd probably offered more words in this session than all our previous sessions combined, and I needed to put an end to that. *My emotions were controlling my tongue and bypassing my brain, and I knew that wouldn't end well. Father had always taught me to consider every word that passed my lips before they found the ears of others, and for the past twenty-two minutes, I completely ignored that particular lesson. Now Oglesby was baiting me, and I knew I shouldn't take that bait, but I couldn't help myself.* "What happened to her?"

I didn't expect him to answer. I had asked this question before and he always fell back on doctor-patient privilege and said he couldn't discuss her case. The doctor surprised me, though.

"Her last foster father raped her numerous times, and when she fought back, he beat her severely. At first, he used a telephone book to prevent bruising, but after several hours, he put that aside and decided he preferred the feel of his own fists on her. Her foster mother, who had been sitting in the living room not ten feet away, listened to all of this for the better part of a weekend before she finally had enough. Rather than call the authorities, she took out a .38 and shot him twice, then tried to hide his body in a crawlspace. Although Libby required medical attention, her foster mother was also unwilling to give up the $512 per month she received from the state for housing Libby, so she left her tied to a bed and pretended none of this happened. Luckily, a neighbor heard the shots and called 911. Libby spent two days at Roper Hospital in Charleston before being transferred to our care." *He leaned forward.* "She needs a friend, Anson. Perhaps you can be that friend."

I said nothing at first. I couldn't imagine the doctor lying about something like this, yet in the back of my mind, Father whispered that he very well might be. "He wants you to trust him, champ. He'll tell you anything. And once you do trust him, he's got you."

Instead of saying anything, I let my eyes wander the office. When they landed on his calendar on the wall behind his desk, I noticed something peculiar, something that jumped out at me. August 29 was circled. The same date that had been circled on the calendar in Mrs. Finicky's kitchen.

35

Clair

Day 5 • 12:10 PM

Clair followed Stout to the elevator, down to the second floor, and through several hallways and corridors. Within minutes, she was completely disoriented and knew if someone were to remove the various signs on the walls, she'd have no idea how to get back to the cafeteria. The mask itched at her face, and her warm breath bellowed beneath the material. Every time she swallowed, the pain in her throat reminded her she was getting worse, and the brisk pace at which they moved was enough to leave her winded. Although she was sweating, she couldn't get warm. Clair knew she had a fever but couldn't bring herself to actually check her temperature. She wasn't sure how much longer she could keep this up. The virus was getting the better of her. She felt that if she were to stop moving and sit down, if she attempted to rest at all, she might not get back up.

At the end of the hall, they came upon two wide metal doors. Stout slid his ID badge over a reader embedded in the wall, and both doors swung open. A whoosh of cold air rushed out at them, and Clair shivered again. A black woman wearing floral print scrubs beneath a white button-down sweater looked up from a desk and pointed at the green door in the far back corner of the room. "She's in the cold room waiting on you."

"Thanks, Bev," Stout said, crossing the room.

All Clair heard was *cold room,* because she couldn't imagine a room colder than this one, then she followed Stout through the green door into what could only be described as the arctic tundra. "Oh, balls," she said through chattering teeth.

The pathology office was much larger than Clair had expected, large enough to rival the medical examiner's offices downtown, and certainly larger than at any other hospital in Chicago. At least fifty by fifty, with large bright halogen lights spaced evenly across the ceiling. The walls and floor were all white tile and there were at least a dozen aluminum workstations filling the space, each positioned over grates in the floor. Five bodies were present—three covered, two exposed. She got the impression they could hose the entire room down, if necessary. Large HVAC vents whirred above, churning out the icy air. The room smelled of bleach, but it wasn't as strong as she expected. Although, with her stuffy nose, she was surprised she could smell at all.

There was a coatrack just inside the door. Stout took a red jacket off one of the hooks and handed it to her. "Here, put this on." He grabbed a green one for himself.

Clair shrugged into the coat. "Why the hell is it so cold in here?"

A woman in her late fifties came around the corner holding a clipboard. Her graying hair was pulled back. She wore protective eyewear and green scrubs. "We keep this room at 36 degrees, the same temperature as the drawers next door. It helps minimize decomposition during prolonged examinations. Abnormal autopsies are performed here, routines such as heart attack, cancer, and the like are processed down the hall under more typical settings in a warmer room." She held out a gloved hand. "You must be Detective Norton. I'm Doctor Amelia Webber."

Clair looked at her outstretched hand and thought of her own without gloves. The look on her face must have betrayed her, because Dr. Webber dropped her hand. "Nobody ever wants to shake the pathologist's hand. Even my husband gives me the stink-eye after twenty-eight years of marriage." She leaned in closer. "Christ, you look like shit. Are they giving you anything?"

"Antivirals and steroids," Clair told her. "I'm fine."

"You're not fine. You should lie down somewhere and give your body a chance to fight the virus. You're starting to swell up, too. That's a side effect of the meds." She glanced at Clair's hands. "You'll want to take off those rings while you still can."

Clair shivered again and tugged the zipper on her jacket up tight. "I was told you have cause of death?"

The doctor eyed her for another moment, then said, "I do. Give me a second, let me get Eisley."

Clair's brow furrowed. "Eisley's here?"

"Not exactly," Webber replied, crossing back through the room and around some tall glass-doored cabinets. She returned pushing a large television on a wheeled stand, a computer mounted below it. A power cord trailed back to the wall. She clicked several buttons, and the screen came to life.

Tom Eisley looked out at them. "Hello Detective, I've been…wow, you look terrible."

A small camera was mounted above the television set and angled down. Clair looked up at it, then back at the screen, unsure where she should face to speak to him. "I'm fine, Tom."

"You don't look—"

"I'm fine," Clair interrupted. "Can we get on with it? I'm under a bit of a time crunch here."

She didn't mean to snap at him, but if he was offended, he didn't show it. "Sure. Amelia, would you like to start?"

Dr. Webber nodded and wheeled virtual Eisley over to two of the occupied tables. Stanford Pentz on their left and Christie Albee on the right. Both were naked. While Pentz had a recently closed Y incision on his chest, Albee had yet to be autopsied. Webber turned to Pentz first. His head had been shaved and twisted to the side as if he were looking off to the left. An incision circled the top of his head. She had opened his skull to access his brain. "He initially presented with signs of cardiac arrest, but when I examined his heart, I didn't find anything to indicate disease or a congenital defect. He was a fit man, his heart was actually in better shape than

I expected, then I found this after cleaning away the blood from the ear removal—" She pointed to a small, dark spot on his neck, just below his missing ear.

"He was injected with something?" Clair asked, leaning in closer.

Webber nodded again. "Nothing came up on the tox screen, and we did a full panel. I had it tested twice and still nothing. Then Eisley suggested I test a sample of brain tissue."

From the television monitor, Eisley said, "Specifically, I asked her to look for succinic acid."

"And I found succinic in quantity," Webber said.

Clair asked, "What is succinic?"

Eisley said, "It's a byproduct of a muscle paralytic drug called succinylcholine, typically used by anesthesiologists. When injected, it paralyzes all the muscles of the body, including those used for breathing. Anyone receiving this drug without the ventilatory support supplied in surgery would die from asphyxia. It's fast, but it would be a horrible way to go—the drug has no sedative effect, only muscular paralysis, so the recipient would be wide awake as they suffocate."

"I would have never looked for that," Webber admitted. "I was focusing on the heart. There are no outward signs of asphyxia. Normally you'd have a blue discoloration to the skin or petechial hemorrhages around the face. We have none of that here."

"The paralytic effect of the drug prevents these things from happening," Eisley said. "I only suggested it because I read about a doctor in Sarasota, Florida who used it to kill his wife—an anesthesiologist having an affair. Apparently that particular drug is a favorite of murderous doctors since it can be difficult to detect. You're in a hospital, there's obvious access, so it crossed my mind."

Clair turned back to Webber. "You said it would be fast. How fast?"

"From injection to death?"

Clair nodded.

"Blood travels the body at three to four miles per hour," Webber explained. "A couple seconds at most for the paralytic to take effect, several minutes to death."

"No time to react or call out," Stout pointed out. He glanced over at the body of Christie Albee. Her head was also turned to the side. "Did you find the same with her?"

Webber shuffled over and pointed to a similar spot below the woman's ear. "Nearly identical injection point—directly into the posterior auricular vein. In both cases, the direction of the needle indicates your unsub came up from behind. I found a definite forward angle. When I take into account the height of both victims along with that angle, I'd say you're looking for someone under six feet tall."

"Someone under six feet tall with access to medications locked away in anesthesiology," Stout pointed out. "I can check the records. Maybe we'll find someone in that department who shouldn't be."

Eisley blew out a frustrated sigh. "That might be the case if I didn't have the same COD with both my Jane Does. Tom Langlin down in Simpsonville was also killed with succinylcholine. I confirmed with the local pathologist about twenty minutes ago."

"What about the salt?"

"Ah, the salt," Eisley said. "As Bishop would say, I've been trying to puzzle that one out but I haven't gotten very far. I can tell you the salt we found on both Jane Does as well as the man in South Carolina is of the type you'd buy in bulk at a large depot store, possibly for a water softener. The salt found on and around both your hospital victims is simple table salt. The Jane Does were stripped naked and completely submerged for some time. Several hours, at least. At first I thought the intent had been to preserve the bodies or possibly to confuse time of death. Now I'm not so sure. Both Pentz and Albee were killed within twenty-four hours of discovery. If the intent had been to destroy evidence, lye would have been far superior and just as accessible. The table salt served no purpose at all, which leads me to believe it's symbolic in nature. Some kind of message. I've been in contact with the FBI, and they're leaning biblical on this. I have to admit, it's been some time since I opened the Good Book. I'm familiar enough with the story of Lot's wife, but that's about it. I'll contact you if I learn more on that."

"Were all these people killed by the same unsub?" Clair asked.

Eisley shrugged. "All were killed with an identical pattern, but I don't see how a single unsub could traverse the distance." His eyes lit up. "We do have one other thing that may prove useful."

"Oh, I need useful right now."

Dr. Webber bent down over the body of Christie Albee and opened her mouth. With the bright lights shining down, it was impossible to miss the red lump of flesh where her tongue used to be. "We believe a scalpel was used to remove the tongue. We've got a near-perfect incision running the length of the terminal sulcus."

"Ah hah," Clair said, choking back the vomit in her throat.

"See the angle here? How there's just a little more of the lingual tonsil remaining on this side versus the other?"

"Ah hah," Clair said again, although she was no longer looking. She squinted just enough to make the world a little blurry. There were some images she just didn't want in her head.

Dr. Webber had stopped talking and was smiling at her.

"Is that supposed to mean something to me?" Clair asked.

It was Eisley who answered. "It means your unsub is left-handed."

"What is Bishop?"

"I performed the autopsies on all of Bishop's previous victims—the ones we know about, anyway. He's right-handed. Or he killed them with his right hand, at least."

"What's Sam?" Clair heard herself ask a little louder than she'd intended.

36

Poole

"This is ridiculous!" Porter snapped.

Poole pressed pause on the DVD player. Bishop's face froze on the screen.

Porter shuffled in his chair. "I've never met Paul Upchurch! Aside from these diaries and the little bit Bishop told me about him, I have no idea who he is."

Porter glared at him, his face red, creases around his eyes. When Poole met his gaze, he looked away. He wanted to believe him, but he couldn't read him and that made him nervous. At Quantico, Poole had taken several courses on kinesics, the interpretation of nonverbal communication through the study of body language. He'd interviewed countless suspects, and with most, once he established a baseline with a series of routine questions, he was able to determine if the person he was speaking to was being truthful or deceitful. This typically came down to one simple fact—when someone told the truth, they did so readily, without the need to put in conscious thought. When someone lied, they accessed the creative portion of their brain in order to construct that lie, and while this may only take a millisecond, there were usually outward signs—anything from glancing off to the side or hand movements or gestures. While Porter demonstrated many such signs, they had been a constant from the moment he entered the room—nervousness, anxiety, anger, frustration—any one of those could muddy the waters of kinesics. Normally, Poole could see through that, but with Porter he found doing so to be difficult. He also had to consider that, as a detective, Porter most likely had also studied kinesics. He most definitely questioned numerous people during his career. He fully understood what Poole would be looking for and might consciously be deploying countermeasures. With the right knowledge, no lie detector was infallible.

"What happened in Charleston?" Poole asked.

"Charleston?"

"Why would he accuse you of killing that woman? He said you did it to cover up something that happened in Charleston."

This time, Porter did glance up, but not up and to the right, which would indicate a lie. Nor did he look to the left, which would indicate truth. He looked straight up, tilted his head back, and ran his hand through his hair with a frustrated sigh. "I did my rookie time in Charleston, that's all. Traffic tickets, petty thefts." He tapped a spot on the back of his head. "I took a bullet from a .22 right here during a dealer takedown. After that, I figured I didn't owe that city anything else, and Heather and I made the move to Chicago to try and get a fresh start."

"You were shot?"

Porter's hands moved back to his lap. "It had nothing to do with this. My partner and I were trying to take down a petty dealer, mostly dirty heroin and some crack. Some kid named Weasel. We cornered him in an alley. I came up from behind, and my partner circled around the block so he could come in from the other side. He saw my partner first, spun around, and panicked when he saw me standing behind him. He was wired, jumpy. He had a gun in his hand and pulled the trigger by accident. He didn't mean to shoot me. The gun wasn't even pointed at me—more of a reflex, really. The bullet hit a Dumpster and ricocheted. I caught it here." He reached up and rubbed the spot again. "The bullet didn't make it through my skull, just lodged in place, caused some pressure to

THE SIXTH WICKED CHILD • 149

build up. They removed it, relieved the pressure, and I recovered. That was that."

"What was your partner's name?"

Porter opened his mouth to tell him, then appeared puzzled. "Huh."

"What?"

He pursed his lips. "It's just…sometimes I have trouble remembering things from back then."

"You can't remember your partner's name?"

He closed his eyes. "This was a long time ago. Derrick something. Hill, Hillman…Hillburn, that's it. Derrick Hillburn. I haven't thought about him in years." He opened his eyes and scratched at the side of his neck. "I heard he left the force, but I haven't spoken to him in a long time."

"The woman you broke out of prison in New Orleans. You never met her before?"

"No."

Poole said, "'She was there, she saw me do it, and she has to go,' you didn't say that?"

"Of course not."

"You didn't shoot her? CSI found gunshot residue on your hand and clothing."

"I took a warning shot at Bishop. Bishop killed her. I told you that. Christ, do I need my union rep here?"

Poole fell silent for a moment, then raised the remote and hit play again.

On screen, Poole said, "Porter hired Upchurch to write the diaries?"

Bishop nodded. "I rode with Porter to the 51st Precinct on the day his wife's killer was ID'd. Some coffee got spilled on his clothes, and we stopped at his apartment on the way back to Metro so he could change. While we were there, he got a phone call from one of the guys on the task force, Klozowski. The IT guy. When he hung up, he told me he knew my real name was Anson Bishop and not Paul Watson. I thought he was going to report me or something, but instead, he told me there was an undercover operation in motion to catch 4MK, something off the books, and we could use this thing with my name if I was willing to help." Bishop shrugged and shook his head. "I trusted him. I asked what he needed me to do. He told me he wanted me to go into hiding. Just stay out of sight for a few days. We both heard the sirens then, and he said we had to hurry. He gave me a thousand dollars in cash and an address for a house on 41st Place. He told me to wait for him there. He insisted there was no time to explain right then, but he'd be there soon."

Poole said, "The green house on 41st Place? Where you attacked me?"

Bishop hesitated for a moment, then nodded. "I didn't mean to hurt you. At that point, months of this had gone by. Porter had me convinced you were involved. I thought you were there to kill me."

"My partner died in the house across the street from there."

Bishop leaned in close and lowered his voice. "Porter showed up right after you. I saw him run around the side of the house when I left. I think your partner may have seen him, too. I think Porter killed him."

"Why would Porter kill a federal agent?"

Bishop tried to throw his hands up, but the chains held him back. "After I left his apartment, he stabbed himself in the leg. I think he killed Talbot at 314 Tower. He may even be the one who kidnapped that girl, Emory Connors. He tried to pin everything on me, said he had to throw me to the press in order to flush out the real 4MK. He had me convinced there was some plan in action. There wasn't, though. There never was. I think he's 4MK. What if he killed *all* those people? He's been playing all of us." Bishop fell back into his chair. "Look, I know how crazy this all sounds. That's why you need to talk to Paul Upchurch. He can back this up."

"How?"

"After what happened at 314 Tower, after Porter blamed me for everything, I hid. Just like he asked. I didn't know what else to do. After a week, though, when I didn't see an end in sight, I started to follow him. He went to Upchurch's house three times that I know of. After that third time, I waited for him to leave. Then I knocked on Upchurch's door. I had nothing to lose. When he answered, I showed him my CSI badge—fast, so he couldn't really read it—and told him I was with internal affairs and I needed to know his connection to the detective who just left. He didn't even know Porter was with the police. He said Porter found him through some ad on craigslist about a year earlier—he worked part-time as an artist; he was trying to get some comic book off the ground. Porter gave him some handwriting samples, asked if he could match them. A few days after Upchurch proved that he could, Porter returned with a ream of printed text and asked him to transcribe it into black-and-white composition books. Offered him ten grand to do it. Upchurch had recently been diagnosed with cancer and needed the money, so he did it. He didn't ask any questions, just did it. Bring him in, he'll tell you!"

"Upchurch passed away about three hours ago," Poole said flatly.

Bishop's face went white, and he slumped back in his chair. "Then it's Porter's word against mine. Oh my God, you have to help me."

Poole stopped the video.

Beside him, Porter had gotten quiet. He hadn't said anything in more than ten minutes. When he finally spoke, his voice was much calmer than Poole expected. "None of this is true. You know that. I wasn't even in Chicago when your partner was killed."

Poole sat there a moment, his gaze fixed on the man across from him. If Porter was lying, there was no outward sign. Earlier, though, when he interviewed Bishop, there were no signs of deception, either. He stood and went to the door. Without looking back, he said, "Excuse me, Sam," and left the room, Bishop's frozen face staring smugly back at both of them.

37

Poole

Day 5 • 12:33 PM

When Poole stepped back into the observation room, Nash handed him a sheet of paper. "Federal warrant for a copy of Bishop's interview. Dalton walked it in here himself. He also said SAIC Hurless is on his way here and he's gunning for you."

Poole looked around the small room. They were alone except for the officer running the recording equipment. "Where's the guy from the mayor's office? Warnick?"

Nash shrugged. "He left as soon as he got a copy of the video. About twenty minutes ago." The skin around Nash's eyes was red and puffy. There was a thin layer of sweat on his forehead.

"You are sick, aren't you?"

"It's just a cold, maybe the flu. I felt it coming on long before Upchurch's house. It's not from there." He reached into his pocket and took out a blister pack of DayQuil and slipped one in his mouth. "I feel better already." Turning his head, he coughed into the elbow of his jacket. When he turned back to Poole, he looked like he had swallowed a mouse.

"What?"

Nash said, "When you were in there, I talked to Clair. They performed preliminary autopsies on the vics at the hospital. They were drugged with something called succinylcholine."

"That's a paralytic. Probably easy to find in a hospital."

Nash nodded. "We've got some discrepancies, too."

"Discrepancies?"

"Bishop's right-handed, and all his initial victims were killed by someone who is right-handed. These latest ones—the two we found and the two in the hospital—were killed by someone who is left-handed. Same with Tom Langlin in Simpsonville. She confirmed with the local pathologist."

Poole considered this and fought the urge to turn back to the interrogation room. "Porter's left-handed."

Nash's eyes fell to the floor. "I promised not to hold anything back so I told you, but this can't be him. You've gotta know that."

"I never told Porter my partner was dead, but he knew," Poole pointed out. "How do you explain that?"

Nash looked back at him. "Maybe Clair told him, or Kloz. He could have heard it anywhere. I even saw it on the news. Doesn't mean anything. Bishop is just fucking with you. We know Porter was in New Orleans when he died."

Poole held out his hand. "Let me see my phone."

Nash fumbled through his pockets, pulled out the iPhone, and handed it to him. "That thing rings more than a hooker at a naval base."

"I'm not sure what that means," Poole muttered, sliding through all the missed calls on his notification screen. Dozens from SAIC Hurless. Several he didn't recognize from a number with a 504 area code.

"It means—" Nash started to explain.

Before he could finish, Poole turned his back on him and tapped on the 504 number.

The voice that answered was gruff, distracted. "This is Warden Vina."

"Warden, this is Special Agent Frank Poole. I was about to call—"

"Something's happened," Vina interrupted. "I'm still trying to piece it together. It's Vincent Weidner. He's gone."

Poole glanced at Nash and put the phone on speaker. "Weidner's gone? Gone how?"

"We had a serious security breach here yesterday, some kind of hack, from what we've pieced together. At a little after nine yesterday morning, doors all over the prison just started to unlock—cell doors, access doors, gates in and out—everything just opened. It seemed random at first, like some kind of system glitch rolling through the hardware. Started at the cellblocks, and when the prisoners started to flood the common areas, outer doors started to open. The guards got overwhelmed, and we went into emergency lockdown. I've got two dead, six in the infirmary with various injuries, and fourteen prisoners unaccounted for, Weidner being one of them. We're on a closed network with redundant backups. Something like this should be impossible." Vina placed his hand over the phone for a moment, spoke to someone, then came back. "We're trying to watch the video footage right now, and it looks like that got hacked, too. All the time stamps are off. Everything is out of sequence. How does that even happen?"

Poole closed his eyes and sighed. "So if I were to ask you for video footage confirming Detective Porter was in your prison two days ago, something definitive, would you be able to provide it? Or maybe a photo of the woman who claimed to be Sarah Werner?"

Vina laughed. "I just watched tape of myself walking from my car to Gate Seven, footage I *know* was from this morning, and the time stamp says it's from three weeks ago. My tech guys are going to try and restore data from the backups, but they don't look very optimistic. I don't understand half the shit they're saying, but from what I gather, whatever caused this has been in our system for a while now, and it might not be reversible. Can I tell you Porter was here? Absolutely. I sat across from him. He was in my office. Can I prove it? No. Not right now. Maybe not ever. I've got a meeting in twenty minutes, and I've got to explain all this to my superiors. I have no clue what I'm going to tell them. After that, if I still have a job, I get to go back on local television and explain to the good people of New Orleans that fourteen of our guests are still missing and probably mixing it up out on Bourbon Street, breaking into their homes, car-jacking, and God knows what else. All of them out on my watch. My responsibility. As far as Weidner goes, my gut says he's coming to you if he's not there already. When we picked him up at his apartment the other day, he had a bag packed, two thousand in cash, and a bus ticket to Chicago. That's a guy with a plan. All we did was slow him down. I've got APBs out on him nationally, and we're getting a photo out to the press. Him and all the others. We'll get him."

"Do you know if Weidner's left-handed or right?"

Vina thought for a moment, then said, "I'm pretty sure he's right-handed. Why?"

"I'm afraid I can't say, but I need to know for sure. Can you look into it?"

"Sure, I'll put that right at the top of the list of things I need to do today. I gotta go." He disconnected before Poole could reply.

As Poole lowered the phone, Nash said, "If Weidner's here, he might be responsible for the women we found, maybe even the other dead body at the hospital. If he somehow managed to fly, he had time to go to Simpsonville, too."

"You're assuming Porter is telling the truth."

"I'm sure as shit not gonna believe Bishop," Nash replied. "I was there when he found the first diary."

"I read your report," Poole replied. "Porter found the diary after you searched the body. Could he have planted the book somehow?"

Nash frowned. "What, like some sleight-of-hand magician shit? With all of us standing around him and the body? No way. He's not Copperfield."

Poole dialed another number. He called the agent running the investigation at Montehugh Labs. The video footage there had been compromised, too. Whoever broke in had little trouble bypassing their security. He got in and out without leaving a single shred of evidence behind. They were concentrating their efforts on the staff, but it could have been Bishop, Porter…anyone.

On the opposite side of the observation window, Porter was reading again, his eyes lost in another one of those composition books, Bishop's *Diary*, and Poole wondered—was he really as enthralled as he appeared to be, or was all of this some kind of elaborate act?

Poole shook his head and turned to the two guards standing in the hallway. "Other than bathroom breaks, neither of these men are to leave these rooms, understand? Get them both some lunch, something to burn time." He reached into his pocket and took out two business cards, handed one to each man. "If anyone tries to get in to speak to them, *anyone*, you call me first to clear it. We'll be back in an hour."

Both officers nodded and took the cards.

"We? Where are we going?" Nash asked.

38
Diary

"What is August 29th?"

I found Libby in the loft, as I had on each previous night during the past week, curled up in our corner under a blanket. I called it our corner because on the third night, we moved her wooden crate and lamp from where I had found her on that first night to a corner on the opposite side of the loft—this one near a window where we could watch the house. We had several books—I was reading Of Mice and Men and she had a scary book by some guy named Thad McAlister. We didn't read when we were together; the books were for the waiting—me waiting for her and her waiting for me. When we were together, we talked, and I found it very easy to talk to her.

I found her to be very pretty.

I can admit that now, although I don't think Father would be pleased. He would say her beauty clouded my judgment. Several years ago he told me beauty had a way of draining the blood from the brain and reason went with it. "Why did the man try to cross the road?" he asked me. "To get to a beautiful woman," he replied before I could answer. "That same man watched her smile as a Mack truck cut him in half because he was too stupid from beauty to bother to look right, left, then right again before hopping out into that road. Beauty has started many wars, but it has yet to end one. Beauty has a taste unlike any other. It's the sweetest of poisons. You'll crave more even as it snatches the life from you."

I thought he was silly when he said all that, but he hadn't been smiling. And I never understood it until I saw Libby standing in that hayloft wearing a short flowered dress with the moonlight on her back. Most of her bruises were gone now. Only a couple stubborn ones held on, but even before they faded I saw through them to the girl beneath. To say I was attracted to her would have been a serious understatement. She became my last thought as I drifted off to sleep and my first when I awoke. My hand felt empty without hers.

"August 29th?" she repeated. "I have no idea, why? Should I?"

I told her the date had been marked on both Dr. Oglesby's calendar and the one in Finicky's kitchen.

"Maybe it's somebody's birthday?"

I didn't think it was. Who could both Dr. Oglesby and Ms. Finicky possibly know other than Detectives Welderman and Stocks? I couldn't imagine anyone celebrating their birthdays.

"Or possibly the day the state fair arrives in town?"

Libby had turned back around and was leaning on the windowsill looking out. She stood balanced on one leg while her other was bent behind her, her white tennis shoe dangling precariously from her toes. In the light of the almost full moon, her dress appeared nearly translucent, tracing every curve of her body. Her legs were highlighted, and I couldn't turn away if I wanted to. I knew at that moment Father had been right about what he said. I also knew I didn't care.

"Does the state fair even come here?" I heard myself ask. The farmhouse was remote. I had gathered that much from my twice-weekly visits back to Camden to talk with Dr. Oglesby. There was very little of anything but farm country and open fields.

Her shoulders shrugged. Her locket dangled from her neck. "I don't know. But I've always wanted to go to a state fair."

Libby's backside swayed from side to side as she stood there, and I found it maddening. I wondered if this was a conscious effort on her part or just a feature built into the machinery at the factory as involuntary as breathing or the beat of a heart.

"They're back!" she said in a loud whisper, and she ducked down even though I knew nobody could see us from the house as long as the lamp wasn't burning.

I crawled over from my spot against the wall and I peered out the window. Libby nestled in beside me and looked back out, too. I hadn't kissed her yet, but I most certainly wanted to. The warmth of her felt so good, I never wanted to leave. Foolish, I know. All good things eventually ended, and I knew this good thing would one day end as well, but I wanted to do everything in my power to make it last as long as possible.

Detective Welderman's Malibu was in the driveway, still running, doors closed.

"Who's in there? Can you tell?" she asked.

I shook my head.

Most nights it was Kristina or Tegan, sometimes both. Welderman drove me to and from Oglesby's office, but those trips were always during the day. It was nearly three in the morning now, and I knew enough to understand they hadn't been visiting Camden. Libby had asked Tegan where they went, and all the other girl would tell her is "you'll know soon enough." Paul had taken that ride last week, and he wouldn't talk about it, either. In fact, he didn't talk for nearly two full days after he got back.

Welderman stepped out of the driver side, and Stocks got out, too, a cigarette burning between his fingers. Welderman opened the back door, spoke to someone, then reached inside.

"Get your fucking hands off me!" Vincent Weidner shouted back at him. "Don't you fucking touch me!"

I noticed Stocks's free hand drift down to the butt of the gun on his belt, and Libby must have noticed it too, because she let out a thin gasp and leaned in closer to me.

From inside the car, Vince shrugged off Welderman's hand and pushed past him out of the car. He was a big kid, nearly as tall as Welderman, and when his shoulder crashed into the older man, he nearly knocked him off balance. Stocks's grip on his gun tightened, but he didn't take it out. Vince stormed up the driveway and into the house without another word to either of them. The two men stood there long enough for Stocks to finish up his cigarette. Then they got back in the Malibu and drove off.

Libby took my hand and pulled me back from the window. "Come on."

39

Poole

Paul Upchurch's house was blue with white trim and sat about midway down the block. A CSI van was parked in front along with a single patrol car. A van from Channel Ten was across the street, engine running, a tail of white smoke pluming up from the exhaust. As Poole pulled his Jeep up behind the patrol car and shifted into park, a hand in the news van wiped the condensation from the passenger window and a face peered out.

"They're like herpes. You think they're gone, and a new rash creeps up on your other ass-cheek," Nash said.

"I don't think herpes works that way," Poole said flatly, looking up at the house.

"I'm just trying to lighten the mood," Nash replied. "You haven't said anything since we left Metro."

"Sorry, I tend to get quiet when I'm thinking."

"Porter and I usually try to talk through the problem. It helps sometimes. Throw all the facts out there, mix it up, come up with a theory. Most things don't stick, but every once in a while we stumble into an angle we might not have considered."

"Could Porter have been running some kind of secondary undercover op without you knowing?"

"No way."

THE SIXTH WICKED CHILD • 161

"That's a knee-jerk reaction. Would it have been physically possible for him to run an op without you catching on?"

Nash tapped his index finger against his lip. "I don't see how. I've worked with the guy for years, and sure, he can be a little secretive at times, but I don't see how he could keep something like that from me."

"When we raided his apartment, you said you had no idea he was still chasing Bishop. You seemed as surprised as the rest of us."

"If we're being honest here, I had my suspicions, but I didn't see the harm in it. Sam's not the kind of guy to let something go, so I figured he was still digging. If he found something worthwhile, he would have brought the rest of us in."

"Did he call you before he ran off to New Orleans?"

"No, but—"

Poole waved him off. "My point is, we think we know the people we work with, particularly when we spend a lot of time with a partner, but that doesn't mean we really do."

Nash turned to him. "He didn't tell us about New Orleans because he wanted to protect us."

"So if he was running an undercover operation, he might have cut you out of that, too. To protect you," Poole countered.

"Sam is a good cop."

"Everyone keeps telling me that." Poole opened his door and stepped out into the frigid cold, started up the walk to the house. Nash followed. They kicked the snow off their shoes against a concrete step as best they could before going in.

A uniformed officer was stationed just inside the front door. He nodded at them both. "Detective Nash."

Nash pointed his thumb at Poole. "This is Special Agent Frank Poole with the FBI. Who's here?"

"Most of the team went out for lunch. Rolfes is upstairs."

"Lindsy Rolfes?"

He nodded.

Poole asked, "You know her?"

"She was there when we found the Reynolds girl under the ice at Jackson Park. Seemed sharp."

Poole's eyes went to a bloodstain on the floor just inside the door, then glanced down the hallway.

"We found one girl unconscious on the kitchen table," Nash told him. "Another in a cage down in the basement. That's where the deprivation tank is. He made it out of an old chest freezer. Upchurch was in one of the bedrooms upstairs, just kneeling there when we came in."

"Waiting for you."

"Yeah."

"Show me."

Poole followed Nash past the kitchen, into the living room, and up the staircase to a little girl's room. Pink and bright. Stuffed animals sat atop a Hello Kitty quilt on the small bed. Drawings covered the walls—some appeared to be drawn by a child, others clearly by a more experienced artist. There was a mannequin in the corner of the room, small, child-size. It was dressed in little girl's clothing—a red sweater, blue shorts.

A reasonable facsimile of the girl in the pictures. Under the only window stood a desk, the drawers all open and the contents spread out on the floor. Sitting in the middle was a woman in her thirties with short blonde hair and glasses. She looked up at Nash as they entered. "Detective."

"Special Agent Frank Poole, this is CSI Rolfes."

She reached out a gloved hand and shook his, then offered a pleasant smile. "What can I do for you?"

"I need to understand Upchurch," Poole said, then realized just how odd that probably sounded out of context. "He may be involved in more than one aspect of this investigation, something beyond his victims."

"Do you mean the forgeries?"

Poole exchanged a glance with Nash. "Forgeries?"

Rolfes nodded. "Looks like he had quite an operation going here. Tough to make a living teaching teens to drive, and he certainly wasn't pulling in enough from his art, so he got creative with his skills to pay the bills. Driver's licenses, passports, that kind of thing."

From under a stack of sketchpads, she pulled out a laptop and set it on the desk. "He was a wiz with Photoshop. In the other bedroom, we've got a professional grade scanner, photo equipment, three different printers. I'd be willing to bet he could get you a driver's license in under an hour without leaving this house."

She clicked the spacebar, and the screen came to life with a template and several photos of two different women. The white background indicated they were probably meant for passports. Driver's licenses tended to use a blue background for people over the age of twenty-one, yellow for under.

"Holy shit," Nash muttered beside him, leaning in closer.

"Yeah…" Poole recognized both, same as Nash. One was the woman found in the cemetery earlier today. The other was the woman found on the subway tracks at the station off Lake Street.

40
Diary

Libby and I were halfway back to the house when we heard shouting. Well, that was wrong—first there was a loud bang, then several more loud bangs, then shouting. A couple lights came on, both upstairs and down, and as silly as it may sound, the only worry I had was whether or not Libby and I would get in trouble for being outside at such a late hour.

Vincent had left the front door open, and the first bang we heard must have been the round table just inside the entrance, because when we stepped into the house, we found that table on its side up against the wall. The vase and flowers, the small plate for car keys, those were on the floor, shattered into about a million pieces. The carpet was soaked from the vase water, and I knew Ms. Finicky would be angry when she saw it. I didn't get much time to think about that, because Libby was tugging my hand toward the stairs, toward the angry voices on the second floor.

We took the steps quickly—no need to worry about creaking boards now—and found Vincent Weidner standing in the middle of the hallway with his arms outstretched, his face flaming red, and blood on his shirt. There were a couple holes in the walls—one on his left and two more on the right—and judging by the cuts on his hands, he'd punched his way through the plaster and lath beneath. The blood on his shirt wasn't his, though. It was Paul's, who was on the floor in front of him with one hand pinching his nose shut to stem the flow from what must have been another punch. He tried to scramble back to his feet, slipped, then fell back on his butt.

"Stay down!" Vincent shouted at Paul. "Stay the fuck down!"

Tegan was standing at her doorway wearing a T-shirt and panties. Weasel and The Kid peeked around the corner of their own door, but neither dared step out. Kristina was in the hallway, reaching for Vincent, trying to calm him down. When her hand found his forearm, he shrugged her off, nearly elbowing her. She looked like she was about to cry. "Vince, it's okay! Come in my room. Let's talk about it. Everything will be all right!"

"I just wanted to help, that's all," Paul said. And I realized his lip was bleeding, too. Vincent must have hit him a few times.

I tried to go to him, to help him up, but Libby's hand tightened in mine and she wouldn't let me go. Tegan must have noticed that too, since she was staring at both of us.

"What the hell is going on here?"

This came from behind us and I turned to find Ms. Finicky standing there in a long, yellow nightgown and a shotgun in her hands. Her eyes jumped from Libby and me to Paul on the floor, the holes in the walls, and finally to Vincent. She leveled the barrel of the gun on him. "What is this?"

Vincent's face somehow managed to grow even redder. "All of you just leave me the hell alone!" I thought he might kick Paul, but instead, he stepped over him. He crossed the hallway to his room and slammed the door.

Everyone just stood there for a moment. I don't think any of us knew what to do.

Tegan's look had gone from a gaze to an outright glare, and Libby's hand fell from mine. I felt her inch away toward her own door.

"Get up," Finicky said to Paul, lowering the shotgun. "Oh, your face! What has he done to your face?"

Paul was still pinching his nose shut with one hand. With his other, he touched his lip, winced, then got to his feet on wobbly legs.

Finicky stepped toward him. "Christ, you children will be the death of me. Tilt your head back—you're bleeding all over the floor." She looked up. "Kristina, get me a rag from the bathroom. The rest of you, get in your rooms. Now."

Weasel and The Kid disappeared like two mice caught in the kitchen when the light turns on. Tegan remained in her doorway for a moment, but she wasn't looking at Paul, her eyes still on me. When I turned to look for Libby, she was gone. Her bedroom door had closed so softly I hadn't even heard it.

"In your room, Anson," Ms. Finicky said, nodding toward my open door. Then her eyes narrowed. "Why are you dressed?"

I didn't answer her. Instead, I slipped inside and shut the door.

I was still awake when Paul finally came in nearly an hour later. The light was off, but I could see well enough. He had a bag of ice wrapped in a green towel pressed to his nose. He didn't say a word as he crossed the room and climbed the ladder to the top bunk. He lay there in silence for nearly ten minutes before saying anything at all. "They'll take you next. You know that, don't you?" His voice sounded nasal.

"Take me where?"

He didn't answer that. And I wasn't sure I wanted him to.

"Everyone goes. It will be Libby's turn after that. Maybe even Weasel and The Kid..." His voice trailed off as he said this. I heard the ice jingle in his bag. "It's different for Tegan and Kristina, even me and Vince—we lived on the streets. They're just kids, though."

I wanted to point out we were all just kids, but I didn't.

Another minute or two passed, then he said, "You were out in the barn, right? With Libby?"

"Yeah."

"Did you see the truck? I heard there's a truck out there," he told me. "We need to see if it runs."

41

Poole

Day 5 • 1:00 PM

"Those photos are recent. Haircuts haven't changed." Nash said, looking down at Upchurch's laptop.

Poole glanced at Rolfes. "May I?"

She nodded.

He slid into the desk chair and right-clicked on one of the photographs, bringing up the metadata on the first image, then the other. "These were both taken in the last week."

Rolfes reached over and clicked several buttons. "He took about a dozen shots of each woman in different outfits. Some with their hair up, others with it down. I'm not sure if that meant he planned to create more than one ID, or if they were just going for the right image."

Poole scrolled through the photo gallery. "How far did he get? Did you see any names?"

She shook her head. "No names for these two. Doesn't look like he finished with them. There are hundreds of others, though, dating back more than a decade. Not just Illinois licenses but Louisiana, the Carolinas, New York too. He's been at this for a while."

Nash clucked his tongue. "Sam mentioned two women's names when you first went in to talk to him, from the diary. Do you think...?"

"Kristina Niven and Tegan Savala," Poole recalled. "I don't know, could be."

Looking back at Rolfes, Nash asked, "Can you get copies of all this to Kloz?"

"Already did. A few hours ago."

Poole opened his mouth to object, but instead, he took a business card from his back pocket. "Contact SAIC Foster Hurless at this number and make arrangements to get copies to the Chicago Bureau office, too."

She placed the card in the breast pocket of her blouse. "Absolutely."

Poole stood from the chair and glanced around the cluttered room. There was a disposable phone on the desk in an evidence bag. "Anything useful on there?"

Rolfes shrugged. "Depends what you consider useful. It's a cheap buy-and-dump model. Upchurch wiped the log after every use, so IT is working on pulling the call logs from the carrier. We should have those in a few hours."

"Call me when you have that too. My cell is written on the back of my card," Poole instructed. "Did you find anything that looks like a diary, a journal, any of those black and white composition books?"

Rolfes nodded toward the opposite side of the room. "Under the bed."

Nash was closest. He turned and bent down, lifting the pink Hello Kitty quilt out of the way.

He let out a deep sigh, then started pulling items out, whatever he could reach—five brand-new composition books still wrapped together in clear cellophane, two loose ones, and several stacks of typed pages held together with heavy binder clips.

Poole stepped over and picked up one of the books. A black pen was clipped to the cover, and several pages of loose paper were folded inside. He unfolded the pages and read:

Hello Sam,
*   I imagine you're confused.*
*   I imagine you have questions.*

I know I did. I have. I do.

Questions are the foundation of knowledge, learning, discovery, and rediscovery. An inquisitive mind has no outer walls, an inquisitive mind is a warehouse with unlimited square footage, a memory palace of infinite rooms and floors and shiny pretty things. Sometimes, though, a mind suffers damage, a wall crumbles, the memory palace is in need of a renovation, one or more rooms are found to be in dire disrepair. Your mind, I'm afraid, falls into the latter. The photographs around you, the diaries to your side, these are the keys that will aid you as you dig from the rubble, as you rebuild.

I'm here for you, Sam.

I'll be here for you, as I always have been.

I've forgiven you, Sam. Perhaps others will, too. You're not that man anymore. You've become so much more.

—Anson

This was the text they had found on the computer screen with Porter at the Guyon Hotel. Only here, it didn't just appear on the printout but was written on the first page of this particular composition book. Poole had seen enough of the diaries to know the shaky scrawl here would be a match for not only the original diary but the ones currently locked up with Detective Porter. Handwriting believed to be Anson Bishop's.

Nash was sitting on the floor with his back against the bed looking up at him. "If that's what I think it is, Bishop could have planted it. This doesn't mean he told you the truth."

He was right, of course, but it didn't look good.

Poole's phone rang.

Nash was still looking up at him. "Hurless?"

Poole looked at the display and nodded.

"As someone experienced with the whole 'dodge the boss game,' I can tell you he will track you down eventually, and the longer you wait, the more pissed off he'll be," Nash said.

Poole reluctantly tapped answer and pressed the phone to his ear. "Agent Poole."

"Why are you at the Upchurch house?"

As with all the agents under his charge, Hurless had access to Poole's phone's GPS data in real-time, but it always made him uncomfortable when the man pointed out that fact.

Poole told him what they had found.

Hurless considered this for a moment. "Have someone bring those pages to our field office. We still have Porter's laptop and printer from his apartment—we need to see if they're a match."

"Yes, sir."

Hurless covered the phone and spoke to someone else on his end. When he came back, he said, "There's an SUV waiting for you outside, a black Escalade. I want you and that detective in it in five minutes."

"I need to get back to Metro and continue questioning—"

"Five minutes," Hurless interrupted.

Then he hung up.

Poole wasn't one to use foul language, but several choice words came to mind.

42

Clair

Day 5 • 1:05 PM

Zero leads.

Nada.

Nothing.

At least not yet.

Clair had just talked to Officer Sutter, and while he had managed to speak to nearly a third of the people in the cafeteria, none had anything useful to offer. If her two victims had any kind of connection, she had yet to learn it. Her two missing officers—Henricks and Childs—were still missing, and had been for over four hours now. She could overlook a quick nap, particularly since none of them had really had any downtime in days, but this wasn't that. The little voice in the back of her head was sounding the alarm, and she could only ignore it for so much longer. If word got out that officers were missing in addition to the two murders, there would be no telling how the remaining people in this hospital would react—law enforcement, professionals, or civilians. This would get ugly. She saw it in the faces—fear, defeat, fatigue, anger—order and civility was an illusion controlled by the majority, and right now, her little group of officers and security guards was far from being a majority.

And now this.

Klozowski had been sharing information as it came in, and the pit in her stomach had grown to the size of a bowling ball. She stared at him from across the small table in their office and swallowed the equally large lump in her throat. "This can't be happening."

"Oh, it's happening," Kloz replied, his eyes glued to the screen. "It's completely fucked, but it's happening."

"There is no way Porter was running Bishop in some undercover thing without the rest of us knowing about it, no way."

"If it wasn't *some undercover thing*, then that means he was just *running Bishop* and that's way worse. That means Bishop isn't 4MK at all. It means—"

Clair grabbed one of the folders and smacked Kloz in the side of the head. "Don't you even think about saying that out loud. Not now, not ever. I don't believe any of that bullshit for a second."

"I'm just trying to be objective here. Strip away what we know about him and look at him as if he's just a suspect, he—"

She smacked him again. "Sam's not a suspect! Don't use words like that!"

Kloz rubbed at the side of his head. "Will you stop hitting me for five minutes and just listen?"

"Sam's not a suspect."

"Okay, person of interest."

"Interested party."

Kloz frowned. "Under the circumstances, I don't think that's grammatically correct."

"I don't care."

He rolled his eyes. "Okay. Whatever. My point is, we have some serious red flags. Have you read Emory's statement? She never ID'd Bishop as the person who took her. She never saw his face. She heard a voice from the top of that elevator shaft, but with the echo and considering her mental state at that point, if we gave her an audio lineup, I seriously doubt she'd be able to pick him out. Frankly, I don't think the DA's office would even agree to try because they wouldn't want to risk her picking the wrong person and blowing the case. That's probably why they haven't brought it up."

It was Clair's turn to roll her eyes. "Why would Sam take her? Why would he kill all those people? We've got motive for Bishop. Sam had no reason."

"Just because we don't have a motive doesn't mean there isn't one," Kloz pointed out. "We haven't looked. And frankly, how solid is our motive for Bishop? That came from Sam—his analysis of the diary and information he said Bishop told him. There aren't any other witnesses to those conversations. Everything came from Sam."

"You were on the phone with him when Bishop stabbed him."

Kloz shrugged. "I heard one side of the conversation. Only Sam. I have no more idea what happened in that apartment than you do. We took Sam at his word." He clicked several buttons on his laptop and brought up the video of Poole interviewing Bishop again. "It could have happened just like Bishop said here. His word against Sam's. How do we know which one is the truth? How do we *really* know?"

Clair wasn't about to accept any of this. "Bishop confessed to Sam right before he killed Talbot."

"Confessed to Sam," Kloz repeated. "Sam alone."

A smug grin spread across Clair's face. "What about the fingerprint? They found Bishop's fingerprint on that railcar with Gunther Herbert's body. At the Mulifax building. If Bishop didn't kill Herbert, why would he be down there?"

"Oh, I've read that report, too." He loaded the file up on his screen and scrolled down to the last few paragraphs. "Mark Thomas with Brogan's SWAT team lifted the print from the railcar, put it in an evidence bag, and gave it to Sam. That was 6:18 p.m., according to the report. Sam carried it in his pocket and handed it off to Nash *three hours later*. He asked Nash to take it in for analysis. *Three hours.* You don't think he had time to switch it?"

"Sam wouldn't do that."

"Forget that we're talking about Sam. We're talking about our 'interested party.' If that person wanted to frame Bishop, they had opportunity. We don't have a single witness who can actually ID Bishop."

Clair snapped her fingers. "What about Tyler Mathers, Emory's boyfriend? Him and his uncle—they collected all that money, stole Talbot's shoes…"

Klozowski opened the report on Mathers, traced a line with his finger, and read aloud, "I never saw him. I don't think Uncle Jake ever did, either. He only talked to him over the phone." Kloz looked up at her. "This is your report. You interviewed him."

"Okay. The people at the park—where Emory was abducted—we have eyewitness accounts…"

Kloz was already shaking his head. "That's your report, too, and all the physical descriptions you got from those people contradict each other. Nobody really got a good look at him. It's like the voice lineup with Emory—the DA won't risk a lineup with those witnesses, considering they were all so far apart on description in your interviews. You bring in a group like that and they pick different people, everything falls apart."

He blew out a breath and leaned back in his chair. "Look, I'm not saying Bishop isn't our guy, all I'm saying is if someone wants to poke holes, they won't have to work too hard."

"Bishop is a fucked-in-the-head, crazy, piece-of-shit vigilante killer. He did it. He did all of it. He's the reason we're here, trapped in this goddamn hospital."

"Is it really so hard for you to believe that a police detective could be a vigilante? Sam wouldn't be the first." Kloz shrunk back and tensed, waiting for another blow.

Clair didn't hit him this time. Instead, she shivered and nodded toward a heavy coat on the floor next to Kloz's chair. "Give me that. I'm freezing."

"You're sweating. You probably have a fever."

"I'm fine."

Kloz handed her the coat. "I don't think the meds they're giving us are helping at all."

She draped the coat over her shoulders and tried to keep her teeth from chattering.

The laptop dinged, and Kloz leaned in closer. "Got another e-mail from CSI Rolfes."

"What's it say?"

He didn't answer at first. Instead, he clicked on the attachment and opened a zip file. About a dozen images filled the screen—pictures of Sam with Bishop at various ages.

"Are those the same pictures they found in that room with Sam at the Guyon?"

Kloz nodded. "I think so."

Clair turned the laptop so she could read Rolfes' note—

> All of these were created on Upchurch's computer. They're fake.
> - Lindsy

"I'm not sure what to make of that," Clair said softly.

"It means either Sam paid Upchurch to make them, along with the diaries, or Bishop had him do it for some reason."

"Okay, but why?"

Kloz didn't answer.

Clair's phone buzzed with a text message from Officer Sutter—

> Need you in the cafeteria. Now.

43
Diary

Shortly before dusk the following day, we did find a truck in the barn. A 1998 Ford F-150 held together by patches of rust and the dwindling remains of yellow paint. Someone had draped a tan tarp over the entire dilapidated mess after rolling it as far into the back corner as possible. It was so close to the back wall, the only way to pass was to jump up on the bumper and crawl over. Prior to placing the tarp, the bed of the truck had been the premier spot for dumping all things that needed to be stored away and forgotten. Libby and I found everything from an old birdcage to shoes and books. There was even a television, the glass cracked revealing the inner workings, the electronic intestines, arteries, and heart of this now dead thing.

All four truck tires were flat. The key was in the ignition, but twisting it didn't even produce a click. The cab smelled musty and stale, the air of an Egyptian tomb opened to the sky for the first time in millennia.

"Phew," Libby said, pinching her nose.

There was an underlying stink there, like something had crawled up under the dash to take a nap and died there. Maybe a raccoon, rat, or family of mice. I poked my head underneath, but without a flashlight, I couldn't see much. The vinyl seats were covered in webs of cracks, yellow stuffing peeking out. When Libby climbed up into the passenger seat and plopped down, a cloud of dust plumed up and sent us both into a sneezing fit. When she finally was able to speak again, she drew a finger through the dust on the dashboard and proclaimed, "This is perfect!"

"It's junk." I twisted the key again. "Somebody left it here to die."

She turned to me and smiled. "We can get it running and drive to California or Canada or maybe even Mexico. Leave all of this behind and start over somewhere!"

"We'll need parts and tools. Heck, we'll need a way to get to those parts and tools. We're at least ten miles from the closest store. And let's say we find a way to get there and back. We need someone who actually knows how to fix this thing. Father taught me how to change the oil and maintain a vehicle, but I have no idea what to do with an engine, how to fix something like that."

Libby's smile fell away, and she turned to me thoughtfully. "You always call him 'Father,' you don't say 'my father' or even 'my dad,' always just 'Father.' Why is that?"

I didn't know the answer to that question. He'd always been Father to me. As long as Mother had been Mother, I supposed. This wasn't a question of this or that, just a statement of what is—as air is air and dirt is dirt. I am—

"Anson," she said, "I'm sorry. I shouldn't have brought it up. It was insensitive. You just lost them. I'm sorry."

She curled her fingers through mine. We held hands all the time now, and it was nice. My hand felt empty without hers. Like Dr. Oglesby, she had mentioned that I sometimes drifted off from a conversation, and unlike Dr. Oglesby, I didn't want to do that with her.

I forced a smile. "It's not that. I guess I just never thought about it before. My parents never permitted me to call them 'Mom' or 'Dad,' only 'Mother' or 'Father.' I suppose everything is normal when you don't know any better." This was like the lock on the refrigerator, but I hadn't told her that. It was like many things that took place at our house—I didn't tell her about those, either. It had been months since I had been home, and I wanted to go there—see my house, my lake. My world had been burning the last time I was there. I was curious what was left, what even the fire didn't want.

"We should tell Paul."

We found Paul where we always found Paul, sitting on his bed with his sketchpad. He didn't look up when we explained what we found, just kept drawing. "Vincent worked in a garage. He'd know how to fix it. But I'm not gonna ask him. Mr. Vincent Weidner is dead to me."

Vincent had done a number on Paul. His left eye was black, and even though he hadn't broken his nose, it was still swollen. The surrounding skin was an odd mix of green and blue. None of us had seen Vincent since last night. He hadn't come out at all, not even to use the bathroom. His bedroom was directly over Ms. Finicky's, and Paul said he was probably relieving himself right out his window onto the porch overhang. "She'll be thrilled about that when the sun comes out," Paul said. But the sun had come out, and nothing happened. I figured he just went when nobody was around.

"We'll talk to him," Libby proclaimed. "Won't we, Anson?"

I didn't want to talk to him. I didn't want to see him. Vincent Weidner scared me. Father wouldn't have approved of me showing fear, particularly around a girl, so I only nodded, and before I could object, she had dragged me across the hall to Vincent's door and knocked.

"Vincent, it's Libby and Anson."

No reply.

"Maybe he's gone." I knew he was in there, though.

Libby knocked again.

"No," Vincent said from the other side of the door.

Libby looked at me, then at the door. "No? No, what?"

"No you. No Anson. No anybody. Nobody. Just no."

"We just want to talk."

"Good for you. Now get the fuck out of here."

Libby just stood there, and I didn't know what else to do so I just stood there, too. Then she knocked again.

Vincent raised his voice. "I will throw both you little shits out the fucking window if you don't leave me alone!"

I let out a breath, thinking it just might be my last. "Vincent, we found a truck out in the barn."

Silence again.

When the door opened, it wasn't Vincent standing there, but Kristina. Her hair was pulled back in a ponytail and she wore a Bangles t-shirt, a pair of pink running shorts, and no shoes. I don't think she had a bra on. "What truck?"

44

Poole

Day 5 • 1:20 PM

As Hurless had said, a black Cadillac Escalade with dark tinted windows waited for them at the curb in front of Upchurch's house. The only occupant was a driver. A man in his late fifties in a neatly pressed black suit. He got out, scrambled to open the doors in the frigid air, and ushered them inside—Poole took the front seat, Nash got in back.

The driver refused to tell them where they were heading.

Poole had never been in a car this clean. The black leather was polished to a factory shine. Not a single speck marred the windows. Aside from the wet winter sludge Poole tracked in on his shoes, even the floor mats were clean, as if someone switched them out between passengers.

"There's a bar back here," Nash said. "A fully stocked bar. Snacks, too. If you look in the back seat of my car, you'd be lucky to find some dried up special sauce on a McDonald's wrapper and maybe half a bottle of water." He reached into the front seat with a Twix bar. "You want?"

Poole ignored him and turned back to the driver. "Whose car is this?"

"I'm not at liberty to say," the man said.

"You realize I'm a federal agent?"

"I'm sorry, sir. I have orders." He made several turns and followed the signs onto 290 East, toward the lake.

When Poole didn't take the candy bar, Nash settled back into his seat and tore open the wrapper. He was halfway through it when he said, "Why is the FBI on this case?"

"You know why."

Nash took another bite, bits of chocolate falling from his mouth as he spoke. "No, actually I don't. We were told you were taking over because Bishop got away and we weren't making headway fast enough. It doesn't work that way, though. The FBI can't claim jurisdiction unless the crimes cross state lines. Not unless local law enforcement invites you. All the initial murders took place in or around Chicago, every single one of Bishop's victims. I know Metro didn't invite you."

"We've got connected murders in South Carolina and Louisiana, too," Poole countered, unsure he even wanted part of this conversation.

"Discovered *after* FBI took over the case," Nash reminded him. "Not before."

"My orders came directly from my supervisor, SAIC Hurless."

"Who picked up the phone and invited *him* to the party? Where did his orders come from?" Nash finished off the candy bar and tossed the wrapper on the floor next to him. "We figure that out, and I think we'll know who owns this car."

The driver exited 290 at LaSalle and made a left on State Street.

"There are other ways." Poole reached forward and opened the glove box.

"Sir, please don't do that." The driver glanced over, then looked back at the road. Traffic on State was heavy for this time of day.

Rifling through the various items in the glove box, Poole found the registration, but it only read *Elite Rentals and Transportation Services, LLC*. He found an old parking ticket, the owner's manual, and a .38 in a leather holster. "Do you have a permit to carry a concealed weapon?"

"Yes, sir. Renewed it last month. I'm at the range at least once each week."

"So, are you a driver or security?"

He didn't reply. Instead, he switched on his blinker and turned onto Wabash.

"Are you with law enforcement?"

The driver made another left, then pulled to a stop at the curb on the right. "We're here, sir."

Looking out the window at the gold awning over the sidewalk, Nash whistled. "The Langham Hotel. Came here for a wedding once and ended up in the pool. They've got twinkle lights on the ceiling. That was one hell of a party."

"I don't think we're here for a wedding," Poole muttered.

The driver stepped out and rounded the Escalade, opened first Poole's door, then the one in the back. "You are to go directly to room 1218."

He left them standing on the sidewalk, arctic air swirling all around.

Poole stared at the front door and cupped his hands in front of his mouth. "I'm not sure I like this. Who even knows we're here?"

"I texted Clair and gave her the room number. If I don't text her again in the next fifteen minutes, she'll send reinforcements."

Poole pushed through the heavy glass doors into the hotel lobby with Nash behind him. As instructed, they ignored the bustle at the registration counter, concierge, and bellhops and made their way to the bank of elevators. When the center lift opened, they stepped inside and rode up to the twelfth floor, where they were greeted by a very large man in a dark navy suit, shaved head, and a goatee, holding a clipboard.

Poole's eyes went from the bulge under the man's left shoulder to another on his right ankle. Two guns, maybe more. This man seemed to do the same, first noting Poole's weapons, then Nash's. If this fazed him, his face didn't give it away. "Names?"

Poole told him.

He scanned the list, flipped to a second page, then took another look at the first. "Give me a minute." Without waiting on a reply, he disappeared down the hallway and around a bend.

"Secret Service?" Nash muttered.

Poole shook his head. "They don't allow facial hair."

"Seriously?"

The man returned a moment later with Anthony Warnick from the mayor's office behind him. Warnick didn't bother with pleasantries. "This way."

Poole exchanged a glance with Nash and followed after him. The man with the clipboard returned to his post at the elevator.

Another man stood at the double doors to room 1218. As they approached, he slipped a key card into the reader and opened the doors for them.

Not a room.

A suite.

Practically an apartment or a small house.

The coffered ceilings were at least ten feet tall, and the far wall was nothing but glass looking out over the lake. Two couches flanked a large table at the center of the room. There was a dining area off to the left and several more doors on the right—a bathroom and two more, which were closed, most likely bedrooms. Ornate rugs covered the hardwood floors, and tasteful prints lined the walls. The furniture was contemporary in earth tones with subtle accents of color.

There were half a dozen people inside, men and women, all bustling about, either on phone calls or talking in small groups. Several looked up at them as they stepped into the room, then went back to whatever they were doing. On a desk near the windows, a woman sat, oblivious to the activity around her. She wore headphones, a beige sweater, and jeans, and her eyes were fixed on the display of a large MacBook Pro. Two video windows were open—one with Anson Bishop, the other with Sam Porter, both from the interviews Poole had conducted earlier. Porter's image was frozen, Bishop's was running.

"What is this?" Poole frowned.

"Madeline Abel," Warnick replied. "She's a leading expert in kinesics. That's the study of—"

"I know what it is," Poole interrupted. "Why does she have access to those videos? Did you even get a warrant for Porter's? Who gave it to you?"

Warnick ignored the questions. "I don't have time for that. I need to know which of these two men is telling the truth. You're not moving fast enough." He shot Nash a disapproving glance. *"Neither of you."*

Nash huffed but didn't say anything.

Warnick placed a hand on the woman's shoulder. She paused the video, removed her headphones, and looked up at them. Her eyes grew when she saw Poole. "Frank?"

Warnick frowned. "You know each other?"

"Agent Abel trained me."

She smiled. "It's just Maddie Abel now. Maddie is fine. I'm private sector. I left the Bureau three years ago."

"I need to know who's lying," Warnick repeated, glaring down at her. "The two of you can catch up later."

The smile left her face. She turned back to the videos. "Well, they both are. They're also both telling the truth. I'll need a lot more time with this. Both men are skilled, they're clearly familiar with kinesics, and they're making conscious and subconscious decisions to mask the appearance of deception. Agent Poole here did a wonderful job asking questions to establish a baseline and with follow-up questions in order to uncover falsities in their statements, but they're both deploying countermeasures on par with his tactics."

Warnick's face grew red. "I brought you in here because you're the leading expert. I need answers, not convoluted bullshit. One of these men is responsible. I need to know which one."

She sighed and rolled her hand over the edge of the table. "Maybe with additional reference material. Can you get me more videos of Bishop? Porter, too, maybe interviews he conducted in the past. Something like that would be helpful. If I can pick up his understanding of kinesics, I might be able to exclude that behavior as I watch this one and focus on aspects he might have overlooked. It's physically impossible to mask every sign of deception."

Warnick snapped his fingers, and a younger man who had been listening behind them crossed the room and got on his phone. Warnick then said, "We can get more on Porter, but there's nothing on Bishop. This is it."

Biting the inside of her cheek, Maddie hit play on the Bishop video again and zoomed in on his temple. She hit pause a moment later. "That's not going to work, either."

"What?"

"Sometimes I can pick up on an unsub's pulse in the video, but the quality on this camera isn't high enough. With Bishop, I'm not sure that would work anyway. He seems to have a good handle on his involuntary actions—breathing and such—I bet his pulse is steady through the entire interview."

"Responsible for what?"

This came from Nash. The only thing he'd said since entering the suite. "You told us you needed to know which of these men was responsible. What did you mean by that?"

For a second, Warnick looked like he might fire back some defensive answer, but he didn't. Instead, he turned toward the far side of the suite. "This way."

They followed him to the door on the left of the bathroom—he twisted the knob and stepped aside.

All the lights were blazing in the large master space—overhead cans, lamps on the dressers, another at a small desk. The ensuite at the back was lit up, too. A king-size four-poster bed stood at the center of the room. The rumpled sheets and duvet were bunched up near the foot. A video camera on a tripod was set up a few feet off to the side, the lens pointing at the bed. Men's clothing was scattered around the floor—suit pants and jacket, shirt, tie, socks, boxers. In the middle of the bed, spreading out from the center and covering at least two-thirds, was a brownish-red stain.

Poole and Nash stepped inside.

Warnick came up behind them. "The mayor's been missing since nine-thirty last night, and yes, that is blood."

45

Poole

Day 5 • 2:00 PM

"The mayor's blood?" Nash took a step closer to the bed.

"I have no idea," Warnick replied. "We found the room like this."

Unlike the others, Poole hadn't moved after entering the bedroom. "This is a crime scene. It should be cordoned off. How many people have been through here?"

"Too many." Warnick walked over to the dresser. "The mayor's security staff wiped down every surface and tried to clean up the mess on the bed before they called me. Spent at least an hour contaminating every inch of this space. Damn idiots."

"If someone hurt the mayor, why would his security staff try to cover it up?" Nash asked.

Poole knew the answer. "Because this isn't the first time the mayor left a mess behind. They thought they were helping."

Warnick eyed him, considering his response. "The mayor's... escapades...can sometimes get rough. Nothing too crazy, the women are always well compensated. They know what they're getting into. We've had bruising in the past. There was a broken finger once. Never anything like this, never blood."

"But because he's hurt them in the past, his staff assumed..."

"They're a bunch of idiots," Warnick repeated.

Nash circled the room, looked under the bed, in the bathroom, the closet. "Where's the woman?"

Warnick shrugged. "They assumed she ran off. There's no sign of her. I pulled the security footage from the hotel and it's all messed up—the time stamps are off, the footage is completely out of order. They've got cameras in all the public spaces, elevators too, but they can't seem to find a single shot of anyone entering or leaving this suite last night."

Poole glanced over at Nash, but neither commented.

Nash had paused at the dresser, next to Warnick. Both men were looking up at the mirror.

When Poole joined them, he understood why. On the mirror, written in what looked like soap, were the words *Father, forgive me.*

Same as the women found this morning. Same as the victims at the hospital and the man down in Simpsonville. He glanced around the room, at the floor. "Did you find salt anywhere?"

"Salt?" Warnick shook his head. "No. Why would there be salt?"

Nash must have thought the same thing. He looked around the room and spotted something near the bathroom door. He went over and knelt down. "There's some here. Not much. Just a little in the carpet."

Poole nodded at the trash can in the corner. The remains of a paper salt packet lay at the bottom. Nash pulled an evidence bag from his pocket and used the plastic to pinch the packet, pick it up, and seal it inside. He shoved the bag back in his pocket.

Poole checked the video camera… empty. "Do you have the tape?" he asked Warnick.

"We found the camera like that."

Poole wasn't sure he believed him. Whether that tape contained evidence or incriminating images of the mayor, it wouldn't be something his people would want in the wrong hands, and Poole quickly got the impression any hands other than Warnick's were wrong. "Failure to give me that tape would be considered tampering with evidence."

Warnick took a step closer. "There is no tape."

His eyes met Poole's, and neither man looked away.

"What do we know about her?" Nash said, leaning over the bed.

Warnick's gaze remained on Poole a moment longer. Then he turned to Nash. "The woman?"

"Yeah."

"That's where things get muddy."

Nash chuffed. "Seriously?"

Warnick ignored him. He turned his head back toward the open door and shouted, "Beddington!"

A moment later a man came in. Heavyset, all muscle, forties with thinning dark hair. The stubble on his face and the condition of his suit suggested he'd been there all night. He had bags under his eyes. Warnick made introductions. "David here has been with the mayor's security detail since election day."

"Before that," Beddington replied. "He hired me when he was still on the campaign trail. Back when he was just on the city council."

Warnick rolled his hand impatiently through the air. "Tell them what you told me, about the woman."

Beddington gave Warnick a nervous glance.

"It's fine. They're under orders—it doesn't leave this room."

Poole wasn't aware of any such order, but he didn't say anything. Neither did Nash.

Beddington shifted his weight to his left leg and looked at the floor. "The mayor has a particular service he uses for these encounters. He's used them for some time now." He reached into the breast pocket of his jacket and took out a cheap phone. "We always call from one of these, never our real numbers, because—"

"We understand why," Warnick interrupted. "Get to the point."

Beddington nodded and dropped the phone back in his jacket. "I was running late, so I called from the car. I got here, and she was already in the bedroom—I caught a few glimpses of her walking around. The mayor, too. He closed the door when he saw me. I had no idea how she beat me in this damn weather, but she did. I didn't think much about it, didn't have a chance. I got distracted by the problem."

"The problem?"

"The mayor's wife. She knows what he's up to, so she calls me. Every time, like clockwork. He says they have some kind of open relationship, but talking to her all these years, it ain't so open. Anyway, I went out in the hall to talk to her, calm her down, ended up taking the elevator to the mezzanine level—service is better there—and we talked for about an hour. She's nice. Easy to talk to. When I came back up to the room, I found a woman from the agency standing in the hallway, *the one I called for*. She said nobody was answering the door—this wasn't the woman I saw inside an hour earlier, this was someone else entirely—younger, blonde. I knew something was wrong at that point. I paid her, told her to leave. Then I used my key card to get back into the room and found this mess." He gestured toward the bloody bed. "I called the other guys, they started to clean things up, and I saw the mayor's burner phone on the dresser. I had figured he phoned the agency, beat me to it, 'cause I was late. When I checked the log, I realized he hadn't made the call either. Other calls were there, but not *that* call. Neither of us called that first woman. That's when I called Mr. Warnick."

Poole turned back to Warnick. "And you're what, the mayor's fixer?"

"I'm the man who called both your bosses and told them we have a serious fucking problem that needs to be handled under the radar for the greater good of Chicago. This can't get out. Not a single word of it." With two fingers, he pointed out the door at Maddie Abel's back, the videos still repeating in front of her. "One of those two men is responsible. We need to figure out which one and get the mayor back before any of this gets out."

Nash nodded at the bed. "That amount of blood most likely means there is no getting the mayor back."

"The mayor weighs nearly two hundred eighty pounds. There is no way a woman carried him out of here. She had a gun on him, maybe a knife or something, but somehow he walked out of here under his own power."

Nash said, "Could have used a laundry bin, room service cart…there are a million ways to get a body out of a hotel this big."

"Maybe Vincent Weidner," Poole suggested.

Warnick frowned. "The guard from New Orleans?"

"He escaped. Porter said he's in the diaries. He might be connected."

Warnick waved a hand through the air. "Fuck the diaries. If Porter paid that Upchurch guy to write them, they're all bullshit anyway."

Poole turned back to Beddington. "What can you tell us about the woman you saw in here?"

Beddington scratched his nose and shook his head. "I saw her for all of a half second. She walked past the open doorway. I didn't get much of a look at her."

"Try closing your eyes. Sometimes that helps."

He did. He chewed on the inside of his cheek. "Short. Maybe five-two, five-three. Brown hair, shoulder length. She was wearing this slinky black dress, gorgeous legs."

"What about her face?"

"I didn't see her face."

"I want the phone number for the agency you called," Poole told him.

Beddington frowned. "Weren't you listening? She didn't come from the agency. She was already here."

"So how did she get here? If the agency didn't send her, how did she know to come to this hotel to this specific room when she did?"

"There's no mystery there," Warnick said. "The mayor does this every Monday—same time, same room. You can set a clock by his penis. That's how the wife knows. That's how his staff knows. People here at the hotel know. I've already spoken to the agency— it's a dead end. I don't want you wasting time on them. This woman somehow got wind of the mayor's schedule, knew he'd be here, and worked this out from there. She may not be alone, but she's not with them."

"Was it Carmine's Pizza?" Nash asked.

Warnick turned on him. "How do you know that?"

"Carmine's came up on a list of Arthur Talbot's businesses a few months back when we checked out his finances. It had also been red-flagged by vice as a front for a high-end escort service. They've been under surveillance for the better part of a year." He turned to Poole. "When we get back to Metro, we can pull the records, but I think Warnick's right. She wouldn't have come through them. Too easy to get caught." Nash turned back to Beddington. "Does the name Sarah Werner mean anything to you?"

Beddington shook his head.

Warnick frowned. "The woman Porter said he was with in New Orleans? You think it was her?"

Nash shrugged. "Similar description. Brown hair, shoulder length."

"Why would she attack the mayor?"

Nobody answered that. Frustrated, Poole looked back at the bed. "We need CSI in here. Do either of you know the mayor's blood type?"

"Oh no," Warnick countered. "No CSI, no photographs. Nobody else sees this room. Nobody knows the mayor is missing, and it needs to stay that way."

"Then what exactly do you expect us to do?"

"I expect you to figure out who took him and find him without putting up a signal flare. I want the mayor tucked back in his bed by midnight like none of this happened and Porter or Bishop, whoever is responsible, rotting in a cell somewhere. I want the people of Chicago to think everything is just fine and it's safe to be out on the streets. I want the two of you to do your goddamn jobs," Warnick said. He produced a knife, went over to the bed, and cut a small strip of the bloody sheet and held it out. "Here's your blood sample. The mayor is A positive."

"You can't be serious."

"No?" With his free hand, he took out his cell phone and dialed a number on speaker. Poole recognized the voice who picked up immediately. Warnick said, "Hurless? Tell your boy here to do his job."

"Sir?" Poole said.

On the other end of the line, SAIC Hurless cleared his throat. "Do as he says, Frank."

"This man has contaminated a crime scene and is attempting to cover it up."

Hurless said, "Nobody's covering up anything. The room will be sealed. The evidence isn't going anywhere. At this point, our priority is finding the mayor without creating a panic. Return to Metro and question Bishop and Porter. One of them knows exactly what's going on. That's our best bet."

"I'm not comfortable with this," Poole shot back. "Not at all."

"We're locking it down for three hours. If you haven't found the mayor by then, I'll get an Evidence Response Team to tear that room apart. We'll involve the press, if need be, but right now we don't risk a leak." He paused a moment, then added, "I'll bring in someone else if I have to, but I don't want to waste time getting another agent up to speed."

Warnick's face flushed red. "Nobody else. Another agent means another possible leak. Wasted time means more possible deaths, we—"

Hurless cut him off. "Did you show him the box?"

"Not yet."

Poole glanced back at Warnick. "What box?"

On the phone, Hurless said, "Finish there and get back to Metro. We've got a ticking clock."

He disconnected.

"What box?" Poole repeated.

"It has nothing to do with the mayor," Warnick said. "You need to understand that."

"He's right," Beddington said. "He's not into that kind of thing. I've known him a long time. I'm sure of that."

Poole was getting frustrated. *"What box?"*

Warnick went back to the dresser and tugged open the top center drawer, then stepped away.

Poole and Nash looked at each other, then walked over and peered down into the drawer.

The box was white, no bigger than eight and a half by eleven inches, the size of a sheet of paper. The lid and a black string had been tossed off to the side when someone opened it. Inside the box were at least a hundred Polaroids of teenagers—boys and girls, all in various stages of undress. Some smiling at the camera, most appearing nervous, watching something or someone off camera, near or behind the photographer.

Poole looked at Nash again, then took a latex glove from his pocket and slipped it on. He reached for one of the pictures and turned it over. On the back, written in a neat hand, was: 203. WF15 3k. LM.

They'd both seen pictures like this before. In a much larger box found in Anson Bishop's apartment.

"The mayor's not into kids," Beddington said.

Poole wasn't listening. He was peering down at something else, something written on the front of one of the pictures in faded black ink. It said, *Hey, Sam, remember me?*

Strangely though, it wasn't the writing that had grabbed his attention. It was the boy's sweatshirt, emblazoned with the logo of a baseball team—the Charleston Riverdogs.

46
Diary

Vincent only managed to open the hood of the truck by forcing a pry-bar under the metal while I pulled the hood release cable from the cab and Kristina held some kind of latch at the center of the hood. It rose with a reluctant shriek, as if it had closed one final time years ago, had come to terms with its fate, and was now being disturbed in death by the shovels of grave robbers.

Vincent used the pry-bar to prop the hood open and peered inside. "The battery is shit. We'll need a new one. Half the cables are either rotted or got chewed up by something." He reached down inside and pulled out a handful of hay and dirt. "Something made a nest in here."

"Can it be fixed?"

This came from Libby. She was standing next to me, holding the driver side door open.

"Sure, I'll just need about five hundred dollars to buy parts, another car to get those parts, a shit-ton of tools we don't have..." He lowered his head. "Do you have a piggy bank stashed away somewhere, 'cause if not, you know Finicky ain't gonna give it to us. She doesn't want us going anywhere." He turned back to Kristina. "I'm packing a bag and walking out of here tonight, just like I said. You want to come with me, be ready at midnight. I'm not staying another night."

I had no idea what happened to him last night with Welderman and Stocks. Neither did Libby. I suspected Tegan and Kristina did, but none of them would tell the rest of us. The look that flew between Kristina and Vincent said as much.

"What did they do to you?" I asked.

He just snorted and shook his head. "You'll see soon enough. I hear your girlfriend is next—tonight. You're probably on deck after her. There's no sitting this one out. I'm done with it. I'd rather walk out of here and take my chances on my own."

"I'll go with you," Kristina said, reaching for his arm. "I already told you I would."

He gave her a sideways glance. "Whatever. You better not slow me down."

"You'd leave the rest of us here?"

The voice came from the open door of the barn. All of us turned to find Tegan standing there. She stepped inside, the setting sun backlighting her. "What about Weasel and The Kid? They can't get out of here on their own. You'd leave them?"

Vincent turned back to the engine. "I don't give a shit about any of you. My mother was a coke whore, and I never met my dad. I've been taking care of myself for as long as I can remember. I'm nobody's babysitter. The earlier they realize they're on their own in this world, the better. They got a roof over their heads and food, same as all you. Everything's got a price. I know what you're thinking—you're thinking we get this truck running, all pile in, and drive off to someplace better. Well, guess what, there ain't no place better, only different. This whole world is a cesspool. All you can do is pick the cleanest corner and deal with the stink of it for as long as possible, then move on to someplace else. I caught a glimpse of the price tag to stay here last night, and I'm telling you, for me, it's too fucking high."

Tegan said, "You really think Finicky will let you go? Even if you manage to sneak out, how far will you get before she's on the phone with those cops, they call their buddies, and they pick you up and do who-knows-what to make an example of you. How many pictures are hanging in that house? Where do you think they all are right now? They're not living upstate in a nice, big house with a good family making plans for college. They're gone. I've been here long enough to know what will happen if you try to run off. They will pick you up before you get close to anything resembling civilization, then they'll beat the hell out of you. If that doesn't work, guess what? You'll be gone for good. There'll be a free bed here at Finicky House, and some new kid will take your place within a day. You'll be another picture gathering dust on the wall." She nodded toward the truck. "With that, we've all got a shot. We all get out of here."

Vincent reached inside the engine and tugged out a rat's nest of rotten cables. He tossed them on the floor. "How do we even work on this thing without Finicky finding out?"

"Finicky's a pill hound. When the detectives bring us back, and she knows we're all in the house for the night, she pops whatever she's got on hand and she's dead to the world fifteen minutes later. I've been in there— I've gone through her closet, all her drawers, the crap under her bed—she never budges, just snores and drools on herself. She's not much better during the day. She's passed out right now."

I slid off the driver's seat and stood beside Libby. "Does she have money hidden somewhere?" I was thinking about the jar Mother kept in the kitchen cabinet above the stove. Her rainy-day fund, she called it. She once told me everyone needed a rainy-day fund.

Tegan shook her head. "I'm sure she does, but I've never found it, and I've looked everywhere." She glanced over at Kristina. "We can get money, though, can't we, Kristina?"

The other girl must have understood what she meant, because her face went a little pale and she nodded reluctantly. "If we have to."

Tegan turned toward Libby. "If you're going tonight, you can too."

"What would she have to do?" I said this before I realized I spoke. I inched closer to Libby and felt her take my hand. She leaned in and whispered softly, "It's okay."

It wasn't okay, though.

47

Porter

Day 5 • 2:15 PM

Sam Porter heard a bang.

That bang was followed by a heavy thump somewhere else in the building. Not like an explosion, more like something falling from a shelf to the ground several rooms over. Somebody tripping in the hallway, maybe landing hard against a wall or the floor.

He lowered the diary.

He listened.

Shuffling feet.

Movement in the upper right corner of the interview room caught his eye. When he glanced up, he realized it wasn't movement at all but that the light on the security camera—the one that always burned red—had blinked out and gone dark.

The clock under the camera read quarter after two in the afternoon.

He heard a shout then, there was no mistaking it. A male voice. He couldn't make out the words, but the voice sounded both angry and frightened.

Standing from the metal table, his body groaned in protest. He'd been sitting still for hours and had to take a moment to stretch, give the blood a chance to find his legs.

Another bang, followed by two more.

He told himself it wasn't gunfire, not within the halls of Metro, but that was exactly what those reports sounded like, and the cop in him reached for the empty space under his shoulder, where his gun usually rested snug in a leather holster.

Porter went to the door.

There was a small window at eye level, designed to give someone entering or leaving a chance to clear whatever was on the other side, and through that window, he saw the back of a head—the officer tasked with guarding him, no doubt. The head swiveled side to side, looking down one side of the hallway before twisting back to look down the other. This wasn't the casual movement of someone caught at a post for hours on end but more of a panicked herky-jerky movement.

Porter knocked on the door.

The head quickly turned, and when Porter saw the man's eyes, he knew something was very wrong. The officer only glanced at him for a second before turning his attention back to the hallway.

Porter reached for the doorknob.

Locked.

He knocked on the door again. Banged on the metal. "What's going on out there?"

This time, the officer didn't look back at him, something else grabbing his attention.

Three more pops in quick succession.

Porter banged on the door again. "Who's shooting out there? What's happening?"

With one quick glance back at the window, the officer darted off to the left and disappeared. The detention cells were that way. There weren't many, since they were meant for temporary confinement while processing. Limited holding before transportation to central or county. Several large cells for groups, and a half a dozen smaller ones for individuals or pairs. Two large metal doors separated that half of the floor from this one with a guard station between them.

An alarm went off.

On the wall of the interview room next to the clock, a red and white strobe started to flash. Someone had tripped the fire alarm.

Porter beat on the door again. "Someone let me out of here!"

Three more people ran past his door—two heading toward the detention cells, another running away, a man in handcuffs with long, stringy black hair and tattoos all over his face. Someone who looked a lot like he was behind bars only a few minutes ago.

From the ceiling came a sputtering sound and the sprinkler system came to life—water rained down. Icy cold.

Porter turned back to the table, the diaries. He scooped them up, piled them back in the box and got the lid over them. He carried the box to the door and beat on it with the back of his fist. "Open the fucking door!"

A click.

He reached down and tried the knob again. This time, it turned. And when he opened the door, three more people rushed by, dressed in tactical SWAT gear, the force of them nearly throwing him back. His eyes followed them down the hallway. The doors leading to the cells were both unlocked, and when the three men pushed through to the other side, Porter caught a glimpse of the chaos in the next room. All the detention cell doors were open. The hallway was filled with both cops and the people who had been locked up. Someone swung a pipe at one of the approaching SWAT officers, caught him in the arm, and—

The door swung shut again, leaving Porter on the other side.

Water sprayed down everywhere, the tile floor slick with it.

Although there were several interview rooms in this hallway, from the video Poole had shown him, he knew which room Bishop had been in and when he looked at that door it was open, same as his. He held his free hand over his eyes in an attempt to block the water raining from the sprinklers and peered down the hallway.

He saw him. Fifty feet ahead. Not running, but walking at a brisk pace.

"Bishop!"

Anson Bishop turned only long enough to see him, then disappeared around a corner.

Porter went after him, and when another SWAT officer rushed by heading in the opposite direction, he grabbed the man by the arm. "Anson Bishop is getting away!"

If the man heard him over all the noise, he gave no indication. He shrugged out of Porter's grasp and continued on toward the cells.

Porter turned the corner at the end of the hallway and spotted Bishop again. Further ahead now, ducking into the stairwell. Doors were open everywhere, as if someone had tripped every remote lock in the building and disengaged them. Even the fire doors stood open. All of them should have closed with the alarm.

Reaching the stairwell, that door open too, he looked both up and down but didn't see Bishop. People were running in both directions, but most were heading down, toward the exits.

Porter ran down with them. He nearly dropped the box several times as people jostled him, pushed and shoved. Panicked, yet trying to remain calm.

On the first floor, at least a hundred people crowded the hallway, all attempting to get to the exits. They moved at a snail's pace. He tried to push through, move faster, but it was nearly impossible. A wall of people all heading to the same place. Nearly two minutes passed before he escaped the building.

Soaked to the bone from the sprinklers, running into the arctic air was like being slapped by a blanket of ice. Snow fell all around, clung to him, the box still clutched under his arm.

Porter saw Bishop then, climbing through the passenger door of a silver Lexus. The driver spotted Porter and first frowned, then smiled. Then she waved delicate, thin fingers. It was the woman he knew as Sarah Werner—Bishop's mother. They disappeared out into traffic as Porter reached the curb.

48

Clair

Clair heard the shouting, yelling, screaming, and otherwise mad mess of chaos from the hallway long before she made it to the cafeteria. Angry voices, all fighting to be heard over each other. Men and women. There were children, too—high-pitched cries unwilling to be outdone by their parents.

Officer Sutter met her in the hall. The doors leading to the cafeteria, normally open, were both closed behind him. "It's that Barrington guy. He's got everyone all riled up."

Clair peered through the windows in the doors at the cafeteria beyond and couldn't tell what was going on—arms flapped and pointed in time with the shouts. "What did he do?"

"It's not just him. He's got several others siding with him. They're forcing everyone who's sick to dress in yellow scrubs and move into the employee lounges at the back, out of gen-pop."

"Gen-pop?" Clair frowned. "Like a prison?"

"That's what he's been calling the main cafeteria—general population, gen-pop."

Clair narrowed her eyes. "If yellow means sick, what does blue and green mean? I'm seeing three colors in there."

"Blue means symptomatic—achy bones, headache…generally not feeling well but not showing any clear symptoms. Apparently some of these people feel sick just because they're around other sick people, but they're not. It's in their heads. Green means no symptoms at all."

"Lovely." Clair sniffled and fought back the urge to sneeze. There weren't many people wearing green scrubs. She spotted Barrington in the far corner of the room next to a table piled high with scrubs, arguing with some other man. "If I'm not out in five minutes, come and get me."

She pushed through the door and went straight for Barrington. As people spotted her, they crowded around, shouted, so many she couldn't make out a damn thing. When she reached Barrington, he held a hand up in front of her face and continued yelling at the other man.

In that instant, Clair thought of at least a dozen ways she could kill this man without the use of her gun, possibly with only one hand. And then, she might still use the gun. One or ten shots to the face, that ought to do it. "Do you have any idea how dangerous it is to shush an angry black woman?" Barrington shot her an irritated glance, then turned back to the other man. "Give us a minute, Walter."

Walter—Dr. Shanahan, according to his name tag—shook his head and walked away.

When Barrington turned back to her, Clair spoke before he could. "What the hell are you doing? You're supposed to be calming these people, not creating some kind of 'us versus them' *Lord of the Flies* bullshit."

Barrington held up both hands. "I'm only doing what Maltby told me to do."

"The CDC guy?"

Barrington nodded. "He told me to identify and segregate the sick. Isolate them, if possible."

"Wasn't the plan to cordon off a space on the second floor and move the sick up there? Get them away from here?"

"We did that, but those beds are long gone. They brought in cots, blankets…they don't have any more room."

"How many people are sick now?"

"I lost track," he told her. "Too many." Reaching to the table, he picked up a set of yellow scrubs, still wrapped in plastic, and handed them to her. "You need to put these on."

"I'm not wearing those."

"You're not even wearing your mask. You're clearly symptomatic. Right now, you're part of the problem."

"I'm in charge here. People see me in that outfit and everything falls apart."

Barrington chuffed. "Yeah, you're doing a bang-up job. Look around. Even your own officers have deserted you."

"Watch it."

"Sorry. I'm just frustrated." He leaned in closer. "People know you're sick. Have you looked in a mirror? This isn't something you can hide, not in a room full of doctors. They see you running all over the hospital, or ducking into your private little space down the hall, while they're stuck out here coughing on each other. What do you expect them to think? I've got news for you. We're about an hour away from these people either rushing the doors or other parts of the hospital. As more and more people present symptoms, those of us who aren't sick will get desperate."

"So you're going to lead the charge, is that it?"

He shook his head. "No, that's not what I mean. I'm on your side here, but I'm in the minority. A minority that is quickly shrinking. And I'm running out of ways to keep the peace." He thrust the package into her hand. "Please, put these on. Lead by example."

Clair took the package. "I'll do it in a minute. Where is the CDC on a treatment?"

Barrington pursed his lips. "There is no treatment, not really. No cure, no antidote. All they can do is pump up the immune system of those who are infected and hope for the best. Oxygen, fluids, that helps, too. SARS is a highly aggressive virus. The strong can beat it and the weak will not. Ultimately, it comes down to that simple fact. When I look around this room, I see the truth. In another week, many of these people will no longer be with us."

"You're a ray of sunshine."

"I'm a realist."

Clair's phone rang. Jerome Stout, head of hospital security. She answered. "Norton."

"Detective, can you come up to my office?"

"I'm on my way." She disconnected and looked back at Barrington. "Give these people something to cling to, give them hope."

He only looked down at the package in her hand. "Please put those on."

She waved to him, tucked the package under her shoulder, and made her way down the hall to the elevators, ignoring the many eyes burning a hole in her back.

When she pressed the button, nothing happened.

She pressed it again.

Nothing.

Clair pressed it a dozen more times, fast and hard, nearly pushed the button through the other side of the wall, then kicked the door and let out a frustrated grunt. That didn't seem to work, either.

She dialed Stout back. "There's something wrong with the elevators."

"We shut them down on that level, you'll need to take the stairs."

"Why?"

"Orders from Maltby with the CDC. He's trying to limit traffic in the hospital. If you take the stairs to the next floor up, you can get the elevator there."

"Wonderful."

Clair hung up, located the stairwell, and pushed through the heavy door. She took the steps two at a time up to the next level. When she reached the door, she found it locked.

She *did not* have time for this.

She banged on it for nearly a minute, but nobody answered.

Back on the stairs, she went up one more floor. That door was locked, too.

In such a hurry, she nearly dropped her phone pulling it back out of her pocket.

No signal.

Double fuck.

That's when the lights went out.

The arm that came up behind her was quick, strong, and utterly silent. She didn't realize anyone was even there until the needle slipped into her neck.

49
Diary

From my bedroom window, I watched Tegan, Kristina, and Libby drive off. Welderman and Stocks had arrived a little after eleven that night, and as usual, they didn't come in. Welderman tapped the horn twice, and Stocks got out for a cigarette and the two of them waited about five more minutes until the girls came out and climbed into the back of the car. Libby had looked up at my window, and when she saw me standing there, she smiled, but it was forced and did little to hide the fear and uncertainty in her eyes.

Libby looked beautiful. Tegan and Kristina had gone to work on her shortly after dinner, a primping and pampering fest behind closed doors. There were giggles and nervous laughs, hushed questions and even quieter answers. They had dressed her in a sleek, black tight little thing that fell off her shoulders on thin straps and stopped about halfway down her thighs. She wore heels, too, and I could tell by the way she made her way from the house to the car this was something new to her. One hand held onto Kristina's shoulder most of the way, and with each stumble came more nervous laughter. They'd applied makeup. Not just on her face but over the fading remains of her bruises—they'd vanished under a thin coat of powder, liquid, or gel, or whatever it was that girls kept hidden away from the prying eyes of boys. They'd swept her hair up on one side while the other flowed down over her shoulder.

Tegan and Kristina were equally beautiful in dresses I'd never seen before. But while Kristina walked beside Libby, helping her along, Tegan hung back a little, her eyes on the backs of the other girls, and I couldn't help but think of the night before when she noticed Libby and me holding hands.

The car was gone a moment later with the three of them inside. The knot in my stomach grew as the taillights faded away.

"Cattle to the slaughter," Paul said quietly from the bunk below me. He hadn't said much in the past few days. I wanted the old Paul back. When we got back from the barn, I told him about the truck and how Vincent planned to help repair it. The girls' promise to get money. None of that had put a smile on his face.

"I think Tegan likes you," I said in return, not sure what else to say.

Paul grunted. "She doesn't like me. She likes you. *Libby likes* you. *Kristina is with Vincent. Hell, even Weasel and The Kid have each other if they decide to swing that way when they eventually grow up. As usual, I've got nobody. Little Paul, all alone again. Maybe I'll make a run at Finicky. She's not half bad. I'd be open to a Mrs. Robinson thing. At least she's got a house—all the makings of a solid sugar momma. Everyone needs a little lovin'."*

"Can I see what you're drawing?"

He seemed to consider this for a moment, then turned the notepad toward me. It was Tegan. She was naked and smiling seductively out from the page. He had her suspended from the ceiling with a rope, the tips of her toes dangling inches above what looked like a giant meat grinder. I wanted to tell him her breasts were all wrong, her real nipples were smaller than the ones he depicted, but I was fairly certain that would do little in the way of cheering him up.

"I call it the Man-eater-eater."

"It's, ah..." My face was flushed red.

He seemed to take this as a compliment. "Do you want me to draw Libby for you?"

"Like...that?"

He flipped to a blank page. "No, not like that. Something nice. Tasteful. But naked. Gotta be naked."

I thought about this for a second, then shook my head. "No thank you."

"No thank you," he repeated in a mocking voice. He quickly began to draw, and in under a minute, I saw the start of her—Libby, lying naked on a bed amid rumpled sheets, one finger at her lips, her other hand—

I reached over and tore the page out, crumpled it up. "I said no."

Paul raised both hands defensively. "Sorry, buddy. I was just messing around. No harm, no foul." He flipped back to his drawing of Tegan, grabbed a pencil, and started shading.

The crumpled drawing of Libby in my hand, I started for the door.

Paul said, "If you're going to beat the Bishop, Bishop, I can color it in for you first."

"I'm going to take it out back and burn it."

"Suppression of artistic license is an offense punishable by death in several European countries."

He said something else after that, but I didn't hear him. I was halfway down the stairs. I would have been all the way down the stairs, but I stopped when I found my picture hanging on the wall with the others. It hadn't been there before. It was one of the pictures Paul had taken the other day in the parlor. There was a half-smile on my face, and my back was up against the wall. I told myself I looked confident, but I knew I really looked uneasy and stiff. Not my best photograph. Not my worst, either.

The picture was at a slight angle, and when I tried to straighten it out, it fell from the wall. Luckily, the glass didn't break. When I went to hang it back up, I noticed something written on a thin piece of white tape on the back. It said: 124. WM15 1.4k.

I removed several others and found similar messages written on the backs of those.

"What are you doing?"

I hadn't heard Ms. Finicky come up behind me. She was standing there with a drink in one hand and a tattered paperback in the other.

"I was just—"

"Put them back. All of them. You're a guest in my house, and I expect you to respect my possessions."

"Yes, ma'am."

"It's late. You should be in bed. You'll need your rest." She took a sip of her drink. It was strong, whatever it was. I could smell it from across the room. "Tomorrow night you'll go with the detectives, and I expect you to be on your best behavior."

My stomach sank, but I said nothing.

50

Poole

"You saw the sweatshirt, right? In the picture?"

"Charleston Riverdogs," Nash said flatly. "Where Porter did his rookie time."

They were back in the black Escalade, a few minutes from Metro.

Poole scratched at the stubble on his chin. "When I first saw that box you and Clair found in Bishop's apartment, I got the impression it was related to some kind of human trafficking. Accounting records, photographs, all of it."

"We did too, but Kloz digitized everything in that box, compared the photos to all the missing child databases, and he couldn't find a single match. We didn't get far with the spreadsheets. They were too cryptic."

"The way I see this, we've got one of two scenarios here," Poole said, thinking out loud. "All the victims are connected, including the mayor. If Bishop is to be believed—"

"I don't believe Bishop."

Poole silenced him with a glance. "*If Bishop is to be believed,* Porter is somehow behind everything, attempting to cover up something that happened to him in Charleston. 'She was there, she saw me do it, and she has to go,' that's what Bishop told me Porter said before he killed that woman at the Guyon." Before Nash could object, he said, "I know, I get it, that's *if* Porter killed that woman. I'm not willing to go there yet, either. I'm trying to keep an open mind."

"Okay, I'll play," Nash said. "If *Sam* is telling the truth and Bishop is behind everything, that means Bishop is trying to point us at something that happened in Charleston, something related to the kids in those pictures. I doubt he'd kill all these people to cover it up He'd be killing them as some kind of revenge. We know Talbot was close with the mayor. That could be linked, too."

"Neither man is operating alone," Poole pointed out. "Can we at least agree on that?"

Nash nodded. "There's just too much for one person, and even with both under lockdown, things haven't slowed down. My money is on Weidner. Maybe that woman Sam said was in the Guyon with Bishop. Werner. Maybe both. I don't know."

Poole glanced back out the window. "I've been thinking a lot about the virus."

"And?"

"And it doesn't feel right to me," Poole said. "4MK's kills have always been close, personal—eyes, ears, tongue—the theft of the virus, using it the way he did, it's the opposite of personal. He wouldn't know who would be impacted. There's no specific target."

"It got him what he wanted with Upchurch," Nash pointed out. "They rushed that specialist right in."

"I suppose there was that. But it feels…off. Remember when we were in the War Room and I told you about noise?"

"You said we needed to get rid of the noise, that it was a distraction."

"I think the virus is noise."

"Maybe."

Both men fell silent for a moment, then Poole said, "If Bishop is telling the truth and Porter is behind everything, how does the virus help Porter?"

"I'm not going there."

"You said you would keep an open mind."

Nash sneezed three times, wiped his nose on his sleeve. "Sorry. It's just a cold, I swear." He sneezed again, bent over, and held a hand up. He looked like he was holding his breath, willing it to stop. When the sneezing finally did, he settled back in the seat, his eyes red and puffy. "Sam has zero reason to release a virus or go after the first responders. Especially knowing first on scene would probably be me or Clair."

Poole didn't respond to that. Not at first. He wanted to choose his words carefully. "There's something I haven't told you. I've been trying to figure out how. You need to know, though. Because it's important. After I spoke to Porter this morning, I put in a request for contact information on his old partner in Charleston. I figured Bishop was lying, but I like to be thorough. If something happened with Porter in Charleston, I wanted to know what it was." He paused for a second, glanced out the window, then back at Nash. "I was told Derrick Hillburn hung himself in his basement six years ago. I don't have all the details, but even though it looked like suicide, the locals investigated it as a potential homicide. Apparently, there was a note, a short one, but the handwriting didn't match Hillburn—that raised the red flag."

"What did the note say?"

Poole licked his lip. *"Father, forgive me."*

Nash recoiled, as if disappearing in the plush seat.

Poole didn't want to say the next part, but he felt he needed to. "If Porter wanted to kill you, Clair, or some of the other first responders, the virus would be the perfect way to do it. Pinning it all on Bishop puts a neat little bow on things. If he's covering something up, something big, he might not want to leave any potential witnesses behind."

"What could he possibly be covering up?"

"A lot of people have died around him."

Nash scoffed. "He's a homicide detective. That's like saying there are too many shitty cars parked around a used car salesman."

"Hillburn died under mysterious circumstances six years ago. That's just before the first 4MK victim."

"That's coinci—"

"You know I don't believe in those."

"Neither does Sam. And he'd never purposely hurt Clair or me. No way."

"I worked a case about eight years ago," Poole said. "A cop in Cincinnati, name of Ben Preece. The guy had been on the force for nearly fifteen years, had won more citations than half his squad combined. He could have easily made captain, but he wanted to stay in vice, insisted he did the most good there. Internal Affairs received a complaint from Narcotics—Preece had been spotted in a sketchy part of town at three in the morning. He was staking out the same dealer the Narcotics team had been there to watch. There was no reason for a member of vice to be there, certainly not at that hour. They didn't approach him, just snapped a couple pictures and turned the information over to IA. That dealer turned up dead about a week later, heroin overdose. IA, being IA, put a tracker on Preece's car, his personal vehicle. Got an order to monitor his phone, too. They noticed something strange—three or four nights a week, Preece would go out but leave his phone at home—the GPS data on his car didn't match his phone. They started to tail him, caught him on surveillance ops that had nothing to do with his job, watching people like that dealer. IA started fishing around closer, loaded a monitor on his work computer and personal. Turned out the computer on his desk had been assigned to a Narcotics officer a few years earlier, and when IT repurposed the machine, they didn't wipe the drive as per protocol. They just created a new user account. Not easy to find unless you know to look for it, but apparently Preece knew to look for it. The previous officer had used a program called PassVault to store all his passwords, so if Preece logged into the computer as him, he had access to all his accounts, including the database used by the Narcotics department. They checked the logs, realized that was how Preece was getting his intel. Meanwhile, they connected six other deaths to him dating back nearly three years. He'd been at this a while. IA kept him in play but watched him close as they put a case together. They found two more deaths, one in Indiana, another in West Virginia—that's when I was brought in. I linked three more deaths to him, all cops. *Bad cops*, mind you—we figured that out later—but dirty or not, we knew he killed them. He covered his tracks, but it doesn't matter how many times you sweep the floor; some footprints stick. When we finally confronted him, we had fourteen murders tied to him, at least three more we couldn't prove. He admitted to everything, didn't ask for a union rep. We didn't have to twist his arm. He was relieved. Preece said he wanted to stop and couldn't. Said maybe now he'd be able to sleep. Then he told us about his partner."

"What about his partner?"

"He said his partner knew what he had been doing, figured it out about a year earlier, and he'd been paying him to keep quiet. His partner was diabetic, and Preece said he swapped out one of his insulin bottles with saline. He told us now that the truth is out, his partner didn't have to die."

Without looking at him, Nash said, "Sam would never hurt me, or Clair, or anyone else. You're way off base on this."

"Preece's partner was his cousin...family," Poole responded. "The people we are in public aren't the people we are behind closed doors. Vigilantes are born out of frustration with the system. Every one of the 4MK victims got traced back to some kind of criminal activity, retribution for their activity. We can't discount that. Who had more of a motive? Some kid caught up in the foster system, or a detective who has seen his share of bad guys walk?"

Nash closed his eyes and leaned back in the seat. "Charleston."

"What?"

"Whether you believe Bishop or Sam, both theories lead to Charleston," Nash said. "You asked me to be objective. This is me being objective. Bishop is pointing us at Charleston, and Sam might have something there he doesn't want us to know. I'd be willing to look if it put an end to all this."

He took out his phone and dialed Clair. The call went straight to voice mail. He opened his messaging app and began tapping out a message.

"What are you doing?"

Without looking up, Nash said, "Telling Clair and Kloz to look for a Charleston connection on the victims in the hospital."

"Nothing on the mayor," Poole told him. "Not until we figure this out."

Nash didn't reply. He finished his message, hit send, and pocketed the phone.

The driver braked a little too hard, and the back of the Escalade slid awkwardly to the left, then back to the right as he regained control. Both Nash and Poole glanced outside. It wasn't his fault. Traffic ahead was at a standstill, with brake lights burning and cars attempting to avoid a collision in the snow. "Sorry," the driver said. "The salt doesn't work well at these temperatures. It stops melting the ice at around five degrees."

Nash sneezed again. "How cold is it?"

"Three right now. With the wind, it's more like negative ten."

Poole peered out the windshield. None of the traffic on Michigan Avenue was moving. "Can you tell what's happening up there?"

Keeping his hand on the steering wheel, the driver pointed forward with his index finger. "There's a crowd outside Metro. Maybe some kind of evacuation?"

Nash's phone dinged. He fished it back out of his pocket and stared at the display.

"What is it?"

He didn't say anything.

"Nash?"

"I just got a text from a restricted number."

"What does it say?"

"'You can't keep me safe. None of you. He won't stop until we're all dead.'" Nash paused for a second. "It's signed AB."

51

Porter

Porter's teeth were chattering, and he couldn't make them stop. He stood, did jumping jacks, paced quickly in a little circle, tried sitting back down on the park bench with his hands under his thighs. None of that made much of a difference.

Outside Metro, he managed to flag down a cab but quickly lost the Lexus in traffic. In the movies when someone tells a cab driver to *follow that car*, they do. When he tried it in real life, feeling foolish even as the words left his mouth, the driver had just stared ahead at the hundreds of cars rolling up and down Michigan and asked, "Which car?" By the time Porter told him, the silver Lexus was gone—Bishop and his mother with it.

He'd given the driver two hundred dollars in soggy bills for his coat and another hundred to use his cell phone, turning the ride to A. Montgomery Ward Park in River North into the most expensive cab ride he'd ever taken. When Porter put the coat on over his wet clothes and told the driver to let him out near the playground, the driver looked at him as if were a crazy person.

That was only twenty minutes ago, and Porter was beginning to agree with that assessment. With the temperature in single digits, his wet clothes were well on their way to freezing stiff. Within the coat, his body heat fought valiantly but futilely with the dampness.

And Porter wished for a hat, because the only thing worse than standing outside in the dead of winter in wet clothes was standing outside in the dead of winter with wet hair.

Porter got to his feet again, did another lap around the bench, and blew into his hands. Every inch of his body shivered, quivered, and revolted.

When a horn blew from the road behind him, it took a moment for his brain to process what he heard, which he blamed on the hypothermia. He turned, started for the SUV, then realized he'd forgotten the box with Bishop's diaries on the bench. He scrambled back as quickly as he could on the slippery ground, retrieved the box, and stumbled back toward the awaiting vehicle, icy wind swirling all around.

There was nobody in the passenger seat, but he climbed into the back anyway, thankful for the tinted windows. The heat wrapped around him like a heavy quilt, and when he tried to speak, his throat didn't cooperate. "Elo, Mree."

Emory Connors turned in the driver's seat, her mouth hanging open. "My God, Sam. Do you have any idea how cold it is? You're soaked! You could have died out there!"

From the floor of the passenger's seat, she grabbed a black backpack and handed it to him. "You need to change out of those wet clothes. I grabbed some of Arthur's old things—socks, under-wear, a few pairs of pants and shirts. I keep meaning to donate them to Goodwill or something, but... Anyway, just...just change right there. I won't look. Before you get sick or something!"

The last thing on Porter's mind was modesty. He stripped off the wet clothes, piled them on the floor, and dressed in the clothes Emory pilfered from her murdered father's closet at her apartment. As he did, he glanced up into the rearview mirror. True to her word, Emory had her eyes pinched shut. Her knuckles were white, she was gripping the steering wheel so tight.

"You cut your hair," he said, buttoning the shirt. It was a little tight on him but close enough. "It looks nice." His throat felt raw, but his voice was returning.

Her eyes still closed, she reached up and touched her brown hair where it curled up just above her shoulders. "I needed a change. Is it okay to look now?"

Porter threaded a black leather belt through the loops in his borrowed pants. "Yeah." He nodded at the radio. "What are they saying on the news?"

Emory put the SUV into gear and pulled out onto Kingsbury, heading toward I-90. "Nothing about what happened at Metro, not yet. All the news channels keep bouncing back and forth between Stroger Hospital and that video of your partner kicking Bishop."

"Nash kicked Bishop?" He hadn't heard anything about this.

She told him about Bishop's arrest, how he claimed Porter and Nash were dirty cops live on the air as he surrendered, all of it.

Traffic picked up the pace when Emory followed the signs from I-90 to I-55 South with the skill of a seasoned professional. "I didn't know you had your license yet."

At this, Emory's face flushed. "I have a learner's permit. Arthur insisted I start private lessons last year. I went to a school for a little while. Then my bodyguards started to take me out to the track in Woodstock, which was way more fun. They taught me all kinds of cool stuff like PIT and PIN maneuvers, threat recognition, weight transfer..."

"Everything a teenage driver needs to know?"

"Exactly."

"I hope somebody squeezed parallel parking into your lesson plan. That's what gave me the hardest time." Porter pulled a pair of black leather shoes from the bag—John Lobbs, Talbot's favorite. They were a size eleven, and he normally wore ten and a half—close enough. When he finished, he looked up at her. "Did you bring the rest?"

She glanced at him in the mirror, her face filled with concern. "Are you sure about this?"

He nodded.

Reaching over to the glove box, she pressed the release and re-moved two paper sacks. Emory handed them both to Porter.

Inside the first were two stacks of bound twenties. Four thousand dollars in total.

The second bag contained a .38, a leather belt holster, and a box of ammunition.

"None of that is traceable," she told him. "Arthur had it in his safe. The gun doesn't even have a serial number."

He twisted the weapon and looked at the underside. She was right. If the number had been filed away, someone did a bang-up job. There were no tool marks. It looked more like the gun had been manufactured without one.

Porter slipped the gun into the holster and clipped it to his belt. He placed the ammunition and money in the backpack. He transferred Bishop's diaries from the wet box to the bag, too.

She took exit 286 from I-55 South and followed the signs for Midway Airport. When the speed limit dropped to twenty, she veered to the left and took a narrow exit toward the private hangars. At the guard gate, she didn't even stop. The guard leaned out the small building, recognized her, and waved her through. Weaving through a series of buildings, she pulled through the large open door of Hangar 289 and parked next to glimmering white jet with *Talbot Enterprises* painted on the tail. "This was Arthur's favorite," Emory said. "It's a Bombardier Global 5000. Swank and fast. There's a couple more here in Chicago, but this is the one I like to take."

Porter tried to imagine a world where an individual had several private jets at the ready, as an adult or a teenager. That reality was so far removed from his own one-car, small apartment existence, he couldn't wrap his brain around it. How this girl managed to keep a level head, he'd never know.

"I'm going to leave this car here for you," Emory continued. "GPS is disabled. The plates are registered to one of Arthur's shell companies. Nobody will be looking for it, and if someone does, they won't find it."

"How will you get home?"

She nodded toward the mouth of the hangar. "My security staff followed me."

When Porter looked out the window, he realized another SUV had pulled up behind them. A cloud of exhaust rose from their tailpipe. There were at least two people inside.

"They don't know who I picked up at the park. I told them to follow two minutes behind me so they wouldn't see you." Emory turned back toward the jet. "The plane is fully fueled, and the staff has been instructed to take you anywhere you want to go. Your name won't appear anywhere, and they won't file a flight plan until just before takeoff. I figured it's better if you tell them where you're heading instead of me. This way, if someone asks, I can tell them I really don't know. Once they have your destination, they'll arrange for another car to be waiting for you at landing, like this one, untraceable." She bit her lower lip playfully. "Apparently there's a service for that kind of thing. Who knew?"

"I imagine Arthur did."

"Yeah, I suppose he did," she agreed. "Wherever you land, they'll wait for you. If you need to go somewhere else, they'll take you." Her voice dropped off for a moment as she weighed what she wanted to say next. "I...I called one of my attorneys after you called me, just to determine what I could and couldn't do. I hope you understand."

Porter *did* understand. "I'm glad."

Emory went on, "I was told since you haven't been charged with anything, I'm technically not breaking any laws here. If they do file charges against you, he said I can wait up to four hours before calling the authorities and telling them what I know. He said that's an 'acceptable window.'" She made air quotes to emphasize her point. "So, if you're charged, I'll tell them you asked to use one of my jets. I'll tell them the truth—I have no idea where you went. I don't know how long it will take them to figure things out from there, but the clock will be ticking. I'm not sure even the cars will be safe at that point. You might want to consider ditching whatever my people line up for you and take something else, get a little more time...you know, if things come to that."

She seemed a little embarrassed by this last statement, and she looked away.

Porter sat back in the seat and took a moment to catch his breath, to look at the beautiful young girl in the front seat. "I owe you for all this, Emory. You might be the strongest person I know."

She smiled. "You will never owe me. Not now, not ever."

More than anyone, he understood the sacrifices she had made, the lengths she had gone to.

He watched as she climbed out of the SUV and ran back to the awaiting car on the tarmac. They were gone by the time he got out with the backpack in hand and made his way to the steps of the Bombardier and disappeared inside.

52
Diary

Libby wouldn't talk to me when she got back. I fell asleep in the hallway leaning against her door and didn't wake until I heard the girls shuffling up the stairs. My eyes fluttered open, and the three of them were standing there, staring at me.

"Move," Tegan said.

My eyes found Libby. "Are you okay?"

She turned away, and a moment later she walked briskly down the hallway to the bathroom and slammed the door behind her.

I scrambled to my feet, tried to go after her, but Tegan got in my way. "Just let her be. You can see her in the morning, but don't ask her about tonight. Don't ever ask her about tonight, understand?"

I nodded my head, but I didn't understand. I wanted to know. I wanted to help her.

Tegan went after Libby, and after a soft knock at the door, was ushered inside. When Kristina and I were alone in the hallway, she reached into her purse and took out a wad of cash. "There's three hundred and fifty dollars here. Give it to Vince. Tell him we'll get the rest next time."

Before I could reply, she shoved the money in my hand and disappeared down the hall and into the bathroom. If the three of them spoke, I couldn't hear them, and as much as I wanted to press my ear against that door, I didn't. I told myself Libby would talk to me about it when she was ready.

Vincent's door was locked, and he didn't answer when I knocked.

53

Poole

Poole and Nash left the SUV sitting in traffic and ran the last few blocks to Metro. Most of the staff was outside on the sidewalks. Some had gone into area coffee shops and restaurants to keep warm. SWAT stood guard at the door, and nearly forty minutes went by before they were permitted back inside.

Both interview rooms were empty.

Bishop and Porter were gone.

The walls, floors, furniture, everything was wet. The text on Porter's whiteboard was an unreadable mess, and Poole did everything in his power to keep from punching a hole through the wall while Nash spoke to his captain out in the hall.

He stepped into the surveillance room. The equipment was all ruined. Shorted out. He'd hoped to at least watch the minutes before their escape. This was a closed system, unlike building security, which had already proved to be useless. From what they pieced together, someone hacked the building. Like the video footage at Montehugh Labs, the prison in New Orleans, and the Langham Hotel, that someone had planted a virus that scrambled everything—time codes, footage, everything. None of it was cohesive anymore. Completely useless. They then overrode every electronic lock in the building and triggered the fire suppression system in order to create cover. Poole had no doubt whoever did it, did it to free Bishop, Porter, or possibly both. CCTV at Stroger had also been compromised. By the same perpetrator. Had to be.

This wasn't just about escape, it was about creating chaos. More noise.

He needed to focus. All these dead bodies. All connected.

Bishop. Porter. Both.

Neither?

The thought popped into his head. A whisper at best.

Focus.

Opening and closing drawers, he found a notepad and closed his eyes, drew in a deep breath, calmed himself. He pictured Porter's whiteboard as he last saw it, a snapshot in his mind. Poole tugged the board close, brought it into focus. When he could see it clearly, he began recreating all the text, writing everything out as Porter had organized it. Within a few minutes, he was done.

EVIDENCE BOARDS
LAKE / RESIDENCE / SIMPSONVILLE, SC
12 Jenkins Crawl Road
Simpsonville, SC

- Anson Bishop's childhood home
- Destroyed by fire (ruled arson – Bishop's mother = suspect)
- Three male bodies found inside / COD undetermined due to fire / unidentified (one thought to be Bishop's father)
- Mother never found
- Only survivor = Anson Bishop / transferred to Camden Treatment Center (closed now). Age 12
- Trailer behind house rented to Simon and Lisa Carter / both missing
- Five complete bodies found in lake (unidentified)
- One dismembered body found in lake (believed to be Simon Carter)

CHICAGO / INITIAL VICTIMS
1. Calli Tremell, 20, March 15, 2009
2. Elle Borton, 23, April 2, 2010
3. Missy Lumax, 18, June 24, 2011
4. Susan Devoro, 26, May 3, 2012
*5. Barbara McInley, 17, April 18, 2013 (only blonde)
6. Allison Crammer, 19, November 9, 2013
7. Jodi Blumington, 22, May 13, 2014
8. Emory Connors, 15, November 3, 2014 (alive)

*Gunther Herbert / Talbot's CFO
Arthur Talbot

CHICAGO / SECONDARY VICTIMS / WITH PAUL UPCHURCH
Floyd Reynolds
Ella Reynolds
Randal Davies
Lili Davies
Darlene Biel
Larissa Biel (alive)
*Libby McInley
Kati Quigley (alive)
Wesley Hartzler

TERTIARY VICTIMS (CHICAGO & SIMPSONVILLE, SC)
Jane Doe – Rose Hill Cemetery
Jane Doe – Red Line tracks / Clark Station
Tom Langlin – Simpsonville courthouse steps
Stanford Pentz – Stroger Hospital
Christie Albee – Stroger Hospital

*Not Bishop's victims?

FROM DIARY
Finicky Home for Wayward Children
Camden Treatment Center
3 girls, 5 boys, ages 7-16
Anson Bishop
Paul Upchurch
Vincent Weidner
Weasel!
The Kid
Libby McInley
Kristina Niven
Tegan Savala

Detective Freddy Welderman
Detective Ezra Stocks

Other Locations of Concern
Montehugh Labs
426 McCormick

54

Poole

Day 5 4:06 PM

Poole was studying the notepad when Nash came into the surveillance room and closed the door. When he spoke, he kept his voice low. "Whoever is pulling the strings on your boss is working mine too," Nash said. "By all accounts, I should be suspended right now. The press is playing that video of me with Bishop on a damn loop. Even *I* hate me. But he told me the same thing Hurless told you—until the mayor is found and we have this under control, I'm to stay on it."

"What about Bishop and Porter?"

"They've got everyone with a shield out looking for them—feds and Metro combined. Airports, buses, trains, they're all locked down. They know 4MK has a male victim, but the captain said they told everyone the man's identity is unknown but he's believed to be alive. He said I can't discuss the mayor with anyone other than you, not even Klozowski or Clair. Which is bullshit, because I tell them everything." He held up a scrap of paper. "I got an address on Carmine's Pizza. I think we should go there next. I don't trust Warnick. He may be right, but—"

Poole didn't look up from the notepad. "I'm going to Charleston."

"Now? Do we have time for that?"

"We keep chasing leads, and we're only getting deeper. I want to get ahead of whatever is happening. We need to take control. You said it in the SUV: Everything points to Charleston. I think if we figure out whatever happened there, we'll know who's killing these people and why." He tapped at a name on the notepad. "There's this, too."

Nash looked down. "Weasel?"

"It's the name of the kid who shot Porter. According to this, he also appeared in those diaries."

"I thought you didn't believe the diaries?"

Nash looked around the room, then through the one-way window into the interview room where they had last seen Porter. That's when he understood. "Porter took the diaries," he said softly, still working it out. "If he paid Upchurch to fake them, he would have left them here for us to read."

"Maybe he just didn't want them to get ruined. Maybe he just stashed them somewhere else," Poole said, but he knew he didn't sound convinced.

"He took them because he wasn't done reading," Nash went on. "He doesn't know what they contain any more than we do."

"I don't want to jump to conclusions." Poole held up his phone. "I have a digital copy on here. I'll read them, too. Maybe it will help me get inside his head."

"Or Bishop's."

Poole looked back down at the notepad. "Real or fake, those books are bread crumbs being followed by one or both of those men. Something from their past resurfacing. Everything we've learned points to Charleston. We need to understand what happened there. That's the missing piece. We figure that out, we get out in front, we solve the murders and find the mayor."

Nash looked out the small window back into the hallway before lowering his voice even more. "They're not gonna let us go. Not now. They want us here."

"That's why we're not going to tell them."

55
Diary

I didn't remember going back to my own room, but I awoke lying on my own mattress, the sun on my face. I heard Weasel and The Kid playing in their room, but everyone else was missing, including Paul. The girls' doors were all open. They were gone too.

I found Vincent in the barn, the hood of the truck braced up and parts lying all around. When I handed him the money, he just shoved it in his pocket. "How are we supposed to get to the store to buy anything?" He pointed at various engine parts on the ground with the head of a Phillips screwdriver. "Spark plugs, piston rings, air filter, belts, wiring harness for the plugs...the more I dig, the worse it gets. At least the tires aren't completely shot. Looks like they just need air, but we'll need a pump or compressor for that..." His head was back inside again, and I didn't hear the last part.

"We should hide all this. What if Ms. Finicky sees it? She'll know what we're doing."

Without looking up, he waved a hand through the air. "Finicky never comes out here. She sticks to the house. Those detectives, neither. Not that I've seen, anyway. They just—ah, fuck!" He jumped back out of the engine compartment and looked at his finger. It was bleeding. He put it in his mouth. His hand was black with grease and oil, but he didn't seem to care. "Goddamn piece of shit!"

I found a rag on an old workbench and handed it to him. He wrapped it around his index finger. The cut didn't look deep enough for stitches, but I bet it still hurt. He slumped down on the bumper. The metal groaned under his weight. "How are we going to get parts?"

I had no idea. "Can you make a list? Maybe the girls, when they're out can—"

"They don't leave us alone," *Vincent interrupted.* "Finicky takes the girls to town to buy groceries and some clothes, but she'll keep them all close. Even if we found a way for one of them to somehow sneak off and get to the auto store, they'd never be able to get all the parts back here without her seeing. We just need too much. These aren't the kind of things you can hide in a purse."

If Father were here, he'd tell me to puzzle it out. He always said every problem has at least three possible solutions, and even if you think you know the perfect solution, you should spend the time to determine the other two so you could weigh them all against each other. Sometimes the easy or obvious wasn't the best, and sometimes the best wasn't obvious or easy. "I'll puzzle it out."

"You'll what?"

I hadn't realized I said that aloud. "I'll figure it out."

"You're fucking weird," *Vincent muttered before standing and returning to the engine.*

"You found tools," *I said, changing the subject. There were several screwdrivers and two wrenches on the ground at his feet.*

"Under the sink up at the house," *he replied without looking up.* "Not everything I need, but it's a good start."

Although we didn't speak much, I stayed in the barn with Vincent most of the day, handing him tools, helping when I could. It was a welcome distraction.

Ms. Finicky returned with the girls at around six in the evening. All of them climbed out of her Toyota Camry with shopping bags in hand. Libby wore a yellow sundress and white tennis shoes. Her hair was pulled back in a ponytail. She didn't see me watching her from the field.

When I returned to my room, I found a new pair of black loafers, dark slacks, and a light blue button-down shirt on my bed. A note written in Ms. Finicky's hand sat atop the pile of clothes. It read—

After dinner, shower and change. Make yourself presentable. Be ready to leave by eight.

Paul was on his bunk, but he didn't speak to me. Instead, he eyed the clothing for a moment before turning his back to me and facing the wall.

56

Clair

Day 5 • 4:58 PM

Clair's eyes fluttered open in utter darkness. Not a scrap of light, and her first thought was of Emory Connors handcuffed to a gurney at the bottom of an elevator shaft.

Her second thought was of 4MK, and she quickly raised her hands to her head, checked both ears (still there), and rubbed at her eyes (still there, too). She was on the floor, her back slumped against the wall, and even through her congested nose she was able to smell mildew, must, and rot.

She wasn't handcuffed.

She hadn't been injured.

There was no gurney.

Clair screamed, and even though her throat was raw, she forced out the loudest, most frightening, bone-chilling scream she could muster. Anger, fear, and frustration vocalized in a primal cry that would go unmissed by anyone within earshot. Her voice echoed off unseen walls, back at her from above, and off the damp floor beneath her, and when she finally stopped, she listened to the echoes as they faded and died.

Then the space went quiet again, all forgotten as if it never happened. Nothing left but the sound of her breathing.

Her fingers went to her neck, found the tender place where she had been injected. Someone had taped a cotton swab over the injury, cleaned things up nice and neat. She tore it off and tossed the bandage aside.

Her gun was gone, but the holster was still clipped to her belt.

When she forced herself to stand, her head swooned as if it were filled with water sloshing from side to side. The start of an epic headache pressed from behind her eyes, at the bridge of her nose. She forced herself to breathe in the stale air. "Hello?"

The echo again, but nothing else.

As Clair began to feel along the wall, taking slow, tentative steps, thoughts of Emory again came to her. The girl had recounted how she had done the exact same thing when she first awoke. Emory had circled her prison several times before realizing there was no door.

Clair moved no more than eight feet before she found one.

Metal, both door and frame. The knob turned and rattled. The dead bolt above it did not. There was no thumb latch, only a keyhole. The door itself didn't move at all, even when Clair slammed her shoulder into it.

She beat on it for a minute or so with the back of a closed fist, because it felt like the right thing to do, but she knew nobody would come running.

She ran her fingertips over the wall again. Not concrete or cinderblock, but stone—course and rough. Stacked and cemented together.

Clair reached up, felt nothing. She bent her knees and jumped, still found nothing. She knew there was a ceiling; the echoes told her that. She was also in good shape and knew her reach—the ceiling was at least nine or more feet above.

The floor was damp concrete. Filthy.

She wiped her fingers on her jeans.

Clair had been in enough old Chicago basements to recognize the similarities, but this didn't feel residential. She couldn't put her finger on exactly what was off, but something was. Whoever drugged her had done so in the hospital stairwell. Theoretically, they could have gotten her to the hospital basement unseen, but she had been down there several times and this felt different from that space, too. Older, maybe?

Could someone have gotten her out of the hospital?

She held up her wrist to check the time but couldn't even make out the shape of her watch in the dark, let alone how long had passed.

Klozowski would be looking for her. Stout, too. Even Barrington was unlikely to go very long without trying to find her to complain about something. The security staff, her officers, Sutter, someone…

Then she thought of her missing officers, Henricks and Childs. Nobody had looked for them, not really.

She should have. Who else could be expected to?

Too much commotion. Everyone was worried about themselves. Nobody would look.

Clair shivered, wrapped her arms around herself. She knew she had a fever, which would not be helped by this damp and musty room, and had meant to take something for it. Some aspirin or ibuprofen.

But you didn't. Did you? And now you'll die here. Wherever here *is.*

Clair screamed again. Not because she wanted to, but because she *needed* to. And when she did, she heard a loud click.

Above her, fluorescent lights sparked to life, and when her eyes adjusted, she realized the metal door had a thick window, the kind with wire mesh embedded in the glass for security. The kind that can't be easily broken.

From the other side of that glass, a face watched her, tilted slightly as he watched her.

Clair froze. "Sam?"

57

Nash

Day 5 • 5:03 PM

Carmine's Pizza occupied the bottom floor of an old three-story building on West 26th in an area of the city known as Little Village. Nash partially skidded, partially jolted his Chevy Nova into a parallel parking spot on the north side of the street and listened to the motor cough as he studied the red, green, and white storefront. Several employees pushed out the door into the cold with insulated pizza bags in their hands. Some walking up and down the street, others heading to cars parked in the alley two buildings over. As Nash sat there, a man in his sixties held the door for one of them and stepped inside. He came out five minutes later with a pizza box in his hand. A teenage girl clad in a puffy pink coat, scarf, hat, and gloves ducked in a moment later and came back out holding two boxes and a bag before running back to an idling car driven by a woman who was most likely her mom.

From the street, not a damn thing screamed escort service. In fact, the longer he watched, the hungrier he got. His stomach had started rumbling about five minutes ago. The report he received from Vice said the escort business had been running out of here for the better part of a decade. They also said Carmine's had a four-and-a-half star rating on Yelp.

While operating an illicit business under the guise of a legiti-mate one was nothing new, Nash found the location of Carmine's completely baffling—it was less than a block away from the Cook County Department of Corrections. A ninety-six-acre facility housing at least 6,500 prisoners, 3,900 law enforcement officials, and 7,000 civilian employees. He could see the corner of the large structure from his car. He couldn't help but wonder how many of those pizzas went to members of Chicago's finest every day. He'd be willing to bet they were accompanied by a secret handshake or a wink because there was no way a fuck-for-hire shop operated *that* far below the radar. Vice knew. DOC had to know, but nobody gave a shit. Must be damn good pizza.

Nash shut off the engine, climbed out of the Chevy, and darted across the street. He nearly slipped on a patch of ice at the edge of the sidewalk, regained his footing, and tugged open the door to Carmine's, stepping inside.

The smell was godly.

A kid of about sixteen in a sauce-stained Carmine's T-shirt looked up from behind the counter, a paper hat on his head. "Slice or pie?"

The kitchen was behind the counter, all open, completely visible. At least half-a-dozen ovens were in use, with five other employees toiling away—making sauce, washing dishes, kneading dough. Christ, this was making Nash hungry. He tried not to look. "Can I speak to your manager, please?"

The kid rolled his eyes and shouted over his shoulder. "Addie, got another cop out here!"

"Another cop? Do you get a lot of us?"

The kid didn't answer, just walked away, headed toward the back of the kitchen without another word.

A moment later, a woman in her fifties came out of a door next to the sink. She was dressed in a white sweater, black yoga pants, and must have weighed three hundred pounds. Nash watched as she turned sideways to squeeze between the tables and ovens to get to the front. When she reached the counter, she looked Nash up and down and smirked. "What?"

"I'm not here for the pizza," Nash said.

"Well, that's bullshit. Even the cops who shake us down take the pizza. Come on."

She turned and started back the way she'd come.

Nash followed.

She led him to a small office space cluttered with boxes and told him to close the door. When he did, she dropped into a swivel chair behind the desk and leaned back. "I told that guy Warnick everything I know. He said you'd come down here anyway. Said you might even bring the feds to try and shake me down. Waste of time, but do your damnedest if that's what you're here to do. Just wrap it up before the dinner rush kicks in."

"You don't seem very worried."

She huffed. "What can you do to me? Nothing illegal going on. I'm a matchmaker, that's all. What those *adults* do on their own time is their business, not mine. I've been in and out of court more times than I can count, and the charges never stick." She leaned forward and lowered her voice. "And frankly, if you knew some of the names on my client list, you'd know there was no chance in hell of me getting in trouble. I've got copies of my client list with friends all over the country. Something happens to me, and things will start to slip to the press. You'll see my Instagram account switch from cuddly cat pictures to photos of politicians dressed like Little Bo Peep sucking on a ball-gag. I could shoot you in the middle of 26th out there if I wanted to. Nobody's touching me. So again, it's after five. We need to hurry this up. What do you want?"

There was another chair, this one in front of the desk. Nash removed the stack of opened envelopes from the seat, placed them on the desk, and settled in. Got comfortable.

She frowned. "That's not how we do this fast."

"Nope."

Sighing, she said, "Look, like I told Warnick, I sent over Latrice. Blonde hair, blue eyes, twenty-two years old, and willing to put up with the mayor's little kinks. She'd been with him twice, knew what to expect. She'd been with me for three years, so I told her what to expect if he tried the unexpected, because those guys tend to evolve, or devolve, depending on your position. I've seen enough of them in my day—he's not a surprise or an anomaly, he's just a different checkbox on all the bullshit that is today's man. She went in prepared, as all my girls do. She arrived within three minutes of the time I expected her to, and she left thirty-eight minutes early. No surprises, not from my end. I don't allow for surprises. I have no idea who your brown-haired girl is—she didn't come from me."

"Do you have any records?"

"You seriously think I'd let you see them if I did?"

Nash shrugged.

She glanced over at the battered laptop on the corner of her desk. "Couldn't show them to you even if I wanted to. My computer caught some kind of virus. All my files are screwed up. I'm waiting for my tech guy to come by and fix it."

Nash loaded images of the two women they had found on Up-church's computer and slid his phone across the desk. "Have you ever seen these two?"

At first she didn't look. Like if she stared at him long enough he'd rescind his request. When she did, she just shook her head. "No, they're not mine."

He then showed her a photograph of Porter. "What about him?"

On Sam's picture, she paused and at first Nash thought it was because she did recognize him. Then he realized she had seen so many male faces over the years it took just a little bit longer to browse through her mental Rolodex. "He's not a client," she finally said, leaning back in her chair.

A relief settled over him before Nash realized a small part of his mind thought she might actually recognize Sam, and that worried him, because that singular thought came from the detective buried deep in his subconscious. Some people called it insight, others called it intuition. Porter had once told him to trust that voice. He said the subconscious had a way of piecing things together at a slightly faster pace than the conscious mind, and once he learned to trust that voice, *listen to it*, he'd become a better detective. Nash had told him he needed to stop listening to *all* the voices in his head. Maybe he needed to heed his own advice.

He changed the subject. "When did your computer get the virus?"

She frowned at the laptop. "About a week ago. It was like it went senile and started forgetting shit. All the dates scrambled, that's the worst part—every file I've looked at, even within files, like spreadsheets and Word docs—every single date changed to some random other date. I'm still not sure how it even happened. I'm not one of those people who clicks on links in e-mails or random websites. My IT guy said it's not even possible with the software he has running on here. He's clearly a fucking tool."

"I've got someone who could probably fix it. Want me to run it by him?"

For the first time since he got there, she smiled. "That might be the funniest shit I've heard all week." She grinned. "Sure, Mr. Copper. Take my laptop and make it all good again, just don't peek at nothin', I can trust you, right? Fuck you." The chair groaned under her weight. "I think we're done here."

"One more thing." Nash scrolled through the images on his phone and found the one he wanted. It was the back of one of the Polaroids from the box in the mayor's suite at the Langham Hotel. He pinched the image and enlarged the handwritten text—203. WF15 3k. LM—and slid the phone back to her. "Does this mean anything to you?"

She leaned forward again, turned the phone so she could read the words. She didn't say anything, not at first. She didn't need to. The color left her face, and her mouth fell open for a short second before she regained her composure and slid the phone back to him. "Nope."

"Now is not the time to start lying to me."

"Talk to Warnick. I'm not getting in the middle of that."

"Warnick knows what this is?"

"You need to leave." She stood and started for the door. Reached for the knob.

"Is it related to Charleston?"

This gave her pause. "Charleston? No...I'm not sure what you...just talk to Warnick."

"How about the Guyon?"

She quickly shook her head, flustered, trying to regroup her thoughts.

Someone knocked on the door, and Addie pulled it open. A girl of about nineteen was standing there in a gray cocktail dress and red heels. She frowned when she saw Nash. "I'm sorry, I didn't realize you were in a meeting." She looked back at the other woman. "I need a ride."

Addie frowned. "Michael will drive you. Unless Detective Nash here wants to give you a lift. He's leaving."

At the mention of the word *detective*, the girl's eyes widened.

Nash stood. "How about I take you to a shelter?"

"How about you leave," Addie said, opening the door wider.

Nash smiled at the girl, tried to look reassuring, and felt a sneeze tickling the inside of his nose. The girl took a step backward, away from him. He walked out of the office, past them both.

From behind him, the woman said, "This ain't nothing new, Detective. None of it. It's been going on since the first time Eve told Adam, 'you want me to do *that*, you best give me an apple.' All I'm doing is keeping things organized and safe. You should be grateful. Better those girls work for me than run around on the street on their own. We both know how that story ends."

Nash did.

He grabbed two slices of pizza fresh out of the oven, and he left. Not because he wanted to, but because this wasn't his fight. At least, not today.

58
Diary

I'd grown fairly used to the detectives driving me around town. They took me to and from my meetings with Dr. Oglesby twice each week, and I'd seen them drive the others more times than I could count. I knew it was odd for police detectives to do such a thing, but I never asked why they did. All people had reasons for their actions, and I was sure their particular reasons would present themselves soon enough.

For the most part, we all settled into our usual roles in the car—Welderman at the wheel, Stocks in the passenger seat doing his best to stink up the vehicle with the stale cigarette smoke that always seemed to loft off his clothes, and me in the rear, watching the backs of their heads, wondering if my seat belt would hold if I were to shove an ice pick into Welderman's neck and he lost control of the car. For the record, I didn't have an ice pick. I didn't even know where I could find one, but such a thing didn't keep a boy from wondering.

Normally, we didn't speak, but today was proving to be anything but normal. Welderman said, "Did your father die in the fire, Anson?"

"Yes," I replied, perhaps a little too quickly.

Welderman's eyes remained on the road. "Of the three men found inside your old house, two have been identified as working for a man named Arthur Talbot. Does that name mean anything to you?"

I saw the vans outside my house, the ones with Talbot Enterprises written on the sides, but I wasn't about to tell him that. I didn't say anything.

"That only leaves one unidentified body, but here's the thing—we pulled some clothing out of your old house. There wasn't much left, mind you. The fire was fairly thorough, but one of the pairs of pants we found held up pretty good. Dress slacks with an inseam of thirty-four inches. They were found inside what was left of a dresser in your parents' room, so we can reasonably assume they belonged to your father since who else would store their pants there, right? A thirty-four-inch inseam would fit a man between five-eleven and six-one or two, a fairly tall man. Was your father a 'fairly tall man,' Anson?"

Again, I didn't say anything. Out the window, I watched the small, narrow roads of farm country fade away behind us and make way for the wider lanes of the highway. This wasn't our usual route. We weren't heading toward Camden Treatment Center. We were heading toward Charleston.

"We believe he was, because the seat in his car was pushed nearly all the way back." He drummed his fingers on the steering wheel. "Anyway, that last unidentified body from your house, he was only five-foot-nine. Not much left of his pants on account of the fire, but you know what we do know? His inseam sure as shit wasn't thirty-four. A man like that tries to wear pants with a thirty-four-inch inseam, and he'd have to roll up the cuffs at the bottom. Doubtful he did that. We're thinking both your parents survived that fire, not just your mother. What do you think about that?"

"I wish my father were still alive, but that doesn't make it true. No matter how hard I wish."

Welderman glanced at the man beside him. "Hey, you know what I don't get?"

Stocks cleared his throat. "What's that?"

"If that kid's parents are still alive, how the hell do they let him roll into a night like tonight without doing anything about it? Can you imagine just standing by and watching something like that happen to your son? Your only son?"

Stocks shrugged, and I swear I saw a puff of cigarette smoke rise up off his shoulder. "If they're alive, they're living nice off all that money they stole with the neighbors... Maybe they care more about that than they do about him."

"Yeah, maybe."

I knew they were just trying to push my buttons, get me to say something I normally wouldn't, but I wasn't about to do that. Father had taught me all these little tricks, taught me how to watch out for them. These guys weren't good cops, they weren't even bad cops—they were dirty *cops. I gave them something else to think about. "My father was a very patient man. If he were still alive, he'd wait until he learned everything he needed from the both of you, watch you, maybe even follow you for a while—he might even be behind us right now—then when he got everything he needed, and you were no longer useful, he'd find a nice, quiet spot in your house or your apartment or wherever you sleep at night and he'd settle into the shadows until you laid your head down to rest. You wouldn't even know he was there until you were in some half-slumber and felt something warm around your neck. And when you woke and realized that warm-something was your own intestines, and you'd been cut from your throat to your cock, he'd grin down at you and tell you that you should have been nicer to his boy. He's not alive, though, so I guess you don't have to worry about that." I fell silent for a moment, then added, "I can't imagine what Mother would do. She wasn't so patient. Not like Father."*

Welderman glanced at me in the rearview mirror but didn't say anything, Stocks didn't, either. They both turned their attention back to the road.

I'd been making mental notes of each road sign, exit, and turn, and I was grateful for the quiet so I could concentrate. After we left the highway, Welderman pulled into the parking lot of a rundown motel painted yellow with lime-green trim. He parked next to a white panel van. A man in a navy blue trench coat got out.

59

Clair

Day 5 • 5:03 PM

Not Sam.

It couldn't be Sam.

At least, she couldn't be sure.

The face on the other side of the glass wore a black ski mask with a pair of sunglasses beneath to hide his eyes, and for a moment, Clair was grateful for that. Something about seeing eyes, recognizing eyes, would have been too much for her.

This wasn't Sam. Because Sam wouldn't do *this*.

She didn't feel well.

She had a fever. Her thoughts weren't quite her own.

The face on the other side of the glass tilted back in the opposite direction, righted itself.

Clair couldn't see his mouth. The mask had no mouth hole.

Smooth.

Empty.

Blank.

She told herself she couldn't be sure this was even a man. She stood on her toes, tried to get a better look—shoulders, chest, something—but the face leaned in closer, blocked her already limited view.

"What the hell do you want, you crazy fuck?"

The face tilted again, and she could almost feel a smile from the other side of that material. Brown teeth and rancid breath—that's the kind of smile she'd find if she could reach out and pull the mask away, she was sure of that. Maybe pointed teeth like a snarling dog, not human at all.

Get your shit together, Clair. This isn't only a man, this is a weak *man. The kind of man who had to drug and lock you away because—*

Because, why?

There was a reason. There had to be a reason. Had she somehow gotten too close to something and not even realized it?

Two missing officers. Two people dead. Maybe this guy didn't wait for you to stumble into anything. Maybe you were just next on the list.

"How about you grow a pair and open this door?" She took a step back. "I'll even count to three and give you a chance to run before I come out there and beat the living shit out of you!"

He only stared.

Glossy black bug eyes behind a mask.

She reached for the doorknob and pulled at it. "I'm sick. You can't leave me in here! I need medicine! Christ, I don't even have water in here!"

There was an audible click, and the lights went out again.

The door vanished.

The small window.

The man.

There was nothing but darkness.

Clair cursed herself for not taking a moment to look around the room when she had the chance. She had no idea where she was. No idea if there was anything she could use to get out.

She shivered.

The cold tickled across her flesh, reached under her clothing and caressed, felt along the nape of her neck and chilled every inch of her. She might as well be standing in a freezer, she was so cold.

Things couldn't get worse. Couldn't possibly.

Then she heard a scream. A man's voice, in horrible pain. He sounded as if he were no more than five feet away in that murky dark.

60

Nash

Day 5 • 5:07 PM

Nash hesitated outside Porter's apartment for several minutes before finally deciding to go in. When he came here with Clair a couple days ago, they had done so out of concern for Sam. They were worried about their friend, wanted to help. This time, Nash was going behind his back, snooping. This was a betrayal, no matter how he tried to sugarcoat it.

No crime-scene tape marked the door. Technically, no crime had been committed. No reason for tape. Yet, Nash had that same feeling in his gut that came when he was standing outside a crime scene. A twisting, churning, stirring of things better left alone.

He'd knocked. Several times.

A small part of him hoped Sam would open the door, usher him inside with a smile, maybe offer him a beer, and tell him how they got all this wrong. Nobody answered the door, though, and Nash was beginning to wonder exactly what they'd gotten wrong.

Bishop or Sam.

Sam or Bishop.

Both.

It was the text from Kloz that really spooked him. Prior to that text, the bits of evidence piling up around Sam had all seemed like nothing more than smoke kicked up by Bishop, some fabricated tale to reposition the spotlight. Then the text came in when Nash was about halfway back to Metro:

I found four cash withdrawals from Sam's checking account—twenty-five hundred each in September of last year. Also found corresponding deposits on Upchurch's side—same amounts, within forty-eight hours of Sam's withdrawals. Anything over $3K would be reported to the IRS due to the Patriot Act—Sam would know that. He tried to keep this below the radar.

This was followed by a second text a moment later:

Facial recognition matched the images on Upchurch's computer to the two victims found this morning. I haven't found a way to confirm whether or not they are Kristina Niven and Tegan Savala—I'm not sure those names are even real—no matches in social security or birth records. Still digging...

P.S. I feel like shit. You?

"I feel peachy." Nash rubbed his tender nose and tried to call Kloz to get more detail, but he got voice mail, same thing with Clair. That damn hospital was a giant black hole for cell service. Always had been.

He reread the texts standing out there in Sam's hallway before finally taking out his keys and letting himself inside.

The air felt oddly still, almost stale, like stepping into a tomb. He remembered coming here for dinner, not that long ago, Sam and Heather rushing around to make him feel comfortable. The Bears on the television, down by seven in the second quarter. The volume was off. A radio played classic rock from the corner of the room—"Hotel California" by the Eagles—funny how music could bring you back.

No music now.

Light filtered in around the drawn drapes. Dust floated silently through the air.

"Sam, if you're here, I'm coming in."

He knew Sam wasn't there, but it seemed like the right thing to say. If not for that text from Kloz, he might have turned and left.

His eyes scanned the apartment. Not sure where to start, not even sure what he was looking for. The FBI had already done a number on the place—Sam and Heather's books were all stacked in front of the various bookcases instead of on the shelves—every page had been flipped—nothing hidden in or around them. Half the kitchen cabinets were closed. The rest stood open, contents scattered about, same with the drawers. Nash went to the refrigerator and found nothing inside but some spoiled milk, stale bread, and slimy sandwich meats. Nothing in the freezer but ice. A crumbled piece of foil labeled *ground beef* was on the counter. He knew Sam hid money in there, but that had been gone before he went to New Orleans. When he retrieved the diary from—

Nash returned to the living room. He hadn't noticed when he first walked in, but he should have. Sam's La-ZBoy, which Sam had flipped on its side to retrieve the hidden diary, and had still been on its side when he and Clair were here two days ago, now stood upright.

Sam had come back at some point after escaping Metro.

With one hand under the chair and another on the armrest, Nash turned the heavy chair back onto its side and knelt down near the bottom. The material was pulled tight and fastened, the internal workings sealed away as it should be. Not how the chair had been left.

He grabbed a corner and tugged the velcro, peeled the black cloth aside. With the flashlight from his phone, he looked up inside the chair. A white plastic package of some sort had been duct taped against the plywood and metal frame, nearly out of reach. Nash stretched, got his fingers around a corner, pulled the package out, and set it on the floor in front of him.

A white plastic trash bag holding square contents, tied off with black string around

Not the diary.

Something larger.

Nash tore the tape from the edges, untied the string, and unfolded the plastic before he realized he wasn't wearing gloves. He took a pair from his pocket and slipped them on, then dumped out the contents of the bag.

And sneezed.

It was the dust. Not the cold, or flu, or whatever, but the giant plume of dust that jumped up at him as four pieces of drywall fell to the floor. The first three contained poems, the last one a single sentence:

You can't play God without being acquainted with the devil.

61

Diary

Welderman and Stocks exited the car, spoke to the man in the navy blue trench coat for several minutes, then Welderman opened my door. "This way, Anson."

I looked out at all three of them and made no effort to leave the seat. I may not have liked Welderman's car, but I was smart enough to know whatever was coming if I followed those three men wasn't good. They weren't going to kill me, I knew that much—they would have killed me back at the farm where they had seclusion—but the way Stocks stared down at his shoes, the nervous glances around the parking lot from Welderman, that told me there was something else to fear. The look on Vincent's face the other night when he returned from a similar trip was enough to confirm those thoughts.

The man in the trench coat handed Welderman a key, nodded back at the motel, and said "fourteen" in a low tone before getting back into his white van and closing the door. He didn't leave. Instead, he sat there, his eyes scanning the parking lot—the people moving across the street at some fast food place, an older man filling up his station wagon at the Phillips 66 next door. I knew what a lookout was. I had played the role plenty of times for Mother and Father. This man was a lookout.

Stocks's cigarette-stained fingers reached into the car, wrapped around my collar, and pulled me out. I let my legs go weak and fell to the ground.

Welderman let out a sigh and made a show of pulling the corner of his jacket back just enough so that I could see the gun holstered on his belt. "Are you going to make me shoot you, kid? If you think I won't, you're kidding yourself. I've got no problem putting a bullet in you and walking across the street and grabbing a burger while Stocks cleans things up. You wouldn't be the first. We could knock you around a little too; that's what we had to do with Weidner. Even your little friend Libby put up a good fight until I added a bruise or two to the patchwork already there." He knelt down next to me and looked me in the eyes. "My point is, this will end in one of two ways: either with you dead or you walking voluntarily to that room. There is no Option C. If you decide you'd like to survive the night, then the sooner you take the walk to that room, the sooner you'll be back home tucked in your own bed, trying to convince yourself none of this ever happened. The first time is tough for everyone, but it gets easier. I can promise you that."

He stood back up then, glanced back across the road at the fast food place. "I'm hungry, so make up your fucking mind."

The man in the van was watching us, too. He didn't appear very concerned—just another day, been there, done that.

I stood back up and brushed the dirt from my pants. I couldn't take on two men with guns, definitely not three. I looked over at the motel behind us. "Room Fourteen?"

Welderman nodded. "Yeah."

I started across the parking lot, with Stocks shuffling along behind me, Welderman behind him.

Room Fourteen was on the first floor in the far right corner. The light was on inside. Most of the other rooms were dark. When we got to the door, Welderman slipped the key into the lock, twisted, and pushed the door open.

There were two beds, both covered in matching floral print comforters. A small, round table stood inside the room to the right of the door. There was a counter and sink at the back of the room, a bathroom to the left. A television droned from a chipped dresser across from the beds. I didn't see anyone, not at first. Then a toilet flushed and a man came out of the bathroom, glanced at us, and turned to the sink to wash his hands without a word.

Either Welderman or Stocks pushed me into the room with a hand to my back. I couldn't tell which. Welderman said, "You have fifty minutes."

The door closed behind me. The man reached for a towel to dry off. And I stood there.

62

Nash

Black handwriting, large block letters scrawled onto drywall over faded and chipped paint. Nash hadn't seen these before, but he knew exactly what they were. Someone had cut them out of the walls at an abandoned house on 41st, the same house where Special Agent Diener was killed. Anson Bishop had been holed up across the street.

Poole wrote the text from memory on one of the whiteboards back at the War Room. They assumed Bishop didn't want the text to be found for some reason and cut them out when he killed Diener. In the video earlier today, Bishop said that Porter killed Diener, which meant he would have removed the drywall...and hid the pieces here?

Even if Sam did take them, why would he hide them in his own apartment?

Planted. Had to be.

Then why would Sam give cash to Upchurch?

Nash laid out the four squares on the floor. The first said:

Because I could not stop for Death,
He kindly stopped for me;
The carriage held but just ourselves

And Immortality.

The second read:

A telling analogy for life and death:
Compare the two of them to water and ice.
Water draws together to become ice,
And ice disperses again to become water.
Whatever has died is sure to be born again;
Whatever is born comes around again to dying.
As <u>ice</u> and <u>water</u> do one another no harm,
So <u>life</u> and <u>death</u>, the two of them, are fine.

And the third was shorter:

Let us return <u>Home</u>, let us go back,
Useless is this reckoning of seeking and getting,
Delight permeates all of today.
From the blue ocean of death
Life is flowing like nectar.
In life there is death; in death there is life.
So where is fear, where is <u>fear</u>?
The birds in the sky are singing "No death, no <u>death</u>!"
Day and night the tide of Immortality
Is descending here on earth.

As Poole had remembered them, several words were under-lined:

Ice
water
Life
death
Home
fear

Death

They thought they had figured out the meaning—Upchurch had placed the bodies of his victims in ice, under the water after drowning them repeatedly in a tank of saltwater in his basement. From what they learned from the two survivors, he was trying to determine if they saw anything after they died, after he brought them back. Poole felt that was why the word *death* was underlined twice. All the underlined words fit their theory except for *home*. They never did figure that one out.

None of this explained why someone (Bishop or Porter) would take the time to cut these particular blocks of text from a graffiti-filled wall and hide them somewhere. Particularly after killing a federal agent, knowing another was just across the street.

There was something else here, something they missed.

Nash took pictures of each board and texted them to Clair, Klozowski, and Poole along with the message *Found these in Sam's apartment.* He knew they'd ask, and at this point, he saw no reason to keep anything from them. They'd sort things out.

A tickle crept through the inside of his nose again, and he turned his head and sneezed. Three of them, rapid fire. When finished, he stood and looked around the room for a tissue. If Heather were still around, he was sure there'd be a box in every room. Sam was slowly reverting back to bachelor status, though— no tissues and the paper towel holder in the kitchen held nothing but an empty cardboard tube.

Even the worst bachelor kept toilet paper on hand, so Nash made his way through the apartment to the bathroom off the bedroom, turning on lights as he went.

He didn't see the body, not at first. If someone hadn't taken the time to wrap it in plastic before dumping it in the bathtub, he might have smelled the decomposing flesh from the other room. The salt probably stifled the smell, too, or maybe it was just his stuffy nose.

63

Porter

Day 5 • 5:2I PM

True to her word, when the Talbot Enterprises jet touched down at Charleston Executive Airport, Emory had arranged for an SUV to be positioned at the private tarmac. They rolled to a stop less than fifty feet from where it was parked, and a man wearing Talbot Enterprises Air Service overalls met Porter at the base of the steps and handed him the keys. "She's fueled, and there's a prepaid cell phone in the center console should you need to place a call. Feel free to dispose of it when you feel appropriate." He handed Porter a business card, also Talbot Enterprises. "My number's on the back. You need anything, you call me. We're under instructions to keep the jet here on standby for your exclusive use. Your pilots will remain on airport grounds. On average, we need about thirty minutes to prep the plane for takeoff, so if you're in a hurry, try to phone me in advance and we can minimize your wait."

"Thank you." Porter took the keys, slipped the card in his pocket, and made his way to the SUV with the backpack slung over his shoulder.

Among every other luxury Porter could possibly imagine, the jet had several laptops equipped with high-speed Internet access. Once online, it didn't take long to find what he was looking for. As he settled into the driver seat of the SUV, he studied the directions he'd written down, then started the vehicle and followed the signs to I-26. He pulled into the parking lot of Camden Treatment Center less than thirty minutes later.

The building was white, single story, with a flat roof. The grounds were carefully maintained, trimmed trees and blooms that managed to provide color even during these winter months—not that South Carolina winters in any way compared to Chicago's. He was fairly certain snow was nothing but a myth this far south. Considering the time was after five, past quitting time, there were only a couple of cars in the parking lot.

He considered bringing the backpack, then thought better of it. He tucked it down on the floor in front of the passenger seat. If he needed the diaries, he could always come back out for them. As in New Orleans, for people to believe he was a working cop, he needed to look the part, and cops didn't carry backpacks. They *did* carry guns and badges, so he left the holstered gun on his belt. There was little he could do about the missing badge. Emory had done her best with the clothing, but he had to admit, everything he wore was far beyond a cop's salary. He glanced at his reflection in the mirror only long enough to confirm he didn't have food on his face, then left the SUV for the building's entrance.

Pushing through the door, he found himself in a carpeted lobby, the walls a mix of beige and white tastefully decorated with painted landscapes. A woman in her early twenties looked up from the computer at the reception desk and smiled. "May I help you?"

Porter handed her one of his business cards from Metro. "I need to speak to someone about a former patient. About twenty years ago."

"Twenty years?"

Porter nodded.

"Patient's name?"

"Anson Bishop."

The woman eyed him for a moment, then picked up her phone and spoke to someone in a hushed tone. Porter couldn't make out the words. When she hung up, she nodded toward a group of chairs against the opposite wall. "If you'd like to have a seat, our director will be with you in a few minutes."

The last thing Porter wanted to do was sit and wait, but he had little choice. He crossed the room and lowered himself into one of the silver and black leather chairs and glanced at the stack of outdated magazines on the table at his side. He really didn't care what the royal family was up to or who Jennifer Aniston was dating. Johnny Depp's financial concerns were slightly intriguing, but before he could scoop up that particular issue, he heard a male voice talking to someone behind the door at the back of the lobby. Then the door opened with an electronic buzz and a man in his late fifties, early sixties looked around the room, settled on Porter.

At first, the man seemed to stare, a slight look of confusion on his face. Narrow eyes behind thin glasses. Porter had told himself that if someone recognized him from television or anywhere, he'd just leave. He could be on the road and gone long before they could call someone. Definitely before that someone could get here. He needed to remain mobile now. He'd lost valuable time locked up at Metro.

The man glanced over at the woman behind the desk. "If anyone calls, tell them I'm in a meeting?"

She nodded in reply.

He turned back to Porter. "Follow me, Detective?"

A statement set in the form of a question. Porter had spoken to his share of shrinks over the years, like every cop does, and this was a particular skill they all seemed to share. Nearly every phrase leaving their mouths did so in the form of a question. He found it as annoying now as he did every other time. He smiled back at the doctor, though, and followed him through the door, a sense of déjà vu rushing over him.

The nurses station on one side, a sealed guard booth on the other. The hallway stretching back about fifty feet. Bishop had described all of it in his diaries. The nurses station was empty, but Porter could picture Nurse Gilman sitting there, watching them as they walked by. The guard only glanced in their direction, then returned his gaze to the bank of computer monitors on his desk—dozens of cameras, watching everything from the lobby to some kind of common area and what could only be patient rooms and offices.

There were cameras at either end of the hallway, dark, black eyes staring down from small bubbles in the ceiling. I had not found a camera in Doctor Oglesby's office, but I was fairly sure he had one. The one in my room was hidden in the air vent next to the fluorescent light, watching from above, it did not make a sound but I felt it blink.

Porter located the various bubbles on the hallway ceiling and tried not to stare.

The doctor ushered him into the second office on the left, asked him to take a seat at the desk, and closed the door before settling into a large leather chair opposite him. He removed his glasses and let them fall against his chest, held there on a silver chain. He wore an argyle sweater of the most hideous shades of red and green, Christmas colors gone wrong. His hair, no doubt once black as coal in his youth, was peppered silver. "It's been a long time, Detective."

This took Porter by surprise. He was good with names and faces, and he had no recollection of ever meeting this man. The nameplate on his desk said *Victor Whittenberg, Ph.D.* That didn't ring any bells, either. "I'm sorry, do we know each other?"

Whatever thoughts this brought on in the doctor, his face didn't betray them. He simply settled back in his chair and studied Porter. Maybe contemplating if he was wrong.

During the five-year period in which he'd hunted 4MK, Porter had spoken to dozens of professionals. It was possible he'd spoke to Whittenberg at one point or another, maybe at a press conference. In those situations, he met so many people at once that he always found it difficult to catalog them. As the person holding the press conference, they always seemed to remember him. That was just the dynamic of such a thing. Or this could be the same situation he ran into with so many others—the doctor had seen him on television at some point and recognized him from there.

The doctor spoke first, his voice reserved. "Perhaps I'm mistaken."

"I have one of those faces."

"I suppose you do." There was a silver micro-cassette recorder on his desk. He thumbed a red button on the side and the tape began to turn. "Do you mind if I record our conversation?"

Porter did mind. "For what purpose?"

Whittenberg reached for his glasses and returned them to the bridge of his nose. "You're a police detective, no doubt about to ask me for privileged information about one or more patients. A conversation I probably shouldn't participate in at all, but if I am to do so, or simply consider doing so, I'd feel more comfortable knowing there was a record."

Porter knew if he pushed the issue, this man would probably end the meeting and send him on his way. He really didn't have much of a choice. "Just keep in mind, this is part of an ongoing investigation and discussing our conversation with someone else could be considered obstruction and lead to possible charges. Obviously, just playing this tape for someone else could be problematic for you. Please keep that in mind."

"Understood." Whittenberg pushed the recorder to the center of his desk, between them both.

Porter tried not to look at it and cleared his throat. "Is Dr. Oglesby still on staff here?"

"Oglesby?"

"Yes."

The glasses came off again, fell around his neck. "I don't know that name."

"How long have you worked here?"

Whittenberg thought about this. "Going on twenty-three years now."

Porter found himself studying the man's sweater, the argyle patterns all twisted together in a chaotic mess. "He would have been here in the late nineties. As recent as ten or fifteen years ago."

"I...I would surely have known him then. This facility isn't very large. The name escapes me, though. Are you sure he worked at Camden?"

"I'm certain. He was the doctor who treated Anson Bishop."

"I see."

Porter found himself getting frustrated. These canned, unclear responses. "Do you have Bishop's file? Maybe we should just start there."

"Detective, I find your behavior to be very disturbing."

Porter wondered how the good doctor would feel if he reached across the desk, grabbed him by that hideous sweater, and tossed him aside as he rummaged through the drawers. He drew in a breath, calmed himself. "I apologize. I haven't slept much. Investigations like this can fray your nerves. Let's see what we find in Bishop's file and go from there?"

A statement in the form of a question.

Take that, you shit.

The doctor glanced down at the recorder, confirmed it was still running, then stood. "Give me a moment."

He left Porter in the office and was gone for several minutes. When he returned, he held two files—one thick, one thin. He sat back in his chair and pushed both folders across the desk to Porter.

Porter drew them close and studied the names typed neatly on the tabs. The thin folder was labeled *Bishop, Anson*. It was the label on the thick folder that grabbed his attention, reached around his heart, and squeezed hard enough to cause his body to jerk. He looked up at the doctor. "What's this?"

"You tell me."

The thick folder was labeled *Porter, Samuel.*

64
Diary

Without turning, the man said, "What's your name, kid?"

"Anson."

"Anson," he repeated in a low voice. He folded the towel and placed it back on the rack.

I could see his face in the mirror. He looked to be in his thirties with short, thinning dark hair and round wire-frame glasses perched on his nose. He had a mustache, but no beard. He'd been wearing a suit, but the jacket sat over the back of the chair near the door, his tie was loose, and the top button of his shirt was open. He'd rolled his sleeves up, too. He was a short man, maybe five-foot-six.

He checked himself in the mirror, then faced me. When he smiled, I saw his crooked, teeth, and I wanted to look away but held his gaze anyway. "You look just like your picture. That's good."

I almost asked him who he expected me to look like if not myself, but that seemed as silly as his statement.

"My name is Bernie. Is this your first time?"

I didn't answer, only stared at him.

After a half dozen seconds, he said, "I paid extra, so I need you to tell me that it is. I don't trust those men. They lie about that sort of thing all the time."

I wondered exactly how many times Bernie had done this. He didn't *look nervous, and I think that frightened me more than anything because I was fairly certain I knew what this was, and I didn't want to know anyone who was comfortable in this particular moment.*

I nodded and was grateful when he finally turned away from me and fished his wallet from his pants pocket. He took out several bills and placed them on the counter next to the sink. "I already paid them, but this is for you." Replacing his wallet, he took several steps toward me and gestured toward a brown bottle on the nightstand between the two beds. "Do you want a drink to help take the edge off?"

I'd only drank twice in my life. The first time with Mrs. Carter, and that didn't end well for me. The second time was with Father the following morning. Hair of the dog, he had called it. A means to lessen my hangover. I'd lost my wits somewhere in that bottle with Mrs. Carter and found them again with Father. I certainly didn't plan to do that again here, so I just shook my head. "You can have one, though. If you want, I mean."

He did want, because he nodded and filled one of the motel glasses with about an inch from the bottle and drank it in a single swallow. He shivered, then set the glass down and sat on the edge of the bed. He patted the comforter next to him, and I noticed he had chewed his nails down to the quick. His fingertips were stained yellow, and I pictured him an hour from now standing outside with Stocks, the two smokers huddled together in their secretive little club, a lighter and bad stories passing between them.

"Sit," Bernie repeated. "I'm not gonna ask you again."

I sat. Not because I wanted to, but because doing anything else would escalate the situation, and it didn't seem wise to do that.

Bernie was nervous, and nervous people don't always act rationally.

I grew up playing chess alone, both sides, white and black. Not because I had no one to play with, but because Father wanted me to learn to anticipate an adversary's next move. When you play chess alone, you're forced to spend a moment as your opponent, thinking through every possible move before them, every possible action, then you return to your side of the board with that knowledge, and because of it, you are forced to reconsider your countermove based on complete knowledge of what that opponent can do next.

Sweat moistened my palms, and I wiped them on the comforter. As I did so, I considered everything Bernie might do next. I also thought about Welderman and Stocks—no doubt across the street ordering burgers—as well as the man in the van; close, but still far.

Bernie inched closer to me and unfastened the top two buttons on my shirt.

I let him.

He leaned in closer—his breath stank of salami, coffee, and stale smoke. His crooked stained teeth matched his fingers. His eyes fluttered closed. Not completely, mind you. Apparently Bernie wanted to see what he was doing, but they closed to slits and he looked like a snake to me, a writhing, oily thing meant to creep across the ground.

"Not yet." I said this quietly as I turned my head to the side.

I knew what this was. I'd be lying if I said I didn't. My friend Bo Ridley had once shown me a newspaper story about a man in town who liked to corner little boys in dark places and do the kind of things that should never happen. The police hadn't caught him, but some local man did, and that man had cut off the other's penis and stuffed it in his mouth before slitting his throat, then left the body in an alley behind the supermarket with a CLOSED sign lying on his chest. I imagined Bernie holding a CLOSED sign under his chin, under those crooked teeth.

"We should get undressed first," I told him in a voice even softer than my last words, because I knew that was what he wanted. Those narrow, slitted eyes of his opened then, wide and bright, and he backed away from me slightly, a smile playing at the corner of his lip. His heart sped up. I could see a little vein throbbing on his temple, a crazy pitter-patter of excitement.

He removed his tie, folded it neatly, and set it on the nightstand. He cleared something from his throat, then took off his shoes. He unbuttoned his shirt after that, removed it, and placed it on the empty bed across from us. When his hands went to his belt, he paused. "You too."

I nodded and reached down to my shoes. They were brand new black dress shoes, still glimmering with polish. I tugged at the laces.

Vincent said he found the tools under the kitchen sink up at the house, and I wondered if sometime after I left, he had reached for the flathead screwdriver on the ground at his feet and noticed it was missing. He'd probably looked around the truck, maybe in the engine, trying to remember where he'd last used the flathead or set it down. It was only about six inches long, but fit nice and snug in my brand new sock. The tip was rusty but sharp.

Bernie was fuddling with his pants when I came up with it. He managed to scream, but not for very long.

65

Poole

Day 5 • 8:03 PM

Poole managed to catch a flight out of O'Hare direct to Charleston, but flying commercial had slowed him down. He'd arranged for a rental car while standing around the terminal in Chicago, but even that had proven to be time-consuming. After the plane touched down at Charleston International, they sat on the tarmac for nearly twenty minutes in some kind of line before they could get to a gate. Once off the plane, he'd run through the airport, dodging families, business people, and airport workers in golf carts, got to the rental car counter only to stand in another line. He fought the urge to pull out his badge every step of the way, knowing the moment he did a record would be made, and an entry in the wrong database would end up in SAIC Hurless's inbox.

Twenty-eight minutes after arriving at the rental car counter, he left airport grounds in a Toyota Rav4 smelling of cigarette smoke and industrial cleaner. Another forty-one minutes to get to the Charleston Police Department on Lockwood Drive, four minutes to explain what he needed to the desk sergeant, and twelve more sitting in a cluttered conference room…waiting.

Poole was eyeing the stained coffee pot on a credenza at the far end of the room when a man knocked twice on the door, came in, and introduced himself as Byron Locke, Assistant Chief of Police.

The first word that came into Poole's head at the sight of him was "beefy." About five-ten and maybe two-hundred-twenty pounds, the man was all muscle and no neck. He wore navy slacks, a white dress shirt with the sleeves rolled up past his elbows, and a loose blue tie. His gun and badge were clipped to his belt. He set two folders on the table and settled into a chair opposite Poole. "So, Officer Samuel Porter."

"Officer Samuel Porter," Poole repeated.

"Only a few of us still here from those days," Locke explained. "Amazing how fast the years go by. Feels like a week ago."

"You were here when Porter did his rookie time?"

Locke nodded. "I'd been on the force for two years when he signed up. We didn't work together, but I knew him. Hillburn, too. Both good men, from what I remember. Pulled their files to refresh my memory. I'm afraid there's not much here. Are you looking for something specific?"

Poole had put a lot of thought into that, but the truth was, he had no idea. In broad strokes, Bishop said Porter was trying to cover up something that happened in Charleston. Poole silently ran through his exact words—

He said she knew him, from his time in Charleston as a rookie. He said she was one of the last people alive who knew the truth about him. She was there, she saw me do it, she had to go.

Poole took out his phone and showed Locke a picture of the woman shot at the Guyon. "Do you recognize this woman at all?"

Locke studied the image. If the bullet hole in her forehead phased him at all, he didn't let on. After more than two decades in law enforcement, he'd most likely seen worse. "Should I know her?"

"We think she was involved in a case Porter worked on here in Charleston. Her name was Rose Finicky."

Locke reached for the phone in the center of the table and dialed an internal extension. When someone picked up, he repeated the name. A moment later, he placed his hand over the receiver and looked back at Poole. "Nothing by that name in our database. Do you have anything tying her to this area? Maybe an address or ID?"

Poole wasn't sure how much he wanted to share. "She may have run some kind of foster home or halfway house."

Locke spoke into the phone again, held up a finger, then shook his head. "Nothing in Department of Child Services, either. She'd be registered there if she worked in the system. You didn't get anything from her prints?"

Poole shook his head. "Nothing with photo recognition, either. I ran her through all the federal databases."

Locke hung up the phone and returned Poole's cell. "You've obviously got better resources than I do. If you can't find her, I'm not sure I can help you."

"What about Porter's case files? Would it be possible to get a look at those?"

"Porter was a beat cop. He didn't have case files. He was on traffic stops, domestic calls, that sort of thing."

"He told me he got shot trying to take down a local dealer. Made it sound like a case."

Locke considered this, flipped through the top file. "There's nothing here like that. His HR record lists the injury and his time out, but nothing to tie back to a specific case. I suppose he and his partner might have been working something—when you catch a specific beat you get to know the locals, both good and bad, you make your Santa list—those who are good and those who are bad—and your focus tends to narrow. If they were chasing a particular dealer, it wouldn't have been part of an official case. If it was, Narcotics would have worked it, not two rookies."

"The dealer's name was Weasel."

Locke held up his finger again, dialed another extension on the phone, and repeated the name to someone. He frowned before hanging up. "No Weasel in past or present narc cases. I'm sorry."

Poole looked down at the folders. "May I?"

Locke slid them across the table.

They didn't contain much. There was a photo of a much younger Sam Porter, one of Hillburn, too. Time-clock records. HR data. No citations. No notes. Nothing Poole couldn't have accessed from back in Chicago. Loose, at the back of Hillburn's file, was the report of his death.

"Wasn't sure if you wanted to see that," Locke told him. "I investigated that one myself. Ruled suicide in the end. His widow said he'd been depressed for nearly two years. Medicated for the last one. She caught him once with his service revolver in his mouth. I didn't hear about that until after, or we would have suspended him, gotten him help. He waited for her to go grocery shopping, then strung himself up in the basement." Locke slumped back. "The job gets to you after a while. I suppose I don't need to tell you that. Some of us learn to talk it out, work through some of the nastiness we see, others bottle up the bad things. I never took Hillburn for a bottler, but it's not always so obvious."

Pooled picked up a photograph of the note. "What can you tell me about this?"

Locke shrugged. "Bothered me, bothered everyone, I suppose. The handwriting was inconclusive. Most likely his but written under duress. Understandable, considering what he was about to do. Hillburn attended church, never struck us as an overly religious man, so 'Father, forgive me' wasn't completely off base, just odd. His own dad had been dead going on fifteen years. Seemed like a strange choice of words, not the kind of thing you think of on the fly, more like something you decided on after some thought. But I've never been much of a religious guy, so who knows."

"Did you ever suspect this was anything but suicide?"

Locke nearly laughed at that. "After this many years in law enforcement, somebody wishes me happy birthday and I suspect they're lying. I looked at everything I could find back then, but other than the note, nothing indicated foul play." He pulled a pen from his pocket and circled an address on one of the pages. "That's his widow. You can try talking to her. She's had plenty of time to think on it. Maybe she can help you."

66

Nash

Day 5 • 8:07 PM

Nash was standing in Porter's living room when Eisley finally came out of the bathroom. He needed to sit down, but between the federal and local CSI agents combing over every surface, there wasn't a chair to be had. When the feds arrived, he told them about the drywall in the La-Z-Boy. He didn't mention the diary that had previously occupied that space, no need to go there, but he couldn't hide the drywall. He was in this deep enough already. The four pieces were still on the floor, an evidence tag next to each. They'd been photographed by at least three people, and some agent he didn't recognize was hovering over them now, glaring down at them as if he could stare at them long enough that their true meaning would come to him like Vanna White turning letters.

Nash needed to sit because he felt like he might pass out. His stomach was a churning mess. He'd tried drinking a glass of water, and the moment the liquid hit his throat, it wanted out. He'd thrown up in Porter's kitchen sink. CSI wasn't too happy about that. He told them it was on account of seeing the body in the bathtub, but he knew he wasn't fooling anyone. One glance in the mirror told him he looked like the walking dead. When Eisley had arrived, he'd given Nash a surgical mask and told him to put it on. He'd assured Eisley it was just a cold or the flu. Eisley said that whatever it was, the mask would help prevent airborne contamination. He then told Nash to go home and rest. Nash couldn't do that. Instead, Nash watched everyone work and tried his best to stay on his feet.

Whatever didn't get upended by the feds got inspected by Metro's CSI. Nothing was overlooked. One agent had opened every seam in Porter's mattress and was busy inspecting between the coils. Another crawled along the floor and pulled up every board showing the slightest sign of being loose or tampered with. Nash remembered when Porter and Heather moved in here. She loved the hardwood floors. He hated the squeaks. He'd spent the better part of their first year nailing boards down, spreading baby powder and oils, trying anything he could to tone down the noise. He finally gave up. All those boards were up now as flashlight beams peered beneath.

"Maybe you should go to Stroger."

Nash jumped. Eisley was standing a foot away from him, and he hadn't noticed the man approach at all.

"You're sweating. Do you have a fever?"

"No," Nash lied.

Eisley rummaged through his pocket and produced an electronic thermometer. Before Nash could object, he brushed it over Nash's forehead. Nash tried not to think about where that thermometer had been.

"Hundred and one," Eisley said flatly. "Figured as much."

Eisley's eyes narrowed. "Were you exposed to those girls at the Upchurch house?"

"No," Nash lied.

"Then you most likely have the flu," Eisley determined. "You're going to fall over if you keep this up. You need to rest." From another pocket, he took out a pill bottle and handed it to Nash. "I had someone bring these over for you. Tamiflu. Should help. Take one now and two more in four hours."

Nash took three of them without water and dropped the bottle into his pocket. "Thanks."

"Porter's got ibuprofen in the bathroom. You should take a couple of those, too. They'll help with the fever."

Nash nodded. "How are you coming along in there?"

"Easier to show you."

Before Nash could respond, Eisley started back across the room, stepping around people, the missing floorboards, and various items tagged into evidence. He'd insisted nobody else enter the bathroom but him.

Like in most of these older buildings, Porter's bathroom wasn't large. Toilet, single sink, a small closet for towels and various sundry items, and a bathtub/shower combo. The curtain had been removed and placed in an evidence bag, same with all the items Porter had left on the counter around the sink. Just outside the door, Eisley had set up a small table, the surface covered with small vials filled with liquids of varying colors. Stacked beneath the table were more than a dozen evidence bags, each filled with salt. "I removed what I could without disturbing the body," Eisley said. "We'll get the rest after we take him out."

From the doorway, Nash could see the naked man in the bathtub. Eisley had slit the plastic open down the center and peeled it back like a cocoon, revealing the man inside. "What did he..."

The words trailed off as Nash tried to make sense of what he was looking at.

"He was tortured," Eisley said. "Nearly every inch of his skin. Someone wrote on him with a razor blade, or possibly a scalpel. *Hear no evil, see no evil, speak no evil, do no evil*...over and over again. I found a few *you are evil* mixed in there, too. *I am evil* on his forehead."

"Like Libby McInley?"

Eisley nodded. "Exactly like Libby McInley."

"Was he killed here?"

"No. Whoever did this took their time. It would have produced a lot of blood. He was awake for most of it. Neighbors would have heard the screaming. You've got a primary crime scene somewhere else, and he was transported here later."

"Is that why he's using salt? Like some kind of preservative?"

"I've been learning a lot about salt today." Eisley turned back to his table. "As a preservative, salt inhibits the growth of micro-organisms by drawing out water through osmosis. This prevents decomp and significantly distorts time of death. I'm working on a method to use the remaining saturation levels in the body to determine TOD, but I'm not there yet. Right now, I couldn't tell you if this man died forty-eight hours ago or a week ago. I don't think it's longer than that. He certainly didn't die today. Here's what interesting, though. I've got two types of salt here. The first isn't designed for human consumption at all—it contains high levels of sodium ferrocyanide and ferric ferrocyanide. He was exposed to that the longest. The second salt is primarily potassium chloride, consistent with the kind used in water softeners." He gestured at the plastic evidence bags. "That's what most of this is."

Nash tried to focus on this, but his thoughts were all muddled.

Eisley went on. "The two women found earlier today, the salt on their bodies matched both types. The first salt appears to be the same as the kind used on the roads to prevent icing. The second is used in water softeners."

Nash said, "Okay, so these people were killed, then stored in road ice?"

Eisley nodded. "When this body was placed here, someone poured water softener salt, the kind you can buy in large bags just about anywhere, on and around the body, then filled the bathtub with water. That caused the salt to leach in and around the plastic, partly contaminating my first sample. They might have done that to try and mask the original salt."

"To prevent us from figuring out where they're storing these bodies?"

"Storing the bodies *locally*," Eisley pointed out. "The body down in Simpsonville only had exposure to water softener salt. I confirmed about an hour ago with their local pathologist. I think that was just meant to confuse us, try to make them all look the same."

"Because they don't salt the roads in South Carolina," Nash thought aloud. "The killer wouldn't have access to that type."

Eisley nodded. "If I'm correct, you'll want to check all the salt storage buildings in and around the city. Your unsub killed these people and brought them to one for an undetermined length of time, then placed the bodies where you found them." Eisley lowered his voice and took a step closer to Nash. "With this victim, the question we really need to ask is, 'did our killer place him here to frame Sam or—'"

Nash interrupted him. "—or was Sam soaking the body, getting it ready for placement somewhere else? Is that what you're getting at? He wouldn't do that in his own apartment."

Eisley shrugged. "Sam's a smart guy. He knows all our countermeasures and methods. He might do it here simply because it's blatantly *not* the best place to do it."

Nash didn't respond to that. Instead, he stepped into the bathroom, opened Porter's medicine cabinet, and found the ibuprofen. As he took four pills, he looked back at the body. "Do you have any kind of ID?"

Before answering, Eisley glanced up at the words written in soap on the mirror. *Father, forgive me.*

"His prints came back as Vincent Weidner," Eisley said.

67
Diary

The man from the van was first through the door. Either Welderman had returned the key to him or he had another, but he got there fast and it made me wonder if the room was bugged and he had been listening in. Bernie was loud, but not so loud that the man should have heard him from across the parking lot. Or maybe he had. There was no way for me to be sure, with things moving so fast.

The tip of the screwdriver entered Bernie the first time just under his chin. I think it pierced his tongue before getting stuck in the roof of his mouth. I'd hoped it would get to his brain, but it wasn't long enough. His scream was more of a yelp, cut short by the impaled tongue, but you'd be surprised how much noise a person can make in a second like that. Without the use of his tongue, the scream turned into a guttural moan, still loud, just different. I tried to pull the screwdriver back out, but it was stuck good. I grabbed the phone off the nightstand instead and smashed it into Bernie's head. That quieted him down.

Van Man came through the door with his trench coat snapping in the wind, slammed the door at his back, took in Bernie on the floor trying to stand (and failing) before turning on me. I'd never seen a face as red as his, and I found myself shrinking deeper into the room, toward the bathroom at the back. He ran at me, shoulder first, and slammed into my chest. I fell back, and when I hit the ground, he came down on top with all his weight. *My right arm folded awkwardly beneath both of us, and I heard a sickening SNAP! like a branch under a car tire, and the worst pain followed a moment later, running down my arm to my chest. I let out a scream of my own. Bernie was still louder, though. Somehow he had managed to find his voice even with that screwdriver sticking through half his face.*

Van Man climbed off me, crossed the room over to Bernie, and did something I didn't expect. He snatched a pillow off the bed and pressed it against Bernie's face with his left hand while his right produced a hand-gun. The pillow reduced the blast to a muffled thump.

68

Poole

Day 5 • 9:07 PM

"I should have moved, but I just couldn't bring myself to do it. My parents left me this house. I grew up here." The widow of Derrick Hillburn, Robin Hillburn, looked up from the cup of tea in her hands and nodded toward some marks on the kitchen door jam. "Those are all me, when I was a little girl. One mark for every month from the time I was able to stand until around fourteen— when I was too cool for that sort of thing and made them stop."

Poole sat across from her at the Formica table. His hands wrapped around a mug of tea he had yet to drink. By the time he'd left Charleston PD, it was well after eight. He considered getting a hotel room for the night and starting fresh in the morning, but he knew he wouldn't be able to sleep, particularly after Nash called and told him about Vincent Weidner's body in Porter's apartment.

Robin Hillburn was in her mid-fifties, at least fifty pounds over-weight, and dressed in a gray sweatsuit. Her straggly hair was pulled back in a loose ponytail, and she wore no makeup. When he knocked on her door at a little after nine, she'd stared at his badge from the other side, the chain between them. When he told her why he was on her doorstep, he half expected her to slam the door, but she didn't. Instead, she sighed and let him in. "Every couple years, one of you seems to come by. Suppose tonight is as good a night as any."

She'd led him through a crowded living room to the kitchen, the house itself caught in a time capsule of shag carpet and wallpaper, knick-knacks, and dusty furniture. From the television, a preacher droned on about the failure of social society and how the Internet was raising our kids.

Robin took a sip of her tea and wiped the side of her mouth with the back of her hand. "When Derrick...when he died...all I wanted to do was run, get as far away from here as I could. I went to stay with my sister in St. Louis for a few weeks, but after a while, I got so homesick. I came back and Derrick was gone, all his stuff was packed up. All the other things that reminded me of home—things I missed—those were still here. After a couple days, I settled back in. Like an old blanket or a familiar chair. I couldn't picture myself anywhere else. I still saw reminders of Derrick around, but this place was my home long before I met him, and I knew it would continue to be my home."

There was no delicate way to ask this, so Poole came right out with it. "Did you find him?"

Robin nodded. "I'd been grocery shopping, and when I came home, I yelled for him to help me unload. His car was in the driveway, so I knew he was home. The second I stepped through the door, though, I was sure something was wrong. I checked upstairs first, then the bathrooms, looked out back. Didn't think to check the basement, not right away. Nothing down there but the laundry, and he avoided that like the plague, but after I checked everything else and didn't turn him up, I went down there." She paused a moment and blew on her tea. "Didn't seem real when I first saw him. Felt like watching a scene from a movie. He was just hanging there from the rafters, all quiet, nothing moving. The first thing I thought of, can't explain why, was where did he get the rope? I didn't recognize it. Turns out the receipt was in his pocket. He'd bought it that morning." She waved a hand around. "There was all this hushed talk—he didn't do it, someone else did it, especially after reading the note. I knew he did, though. It was that damn receipt that convinced me."

"Could someone have planted the receipt?"

"Nope. Not a chance."

"How can you be sure?"

Robin sighed. "Derrick did this thing with receipts. He liked to roll them. I'd find them in his pockets all the time like that, never failed. This one was rolled the same way as any other."

A partner would know to roll it. Partners new each other better than most married couples.

Poole shook the thought from his head. "Did he ever mention the name Rose Finicky to you?"

She shook her head.

"Vincent Weidner?"

"Nope."

"How about a Detective Freddy Welderman or Ezra Stocks?"

"I think I'd remember a name like Ezra. He never mentioned anyone named Freddy, either."

"Anson Bishop?"

She took another drink of her tea. "I know that one from TV, but Derrick was long gone before all that business ever came up."

"What about a drug dealer named Weasel?"

She shook her head again.

"Did he discuss his work with you at all?"

"Only that he didn't like it much and was considering a change. Talked about that a lot, but it was mostly talk. He got into law enforcement because he wanted to help people. Derrick was a kind soul like that. Like any other boy, he grew up idolizing cops, but once he got into that world, he realized it was nothing like television. I imagine you know what I mean. He spent shift after shift with the worst humanity has to offer, and it took a toll on him. We were both raised on the Good Book, and he thought he could help everyone. After a number of years on the job, he realized that wasn't the case. Rather than him showing them the light, they showed him the dark. The dark engulfed him. Derrick got depressed. Obviously, more so than even I realized."

"Did he get along with his partner?"

"Which one? He had a couple."

"Sam Porter."

"Is he the one who got shot?"

Poole nodded.

"Those two were thick as thieves for a while there. Like brothers. When Sam got shot, that spooked Derrick. Looking back, I think that was the start of his slide. He blamed himself. I guess any partner would. Took to drinking for a little while after Sam left. Luckily that didn't stick. Suppose if it did, he wouldn't have hung in with the job as long as he did. I can tell you one thing—Sam was the only partner he ever brought home for dinner. I think he vowed never to get too close to another after all that business. He spent a lot more time at home after Sam, that's for sure."

"Derrick traveled?"

Robin nodded. "He and Sam took a few overnight trips for some case or another. Never said what it was about. I didn't ask. Figured he'd tell me if he wanted me to know."

"Do you know where they went?"

She shook her head. "They drove, so not too far."

Poole glanced around the kitchen, at the cluttered shelves. "You said after Derrick died, you stayed with your sister for a few weeks and while you were gone, somebody packed up his belongings?"

She nodded. "Some of the guys from the force. They boxed up everything and put it out in the garage. It's all still out there. You're welcome to go through it, if you like. Just do me a favor—whatever you don't want, put out at the curb. I think it's time I rid myself of all that."

69

Porter

Day 5 • 9:08 PM

Porter took the files.

He wasn't going to apologize for that.

He'd pulled over on the side of Mount Cleary Road just before the I-26 on-ramp, about three miles from Camden Treatment Center and looked down at the two folders on the passenger seat.

Bishop's folder was damn near empty. He was brought in immediately following the fire at his home and only stayed for a handful of weeks. He received several medications, mostly for anxiety, and was released into the foster custody of David and Cindy Watson, residents of Woodstock, Illinois, just as Bishop had said in his interview with Poole. Not a single scrap of paper was signed by Dr. Oglesby—he wasn't mentioned at all, only Dr. Victor Whittenberg. As *he* had said. Porter grilled him on it for nearly three hours, and the man didn't falter. His story didn't change at all. Porter ran him through it forwards, backwards, and sideways, and he didn't slip once. Whittenberg believed every word he told him.

It was the look on Whittenberg's face that made things worse. Pity, misplaced compassion—whatever it was, Porter hadn't liked it one bit. This only got worse when they talked about the contents of the folder with *his* name on it.

Porter felt this distinction was important.

The folder had his name on it—but he didn't consider it *his folder*. He'd read the stack of lies three times with the doctor watching him curiously, like some caged animal. His eyes darting to that little recorder on his desk from behind those ridiculous glasses every few minutes to ensure the device was still working.

Porter had taken that, too. Right along with the files.

Fuck him.

He wasn't there to make friends. He was there to get answers.

Nothing in the folder with his name on it made sense.

Porter knew he had lost time. The bullet to the back of the head had seen to that. Fluid elicit retrograde amnesia, that's what they called it. When he'd woken from the coma, that first time he'd seen his future wife, Heather, they discovered the damage. Most of his memories were intact; childhood, teen years, even recent events were all still there. But there were big blank spots, entire months and years missing. He remembered the tests for this at the hospital in Charleston, always with Heather present. He remembered his extended stay there, the ensuing treatment and rehab leading up to his release. He recalled taking and passing the necessary steps to get back on the force, to be reinstated—Heather with him every step of the way.

Not once did he set foot in Camden Treatment Center.

Not once did he meet this Dr. Victor Whittenberg.

Whittenberg never treated him.

Yet, this file said otherwise. Nearly four months meticulously documented. His release from the hospital in Charleston to his extended stay at Camden—paperwork, insurance records, notes, progress reports.

Porter stomped the gas and pulled back out onto the road.

Fifty.

Sixty.

Seventy miles-per-hour.

None of it could possibly be true, because that would mean everything else was a lie, including his early memories with Heather, and that was not something he was about to accept.

Porter rewound the microcassette and hit play. Static poured out of the tiny speaker. After about thirty seconds, he hit the fast-forward button, then play again. More static. Fumbling with the buttons while trying to keep an eye on the road, he hit fast forward again and still only found static. He tried three more times before finally giving up and throwing the recorder down into the passenger foot well.

Bishop is fucking with you.

All Bishop. Had to be. The files. The tape. All fake, just like the Simpsonville property records.

Porter told himself that, repeated it several times, because there was no other explanation.

Focus, Sam. Stay focused.

It took every ounce of his willpower to keep from throwing everything out into the street and watching the wind take it all away.

Sam drew in a breath, forced his head to clear, and consulted the notes he had made on the plane. It was going to be a long night.

A minute later, he was back on I-26 south pushing his borrowed SUV well above the posted speed limit.

70
Diary

They didn't want to take me to the hospital, Van Man and Stocks; it was Welderman who insisted. Not because he cared about me or the amount of pain I was in. No, he was just as mad as the other two. I heard him say that if my arm didn't heal properly, the deformity would cost them on the back end.

"Then we write him off," Van Man replied. "No hospitals. If you need me to call the boss, I will, but he won't be happy. Not at this hour."

That seemed to settle that.

No hospital.

A very angry Welderman dragged me back to the Malibu while Van Man and Stocks wrapped Bernie in a comforter and loaded him into the back of the van. Stocks asked me what I touched in the room and I told him. Then he was gone again. I knew there was blood everywhere— Bernie was a bleeder, and I knew he'd made a mess. I was covered in it, but apparently they were more concerned with prints. I expected someone in the motel to hear all the noise and come out to see what was going on, or call the police, or something, but nobody did. We were back on the road in under fifteen minutes.

I cradled my broken arm against my chest. With each bump in the road, I felt the two sides of the broken bone grind against each other. The break was just below my elbow—the ulna bone, I would learn later—and my arm was swelling up fast. The skin had grown hot and purple in color.

More than once, Welderman shouted for me to shut up, but I couldn't stifle the whimpers dropping from my lips if my life depended on it (and part of me thought it just might). The ride back to Finicky's might have been the longest of my life.

The white van left her driveway at about the halfway point, cutting out across the field while we drove right up to the front door.

They must have called ahead, because Finicky was standing there under the porch light with a blanket wrapped over her shoulders. "Get him inside, in the kitchen." Then she turned and stomped through the door.

If I thought the ride back was painful, the walk from the car to the kitchen was ten times worse. At one point, Welderman and Stocks tried to pick me up, said I was moving too slow, but something in my eyes must have told them to back off, because they did. The two of them shuffled next to me, about a foot away, just close enough to keep me heading in the right direction.

Dr. Oglesby was in the kitchen. He looked up from a newspaper and nodded at the table. "Put him up there."

I blocked out most of what happened next.

Welderman and Stocks were told to hold me down while Finicky put a leather belt in my mouth and told me to bite down hard and not let go. Oglesby cut away my shirtsleeve and studied the break for a moment. When his fingers stopped prodding at my arm, he tightened his grip, one hand on either side of the break, looked at me for a moment, then—

I passed out then. I didn't think the pain could get worse, but the pain most certainly did, and that wash of hurt came with a blinding white light, then nothing. When I woke, Oglesby was busy wrapping my arm in cloth strips dripping with plaster. I could hear Welderman and Van Man shouting at each other somewhere else in the house.

Finicky saw that I was awake and leaned down next to my head. "If you ever do something like that again, I'll let each of these gentlemen gang rape your little girlfriend while you watch. I'll let them violate every hole in that sorry bitch. And when they get tired of her, I'll slit her fucking throat and drop her out in the fields for the crows to pick at. While you're under my roof, you live by my rules, and you'll earn your keep." She licked at her chapped lips. "You think Bernie was bad? Wait until the next one. Just wait. I'll give the next one a free pass to do whatever the fuck he wants with you. You'll learn. You'll see. Or I'll dig a hole for you out back myself. Welderman kept the screwdriver. It's got your prints all over it. You tell anyone what happened, and he'll make sure you're charged with Bernie's murder." She leaned in closer. "I own you, you little shit."

Oglesby left medication for the pain but Finicky pocketed the bottle for herself. She told me, "I want you to hurt." Then told me to go up to my room.

Paul was awake when I gently lowered myself onto my bed. "You flubbed that up good," was all he said.

71

Poole

Day 5 • 9:15 PM

The two-car detached garage sat behind the Hillburn house at the end of a cracked blacktop driveway under the unkempt branches of a willow tree that looked like it might topple over with the next breeze. Robin Hillburn had given Poole the key, but he found the side door to be unlocked. That didn't mean it was willing to open. Whether from moisture, old paint, or copious amounts of glue, the door was stuck and had been for a very long time. Poole put his shoulder into it, and after several hits the door rattled and finally gave, the bottom grinding against the concrete.

He located a light switch on the right of the door frame, but when he flicked it, the bulb hanging from the center beam only sparked for a brief second before going dark with a dry pop. He activated the flashlight on his phone and swept the space with the beam instead.

Spiderwebs dripped from the ceiling. White, tangled, thick knots of them. Brown recluse spiders were indigenous to South Carolina—he'd read that somewhere—but so were many other spiders. He couldn't tell what had spun these particular webs, and no spiders were visible, but he felt their eyes on him, an intruder in their home.

Of the two parking spaces, the one nearest the door was filled with boxes of all shapes and sizes.

In the second bay sat an old white panel van.

Tires flat, the rubber rotted and split, windows caked with dust. The paint lined with rust and filth. Poole had always found it odd that someone could allow a vehicle to waste away in some dark corner, but he had seen his share over the years. Most likely Derrick Hillburn drove this one, and his wife either had no use for it or couldn't bear the memories it might contain. Easier to forget than to even attempt to sell.

Poole stepped over and around the boxes, swiping at the webs with his forearm, sneezing more times than he could count with the agitated dust. He reached the garage door at the front, located the release handle, and tugged the door up. Like the side door, this one fought back, rollers protesting loudly every inch up their track. But he managed to get the door open and welcomed the rush of cold air from outside.

Several mice scurried from the shadowed mess inside, darted out the opening, and vanished in the unkempt grass. One stopped long enough to look up at Poole. It was possibly the largest mouse he'd ever seen—all twitchy nose and glowing eyes, the rodent stood on its haunches and glared at him before turning and chasing after the others.

From the house, a floodlight positioned under the eaves and pointing back toward the garage door flipped on. Poole shielded his eyes and found Robin Hillburn standing in the window of a backdoor. She raised a hand and offered him a tentative wave before disappearing back into the house.

The light strained to reach into the garage, the mouth of the building somehow holding the light at bay. It was better than his flashlight, though, so it would have to do. There was no simple way to tackle this project, so Poole went at it the only way he knew how—one box at a time. Starting with the first box within reach, he carried it from the garage out to the driveway, opened the flaps at the top, and riffled through the contents. Jeans and pants, a few dozen pairs, all musty and riddled with moth bites. The next five boxes proved to be more of the same—T-shirts, sweaters, socks. He couldn't bring himself to throw these things away as Robin Hillburn had asked so he separated items as he went—anything worth donating went to the right side of the driveway, the rest went on the left. Derrick Hillburn had his share of junk, too.

Forty minutes later, dripping with sweat, Poole hadn't found a damn thing.

He was considering knocking on the kitchen door to get a glass of water when his eyes drifted over to the van.

Derrick Hillburn (or whoever drove it last) backed it into the garage with the driver's side butted against the side wall and the back of the van tight against the back wall of the garage. Poole hadn't thought about it earlier, but this meant that whoever parked the van would have needed to climb out through the passenger door. That made no sense. If they meant to park in such a way to leave as much storage space in the garage as possible, why not just pull in?

Over the years, several towers of boxes had tumbled over against the passenger side, blocking access there too. Poole focused his attention on those boxes, carrying them out to the driveway with the others, checking each as he went, until he'd cleared a path to the passenger door—locked.

He tried shining his flashlight inside but couldn't see much. A partition separated the passenger compartment of the van from the back with a narrow access door positioned behind the two front seats.

Poole checked the exposed wheel wells for a magnetic key but didn't find one. Nothing under the bumper, either—what he could reach, anyway. Glancing back at the house, he noticed all the interior lights were out. Robin Hillburn had most likely gone to bed.

Poole considered breaking the window but knew the noise might draw unwanted attention. Instead, he plucked a wire hanger from one of the boxes in the driveway, straightened out the metal, and fashioned a small hook at one end. He forced the wire between the window seal and glass and twisted it back and forth until the hook brushed over the chrome nub of the door lock. He made five attempts before finally catching the top—he yanked up and popped the lock.

When Poole opened the door, stale air rushed out at him, somehow colder than the garage—ancient trapped air eager to escape. The dust on the cracked leather seat was so thick, he thought the seats were gray until he ran his finger over one and discovered they were originally black.

He opened the glove box. There was a .38 inside along with two boxes of ammunition and a leather belt holster. Vehicle registration. Owner's manual. A half-eaten roll of Rolaids. Nothing else.

In the cupholder near the stick shift sat an old can of Pepsi. Liquid along the rim had long ago gummed up and evaporated, leaving a black tar-like ring behind. An old navy-blue trench coat was bunched up and lying on the floor.

Poole climbed in and leaned over the metal door leading to the back, tried the latch and found it unlocked. The door groaned on tired hinges as it swung back and away.

Flashlight out again, he edged closer and peered into the back.

There was a green duffle bag near the wheel well. Written across the side in black Sharpie, faded with age, was a single word.

Porter.

A gym bag, maybe. Possibly something Porter used to transport his dirty laundry from the locker room at Charleston PD to home and back. Not completely out of place in his partner's van. Not something Poole was about to ignore, either. He'd check it in a moment, because something else had caught his eye.

Some kind of bundle at the far end—black garbage bags or plastic around something entwined in circles of duct tape, sealed up tight.

Unsure of what he'd find in Hillburn's possessions, Poole had been wearing latex gloves, but they were torn in several places and covered in grime. He peeled them off and put on a fresh pair before climbing into the back of the van. He glanced at the bag, but it was the bundle that had his attention, nearly five feet long. He'd carried a knife since he was a kid, and Poole found himself reaching for it in his front left pocket before remembering he'd flown commercial and he left both his knife and gun back in Chicago rather than risk appearing on a list that might cross SAIC Hurless's desk. Even when checking a bag containing a weapon, federal agents were required to disclose the firearm at the counter. That information went into a database which automatically cross-referenced against current assignments. Anomalies were flagged, and Poole had no intention of becoming an anomaly.

Pulling a section of the black plastic tight, Poole poked his finger through.

A sickly sweet scent crept out, one he sadly recognized.

He leaned back on his heels and pinched his nose.

72

Diary

"Christ, kid, that took balls."

Vincent was leaning against the bumper of the truck, Kristina beside him. Libby sat on the ground next to me, with Paul standing near the door, watching the path leading up from the house. Weasel and The Kid were playing in the loft. Tegan had gone to town with Finicky.

For the most part, they all knew what happened last night. I filled in the blanks.

"They buried him out in the field." Paul pointed off into the distance. "I found the spot on my way here easy enough. He's only about twenty feet off the path in the weeds."

"We should call the cops," Kristina said. "They'll take away Finicky. They'll take them all away."

We all knew we couldn't.

Vincent took her hand. That might have been the first time I ever saw him appear even remotely affectionate toward someone else. He let go when he noticed Libby and me watching. "Welderman and Stocks are the cops. They'll pin it all on Anson, just like Finicky said. Then things just get worse for the rest of us 'cause we'll still be stuck here. We need to stick with the plan." He thumped a hand against the truck. "We fix this thing, then we all run together. We get to Charleston or some other big city where we can vanish."

Kristina frowned. "They'll just come after us."

"Welderman and Stocks are the cops here," *Vincent pointed out. "Once we get away, they can't touch us. They wouldn't risk alerting the authorities outside their little circle."*

"We don't know how big their 'little circle' really is," I pointed out.

Vincent's eyes met mine. "And we won't know until we try to run, until we test their limits."

"They'll kill us," Paul said. "Think of the pictures in the house. Where do you think those kids are?" He turned back toward the door and looked out over the large field, at the tall blades of grass, weeds, and patches of wheat waving in the wind. "I'll tell you where—they're all out there somewhere, eating dirt with Anson's buddy Bernie. Finicky's got a revolving door on this place. How many others have we seen come and go? They leave one night and don't come back. There are hundreds of kids on those walls."

I looked up at him. "Last night they argued about taking me to a hospital for my arm. I heard Welderman say if it wasn't set properly, they'd lose money on the back end. They could have killed me, just like you said, but they didn't. They were more concerned with making sure there was no permanent damage."

Paul's eyes narrowed. "What, like you can't sell a car easily if it's got a dent?"

I hadn't thought of it like that, and I don't think I wanted to.

Kristina went pale. "They're planning to sell us? What, so the things they make us do at that motel, that's not enough? No way. Sell us to who? You guys are crazy." She'd gotten down off the bumper and began pacing the barn. She kept talking, but I couldn't make out the rest; she said it too low.

"August twenty-ninth," I said in a quiet voice.

Vincent, who had been watching Kristina, turned back to me. "What?"

"August twenty-ninth is circled on Finicky's calendar in the kitchen. Same with Dr. Oglesby's calendar at his office. Whatever they have planned, that must be the day."

"What's today?"

This was Libby. She'd been silent through most of the conversation.

"The eleventh," Kristina said.

Libby ran her hand over the plaster cast on my arm. "That's only eighteen days from now. This won't heal that fast."

"She's right," Vincent said. "I broke my arm a few years back, and the cast stayed on for six weeks. No way that thing is coming off in less than three."

Paul grunted. "They probably don't care if it's completely healed. Sounds like they're more concerned with healed enough to look normal. The last time mine got broke, the plaster came off in two weeks, and I had to keep it in a sling for another two." He raised his left arm up over his head and twisted it around. "Healed up fine. I just had to be careful with it."

"How many of you have broken bones?" I asked.

Everyone's hand went up. Even The Kid leaned out over the edge of the loft and held a hand out.

"Welcome to foster care, Mr. Bishop," Paul muttered.

I'd never broken anything before, and I certainly had no plans to let it happen again. My arm hurt something awful. Not as bad as last night, but still bad.

"I've had six broken bones," Libby said beside me. "When it happens, they just move you to another foster home, like that's gonna solve everything. Fill out a couple forms and bury it at the back of your file. Maybe a couple of therapy sessions to sort out the details. I'm sure there are good foster homes out there, but there are lots of bad ones, too."

Paul spun an imaginary roulette wheel. "Sometimes you land on black, sometimes you land on red, sometimes your ball stops smack in the middle of black and blue."

Vincent broke a clump of dirt off the truck bumper and tossed it at him. "You're an idiot."

Paul sidestepped, and the dirt flew through the open door. "Watch it. I've got to stay pretty for the big sale." He slid his hands down his sides. "I'm not gonna let all this go to some bargain basement shopper."

"You're a serious fucking idiot," Vincent said, shaking his head.

"August twenty-ninth," I said again. "Can you get the truck running before then?"

Vincent didn't look up. "I don't know. I've got most of the engine cleaned out. The carburetor was a bitch, but I think I got it. I think the tires are okay, but I won't know until we try to get air into them, and we can't do that without a pump. I need to replace a bunch of hoses and belts, the spark plugs—"

"We got you money," Kristina pointed out.

He gave her a sideways glance. "You did. Turns out money isn't really much of a problem anymore. I found something." He slid off the bumper and crossed the barn to a stack of crates near the back corner and pulled several away, then tugged at the floorboards. They came up far easier than they should. The rest of us followed over.

Paul was the first to whistle. "Oh, man."

There were dozens of bundles—stacks of cash wrapped in plastic. Some loose, others in bags.

"Are all of those bags filled with money?" Tegan said quietly, barely audible.

Vincent blew out a breath. "I wish they were."

He grabbed a red backpack and pulled the zipper open. The bag contained girl's clothing, damp with mildew. "About half are filled with clothes, boys' and girls'. The rest have money. Might be a few hundred thousand dollars here. I tried to go through everything without disturbing it much. We don't want them to know we found all this."

"From the other kids," Paul said.

"Yeah, some of them, anyway." Vincent sealed up the red backpack and put it back where he found it. "Doesn't really matter if we have all the money in the world if we can't buy what we need."

"There's a Discount Auto across the street from the motel, about a quarter block down from the gas station. I saw it last night," I said.

Vincent's eyes were back on the ground. "Yeah, I've seen it too. Can't get to it, though. Not with those guys hovering over us. It might as well be a thousand miles from here."

Father would tell me to puzzle it out. He always said every problem has multiple solutions, and even though they may seem distant or impossible to grasp, those solutions were only a thought away.

Beside me, Libby said, "Who's going next? To the motel?"

Kristina pointed up at the loft. "Those two, tonight. Tegan said that's why Finicky wanted to go to town today. Finicky was mad because nobody told her she was supposed to buy clothes for them. She could have gotten something when she bought that stuff for Anson. Had to run back out today."

Turns out, I wouldn't be the one to puzzle it out. It was Libby.

73

Poole

Poole knew he'd need to make a phone call. Sifting through someone's discarded life under the radar was one thing, but he was certain there was a body wrapped in that plastic, and that was not something he was prepared to go alone. At a length of only five feet or so, this was either a child, a woman, or someone dismembered. He was fairly certain it had been here as long as the van—the dust told him that. If the van had been here first and the body placed later, the dust wouldn't be so evenly dispersed. Subtle disturbances, the remains of tracks, that sort of thing would be visible. Aside from his own, he saw none of that.

There was a good chance Hillburn killed himself because of that body.

Poole backed up slowly, doing his best to place his feet and knees in his existing tracks to avoid further contaminating the scene. When the dust tickled at the inside of his nose, he sneezed into the crook of his elbow, not once but twice, and he couldn't help but think about how sick Nash looked the last time he saw him. How Nash had promised it was just a cold or the flu.

At the green duffle, Poole settled back on his knees and ran the beam of the flashlight over the material. Like everything else inside the van, the dust formed an undisturbed coating—thicker and gray at the top, fading to the original green down the sides. He took several photos from various angles with his phone, then reached for the zipper and forced it open. Inside, he found a light blue dress shirt, black slacks, a pair of loafers, a dark-colored tie, socks, and underwear. The clothing had been shredded, some torn, other pieces cut, but all in rags. Nearly all of it was covered in dry, crusty blood. Under the clothing, he found an old Canon with a telephoto lens. There was also a black and white composition book identical to Bishop's diaries held together with a rubber band. The band snapped when Poole tried to peel it off.

He brought the light closer and peered down at the first few pages.

Dates, times, random notes and observations. This was some kind of log, possibly from a stakeout. Poole didn't recognize the handwriting. A closer inspection would be necessary, but from what he recalled, this wasn't a match for Bishop. He didn't think it was Porter's writing, either. Maybe Hillburn, maybe someone else entirely. These things were always difficult with the passage of time. A person's handwriting was fluid, always evolving. An expert might be able to match similarities with proper study. Inside the bag, there were also three bundles of cash. Hundred-dollar bills. If the number on the band was correct, each bundle held ten thousand dollars.

Poole stared down at all of this for a moment, then packed everything back in the bag, tugged the zipper closed, and tossed the bag into the front seat before climbing out after it. With the bag in hand, he exited the van. Standing in the driveway, he drew in several breaths of fresh air, then dialed a number.

"Granger," a gruff voice answered.

"Hey, it's Frank. Are you still out at that lake in Simpsonville?"

"We wrapped up there a few hours ago. I'm back at the hotel. Why?"

Poole knew the moment he told SAIC Granger where he was, it would get back to Hurless, but he didn't have much of a choice. He turned back around, faced the garage, and ran his hand through his hair. "I've got a secondary crime scene. It may be connected."

"Where?"

"Charleston. Sam Porter's old partner." He explained what he had found.

Granger took this all in, then said, "Do you have anything tying the Simpsonville body back to Porter? The one at the courthouse?"

Not yet.

"No," Poole replied.

"We'll need to reexamine everything from that angle. If Porter is a suspect, we need to reexamine *everything*."

Poole didn't reply to that. His phone vibrated with another incoming call. He glanced at the display. It read *South Carolina State Police*. "I need to take this."

"Secure the scene—I'll call the local field office and get a team there. I'll drive in, but that will take me a few hours," Granger replied before hanging up.

Poole accepted the other call. "Special Agent Poole."

"This is Lieutenant Miggins with SCSP. My office just picked up an alarm call from that old psychiatric facility, Camden. Possible break-in. Description of a man leaving the scene matches your BOLO for Sam Porter. I've got a unit out there right now—he said one of the offices is covered in blood. The lobby, too. No body, no reported injuries… nothing yet, anyway, but it's clear something bad happened there. I'm heading out there myself but figured best to give you a call first. You're listed as the contact on the BOLO."

"How sure are you it was Sam Porter?"

"A security guard called it in—said he recognized Porter from television. 100 percent certain. He said Porter left in a dark SUV, got a partial plate. I'm texting it to you now."

Poole looked down at the duffle bag beside him, then into the garage.

He caught a movement from the corner of his eye—at the end of the driveway. He turned back around. "Lieutenant? Let me call you back in a few minutes."

The lieutenant said something else, but Poole hung up.

The floodlights cast the man in shadow but Poole could tell who it was. He stood silently at the edge of the driveway. "What are you doing here, Sam?"

Porter took a step closer. "I thought Robin might know something about the night I was shot. Maybe something Derrick told her."

"She doesn't."

"I'd like to ask her myself."

Poole tried to keep his voice calm. "Maybe you should put the gun away first."

Porter's left arm was extended, pointing some kind of small revolver. .38 or .22—he couldn't tell from this distance. Poole regretted leaving his gun in Chicago.

Porter stepped closer. "You're digging around through someone else's possessions in the middle of the night. Someplace you have no business being. This has nothing to do with the case."

"I have a warrant."

"No, you don't. You wouldn't be alone." Porter glanced back at the house. "Where's Robin? What did you do to her?"

"She gave me permission. Put the gun down, and we can talk about it."

Porter shook his head. "Take out your gun, slow and easy, by the butt, and toss it off into the grass."

"I don't have one on me." He told him he flew commercial.

"Take off your jacket, then turn in a slow circle. All the way around."

Poole dropped the jacket at his feet, then shuffled through a full turn until he was facing the other man again.

Porter pointed the gun down toward his ankles. "Lift up the bottom of your pants, both sides."

Poole did that, too, showed him he wasn't carrying any kind of weapon.

"Those were cuffs, right? Attached to the back of your belt?"

"You don't want to go there, Sam. You're already pointing a gun at a federal agent."

"I'm pointing a gun at a rogue law enforcement officer who

took advantage of a grieving widow to conduct an unlawful search of her deceased husband's possessions in the middle of the night."

"I've got backup on the way. I already called this in."

"I heard you."

"Then you also know there's a body in there." Poole nodded back toward the van.

"I don't know anything about that." He glanced down at the green duffle, squinting as he read his name. "That's not mine. I hate green. What's in it?"

Poole told him.

"Did you bring that bag with you? Were you about to plant it in the van? That's what this looks like. You planting evidence."

Poole forced himself to maintain eye contact. "Why would I do that? I found it. In the van."

"Somebody's trying to frame me—Bishop, somebody working with Bishop. Maybe multiple people working with Bishop."

"I have no reason to frame you, Sam."

"I'm not stupid enough to leave a bag with my name on it with a body inside in my partner's old piece-of-shit van, so how exactly did it get there? Who put it there if it wasn't you?"

"It's been there for a long time. As long as the van's been parked."

"Bishop, then. I haven't killed anyone."

Poole started to lower his arms but froze when he saw Porter's finger tighten on the trigger. He stared down the barrel. "If you're not guilty, put the gun away and we can talk."

"I'm going to keep the gun on you to make sure you listen. I can't risk getting locked up right now."

"You're making a big mistake, Sam."

Porter waved the revolver. "Take out your handcuffs and put them on. Cuff yourself in the front so I can see."

Poole considered running. If he dove to the side, out of the light, he had a chance at hitting the ground and getting to cover before Porter could get off a good shot. Revolvers were only accurate at about ten feet, and Porter was nearly twice that far from him. He had to assume Porter was proficient with firearms, though, not the average shooter, and he seemed oddly calm.

"You called this in seven minutes ago. The local field office is a little more than twenty minutes away. If agents are coming in from their homes, they might be closer. I'll give you one minute to do as I say. If you don't, I'm putting one in your leg and taking you out of this fight. I can't risk getting locked up right now," Porter repeated before glancing up and down the empty street.

Poole eyed him. "I do this, then what?"

"I take you with me. We figure this out together."

Poole didn't answer.

"If I wanted to kill you, I could do it right here, right now. You know that. There are no witnesses. Your team would show up, and I'd be willing to bet they wouldn't find any forensic evidence. My prints aren't even on these slugs. I'd be in the wind before you finished bleeding out."

"You wouldn't kill me."

This time it was Porter who said nothing.

Poole reached behind his back.

Porter's arm grew stiff. "Slow."

Poole's handcuffs were in a leather case on the backside of his belt. He unsnapped it and took them out. Moving carefully, not willing to spook Porter, he first locked them on his left wrist, then his right.

"Tighter."

Poole did as he asked. If Sam noticed the light turn on in the second-floor window of the Hillburn house, he didn't acknowledge it. Poole saw a shadow in the window as the curtain moved aside. "Now what?" he asked Porter.

"Now you get that bag and come with me."

Poole nodded and did as he was told.

74

Nash

Day 5 • 10:02 PM

Nash woke in his car, no recollection of getting behind the wheel. He didn't even remember leaving Porter's apartment. He was still parked on Porter's street; thank God he hadn't tried to drive. Through the layer of snow on his windshield, he could still see the various Metro cars, federal vehicles, and CSI vans parked about half a block up the road from him. His engine was sputtering, coughing heat through the vents with sporadic gasps. He was thankful he had at least had the good sense to start the car at some point, even if he had no recollection of doing so. Every bone in his body ached. He couldn't breathe through his nose, and his throat felt like a wild cat spent an hour in there sharpening its claws. It was his phone that had woken him, an incoming call. The iPhone danced in his cup holder as it rang again.

Klozowski.

Nash fumbled with the device and answered the call on speaker. "Yeah?"

"What the hell? I've been calling you for an hour!"

The phone felt like an ice cube in his hand. Nash flicked the heat switch to full and heard something behind the dash groan in protest. He couldn't stop shivering. "I feel like shit, Kloz."

"You too? Ah, man. You probably picked it up at Upchurch's

house. Nobody's told you to come here? You shouldn't be running around. You're probably infecting everyone."

"Gotta find Sam. Gotta find Bishop. Gotta find the…" Nash remembered he wasn't allowed to discuss the mayor and managed to pinch off the word before it got out.

"The mayor is missing."

This took a moment to sink in. Nash's thoughts were all muddy. "How do you know about the mayor?"

"What? No, not the mayor. *Clair* is missing." He dropped off for a second. "Wait, is the mayor missing, too?"

Nash sat up, forced his brain to work. "Did you say Clair is missing?"

Kloz sighed. "You must have a fever or something. Yes, *Clair is missing*. Our Clair. She went to the cafeteria to deal with something, and nobody's seen her since. That was like…wow, eight hours ago now. The head of security has his people looking for her, but with the CDC lockdown, they're having a tough time getting around the hospital. The elevators are all shut down and the stairwells are locked. His people have keys, but the CDC doesn't want people moving floor-to-floor. Two of our uniformed officers are missing, too. They've been gone most of the day. We've got two dead here in the hospital, someone's picking off the law enforcement officers, and now Clair is gone. I'm holed up in our office, but I'm all alone. I'm not sure who I can even trust. For all I know, Stout took her."

"Stout?"

"Christ, aren't you paying attention? He's the head of security here. Whoever is doing this is in the hospital somewhere. They might all be dead. If it's Bishop, can you imagine what he'd do to Clair? He's had eight hours. If this is all Sam…if Clair has seen his face…I don't know what to do, man. I need help."

Nash looked out the windshield again, at all the flashing lights in front of Porter's building. A stretcher was coming out. "I found Vincent Weidner's body in Sam's apartment. He was in the bathtub."

Klozowski's voice dropped lower. "I know. I've been watching all the chatter—texts, e-mails, radio traffic. The feds think this is all Sam. I really don't want to go there…I keep telling myself not to go there, but there's so much evidence. Poole just found a body in Charleston—an old body—hidden in the garage of Sam's old partner. Some of Sam's stuff was there…a ton of money."

Nash pinched his eyes shut and rubbed his forehead. Forced himself to see clearly through the brain fog. "You can see all that?"

"Seriously? I could tell you the last three porn videos you watched on your phone, if I wanted to. Now is not the time to question my skills. We need to get Clair back."

Nash reached for the gear shift, and his hand moved right past it. He actually missed. He tried two more times before he was able to wrap his fingers around it. "I'm coming in. I'll be there soon."

"They won't let you through the doors. This whole building is under quarantine, remember?"

"I'm sick. They have to let me in." When Nash turned to look for traffic, his head tapped against the window glass. He felt like he might pass out. He found the pills Eisley had given him and took three more.

Shutting off the engine, he eyed a patrol officer getting into his car at Porter's building. "Think I'll get a ride, though."

He forced his body to move from the car and flagged the man down. At some point, he hung up on Kloz.

75

Diary

Libby and I huddled at my bedroom window, watching as Welderman and Stocks pulled up. It was a little after nine, and the sun was long gone. There wasn't much of a moon, either, the sky as black as oil.

"Do you see him?"

I rose up a few inches, and she pulled me back down. "Don't—"

The lights were off in my room, so there was no way anyone would spot me, but I ducked anyway. I raised my head just enough to look out past Welderman's car to Finicky's Camry parked to the left side of them. I didn't see him, not at first. Then this long, black figure rolled out from underneath and crouched beside the passenger door.

"There he is," I said, pointing.

Libby had seen him too. I could tell by the way she tensed up. "God, I hope he can pull this off."

"He will," I said with all the confidence I could muster, although I wasn't so sure. Libby had devised a good plan, but there were a lot of moving parts, and any one of them could go sideways.

Finicky shouted up from downstairs. A moment later, I heard the sound of feet as Weasel and The Kid ran through the hallway and thundered down the steps. I tried not to think about where they were going or what was waiting for them. There were far too many Bernies out in the world and not nearly enough of them buried out in the field. Tegan had said it was more pictures, and while that was bad, there was worse.

Outside, Vincent made his way across the open space to the back of Welderman's car. He moved slow, stayed as low to the ground as he could. Welderman was still behind the wheel. As usual, Stocks was standing with his door open and a cigarette in his hand on the opposite corner. Vincent made his way to the driver's side rear tire, twisted off the cap on the stem, and began letting out the air.

"I think he's done this before," I said quietly.

"Vincent has done a lot of things," Libby agreed. "He needs to hurry."

I just hoped he didn't let out too much. The trick was to leave just enough so they could still drive on it, but not enough to maintain integrity. In a perfect world, they'd get about halfway to town before the rim ate through the rubber. Libby had insisted that as long as they got out of the driveway, it would work. With the driveway being dirt and gravel, they probably wouldn't notice the poorly inflated tire until they got back on the pavement, and even then, Welderman might drive a bit on it before realizing something was wrong, if the discrepancy could be felt at all.

Downstairs, I heard Kristina say something to Finicky. The two boys raised their voices in some kind of mock argument.

"She won't be able to stall them all for very long," Libby pointed out. "Vincent needs to hurry."

This wasn't exactly something you could put a rush on. If they came out the front door before he was done, Finicky would surely see him crouching there between the two vehicles, a stem cap in his hand and a blank look on his face. Her Camry only partially blocked him from the porch.

Libby and I both heard the front door of the house open, then the screen door.

"Oh no." Her hand tightened around mine.

Vincent must have heard it too. He had the stem cap back on in a second and dove for the Camry. Stocks's head tilted up, the glow of his cigarette just enough to illuminate his face. Vincent scrambled back under the car as Stocks took several steps in his direction, then stopped.

The porch light came on, and Weasel and The Kid made their way to the car. Tegan's camera dangled from Weasel's neck. Welderman got out long enough to open the back door for them and exchange a couple words with Finicky. Then he was back behind the wheel. Stocks dropped his cigarette and ground it out under his shoe, then got back into the car too. A moment later, they were making their way down the driveway, the back of Welderman's Chevy leaning awkwardly to the left.

"Who's got the envelope?"

"The Kid," Libby said.

The envelope contained a list of the parts we needed, five hundred dollars in cash, a note for whoever The Kid could pass it to at the auto parts store—deliver these parts and we'll give you another five hundred for your trouble. Finicky's address was listed, along with instructions to go straight to the barn. They had also slipped in a very provocative picture of Tegan. This was Paul's idea. "Any male with a pulse who thinks Tegan is waiting for them in some isolated barn will be helpless to resist. The Force is strong with that one," he insisted.

Libby sighed. "If they go to the gas station instead of the auto parts store, we're sunk."

"The garage will be closed this time of night, and I taught Weasel how to disable the air pump out front. They'll have to go to the parts store—there's no place else."

"He might have a spare or could call someone, or maybe that guy in the van will help him...a million things could go wrong."

She was right; a million things could go wrong. "The guy in the van has a job to do. He won't help them. I don't think Welderman's the kind of guy who asks for help, and even if he wanted to, who would he call? He'd have to explain the kids in the back seat. Vincent said the spare tire in a Malibu is probably one of those little donut tires, and I don't see them driving around for very long on that. They'll want to fix it tonight."

"What if they make Weasel and The Kid go to the motel before they go to the store?"

"If this doesn't work, we'll try something else."

"We should just steal Ms. Finicky's car, like Tegan said."

We'd talked about that. We'd talked about it a lot, actually. But it wouldn't work. "Her car is too small to fit everyone, and they'll just report it stolen and bring us all back. We need to get everyone out, or we don't go *at all. That's the plan. They don't know the truck. We have a shot if they don't know what to look for."*

"Maybe we should run away, just the two of us. I wouldn't be surprised if Vincent and Kristina did."

Oh, how I wanted to. And looking back, how I wish I would have said yes. How I wish I had taken her by the hand at that very moment, found a way out of the house, and disappeared into the night with a bag of cash from the barn. Her and I alone. I don't know why I hesitated, maybe for the same reasons she did. We'd promised the others we'd all go together. The Kid and Weasel were too young to try and make it on their own. We all were. We all needed each other. "Remember where I said I grew up?"

Libby nodded. "The house by the lake in Simpsonville."

"If we get separated, I want you to meet me there." I told her the address and made her repeat it back to me until I was sure she had it memorized. "I'll find some way to get there, and I'll wait for you."

This made her smile.

I'd grown quite fond of her smile.

My leg was falling asleep, and when I shifted my weight, a horrible pain shot through my broken arm. It didn't take much to set it off. I'd been taking Tylenol like candy. Finicky wouldn't let me take anything stronger. Libby must have noticed, because she brushed her hand through my hair. "Is it getting any better?"

"A little," I lied. My heart did this little pitter-patter dance every time she touched me. She must have known that. Are all girls born knowing that, or is it taught to them by some older, wiser girl? She was wearing a cotton dress that was probably a size or two too small for her, and the hem rode up on her thigh a little higher than it probably should. She made no effort to tug it back down, even when she caught me looking. I'm not sure whose face flushed the brighter red then, hers or mine.

"If I show you something, do you promise not to tell anyone?"

I nodded.

She led me across the hall to her room, closing the door softly behind us.

76

Poole

Day 5 • 10:08 PM

Handcuffs still on his wrists, Poole drove. The gun didn't leave Porter's hand as he dug through the contents of the green duffle bag. His wild eyes kept darting up to glance at Poole, then back at the road as he occasionally told him where to turn. He tugged the sodden dress shirt from the bag and held it up in the thin light. "This is the shirt I was wearing the night I got shot. My other clothes from that night, too."

"You should wear gloves—you're contaminating evidence. I have some in my right jacket pocket."

Porter ignored him and kept digging. He came up with the camera. "This isn't mine. I've never owned a camera like this. Look at this lens. It's expensive. Or was expensive at the time. How old do you think it is?"

Poole shrugged. "You shouldn't touch it."

"There's film. We need to find someplace to get it developed. See what's on there." Porter pointed at a street sign with his free hand. "Make a left up here on East Bay, then head north."

"Where are we going?"

Porter's brow creased, and he turned to him. "Where's your cell phone?"

"In my pocket."

"Give it to me. Now."

"Why?"

"You know why."

"You'll need to get it. I can't reach with the cuffs, and I'm not about to let go of the wheel."

Porter considered this. "Which pocket?"

"Right front, in my pants."

Porter moved the gun from his left hand to his right, kept the barrel pointing at Poole, then reached over and dug out the phone. When he looked at the display, he frowned. "Granger's been calling you. Why didn't you say anything?"

Poole's eyes stayed on the road. "They'll look for me if they're not already. You destroy the phone, and you'll trigger a response the moment my signal goes dark."

Porter scrolled through the rest of the messages, then smashed the phone against the dashboard three times. When the glass shattered, he grabbed both ends, bent the phone in half, then lowered his window and tossed the device out into the night.

"I just bought that."

Porter rolled up his window and went back to the bag. He took out the composition book and began flipping through the pages. "What do you make of this?"

"Did you visit the Camden Treatment Center?"

Porter's eyes darted up. "Make a left on Queen."

"Answer my question."

"Why?"

"The call I took after Granger, that was a lieutenant with the South Carolina State Police. He said something bad happened at Camden. They found blood."

Porter's eyes were on the street ahead. "I didn't hurt anyone at Camden."

"But you were there."

Porter was leaning forward. "Pull over there on the left. You can park at that church."

Poole glanced at the large church but kept going straight. "Oops."

"Goddamn it." Porter fumed. "We don't have time for games, Frank. Make a right on Church Street. Another right on Cumberland. We'll go around the block."

"You seem to know this area."

"This is my old beat. Me and Hillburn. You drive the same streets enough, and they're in your head forever."

Poole took the right onto Church, drove past two small parks, then took another right on Cumberland.

"Park at the bank. Up there on the right." Reaching into the bag, Porter removed the three bound stacks of bills and placed them on the center console. "I don't think I've ever seen this much money in my entire life. The bills are circulated, nonsequential. The bands aren't stamped with a bank ID. They were most likely bundled privately somewhere. Banks are required to stamp them."

"Whose SUV is this? Did you steal it?"

"Right there, park there." Porter pointed toward the far corner of the lot with the barrel of the gun. "Under that streetlight."

"Good idea. I'd hate to see someone steal your stolen car."

"It's not stolen."

"Then where did you get it? You didn't rent it. We would have flagged that."

"Park. Shut off the motor."

Poole pulled into the space Porter indicated, shifted into park, and pressed the button on the dash to kill the motor. "Now what?"

"Now we get out and walk." Reaching into the back seat, Porter grabbed a black leather jacket and pulled it on, carefully shifting the gun from one hand to the other. He then slipped the gun into the left pocket. "Don't think for a second this isn't pointed at you, ready to shoot."

"I'm not going to run."

"I don't care." Porter exited the SUV, quickly made his way around to the driver side, and opened Poole's door.

Poole held up his cuffed hands. "Somebody might see these."

"That would be unfortunate. I suggest you hide them under your jacket."

When Poole got out of the SUV, Porter nodded toward the side of the bank. "Follow the edge of the building and make a left at the corner. I'm right behind you, so nothing stupid."

Although the bank was closed, several lights were on inside. Through one of the windows, Poole spotted a security guard sitting at his post. He saw them, too. Several people were on the sidewalk, walking in both directions. Foot traffic was high enough, Porter and Poole didn't raise any red flags in the guard's mind. After a quick glance, he returned to the book in his lap.

"Left here," Porter said as they reached the northwest corner of the building.

Poole glanced down the alley. Light trickled in, but not much. A cobblestone sidewalk ran down the center. Hedges and potted plants lined each side. The opposite end was barely visible, nothing but a distant glow between the branches of low-hanging trees. "Is this where you were shot?"

Porter pushed at the small of his back. "Keep going, out of the light."

They followed the sidewalk to just beyond the halfway point before Porter told him to stop. He glanced around, first at the surrounding buildings, then at a fenced-in yard on the left. "There used to be a restaurant here," he said, pointing. "The Dumpster was right here, up against the wall. It wasn't so overgrown back then. They didn't allow all these plants; the trees were cut back more so the trucks could squeeze in."

"What do you remember?"

Porter pursed his lips and knelt, running the fingers of his free hand over the cobblestones. "This is where I fell."

"Tell me what you remember."

He fell silent for a moment, then looked back in the direction they had come. "I chased this kid, Weasel, from Cumberland. I don't think he realized I was so close behind him. He ducked down here. Hillburn circled the block and came in from Queen. Weasel panicked when he saw Derrick and spun around. I was fast back then. At that point, I was nearly on top of him, and he got spooked when he saw me. The gun was in his hand, and it just went off. The bullet hit the Dumpster, ricocheted, then caught me in the back of the head. I went down right here."

"And you remember all that? Exactly like that?"

"Yeah. Every second of it. I close my eyes, and I can play it like a movie. He didn't mean to shoot me. The gun wasn't even pointed at me, it was more of a reflex than anything. I remember the hit, like a hard slap to the back of my head. I stood there like an idiot. Thought I could get back in the car and drive myself to the hospital. I touched the wound, saw the blood on my fingers, and took about two steps before I passed out. Right here."

"It's very odd for someone to remember an event like that," Poole said. "The brain tends to hide certain memories when we undergo something traumatic."

"I remember every second of it…"

"…like a movie," Poole said, finishing the thought.

"Yeah."

"What happens if you try to watch that movie backward?"

Porter frowned. "I don't follow."

Poole took a step closer to him, got near the wall where the Dumpster once stood. "Play the events in reverse order. Start when you're on the ground, right before you lost consciousness, then tick off the events in reverse order. It helps if you close your eyes."

"I'm not closing my eyes."

"I won't run."

"So you've said."

"I think you need to try this. Close your eyes. I'll walk you through it."

"I'm not closing my eyes." His hand was back in his pocket, fingers around the gun.

Poole looked up and down the alley, then back at Porter. "Okay, try this. When did you first spot Hillburn?"

"Hillburn circled the block and came in from Queen."

"That's what you said. I've heard you say nearly exactly that three times now. A few minutes ago, and when you told me about it back at Metro."

"Because that's what happened," Porter said.

"In the movie in your head, did Hillburn have his gun out when he entered the alley? When did you first spot the gun in Weasel's hand? Was your gun out? You said Weasel was a dealer. At what point did he throw his drugs? They always toss their drugs when they're running."

"I don't...I'm not sure."

Poole continued to press him. "Did Hillburn say anything when he entered the alley? Did he shout *police* and tell the kid to drop his weapon?"

"Yes..." Porter replied, but he didn't sound so sure.

"Are you saying that because you actually remember it, or because I suggested it and it fits what should have happened? Did I just add a scene to your movie? Did you yell *police?* Did you tell the kid to drop the gun?"

"....yes," Porter said again, softer this time.

"Your movie just changed, didn't it? Because I suggested it."

Porter's mouth was open slightly. He looked up at the wall, toward the now fenced-in yard.

Poole stepped closer. "Close your eyes. Remember from the middle—you ran down the alley, you got here, to this point, near the Dumpster, and—"

"Hurry, they're coming..." Porter said so quietly Poole nearly didn't hear him.

"What?"

Porter *had* closed his eyes, just for a moment. When he opened them, they went from the cobblestone back up to Poole. "That's what the kid said, Weasel—'Hurry, they're coming.'"

77

Nash

Day 5 • 10:10 PM

Nash took a short nap.

He didn't intend to. The idea of Clair missing (or worse) somewhere in that hospital was enough to jolt him back from the dead.

When Nash's eyes fluttered open, his head was leaning against the passenger window of a patrol car. A bead of drool trickled down the side of his mouth and found a home on his shirt within a collective pool of its friends. He straightened himself up, grateful for the help of a seatbelt, and looked out the windshield, thinking of the shirt. "Mother will not be happy with that."

These words slipped out, and Nash had no idea why. His head wasn't really on straight. He was aware of things enough to at least understand that. He also knew Mother would be very unhappy with the fresh drool stain on his shirt—he'd have to clean that before she saw.

Nash fell back to sleep then.

Not long, maybe a minute or so. When his eyes opened, the car had stopped moving and the patrol officer who had been driving had somehow managed to vanish from the driver's seat and reappear outside Nash's door through the use of some Harry Potter magic bullshit. He was caught up in an exchange with two other people, their voices a frantic mess—

"...he may have been exposed to the SARS virus...first responder at the Upchurch residence. Direct contact with Larissa Biel *and* Kati Quigley..."

A woman's voice. "Why wasn't he brought in sooner? Do you have any idea how this virus spreads? Are there more like him out there? People exposed just running around? Ridiculous...irresponsible...I need a stretcher!"

Another quick nap.

Nash woke again, this time on a bed. A wonderfully soft bed. The walls of his small room were made of white curtains, and there were lots of flashing, pretty lights accompanied by a cacophony of dings, beeps, blips, and thumps. Five or six people hovered around him, maybe more. He found it hard to keep track since none of them would stand still long enough for the count. They all wore white, though, which seemed really strange to him, Labor Day being five months earlier. They talked a lot, too—to each other, to him—he watched all this as if he were sitting in the middle of a favorite television program, witnessing events unfold around him. This was all extremely exciting, but he wished he wasn't having so much trouble following along.

"...for the fever! Need to get his temperature down," someone said. A female someone. "And fluids. He's severely dehydrated."

"He's been taking these—" A hand held up the bottle of pills Eisley had given him. From the bed, he couldn't see who that hand was attached to.

Long blonde hair bobbed into his vision. She looked at the pills, then down at him. "Good. That's good." And she was gone again.

Nash reached up and tried to take his pills back, but his fingers only found air. His hand and arm were so damn heavy, they fell back down on his chest and took a time-out.

"He's slipping out again."

Fingers snapped right above his eyes. Pretty nails. Red. "Detective? Can you hear me? Try to stay awake."

Nash told himself he would do exactly that, right after another quick nap. He was so tired, and it was fucking cold.

78
Diary

When I first arrived at the wonderful Finicky House for Wayward Children, I had been told there was a strict "no boys in the girls' rooms" and "no girls in the boys' rooms" policy. This was rattled off along with several dozen other rules to live by. Yet, Kristina spent many a night in Vincent's room, and Paul would have sacrificed a goat if it meant five minutes alone with Tegan. (I had no idea where Paul was at this particular moment, but I was fairly certain he wasn't in Tegan's room. I got the feeling she thought of him no different than she would a puppy.) Not once did Finicky come upstairs and check to see if any of us were violating this particular rule. That didn't stop me from feeling nervous, nor did it keep me from glancing up at Libby's closed door. If the rumors were to be believed, Finicky would be in her room right now, taking a pill or four to help her sleep. I hoped that was true.

Libby dropped a blouse over the lamp in the corner to dim the light, then gestured for me to take a seat on the floor at the foot of her bed. She went to her dresser and began rummaging through the top drawer.

None of us arrived here with much, no more than a bag, but I had noticed that everyone took the time to unpack and claim their particular space as their own. Everyone but me. I'd lived out of the green duffle they'd packed for me at Camden until it was empty. It wasn't until clothes started to return from the laundry that I began using the two drawers and closet space allotted to me rather than refill the duffle.

Libby found what she was looking for and sat down beside me. It was a book.

"The Complete Poems of Emily Dickinson?" *I read the cover aloud and ran a finger over the embossed lettering.*

"Do you like poetry?"

I didn't know any poetry. I was an avid reader (comic books, mostly), but poetry had never been on my radar. "Sure," I told her, because she was incredibly pretty, and if she asked me if I liked to eat raw toad, I would have nodded enthusiastically if I thought that was what she wanted me to say.

"Dickinson is incredible. Her words flow as easily as water. It's like, I don't know, like if she knows exactly which ones are meant to be together. Like if you took a bunch of words and scrambled them, she'd know exactly what order to put them in."

"Like a puzzle?"

Libby nodded. "Yeah, like a big word puzzle."

"Can I see?"

She handed the book to me, and I thumbed through the pages. Many of the corners were folded over, and each of those pages contained highlighted blocks of text. I turned to a random marked page near the middle and read softly, "'Because I could not stop for Death, he kindly stopped for me. The carriage held but just ourselves and immortality.'" I paused for a second. "Why is 'Death' capitalized?"

"She's saying two different things here with one phrase. She's implying Death is a person or an entity who is waiting for her, and she's also saying that she has no control over when she's going to die. She can try to avoid death, but he'll stop for her anyway. She can't avoid it, or him, any more than the rest of us can. Death comes for us whether we want him to or not. There's no hiding."

"I think if he rolled up in a carriage, I'd at least try to make a run for it," I replied. I tried to run my finger down the page, and a sharp pain shot up my right arm, causing me to wince.

Libby's finger brushed the back of my hand then slid over my cast. "When I broke my arm, I couldn't use it for nearly a month. I learned to do everything with my other one. You should try too. I know it's hard, but the break will heal faster if you don't aggravate it."

"What's gossamer?" Another line in the poem—For only gossamer, my gown, my tippet, only tulle—*"And tulle? What's that?"*

Libby giggled.

"What's so funny?"

"You. It's such a deep poem and you're more concerned with what her dress is made of."

"Well, what is it?"

Libby thought about this for a moment. "If I show you, do you promise to behave?"

I nodded. Because now, I was curious.

Libby stood and did something that caused that pitter-patter in my heart to kick into high gear. She unbuttoned her dress and let it fall to the floor, stepped out of it, and came closer to me. "My bra and panties are gossamer."

My breath caught in my throat and an audible gasp escaped my mouth before I could stop it.

Her bra and panties were made of this thin, white frilly material that was nearly translucent. I knew I shouldn't stare, but I couldn't help myself. My eyes followed the curves of her bare shoulders down to her breasts, to her nipples, both erect and almost visible but not quite. My eyes drifted down over her flat belly. She had a bruise on her left side, nearly healed but still there, and she must have noticed me looking at it—she self-consciously slipped her hand down her side and covered it with her palm. The index finger of that hand curled around the top of her panties and tugged them down an inch or so off her hip, and that was more than enough to distract me from the bruise.

Although Libby's face was bright red, she was grinning down at me. "Tegan picked these out. She said they made my butt look good. They're thongs. I'd never worn them before. They were a little uncomfortable at first, but I got used to them. She said they're the best when you want to hide your panty lines."

She turned in a slow spin, and my brain swirled with her—I thought of Mrs. Carter at the lake, naked for a quick dip in the icy water. Mrs. Carter in the bedroom with Mother, Mother undressing her at the mirror. The photo of the two them in bed together, their naked limbs intertwined.

The photo I had yet to get back from Dr. Oglesby or whoever had it now. I thought of Tegan stepping out of the bathroom wearing hardly anything at all—all these thoughts, all at once, and then I was back with Libby, sweet Libby smiling down at me as she completed her slow spin, her fingers playfully twisting the corners of those panties. She knelt down in front of me and leaned in closer. Her hands left her side and found the fingers of my left hand. She pressed her fingertips against mine, then pulled me closer. "Gossamer is very soft." She drew my hand to her left breast and ran my fingers across the edge of the material. The warmth of her flesh was maddening. A tingle crawled over every inch of me. Her nipple pressed into my palm and her eyes closed, both of us breathing heavy now. I didn't notice her reach around and unclasp her bra. One moment it was there, keeping me from her, then it was gone, and I felt as if the two of us were one. This urge to touch every inch of her, to taste her, all these feelings I had never experienced rushed over me. She held my face for a moment between both her hands, then her lips found mine and she kissed me. Her hair fell over my cheeks and neck, and before I realized I was doing it, I kissed her back. Five minutes. Ten. I don't know. I lost all time.

"You told me to behave," I finally said, the words barely able to get out between short gasps.

"I changed my mind. Girls do that."

Libby reached down and unfastened the clasp on my belt, unsnapped the top button of my jeans. Her mouth rolled over my ear, warm breath. "Have you ever?"

I shook my head.

"Okay."

79

Poole

Day 5 • 10:12 PM

"What's going on here?" Porter looked around the alley, but his mind was elsewhere.

Poole edged closer. "I want you to think about this very carefully before you answer me, give what I'm telling you a chance to sink in. You've told me what happened here in this alley multiple times. You said you remember it vividly. You also said you lost other memories as a result of the gunshot, the pressure from the brainbleed. That's a very common side effect from an injury like that. But you said you remember being shot, every second of it." Poole paused for a moment, choosing his words. "I know you were placed in a medical coma for about a week following the accident. When you woke, who was there?"

"Heather." Porter said this without hesitation.

Poole nodded. "Heather was there, good. Anyone else? Was there anyone else in the room when you first woke?"

Porter nodded. "My partner was there, Hillburn. Sitting in a chair in the corner of the room, near the window. Looked like he'd been there for a while, like he had been sleeping there."

"What exactly did he do when you first saw him?"

"He was reading a magazine. I think Heather said something. He put the magazine down and crossed the room, leaned over me. He smiled. He looked so relieved. I remember asking him how long I'd been out, what happened."

"And?"

"…and he told me. Said Weasel had been fast, ducked down the alley with me behind him. He rounded the block, came in from the other side. Weasel saw him, spun around, and panicked when he saw me coming up behind him. He said the kid was jumpy and the gun went off. The bullet hit the Dumpster, ricocheted, and I caught it in the back of the skull." Porter dropped off for a moment.

"What else? You're remembering something else."

"That's when Heather jumped back in," Porter recalled. "She asked me who the current president was, and I told her. Then she asked me who the last one was, and I drew a blank. A doctor came in at that point, asked Hillburn to wait out in the hallway. There were a few more tests. Fluid elicit retrograde amnesia, that's what they called it. They said the pressure caused some memory loss and everything would most likely come back."

"Okay." Poole was nodding. "I want you to go back to the alley again, in your mind, your thoughts. Try not to think about what Hillburn told you when you first woke. Try to pull from your own memories. Maybe focus on the visuals, the sounds you heard, the smells of this alley. You said there was a restaurant. What did the Dumpster smell like? Recall the temperature of the night air—anything that will ground you, take you back. What do you remember *right before* you got shot."

Porter thought. "I remember chasing Weasel, rounding the corner at Cumberland, and coming down here. Weasel stopped right here, at the Dumpster…" Again, his voice trailed off.

"What is it?"

Porter held up a hand, silenced him, and closed his eyes. He stayed like that for a long moment. When his eyes snapped open, he looked scared. He looked down at the opposite end of the alley.

"What?"

"I remember Weasel stopping here, at the Dumpster. Turning to me, spinning around fast…but…I don't see Hillburn anymore. Then the shot…"

Poole knelt down on the cobblestone next to Porter. "There's something else, right? Don't let it slip away. Tell me before you lose it."

Porter turned to him. Sweat had broken out on his brow. "I don't remember Weasel actually having a gun in his hand. I think he had the camera…"

"Weasel didn't shoot you?"

"I…I'm not sure. I don't think so. 'Hurry, they're coming,' he said…then the shot." Porter gazed back down the alley, looking at nothing in particular, lost in his own thoughts. When he stood, he moved fast, back the way they'd come. "We need to get that film developed."

Poole found himself chasing after him, the handcuffs chafing his wrists.

80

Clair

Day 5 • 10:14 PM

Clair had fallen asleep, and she wasn't happy about that. It was the damn virus, this foreign invader who had taken up residence in her flesh before commandeering resources and energy and leaving her to starve. She'd given up telling herself she'd be okay. She knew her fever had crept up to record levels—she felt like she was standing naked in the Arctic under a fan yet she was dripping with sweat. How her body was able to sweat, she had no idea. She was incredibly thirsty, probably dehydrated, yet her body betrayed her by expelling the water she so desperately needed. Her throat was a raw, angry beast not only from sickness but from the yelling. The yelling made her feel better, like she was doing something about her situation, although she was certain the only other person who could hear her was the man moaning next door.

He'd gone quiet shortly before she fell asleep (passed out, actually, but that meant surrender, and she wasn't about to admit to that, not even to herself). Prior to that, his own screams had peaked at a horrifying crescendo before tapering off, becoming something just a little worse than weeping, then the moans, then nothing.

At some point, Clair wondered if the man in the black mask was out in the hallway listening to their chorus, and that's when she finally stopped. If he took pleasure in their suffering, she had no intention of feeding the degenerate asshole's appetite.

Clair had discovered a vent in her room a few hours ago, and that vent seemed to be connected to the moaning man's room next door. It was too small for her to climb through, but when she leaned down next to it, she could hear him again, muffled sobs. "Hey? Can you hear me?"

The sobs stopped momentarily, then a weak voice replied, "Who are you?"

This took Clair by surprise. She'd tried talking to him several times, but he'd never answered. She tried to clear her throat and immediately regretted that decision. It felt like someone shoved a Brillo Pad down her windpipe and yanked it back out. "My name is Detective Clair Norton with Chicago Metro. Who are you?"

"She cut off my ear. That fucking cunt took my ear. I need a doctor."

She?

"Who? Are you saying the person holding us here is a woman?"

"The bitch from the escort service. Had to be her. She tied me up, that was all good, but then she stuck me with something, knocked me out. My ear is gone. Christ, it hurts."

Escort service? What was he talking about?

"Does anyone know you're here?" Clair asked, not sure she really wanted to hear the answer.

"I don't… Do you know where we are? I was at the Langham. I don't know what this place is. I woke up here."

"The Langham Hotel?"

"Yeah. My staff must be looking for me, right? You said you're with Metro. Are *they* looking for me? Wait, you're locked up, too. Were they looking for me before the crazy bitch grabbed you?"

"Are you sure it was a woman?"

"Are you calling me some kind of queer? Of course, she was a woman. I don't go that way, and I can sure as shit tell the difference."

Dick.

Grating. Egotistical. Clair knew his voice. Through the fever, it took a moment for her to make the connection, but she'd heard him on television more times than she could count. Old-school Chicago accent. "Mayor Milton?"

His voice came louder— he must have moved closer to the vent. "She said her name was Sarah. I thought that was weird. They typically have names like Brandy or Hope or Tiffany. Sarah was different. She was different. A little older than the usual girl, a woman, really, but I didn't send her back. I figured with age came experience. Maybe she'd be a little more fun than the others, a little more open. Then the bitch stuck me."

This was *not* the kind of thing Clair usually heard coming from the mayor, and she could live a perfectly full life without hearing another word of it, even if that life was extinguished soon. She felt so shitty. If her captor were to come in and offer to end things, Clair wasn't so sure she'd fight that hard.

"What did she look like?"

The mayor grunted. "I don't know. Short. Dark hair."

"Sarah what? Did she give you a last name?"

"Ha. That's funny. Yeah, she gave me her last name, showed me pictures of her kids. We talked about her goals and ambitions and climate change. It wasn't that kind of party, Detective." He dropped off for a second. "This is all off the record. Every word. You can't repeat any of it to anyone, understand? You do, and I'll have your badge. I'm only telling you in case it helps you get us out of here."

Clair gave him the finger. She knew he couldn't see her, but it still felt good. "Tell me about the room you're in."

"Stone walls. Concrete floor. Metal door with a small window. There's this little vent on the floor, the one we're talking through. Other than that, no ventilation."

Same.

"Is your ear still bleeding?"

"I don't think so. She bandaged it."

"Leave that on. You don't want to aggravate the wound."

"Sure thing, Nurse Nightingale. How about you focus on getting us out, and I'll worry about my medical needs. I don't suppose you have your gun, do you?"

"No."

"Of course not."

"What is that supposed to mean?"

"Never mind."

"Tell me."

"It doesn't matter. You let them take you, take away your weapon, lock you up. You're no better off than me. They got me when I was vulnerable, took advantage of me, but you've got training. You're a cop. Obviously not a very good one, or you wouldn't have let it happen."

"You're not building a very compelling case for helping you," Clair replied.

"No, but you will. You'll do your job. You don't, and you'll find yourself waiting tables if you get out of here."

Clair was beginning to wish she hadn't spoken to him at all. She liked him better when he was screaming. "You said *them*. Did you see more than one?"

The lights went out.

All of them.

Her room. The hallway. The other side of the vent.

She heard a door open but not her door.

"No!" the mayor said. "Don't! Get the fuck away from me!"

The mayor screamed again, louder than the first time. That wasn't what frightened Clair, though. What frightened her was how abruptly those screams stopped.

81
Diary

We woke to a clatter. Something horrible downstairs. When I heard the first shout, I thought I imagined it. My eyes snapped open, and at first I wasn't sure where I even was. Libby stirred beside me. Her naked body was pressed against my own, her leg curled over my waist.

It was Welderman who was shouting. Someone was crying, too. At first, I didn't realize it was The Kid. He rarely spoke. I never heard him laugh. I certainly never heard him cry.

"Oh no," Libby said softly. She sat up, holding the sheet over her breasts.

The two of us scrambled out of bed and into our clothes. When we opened Libby's door, we found Paul across the hall, leaning out of our room. He'd been staring in the direction of the stairs, and when he faced us, he was ghostly white and his mouth hung open. His eyes bounced from me to Libby and back again, and I'm not sure if he looked that way because of us, because of something he heard downstairs, or both.

"What's going on?" I said as quietly as I could.

Before he could answer, Finicky shouted up the stairs. "All of you— down here, now!"

"Oh no, no, no," Paul stammered.

Libby squeezed my shoulder. "They must have found the note. The money. We're dead."

"They won't hurt us," I reassured her. "They need us, remember?"

This didn't seem to make her feel any better.

Tegan and Kristina came out of their room, both yawning. Tegan wore a white robe, and Kristina was in a loose T-shirt and pink shorts.

"What time is it?" Tegan asked.

Paul glanced back over his shoulder. "Quarter after four in the morning."

"Now! Goddamnit!"

This was Welderman.

Vincent's door opened—he had a wrench in his hand.

Kristina's eyes narrowed. "What are you going to do with that?"

"Whatever I have to." He tucked the wrench into the back of his jeans and pulled the top of his shirt over it, then started down the stairs.

The rest of us followed after him. About halfway down, Tegan leaned in close to me. "Did you get some?"

Libby shot her a dirty look. Neither of us answered.

We found them all in the parlor. Well, almost all.

"Sit," Welderman instructed. "Not a fucking word out of any of you." His coat was open, and I could see the gun under his shoulder. Some kind of revolver.

We worked our way around the room. Libby and I sat on the couch with Paul. Kristina and Tegan sat on an armchair together, the two of them holding hands. At first, Vincent remained standing, but when Welderman's eyes landed on him, he pulled a wooden chair out from under the desk and lowered himself into it. I expected the wrench to drop out the back of his jeans and clatter to the floor, but it didn't.

Welderman and Ms. Finicky stood in the doorway leading toward the kitchen. Welderman's free hand was on Weasel's shoulder. Stocks wasn't there. Neither was The Kid.

82

Poole

Day 5 • 10:41 PM

The CVS parking lot was empty, all lights off. This was the third place they'd stopped in hopes of developing the film.

Porter drove.

There was a moment when Poole followed him out of the alley at a run, when he considered fleeing, but that instant passed when Porter got behind the wheel and reached over to the passenger door and opened it for Poole from the inside of the SUV. He didn't think Porter would hurt him, but he kept reminding himself that he might. Something about his actions, the crazed look behind his wide eyes. This could all be part of some kind of elaborate ruse. If Porter was somehow responsible for the dead body in that van, he's had years to develop a cover story. If that were somehow true, if Porter really was responsible for all these deaths, he could turn on him in an instant. Poole also knew that if he let the man slip from his sights, he'd vanish. Sticking with him, seeing this through, was his only shot at bringing Porter in. And he fully intended to bring him in.

Poole had gotten in the SUV and pulled the door shut with his cuffed hands, knowing in that instant an unspoken trust formed between them. A trust he could use.

A Walgreens parking lot, also closed.

"Dammit," Porter muttered, looking up at the dark sign.

"I'm not sure these places can even develop film anymore. I think they send it off somewhere."

Porter threw the SUV in reverse and squealed out of the lot, nearly sideswiping a white Toyota as he pulled back into traffic. "The one down the street from my apartment does. Heather refused to use a digital camera for important stuff. She said the camera on her phone could never compare to 35mm. I think I still have a coupon on the fridge for developing."

"You need to slow down a little."

Porter swung into the right lane. His hand absentmindedly swiped at the turn-signal knob on the steering wheel about a half second after he made the switch. Someone behind them held their hand down on their horn for nearly thirty seconds. "What were you implying back there? Are you saying Hillburn somehow planted that memory in my head?"

Poole rubbed at his handcuffed wrist. "It's called suggested cognition. For a very short moment, when the mind is coming out of a sleep state, the door between the conscious and subconscious is wide open. You know how when you wake up from a dream for a split second everything about that dream feels real? Then you realize you were sleeping and the thoughts are properly categorized as fiction or forgotten altogether. Your brain is capable of determining that information is false because your brain created the dream. If you're exposed to external information when that door is open, regardless of the source, your brain can improperly categorize. You're not quite awake, so you don't necessarily remember the experience, but your brain stores it anyway, stores it *as a memory*. This is one of the reasons most repressed sexual experiences discovered during hypnotherapy sessions have been debunked—the therapist unknowingly planted false memories when the subject's mind was open to suggestion. Whether intentional or not, Hillburn telling you what happened in that instant when you woke may have planted that memory."

"Or all of that might just be coincidence, and I'm remembering it wrong now."

"Maybe."

"Or I'm lying to you about what I'm remembering to try and cover my own ass."

The bluntness took Poole by surprise. "Yeah, or that."

A phone rang. Porter removed a burner from the center console before he realized the sound wasn't coming from there. He turned to Poole, his face growing dark. "Do you have another phone?"

Poole saw no reason to lie. "I carry a personal phone and one issued by the Bureau. The one you destroyed was my FBI phone."

"Christ, do I need to strip search you? Hand it over, now. Don't answer. Take it out with two fingers and hand it to me."

Poole did what he asked. He removed the Samsung from his jacket pocket and passed it over to Porter as it rang for the third time.

Porter answered the call on speaker with his best impression. "Poole."

"This is Granger. Is he with you?"

"Uh huh."

"Okay, don't say anything. Hillburn's widow recognized Porter from television. News that Weidner's body was found at his apartment has gone national, so his photo is everywhere. When your phone went dark, alarms went off. We're tracking GPS on this line right now. We just missed you back on Cumberland. I've got them holding back out of line of sight. I've got a chopper inbound. We're not sure which vehicle—"

Porter lowered his window and tossed the phone out as they rolled through a yellow light at the intersection of Klondike and Mortin Avenue. He then swung a hard right and doubled back the way they came and quickly took a ramp onto I-526.

The burner phone had fallen to the floor during the turn. Porter reached down and scooped it up, shot Poole another dirty look, then dialed a number. Poole didn't recognize the male voice who answered. Porter said, "We're coming in hot."

"Understood. Get as close as possible."

Porter disconnected the call, tapped out a text message, and dropped the phone back into the center console before turning back to Poole with a scowl. "That was really stupid."

"You would have done the same thing."

"Give me your identification." His free hand had slipped back into his jacket pocket, the one with the gun.

"Why?"

"Badge, ID, driver's license. Give me all of it. Right now."

"Sam, I don't think—"

"Give me all of it, right fucking now!"

Poole took his badge and FBI ID from his jacket pocket and handed it to Porter, then he pulled out his wallet, removed his driver's license, and handed that over, too. Porter threw it all out the window.

"That was another mistake," Poole told him.

"Seems I'm making a lot of those lately." He rolled the window back up and increased speed. "What did they find in my apartment?"

Poole told him about Weidner's body, the pieces of drywall. He held nothing back.

Porter listened without speaking. He kept glancing in the rearview mirror. When Poole looked in his own mirror, he saw it too—a South Carolina State Trooper, three car lengths back. He wasn't sure how long the car had been there.

83

Poole

"You should just pull over, Sam. Turn yourself in before someone else gets hurt."

Porter glanced in the rearview mirror. The state trooper had fallen back four car lengths but was still behind them, one lane over. "You know I can't do that."

"If you're innocent, we'll figure this out."

Porter had both hands on the wheel again, no longer holding the gun. He nodded over his shoulder. "There are two file folders on the floor in the back seat. Put them both in that green duffle and be ready to move."

The SUV was picking up speed again. Poole wasn't sure he wanted to unfasten his seat belt.

"Do it now!"

"Try not to kill us until I'm back in my seat." Poole released the belt and twisted awkwardly between the two front seats. He saw the folders on the floor behind Porter, reached down with both hands, fell forward, then braced himself with both hands before tumbling completely over. "This would be a lot easier if you'd take off the cuffs."

"Hold on." Porter jerked the wheel hard to the right and shot across three lanes of traffic toward another exit.

Poole pushed himself up high enough to see the state trooper attempt the same maneuver behind them, but he was too slow. He shot past the exit, braked, and started backing up before disappearing from view. "If they weren't following you before, they definitely are now." He scooped up the two folders and fell back into his seat. A sign for the Charleston Airport flew by on the right. "Where are we going?"

"Shit, shit, shit." Porter's eyes were on the mirror again. No sign of the state trooper, but there were two Charleston PD cars behind them. Their lights were off, but that could change. They were on an airport perimeter road. The speed limit dropped to twenty miles-per-hour. Porter had slowed to just a little above that. Some vehicles peeled away for ramps leading toward long and short-term parking, but for every car that left, it seemed three more merged in to replace them. Traffic grew thick as they neared the terminals, and the patrol cars fell back. Another Charleston PD car pulled in from an access road a few hundred feet ahead of them. Porter spotted another already in his lane a quarter mile up. "They're going to try and box us in."

"Take off my handcuffs and give me the gun," Poole said. "I'll tell them you surrendered to me."

Leaning over the steering wheel, Porter's eyes shifted wildly from the signs above to the cars around them. Sweat dripped down his brow. He pursed his lips and gripped the steering wheel hard enough to turn his knuckles white. "Hold on."

His foot stomped down on the brake, the SUV lurched in protest, and Poole's seat belt yanked back against his chest. The vehicle behind them slammed into their bumper with a sickening crunch. Poole heard at least two other crashes behind that, and when he looked in the side mirror, he realized at least a half dozen other cars had wrecked, too. A few airbags deployed. Horns everywhere started to blare.

Gridlock behind, open space in front as traffic continued to move forward.

Porter floored the gas. Plastic crinkled behind them as their bumper tore away from the car that had hit them. He crossed the remaining two lanes on the right and took an exit toward the private hangars, an executive airport, picking up speed as he went.

"Helicopter." Poole spotted it first, coming in from the east.

Porter didn't seem to care. They were approaching a small guard house, the gate down.

Poole cringed.

The gate arm swung up moments before they would have burst through it. Porter didn't even tap the brakes.

The helicopter arched down, tried to block their path, then zipped back up into the air when they realized Porter had no intention of slowing. In fact, Porter was still picking up speed. Someone said something over a loudspeaker, but Poole couldn't make out the words.

Porter tugged the wheel to the left. The front tires cried out in protest, then gripped the blacktop. The helicopter came up behind them about a hundred feet above the pavement.

Far in the distance, Poole spotted several other vehicles racing across the tarmac with lights flashing. "Stop, Sam! Stop!"

He sped up. He pointed the SUV toward the open mouth of a hangar and picked up speed. It wasn't until Poole could see people scrambling out of the way inside that hangar that Porter touched the brakes at all. When he did, he hit them hard. His right hand went to the emergency brake and he yanked it up, locking the rear tires. Poole braced himself; they were going to slide right into the large jet occupying most of the hangar. The blacktop gave way to concrete, and Porter jerked the wheel again, pulling them to the right. They skidded into the hangar, the SUV threatening to flip. Above, the helicopter roared over and gained altitude.

A moment later, when the Bombardier Global 5000 jet with Talbot Enterprises painted on the tail rolled out of the hangar and onto the tarmac, the helicopter was still doubling back. The emergency vehicles racing toward them were still a quarter mile away when the jet's engines screamed and the private plane tore down the runway. They were in the air long before anyone had a chance to determine who the plane belonged to or could attempt to ground it.

84
Diary

"Where's The Kid?" I said it because nobody else seemed able or willing to ask.

Welderman's hand tightened on Weasel's shoulder, and Weasel cringed, trying to shrug off the man's grip. This only seemed to irritate Welderman, who dug his thumb down into Weasel's shoulder blade as he glared at me. He reached into his pocket with his free hand and took out the note we'd given The Kid. "Was this your idea? Are you fucking kidding me?" He released Weasel and took a step closer to me. "Do you realize with that broken arm you're worth damn near nothing to us? I'd sooner chop you up into little bits and bury you out in that field than deal with your bullshit."

I felt Libby's hand try to curl into mine, but I pulled away. I didn't want to risk Welderman seeing that. While he didn't, I failed to notice Ms. Finicky watching us, too. I wish I'd seen her. Oh, how I wish I'd seen her. "Yes," I told him. "It was my idea."

Welderman's eyes looked like they might explode out of his face. "First the mess at the motel, now this? Give me one reason not to put a bullet in your head."

I didn't answer him, because I didn't have one. I would have killed me. Father would have killed me. Mother would have certainly killed me. I was a problem, and Welderman knew it. I'm not sure what stopped him.

"Bring that little shit in here!" Welderman shouted over his shoulder.

I expected Stocks, but it was the man from the van back at the motel. He half carried, half dragged The Kid into the room by the collar of his shirt. The material was torn, stained red with blood. The Kid's face was a dozen different shades of red, purple, and black, the skin crusted over with more blood. His left eye was swollen shut, his nose was no longer centered above his mouth but off to the side.

Several gasps filled the room, the loudest from Tegan.

Under Welderman's grip, Weasel squirmed away and went to his friend as Van Man dropped The Kid to the floor in front of us like yesterday's trash.

The Kid crumbled. His legs failed to hold him up. His right arm attempting to stop the fall, but it was nothing more than a casual swipe—his arm, hand, fingers, they fell with him as dead weight does, and for a moment I thought he was dead. He coughed, though. His good eye scanned us all before closing.

Stocks came in carrying a green bag, glanced around at all of us before turning to Welderman and Van Man. "The truck was out in the barn. Looks like they've been working on it for a while now. It's not running, but it was close. No chance of that now, but dammit, they were close." He shook the bag. "They found the money too. Found this on the front seat."

Welderman glared at Finicky. "How the fuck do you let this happen? You're supposed to be watching them. We give you one job. One simple job, and they find the time to rebuild some old rusted out beater right under your nose? Goddamn pillhead."

Finicky opened her mouth to object, but Welderman didn't give her a chance.

Welderman held out his hand. "I want your keys. Nobody is leaving this place until Guyon, understand? Not you, not them, not anyone."

Her face flushed with anger. "Need I remind you, you still need to go back and make good on the appointment—they're still there."

"Fuck!" He stomped across the room, swearing under his breath. "I don't need this!"

"What's Guyon?"

This came from Weasel. One of the few times I had heard him speak. His voice sounded so small compared to Welderman's tirade.

"It doesn't fucking matter what Guyon is." Welderman fumed, his face red, with spittle at the corners of his mouth. He looked like he might kick Weasel, or worse. Instead, he grabbed Tegan's camera off the table and shoved it into the green bag. He pressed the bag into Van Man's chest and nodded at Weasel. "Get this one back there, tell them he's a freebie, give them the money to smooth things over, and get back here. No other stops, understand?"

Van Man nodded and grabbed Weasel by the collar, dragging him out the door.

When they were gone, Welderman pushed The Kid onto his side with the tip of his boot before turning on Stocks. "Look at his face. What the fuck is wrong with you? Whatever that ends up costing us is coming from your cut."

Stocks prepared to argue but said nothing.

"Can we take The Kid upstairs?" I asked Welderman. "We understand. We won't try anything. We should have known better. We all get it now."

Welderman's angry face went from Stocks to me to the rest of the group. "Yeah, get him out of here. I don't want to see any of you right now."

I got down on the floor and tried to help The Kid up, but with my broken arm, I had no way to get a good grip on him. Vincent knelt down beside me and scooped The Kid up into his arms. He didn't say anything as he carried him out of the room toward the stairs. Tegan and Kristina bounded out of their chairs after him, the rest of us behind them.

Upstairs, Vincent set The Kid down on his bed, eased his head onto his pillow. Libby appeared with a bowl of water and a washcloth. She tenderly wiped the blood off his face, careful to avoid his broken nose. I peeled off The Kid's filthy clothes and piled them in the corner of his room. Paul stood in the doorway watching us, Tegan and Kristina behind him. "They'll kill us all," Tegan said quietly.

"They won't kill us. They're going to sell us," Vincent replied. "That's what Guyon is."

Van Man must have locked Weasel in the van. He was back downstairs arguing with the others. Two kids down now, which was all they really cared about.

We all heard it then, above the voices—the sound of a car coming up the driveway. Tires crunching on the gravel.

Paul was first to the window. "It's a cop!"

The words were barely out his mouth before Stocks bounded up the stairs and came through the bedroom door, his gun out and waving through the air. "Get the hell away from the window. Now!"

Paul did.

I could still see, though. The black and white patrol car pulled up behind the white van and came to a stop. Nobody got out, not at first.

The screen door on the front of the house squeaked open and slammed shut. Van Man appeared below. He crossed the driveway and went to the patrol car. When the window rolled down, he leaned in and spoke to the driver.

"Nobody make a fucking sound," Stocks said. His gun was pointed at Libby, but his eyes were on me.

"Who is it?" I asked him.

"Shut the fuck up."

"You know him, don't you?"

"I said, shut the fuck up!"

"Are all the police part of this?"

Stocks raised the gun, ready to hit me, but didn't. Two kids down. I *don't think he wanted to find out what would happen if he hurt me worse than I already was.*

Outside, Van Man was still speaking to the driver. I could see the vague outline of the man behind the wheel, but between the dark and the distance, I couldn't make out his face. Several times, Van Man gestured back at the house. They spoke nearly five minutes, then Van Man stood, tapped the roof of the police car twice, and ran back to his van. When the police car turned and started back down the driveway, the white van followed.

"Is Weasel in the van?" Tegan asked.

Nobody answered. We all knew he was.

Stocks waited for their taillights to fade away before he spoke again. "I want all the girls in the room across the hall and all the boys in here. None of you are leaving my sight."

I didn't see Vincent take the wrench from his pocket, nor did I see him swing. It wasn't until the heavy steel came down against the back of Stocks's head with a sickening crunch that I realized what was happening. Stocks's eyes rolled up into his head, and he fell to the floor with a thump far too loud.

"Stocks? Everything okay up there?"

Welderman downstairs.

All of us stared at Stocks on the floor, clearly dead.

85

Nash

Day 6 • 2:18 AM

When Nash's eyes opened the first time, the harsh light took the opportunity to reach down from above and scratch at his dry pupils. He pinched them shut, blinked several times, and tried again. To him, it felt as if only a few seconds ticked by. Had anyone been watching, they would have told him four hours passed. Nobody had been watching, not the entire time, but when he turned his head he did spot Klozowski sleeping in a chair with his feet up on the corner of the bed. "Kloz?"

Klozowski sputtered, mumbled something, then fell back asleep.

Nash kicked his feet off the corner of the bed.

Kloz nearly dropped out of the chair. He grabbed the arms, scrambled to maintain his balance, and quickly glanced around before realizing where he was. When he saw Nash was awake, he stood. "Nurse! Nurse!"

"Christ, Kloz. Calm the fuck down." Nash's throat was horribly dry and scratchy. It was hard to speak. "Can I have some water?"

Kloz shouted for the nurse one more time, then filled a pink plastic cup from an equally pink pitcher sitting on the table beside Nash's bed and held the cup up to his lips. Half the water went down his throat, the other half covered his shirt. Nash really didn't care, he was so thirsty. He took the cup from Kloz, finished it, and asked for more.

Three cups later, sitting up in the bed, the nurse came in. Red nails, blonde hair, he vaguely recognized her from earlier. "Welcome back, Detective."

"I didn't realize I left."

"You came in with a hundred and four fever. At your age, that's dangerous."

"I'll be sure to put a warning label on my walker." His throat still hurt but nothing like before the water.

She ignored the quip. "We've had you on constant fluids, antibiotics, and anti-virals. Now that we have a handle on what's going on, we have a treatment protocol."

"It's not SARS," Kloz said. "The CDC ruled that out about an hour ago. They're treating us all now." Kloz pointed up at an IV bag hanging above his chair. "I'm not sure what's in there, but I feel a hell of a lot better."

The nurse ran an electronic thermometer over Nash's forehead. She held the display out to him. "Down to a ninety-nine point eight. Much, much better."

Nash said, "If it's not SARS, what is it?"

"A highly contagious strain of the flu. Nowhere near as dangerous as SARS, but still bad if left untreated."

Nash tried to process this. His thoughts were still a little sluggish. "So Bishop didn't inject anyone with the SARS virus?"

Klozowski glanced nervously at the nurse. "Can you give us a minute?"

She nodded and stepped out of the room.

When she was gone, Kloz lowered his voice. "A lot's happened while you were sleeping. Sam's in serious trouble."

"Weidner's body." Nash forced himself to sit up, fighting the wooziness that caused the room to tilt.

"There's more than that," Kloz said. "I took apart the video from Montehugh Labs. I went frame by frame, because it's as messed up as all the other ones related to this case, jumbled by some kind of virus or malware. I found a shot of Sam there on the night of the break-in. It's quick, and I had to enhance the footage to bring up the light, but it's him, no question." He lowered his head. "I had to share it with the feds. They think he's working with some kind of partner. Between the body in Simpsonville and the bodies up here, there's no way he could have killed everyone. They think he's trying to cover up something big, something dating back years, and all this business with the virus was just a smokescreen. They think his partner took the mayor and is holed up somewhere."

"You know about the mayor?"

Conspiratorial guilt washed over Kloz's face. "I've been monitoring all the fed chatter. I pieced it together. Then when Poole dropped off the grid and you showed up here sick, the people upstairs went to the press with the story. They couldn't keep it quiet any longer. He's been missing for more than a day and a half. It doesn't look good. Not after that much time."

"Christ."

"It gets worse," Kloz said. "They found a body hidden in an old van at Sam's partner's house in Charleston. Looks like it's been there for years. There's no ID yet, but it's a kid, a boy."

Nash rubbed at his face; he needed to shave. "How does that tie back to Sam?"

Kloz told him about the bag, what was inside. "Sam showed up while Poole was trying to secure the scene. Sam took him away at gunpoint. There's an eye witness—Hillburn's widow. The feds used GPS to track them down."

"Where are they now?"

Kloz glanced up at the television mounted near the ceiling in the far corner of the room. The sound was muted, and it was tuned to one of the twenty-four-hour news channels. A shaky image of a jet filled the screen, the landing gear in the process of deploying. The corner of the video was labeled LIVE and the scroll at the bottom said 4MK BELIEVED TO BE ONBOARD THIS JET OWNED BY TALBOT ENTERPRISES. "Somehow Sam managed to get on that plane with Poole in Charleston, and they got off the ground before anyone could stop them. They're landing at O'Hare. There's an army out there waiting on them. No way he's going anywhere.

They'll lock him up for sure."

On the television, the plane touched down on the runway, back wheels, then front, and began to slow. As the camera panned out and went wide, Nash saw dozens of law enforcement vehicles parked down at the opposite end surrounded by hastily erected lights. Federal, local, and emergency—two fire trucks and an ambulance. There was a quick shot of Frank's boss, SAIC Hurless before the camera went back to the plane.

That's when Nash remembered. His heart jumped. "Did you find Clair?"

Kloz shook his head. "Not yet. We searched what we could with hospital security but everyone's sick and we're thin on help. We're still missing two uniformed officers too. No sign of them. Captain Dalton told me now that we know we're not dealing with SARS and they're opening the doors, he's sending in reinforcements for a complete search. He told me to stay put and wait for help."

"They can't open the doors. Whoever took her will get out!" Nash started removing the tape around his wrist, freeing the IV line and a blood pressure cuff.

Klozowski ignored him. His eyes were glued to the television. The plane had stopped, the door opened, and the stairs came down, slow and mechanical. Officers in tactical gear rounded several of the cars and pointed weapons at the dark opening. In silence, he watched as they stormed up the steps in a low crouch, rifles at the ready.

86

Poole

"Go! Go! Go!"

From a world of darkness, Poole heard the shouts. He heard the approach of boots—first outside, then on the stairs, then in the cabin of the small plane. He opened his mouth in preparation for a concussion grenade. He'd heard horror stories of shattered teeth and bitten tongues from people who did not open their mouth and relax their jaw during detonation. He recalled his training at Quantico in exactly that and forced his mouth to go slack.

There was no explosion, just the thunder of boots and the jangle of weapons and gear on tactical officers. At least four, maybe six. He couldn't see anything.

"One! Portside! Midway! Appears disabled!" Someone shouted.

"We're coming out!" This shouted too, but from behind a closed door.

"Hands first!" This voice about ten feet away from Poole. "Slow! Show us your hands!"

A door crashed open. Someone thudded against the floor with a grunt. Another person dropped half a moment later.

Through all this, Poole saw nothing.

Boots stomped past him. Someone brushed against his right

elbow, heading toward the back of the plane. More crashing doors behind him. Bathroom?

"Clear!"

"Clear!"

"Where is Sam Porter?!?"

No response.

"Where is Sam Porter!"

"He's not on board." Poole recognized the muffled voice of the plane's pilot. In his mind's eye, he pictured the man in the aisle of the plane, his face pressed to the carpet.

Someone tore the blindfold from Poole's eyes, and he blinked against the harsh light pointing at his face from an LED mounted to the barrel of an MP510 assault rifle. The light fell to the side, and the tactical officer reached up and pulled the gag from Poole's mouth.

"I'm Special Agent Frank Poole with the FBI." Frank found it hard to talk. The gag had been tight, and the corners of his mouth were on fire. "Cut me loose." His hands, arms, legs, and feet were zip-tied to the seat.

"Sergeant?" The man standing next to Poole was looking at one of the other officers standing back near the door for instruction.

That officer looked down at the pilot on the floor. He was holding him down with a boot on his back. "What the hell is going on here?"

"Let me up," the pilot muttered into the carpet.

The officer lifted his foot and allowed the pilot to stand.

The pilot brushed dust from his pristinely pressed dark suit. "Detective Porter told us this man is a suspect in the 4MK investigation and ordered us to transport him back to Chicago. We were told law enforcement would be waiting to pick him up. I certainly don't appreciate the harsh treatment, and you will be held responsible for any damage to this plane."

Frank glared at him, fuming. "I told you—I'm a federal agent."

"You don't have ID. Detective Porter told us not to believe anything you said." The pilot turned back to the sergeant. "The detective ordered us to restrain this man, said he was extremely dangerous. We did exactly as instructed. My phone is in the cockpit. I saved his text message if you want to read it."

The sergeant went to retrieve the phone.

The man beside Poole had a knife out. He went to work on the zip ties. When free, Poole stormed off the plane, down the steps, where SAIC Hurless was waiting along with half a dozen other agents. They'd heard the entire exchange over the open communication line.

Hurless's face went through a series of shades of red. Before he could say anything, Poole pulled the two folders from Camden Treatment Center from where he had hidden them under his shirt and handed them to his supervisor. "This is how we catch him."

87

Clair

Moaning again.

Clair was half asleep when she heard the mayor next door. At first, the moaning was soft, more of a whimper, but he grew louder, more urgent.

Waking?

He screamed. A horrid, pain-ridden belt of a scream, enough to jerk Clair right out of whatever haze of sleep still lingered. She'd been lying in the corner of the room, her legs folded under her, her arms wrapped around her chest, and with that last scream, she found herself on her feet and back at the vent.

"Mayor Milton? What happened? Are you okay?"

Sobbing.

There was something about the sound of a grown man crying, even this man, who she absolutely abhorred, she found it hard to hate in that moment. "Barry?"

She knew his first name from the papers, but it sounded weird coming from her lips.

"She took my…"

"Took your what?"

More sobbing, nearly two minutes.

"My eye," he finally said. "I think she took my eye. I…can't tell for sure. It's bandaged, but it hurts. Oh God, she must have…I need to check."

"If there's a bandage, you should leave it alone. I can't imagine what that's like, but who knows if she cleaned the wound, or gave you any kind of antibiotic. If you remove the bandage here, you risk exposing the wound to infection."

"I need to know."

Clair shivered. She was still horribly cold but not as bad as earlier. The fever was either breaking or at the very least pulling back. She was so thirsty. "Don't touch it. Your hands aren't clean."

"I've got the tape off on one side. I'm just going to slip a finger under it. I won't take the bandage off completely." As he said these things between tears, he didn't sound like a grown man but a small child. A little boy afraid of what might come next.

"You shouldn't touch it."

He didn't tell her what he found. The renewed cries were enough.

88

Poole

"Tell me again," Hurless said.

Frank continued to read, quickly flipping the pages of the files he stole from Porter back in Charleston. His finger skimmed over the text at a fevered pace as he took in every word. "We don't have time for me to tell you again."

"Tell me anyway."

They were in the FBI communications truck, still at O'Hare Airport. Out of shot from the press cameras and microphones. Although the media had been held back from the tarmac, their equipment was just as good if not better than that of the Bureau. Even from a distance, they had the ability to capture video and sound, and Poole couldn't risk the wrong information getting out, not now. Hurless understood that too. He'd ordered nearly everyone out of the truck so he and Poole could talk.

While continuing to read Porter's file, Poole ran through everything that had happened in Charleston again.

When he finished, Hurless rubbed his chin and looked out one of the tinted windows at the plane. "Bishop has been in contact with our Chicago field office four times now. Always from a different number. He doesn't stay on the line long enough for us to trace. He's attempting to negotiate a surrender, but he doesn't feel we can guarantee his safety, not after what happened at Metro. He said Porter is working with a partner, someone high up in law enforcement, but he doesn't know who. Until he's comfortable, Bishop won't come in."

"Do you believe him?"

Hurless shrugged. He looked as exhausted as Poole felt. "We need to bring them both in alive. Get them in custody, then sort this out. Find the mayor, the missing officers, and that detective from Metro, hopefully still alive."

"What detective from Metro?"

"Clair Norton. She disappeared from Stroger Hospital about twenty-four hours ago."

Poole was about to say he didn't think Sam would ever hurt Clair, but he wasn't sure anymore. His finger, still tracing the text as he read, stopped. "Porter was treated for significant psychological issues well beyond memory loss from that gunshot. We've got psychosis, even hallucinatory events."

Hurless frowned. "There's nothing like that in his Metro file."

"There wasn't anything like it in his Charleston PD file either. They'd never let him back on the force with problems like this."

"It's possible they didn't have access. If the treatment at that place wasn't court ordered or sponsored by Charleston PD, it would be considered private. Porter would have had to consent to share the records."

"There are statements here from several members of the staff saying they caught Porter speaking to someone who wasn't there. At least half a dozen of them. When asked about it, he said he'd been talking to a woman about his age with shoulder-length brown hair and a southern accent—native to South Carolina. The physical description here is nearly identical to the one he gave me for Sarah Werner." Poole looked up. "Any luck getting a photo of her?"

Hurless shook his head. "We got one shot. At the courthouse when she went in with Jane Doe down in New Orleans. We've confirmed that was the real Sarah Werner, the one you found dead in her apartment. We don't have anything on the woman who had been with Porter."

Poole considered this. "Do we have any proof she was real at all? Anything beyond his statements?" Before Hurless could answer, Poole found something else at the front of the thick folder. "What was Porter's address when he lived in Charleston?"

Hurless took out his phone and dug through his case notes. When he found Porter's address, he read it to Poole. Poole tapped the patient identification form with his index finger. "Then what's this place?"

"Sir?"

This came from one of the techs seated at the communications equipment to their right.

"Yes?"

"The cell phone taken from Special Agent Poole at the house on 41st just went active. We have a location."

"Where?"

89

Porter

Nearly two hours before the jet carrying Special Agent Frank Poole back to Chicago touched down, Porter stood in a small parking lot next to an auto parts store, staring at the wall, his hands balled into fists.

They'd worked fast at Talbot's hangar. The moment the SUV stopped moving, three of Talbot's employees snatched Poole from the car and pulled him into the plane. Porter was rushed through a door at the back of the hangar to a waiting Ford F150 driven by a man in his sixties with thin white hair under a tattered New York Yankees ball cap. The green bag went in the back, and the moment the plane exited the hangar, they pulled away at a crawl. No reason to draw attention. The driver of the F150 hadn't said much, only grunted at Porter when he got in. With one eye on the flashing lights of the law enforcement vehicles racing across the tarmac, Porter tried to thank him. The man had nodded but didn't offer a name. Probably for the best. The F150 passed through security and left the airport grounds without any fanfare. Porter's driver had offered a half-assed wave at the guard manning the booth, then pulled through. The guard didn't seem to notice Porter at all. His face was buried in a magazine. Across the street from the airport, they pulled into a Sheraton parking lot where they saddled up next to a dark blue BMW. Porter was given the keys. Porter peeled several bills off one of the cash bundles in his green bag and tried to pay the guy in the Yankees cap, but he waved it off without making eye contact.

"I've been well compensated."

These were the only words he spoke to Porter before driving off in the opposite direction from the airport.

Using the key fob, Porter opened the trunk of the BMW and dropped the bag inside. He found a new burner phone on the passenger seat along with contact information for another team of pilots stationed at a small regional airport. He owed Emory. He also deeply regretted that she had become mixed up in all this. She was a good person and deserved better. As he started the car, he vowed to himself he'd find a way to make it up to her.

He was on the road a moment later, about the same time the Talbot jet with Poole inside reached altitude.

Twenty minutes after that, he was back in the center of Charleston. Eight minutes after that, he pulled into this lot, parked, and got out.

He'd spotted the discount auto parts store about the same time Poole's cell phone rang earlier. He'd been ready to pull into this very lot when that phone rang, and he was damn glad he didn't. He wanted to trust Poole, he really did, but that ring proved that he could not.

Although it was the auto parts store that drew his attention, it was the gas station across the street, the motel next to that gas station, that really pulled him in—rundown, falling apart, painted yellow with lime green trim. He recognized the scene immediately, and Porter tried to convince himself he recognized it from the description in the diary, but he knew that was only partly true. He knew this place. He'd been here before.

Porter pulled into this lot across the street from the motel because parking there felt right, felt *familiar*. He knew the moment he slipped the car into park and stepped out into the night air that he'd stood in that very spot before.

The writing was literally on the wall.

His hands were still balled in fists as he stared up at the side of the auto parts store, at the words spray-painted on the brick in red:

We bled for you, Sam.

He heard these words in his head. He couldn't explain why or how, but it was like someone was reading the five words to him. The voice wasn't his own, and it wasn't Bishop's. He didn't recognize the voice, but he *knew* the voice.

Porter stared up at the words on the wall.

We bled for you, Sam.

He had no real recollection of the motel across the street, not really. He'd driven by hundreds of time on patrol, but he couldn't recall a single time he was actually called there. He closed his eyes for a moment and tried to picture one of the rooms or the lobby or even an ice or soda machine, and he came up blank. His only memories of an interior room at that place came from what he read in the diary. Bishop's encounter with Bernie. The aftermath of that encounter.

Porter hadn't been there for that, had he?

He wanted to say no, but the truth was his memories of that time were so muddled in his brain he couldn't be sure. Until a few hours ago, he thought he remembered the moments leading up to when he was shot with vivid detail. Poole had shown him that that detail was a lie.

He could picture the white van across the street. He could even see Stocks and Welderman pulling up next to that white van in their Chevy Malibu, a young Anson Bishop getting out.

Or was it Weasel?

Or Tegan?

Kristina?

Libby?

Even Vincent Weidner.

He could *see* it if he closed his eyes, and that frightened him a little bit. That white van might be Hillburn's. How many times had he ridden in that thing? How many times had he driven it? Hell, how many times had he borrowed it?

About as many times as Hillburn borrowed your coat, his mind shot back. *That old navy blue trench you loved so much.*

He tried not to think about that. No, not that.

She was standing across the street. Porter wasn't sure how long she had been there. Just standing there, watching him from the motel parking lot. Her dark hair fluttered around her shoulders, caught in the night air. She wore a coat of her own, long and black, her hands in the pockets. She stood perfectly still, watching him as cars zipped between heading north and south. If she felt any emotion at the sight of him, her face didn't betray her. Her solemn look was stoic, statuesque.

Sarah Werner.

Or, at least, the woman he knew as Sarah Werner.

Bishop's mother.

A killer.

A liar.

Ghostlike in that silent breeze.

She returned his stare but only for a moment, then got into the same silver Lexus she had been driving in Chicago and pulled out of the motel parking lot, out into the late-night traffic.

Sam scrambled back into his borrowed BMW and somehow managed to keep her in sight, three, sometimes four cars between them. He couldn't tell if she was alone. He dared not get closer.

90

Porter

Day 6 • 1:27 AM

Porter drove with the windows open. This time of year in Chicago, that would have been impossible, but the temperature in South Carolina hovered somewhere in the sixties, and that cool air rushing over him kept him alert, helped him feel alive.

He needed to feel alive, because something about this moment did not. He couldn't put his finger on it, and he'd spent the last twenty minutes thinking about it. He felt present, yet he didn't. If a man could step out of his own body and watch himself, then that was what Porter was doing right now. He was an observer, a bystander as the film reel of his life ticked forward.

Sarah Werner's silver Lexus hadn't violated the speed limit. In fact, she remained one or two miles per hour under. She used her turn signal whenever necessary, and the few times she came upon a yellow traffic light, she stopped rather than increase speed and continue on. About ten minutes after pulling out onto the highway, Porter had given up all pretenses of a clandestine tail. Sarah knew he was following her. She had all but shot off a flare to encourage him. Had they remained in the city, he might have had a chance at remaining hidden, but they weren't in the city, not anymore. He'd followed her onto I-26, then 78, then a series of smaller roads until he gave up trying to keep track. With each turn, the number of cars around them dwindled and now, as he followed her down a narrow two-lane road through open fields, they were utterly alone.

Much like the parking lot next to the auto parts store, there was a familiarity to this drive, and again Porter told himself this was because Bishop had detailed it in the diary. And much like before, telling himself this didn't quash the feeling that *he* had made this drive before. When two grain silos rolled by outside his passenger window, both painted green and tainted with rust, Porter told himself that he had never seen them before, yet he knew he had. The little voice in the back of his mind reminded him that there was no mention of grain silos in Bishop's diary.

Sarah's blinker came on. Left turn from the blacktop to a gravel road surrounded by weeds as tall as Porter. At one point, this might have been a cornfield or maybe tobacco or wheat. Mother Nature evicted the crops in lieu of her own a long time ago. Even the stars seemed to have vanished from this place. The sky nothing more than a tapestry of black, and Porter knew if he found the courage to turn off his headlights, he'd be plunged into a darkness thick enough to taste.

He made the turn and listened to the gravel crunch under his wheels as he left the pavement. She was at least a quarter mile ahead of him now, lost behind several twists and turns, but that didn't matter. He knew where they were going, even if he didn't want to believe that little truth.

When the large farmhouse came into view at the end of the gravel road, a looming structure of white clapboard and tin roof, it did so as a monster might climb from a hole in the Earth. First with only peaks and chimney, then the second floor, followed by the first and the porch. The front door open like a mouth, a hint of light beyond, although all the windows appeared dark. As Porter pulled up behind Sarah's empty Lexus, he realized all those windows weren't dark but boarded. The fingers of his headlight beams reached out across the field behind the house and found the barn, or what was left of it. The roof was long gone. Only three walls still stood, and those appeared to be balanced precariously against each other. A gust of wind in the wrong direction could take the entire structure down.

Porter shut off the BMW, the lights with it, and that left only the glow from that open front door. He found himself on the porch, boards creaking underfoot, without any recollection of leaving the car. Every inch of his skin prickled. His pulse drummed wildly in his neck. He stepped inside and all went quiet, even the cricket song somehow remaining outside.

The glow came from candles, dozens of them, placed on various flat surfaces around the house. They'd been burning for some time, and most were about half gone. Sarah hadn't been here long enough to light them—she had to have done that earlier in the night. All the furniture had been covered with white sheets long ago, thick, gray dust clinging to the cloth.

Porter found her on the other side of an arched doorway in what could only be the parlor, the room filled with shadows, only a single candle on the stone mantle of the fireplace.

Her back was to him.

Kneeling. Her black coat gone. She wore a white gown of some sort. Her head was bowed, and as he neared, he realized her hands were clasped together, her eyes closed.

On a silver serving tray, three white boxes were on the floor beside her. Several pieces of black string.

And a knife.

The light of the candle seemed to like that blade.

91

Clair

Day 6 • 1:31 AM

The mayor was quiet again.

Clair was fairly certain he was still in the room next to hers, but he'd stopped crying and he didn't respond when she called out to him. There was a good chance he was in shock.

When the face appeared at her door—black mask with dark glasses beneath—Clair stood, went to the glass, and glared back at him, her, whatever. "Who the fuck are you?"

The head tilted slightly to the right, this slow movement, then a gloved hand raised a water bottle to the window. The bottle rested on the person's palm and they drew their other hand over the top with their fingers splayed out in a slow caress, like a hand model displaying a product. They then pointed at Clair and gestured for her to move to the back of the room, away from the door.

The last thing Clair wanted to do was obey this piece of shit, but that bottle of water might as well have been a bar of gold dangled in front of an old Arizona miner. Her dry throat ached at the sight of it.

Clair stepped back.

The person didn't move, only held up the bottle at the window. After a moment, their finger bent slightly, gestured for Clair to get further back.

One pace from the door.

Two.

Three.

Her fever may have broken, but she was far from healthy. Clair's legs wobbled beneath her, a light sheen of sweat covered her skin. Simple movement felt labored, exhaustive. If she were to jump this person as they came through the door, Clair was under no illusion she would win the struggle which was sure to follow. Now wasn't the time.

That finger again pointed toward the back corner of the room.

Clair took another step back.

The face disappeared for a moment.

The click of a lock disengaging.

The door slowly swung into the room on squeaky hinges.

When the masked figure stepped through the narrow opening, Clair noted the broad shoulders, the flat chest. About five foot ten. Male. No doubt anymore.

Black jeans.

Black shirt.

Black gloves.

Black mask.

Dark glasses beneath.

He held the bottle in his right hand, reached into the small room, and placed it on the floor inside the door. From the hallway, he retrieved a brown paper sack, set that next to the water bottle, also with his right hand.

He didn't have any keys, but in the door itself, she spotted the nub of a dead bolt. The hallway floor behind him was tiled, although it appeared very old and distressed. The walls were painted a muted gray.

"I'm still in the hospital, aren't I?"

The man looked at her, his eyes appearing buglike behind dark plastic in the mask, but he didn't answer. Instead, he stepped back out into the hallway, closed the door, and twisted the lock.

Clair scrambled for the water.

92

Porter

Day 6 • 1:48 AM

Porter's breath fell from his lips, the air leaving him as if defeated and retreating. As he saw her on the floor like that, perfectly still, he had to remind himself to take in more air, to *breathe,* because his body had become a traitor, no longer his own but a separate thing with thoughts and actions of its own.

Porter stepped deeper into the room, closer to her. "What is this?"

"This is home, Sam. *His home,* where he was forced to live after those horrible events in Simpsonville. After we failed to protect him, our little boy."

"He's not *our* little boy."

"He put so much faith in you, as any child would."

"I'm not Anson's father. Don't imply that I am."

"He counted on you. Looked up to you. You were a hero to him, and instead of rescuing him from this hell, you let him burn. You left all of them to burn."

Porter's head was shaking before he realized he had moved at all. He raised both his hands and gestured around the room. "I don't know what any of this is. I don't know what you're talking about. I don't remember anything."

"Try, Sam."

"I have. There's nothing there."

"But you know this place, don't you? You remember being here? You remember standing in this very room?" She said this without opening her eyes, her hands still clasped. When her voice began to plead, she bit it off, paused for a moment. "Memories are fluid, like water. They can disappear into the smallest cracks in a wall, drip by drip, but they never completely vanish, they fester back there, grow mold, until they can no longer be contained, then they find an opening, they reach for the light. Your memories want to come out. You only need to let them. They're pushing on the backside of those walls."

Porter circled her with slow steps, dust from the carpet pluming up with each footfall. When he faced her, he went still.

Her eyes opened, and she looked up at him, at his hand resting on the butt of the .38 attached to his belt. "Are you going to kill me?"

"Why would I kill you?"

"Like the others, I mean."

Porter didn't remember reaching for the weapon, and his hand fell away. He tried not to look at the empty white boxes beside her, at the knife. "I haven't killed anyone."

At this, she only smiled.

Porter knelt down, his voice growing firm. "I met you for the first time in New Orleans. I met Anson for the first time in Chicago when I got called in to investigate that bus accident, the victim we thought was 4MK. Whatever you're trying to do here is bullshit. It's a lie. It's you and that kid of yours playing some kind of twisted, fucked up game, and I refuse to be part of it."

Her smile grew. "Sam, you've been playing the game longer than any of us."

His face grew red. "What happened to Anson's father? His real father?"

"He was shot, Sam. In the head."

"Like it said in the diary," Sam interjected.

"Not like in the diary," she replied. "Not like that diary at all."

Blowing out a breath, Sam got to his feet. "Why the hell are you doing this?"

Sarah unclasped her hands. "Do you remember the last time you stood in this room?"

"I've never been in this room."

She nodded toward a chair on his left. "Pull the sheet from that armchair, Sam."

"Why?"

"Because your memories want to get out. Can't you hear them?"

Porter shook his head, frustration mounting. He reached for the dusty sheet and tugged the cloth away, let it fall to the floor in a crumpled pile. The armchair was a yellow wingback, tufted velvet with stubby wooden legs. At the center of the seat cushion, up one arm and covering nearly half the backrest, was a dark brown stain. Someone had made an attempt to scrub it out, but Porter knew this was the kind of thing you couldn't wash away. Whoever had worked on the stain only managed to spread it out, creating deep swirling patterns. With this much blood, all you could do was strip it away, burn the material, start over.

Cover it with a sheet and forget. His mind whispered back. *Some things are better forgotten.*

Something horrible happened here. That much blood.

"The couch, too," Sarah said softly.

Before she even had the words out, Porter was pulling away that sheet, the dust rising around him, tickling his eyes and nose.

The stains on the couch were far worse than the chair. The cushions had been soaked so deeply he found himself looking to the sides of the couch to determine the original color because that deep brown had found its way into every crease and crevice on top, and there was no denying someone had died there. Multiple someones had died there. This was too much for only one. He'd been to enough crime scenes to understand that.

Porter reached for another sheet, and when he pulled that one away, he found a broken wooden chair beneath, also stained in death. The next sheet revealed an old roll-top desk, covered in utility bills, the paper and desktop streaked with the remains of some horrific event.

Taking the candle down from the fireplace mantel, Porter held it to the walls and realized the splatter extended even there, drips and lines. And the more he looked, the worse it got. What he first thought were intricate patterns in the wallpaper were something terrible. The room screamed of death. A long-ago massacre.

Porter wanted to ask her what happened here, but he choked on the words. He forced out, "They killed Stocks, upstairs. That's where the diaries I have end. What happened after that? What happened here?"

At first, Sarah didn't reply, and when he finally turned back to her, she was no longer kneeling on the floor. She'd risen to her feet and moved to the arched doorway. "Father, forgive me," she said softly.

"What?" The word came out harsh, his throat filled with dust.

"When I asked him, that's all he would tell me. 'Father, forgive me,'" she said. "He carved the same words in the top of that desk. He said you may have forgotten, but he wasn't willing to, regardless of how much it hurt."

Porter reached for the desk and pulled the roll-top down, the words glaring at him from cherry-stained mahogany, maybe the only place in the room not touched by blood.

93

Poole

Day 6 • 2:29 AM

The address on Porter's file was a rural farmhouse about thirty minutes outside Charleston. Still in the FBI communications truck, en route back to the Chicago field office, Poole and Hurless loaded up satellite images. There wasn't much to see. Even from the distant aerial shots, the place appeared abandoned. County records indicated the property comprised nearly twenty acres. There was a main house and the remains of a barn set back in an open field.

Poole's cell phone had come to life on a tower near that farmhouse.

Hurless read the data to Poole aloud as it came in. "It's been nearly a decade since anyone had the power on out there. Plot data says the property's got a well for water. Last crop record said they farmed wheat, but that dates back nearly two decades. Nothing current."

The deed was in the name of Sam Porter.

"He bought the place seventeen years ago and looks like he left it empty, unless he's running a generator out there for electric."

"He was in Chicago by then," Poole pointed out. "Doesn't make sense."

"I've got a small cabin on a lake up in Wisconsin I visit in the summer," Hurless pointed out.

"Nobody buys a farm as a vacation house."

"Maybe he planned to retire there."

"Maybe." Poole sighed. "Or maybe this is like the place in Simpsonville. Porter claimed Bishop falsified the records."

An FBI tech, who was seated in a chair bolted to the floor across from them, removed her headphones and turned to Hurless. "Sir? I think you'll want to see this." She pointed at a frozen video on a computer monitor. "This is airing live right now on Channel Seven." She twisted a volume knob, and sound came from the van speakers mounted in the ceiling. Poole recognized the reporter as Lizeth Loudon, a local fixture.

"— source within the department who wishes to remain anonymous has told us Bishop claimed innocence, saying that his involvement in the case was as a pawn in a sting operation perpetrated by Detective Nash's partner, Detective Sam Porter. Before any of this could be confirmed, a security malfunction somehow led to the disappearance of both Anson Bishop and Detective Porter. While Detective Porter's whereabouts are still unknown, we just received the following message from Anson Bishop."

Loudon went quiet, staring at the camera. The shot switched from her to one of Bishop and a video that appeared to have been shot with a cell phone. "I don't know who else to go to. I'm not sure who I can trust anymore. When they took me to Metro, I explained everything to the FBI, *everything*, I thought they could protect me, keep me safe. This is bigger than Porter, though—he's working with other people. Somehow, those people triggered the sprinklers in the building, all the doors unlocked, everything, all at once." Bishop ran his hand through his hair in frustration, then looked back at the camera. "Porter tried to kill me. I think he created the distraction, him and the people he's working with. I managed to get out, but I had to run, hide—I don't know what else to do, who I can trust. *I was in federal custody, and he still almost killed me.* Porter won't stop until I'm dead. I know that now." He looked to the ground for a moment, then back at the camera. "I'm going to turn myself in to you, the press, the people of Chicago. I'm not sure what else I can do. I'll be at the Guyon Hotel at six in the morning. I don't think Porter would kill me in public, not in front of a crowd. I want the FBI there. U.S. Marshalls. Anyone who can protect me and safely bring me in. All of you, anyone. My only safety is in numbers. I'll only be safe with *you*. If Detective Sam Porter finds me first, I know I'm dead. I don't know if anyone in law enforcement can be trusted. I'll do what I can to stay alive, but I need help. I need *your* help. If I don't show up, you'll know it's because he found me first, or the people he's working with did. Nothing else will keep me from there. Nothing."

Bishop's face froze, still looking at the camera.

The image returned to the live shot of Lizeth Louden and panned back several feet to reveal that she was standing outside in a parking lot, a large building looming behind her, snow drifting down and catching the bright lights from her camera crew. She turned slightly and gestured back. "The Guyon Hotel is a 1927 Moorish Revival in West Garfield at 4000 West Washington, an area of town that has seen severe decline over the past several years. The one-time home of WFMT and Benny Goodman has been in a constant state of disrepair, and while it has changed hands numerous times in attempts at revitalization, all have failed. In the '80s, the Guyon even hosted President Jimmy Carter while he was in the area working with Habitat for Humanity. Shortly after that, an attempt to convert the hotel to low-income housing was made, but that didn't pan out, either. Since 2005, this once-spectacular Chicago hotel has changed hands at least four times but has remained abandoned. Preservation Chicago, the organization behind the renovated Rosenwald Apartments, believes they can turn the building around, but their efforts have yet to be realized." The camera zoomed back in on Louden's face. She tucked a loose strand of hair behind her ear. "Two days ago, former Metro Detective Sam Porter was apprehended in this building and taken into federal custody. He later escaped and is still at large. I personally plan to stay here at the Guyon and wait for Anson Bishop to turn himself in at six this morning, approximately three and a half hours from now. I welcome all our viewers to join me. We'll see this developing story through to the end together. If you do come out, I advise you to dress warm. You may also want to consider bringing food and water—there are only a handful of businesses supporting this neighborhood, and most likely they will not be able to handle an influx of visitors, particularly at this hour."

Hurless was pale. "Oh, Christ."

"It will be a mob, all gunning for the police. He's trying to turn the public on us."

Hurless shouted up to the driver. "We're moving base—get us over to the Guyon Hotel in West Garfield!" He turned back to Poole. "I'll build a perimeter and get our people in place on this end. I want you to reach out to Granger—his team is closest to that farmhouse. Get him on the phone. I want them out there."

Poole nodded.

Taking out his own phone, Hurless added, "You disobeyed a direct order by leaving town. When this is over, you *will* answer for that. Don't think you won't." He turned his back on him, holding on to the ceiling with his free hand as the van lurched forward.

94

Porter

Day 6 • 2:02 AM

"Five, four, three…"

Porter was still standing at the desk when the woman he knew as Sarah Werner began to count down. Both of them had been silent before that, Porter staring at the words *Father, forgive me* carved into the cover of the roll-top desk, Sarah standing behind him. Several minutes, maybe more—Porter was having trouble tracking things like that, his mind swimming. Then she started counting down.

"Two, one…"

A phone rang.

Porter glanced back at her.

She smiled. "You should get that."

The sound came from the desk. He rolled the top up and fished around under the papers and bills, many of them glued together with ages-old blood.

The phone didn't look like a disposable. UNKNOWN CALLER scrolled across the display before ringing for the third time. Taped to the back was one of his old business cards from Charleston PD, faded and covered in grime. The lettering barely legible. Porter's finger shook as he touched the answer button and pressed the phone to his ear. "What the fuck is this?"

"Sam, you know how I feel about foul language. I thought we were beyond all that."

"I don't understand…what I'm looking at."

"You're home, Sam. You're looking at your home. You left a mess behind."

"I've never—"

Bishop cut him off. "Don't say you've never been there, Sam. That's a lie, even if you're having trouble remembering. You need to see beyond all the lies you've told yourself and find the truth. It's there in your head, somewhere in the back under all the dust. You can bury a bad thing, but those bad things have a tendency to claw their way back out of the dirt. Yours are coming for you, and they're angry. You dismissed us all. You wrote us off. Left us to bleed."

"I was hurt, I—"

"We were all hurt, Sam."

Sam tried not to look at all the blood, blood marring nearly every surface of the room. "Who died here?"

"In many ways, we all did."

"Where did you get my card?"

At this, Bishop did not reply. Instead, he said, "You, Hillburn, Welderman, Stocks, who knows who else—the corruption and dirt is so thick around all of you, I'm surprised you're able to move. At least Hillburn had the decency to take his own life, pay retribution for his sins, but you? You went on without remorse, you carved out a life on the backs of the dead, on the backs of tortured children. How many? Do you even know?"

"I don't know what you're talking about!" Porter shouted. He hadn't meant to shout, he didn't want to shout.

"I saw you there, Sam. We all did. Do you feel their eyes on you now? They're all around you. Can you hear them? I know I do. Not a night goes by that I don't hear those voices pleading for help. Over the years, I've gone back to Finicky's little farm and sat in that very room more times than I can count. I cried with them. I gazed upon them. I longed for one more chance to hold Libby in my arms, knowing I never would. And when a miracle came, when I finally did find her, you took her away from me for good. You and your friends tortured her, left her body in complete disgrace in her own filth in that house on Mckeen Road." He paused for a moment, then said, "Do no evil, Sam. Retribution is at hand. It's time you pay for your sins."

From across the room, Sarah watched him, her face expressionless. Although the phone wasn't on speaker, in the otherwise silent room she probably made out most, if not all, of what Bishop said. Porter's eyes fell on the three white boxes on the floor, the black string, the knife. That was when she smiled.

As if able to see him, Bishop went on. "The boxes aren't for you, Sam. Death would be a mercy. A mercy of which you are undeserving. The children shall pay for the sins of the father; it's only from that pain that the father will find greater or equal suffering. As with all those before you, it should be a child who dies for you, but you don't have any children, do you, Sam? The only children in your life are those like me, the ones you ran through your little hell house with Finicky and the others. Those children have suffered enough. You do have loved ones, though, don't you? Well, you did."

Porter's chest tightened. "Did you kill Heather?"

"A wife is not a child but a loved one nonetheless. Close but not enough. Not nearly enough."

The blood rushed to Porter's head, throbbed at his temples. *"Did you kill Heather?"*

Bishop let out a sigh. "Harnell Campbell planned to rob a convenience store that night. All I did was offer him a ride. Truth be told, I may have left the .38 on the seat, and Harnell appeared quite fond of it. At one point, the gun belonged to your friend Stocks, but he hasn't needed it for some time, and good ol' Harnell said he'd give it a home, so seemed silly not to oblige."

"If that's true, why did you kill him?"

"Loose end. Father taught me the importance of picking up after myself. He was trash, and my need for him was over."

Porter's hand shook, his head buzzed, he nearly dropped the

phone. "Heather never hurt anyone," he managed to say, his eyes filled with tears.

"Heather was a partial payment on your debt. In several hours, you will make good on the rest. Maybe, once we're even, once the offering plate is full, we can part ways as friends, but I'll understand if you don't want to. I've lost Libby, Weasel, Vincent, Paul, Tegan, Kristina…who will you lose today?"

Porter tried to speak, but he couldn't form the words. The lump in his throat held them all back.

"Go to the stairs, Sam. There's something you need to see."

Porter didn't want to, but he also knew he had no choice.

Without a word, Sarah followed behind him as he crossed the parlor back to the hallway, as he made his way to the landing at the base of the staircase, his legs weak. As it said in the diary, the walls leading to the second floor were covered in framed photographs of children—boys, girls, all ages. Some smiling, some not. One in particular caught Sam's eye.

"You see it, don't you?"

He *did* see it. Porter climbed the steps. The picture was about halfway up, the only one facing backward. On the back of the frame, written in black, blocky letters was WM10 5k, and two initials. Sam knew what he'd find even before he lifted the frame off the wall and turned it around so he could see the picture. A much younger face, but one he recognized.

Oh God, it couldn't be him.

"Your friends hurt The Kid bad that night, but he eventually recovered," Bishop said. "Over the years, I realized he was the most resourceful of us all. He came back from those horrors of childhood and found a way to help balance the scale, reclaim what had been taken from him, from us all."

Porter's eyes were glued to the photograph. "Nobody else has to die, this needs to stop."

"I have something of yours, Sam. Something precious," Bishop said. "I tried to get from that farmhouse to the Guyon once to try and save someone. I wasn't fast enough. Let's see if you are. It's *so* far. I think part of me is rooting for you. Heather always had faith in you. Even as the last breath left her body, she held out hope you'd save her."

The line went dead then, and Porter looked down at Sarah, watching him from the bottom step. "Hmm, if only you had a plane," she said. "We're late for a flight."

"I put Poole on the jet."

"Talbot's people had another brought out to Atlantic Aviation just for you, you know that. Don't lie to me, Sam, not after all we've been through together—it's beneath you."

Porter shook his head and dialed another number. "I'm calling the FBI."

"Anson told me you'd try to do that." Sarah stepped closer and took out her own phone. She cycled through several screens before holding it out to him. "He told me you'd throw yourself in front of a bus if you had to. He said when you did, I was to show you this."

The video she played was surprisingly clear. Even though the image was shot from behind, Porter recognized Clair. Although muted, he still heard her screaming as she beat on a door with both fists.

"You're going to power down that phone and it will stay that way until you touch down in Chicago, then you can call whoever you want. You try to reach someone sooner, and she's dead. Do you understand?"

Porter nodded reluctantly.

"You try to call *anyone* before you reach Chicago, and not even her boxes will be found. Power it down, now."

He did.

95

Poole

Day 6 • 3:31 AM

Twenty-eight minutes to mobilize Grainger's team in Charleston, another thirty-one to reach the farmhouse. Nearly one hour after Poole made the call, at a little after three in the morning, they moved into position as he listened from the FBI communications van now parked outside the Guyon Hotel.

"Gwendle, in position."

"Jordan, in position."

"Suarez, in position."

"This is Michaelson, I've got line of sight on the vehicle in the driveway. A silver Lexus, Illinois plate TW84R3. The vehicle appears empty."

"No lights on inside the house. No sign of anyone."

"Stay frosty," Grainger said. "Porter may just be sleeping."

They'd already searched the remains of the barn and found nothing.

"Lonestar One in position, North and West face."

"Lonestar Two in position, South and East. Full line of sight."

Poole knew *lonestar* was code for Grainger's two snipers. Federal snipers didn't use names on communication lines. Based on the satellite photos, they were most likely hidden in the fields, probably found some kind of hill to provide a visual field.

All would be wearing night-vision equipment, thankful for the cover offered by the last few hours of darkness.

Grainger returned to the line. "Gwendle, you head up. Suarez, you take down. Jordan, you've got the ball. Move on my count."

"Copy."

"Three, two, one, mark."

"Federal agents!" someone shouted out.

Poole heard the familiar sound of a battering ram, and in his mind's eye, he pictured the scene as Jordan heaved the heavy metal cylinder back and swung toward the door. Wood cracked and gave way with a satisfying crunch. This was followed by two loud bangs, concussion grenades, no doubt heaved into the house from the opening, then the stomp of running feet. More shouts.

"Hallway, clear!"

"Stairs, clear!"

"Dining room, clear!"

"Bedrooms one and two, clear!"

"Parlor—Don't move! Don't move!"

"Remaining bedrooms, bathroom, clear!"

"Suarez," Grainger said. "What do you have?"

No response.

"Suarez?"

Nothing.

"Gwendle—back downstairs, check on Suarez!"

Suarez then, "Parlor...clear. I've got a body here. Female. Oh, man." He retched, his bone conducting microphone picking up the sound with crisp detail.

"This is Jordan. Suarez is...indisposed. We've got a female. Thir-ties, forties, difficult to tell. Short brown hair. She's wearing a white dress, thin material, almost looks like a nightgown. Someone carved her up. It's bad. Missing ear and eye, looks like her tongue, too. I've got three white boxes sealed with black string. I'll leave those for CSI to open. Cause of death appears to be a slit throat. There's a butcher knife on the floor beside the body. They used something else on her too, maybe a scalpel, something with a fine tip. They carved her up—wrote all over her face, neck, arms...all exposed skin...see no evil, hear no evil, speak no evil, do no evil. We'll...we'll have to ID her from prints or dental. That's not all, though. We've got blood all over this room. Old, not from her. Under the dust, might be years old. Something else. Somebody carved *father, forgive me* in the top of a desk in his room. I don't see any wood shavings. Hard to tell if it's recent or not."

"Grainger? This is Gwendle. I found blood in one of the upstairs bedrooms as well. Old too, like down here. Not a recent crime. There's a lot, though. Very possibly fatal."

Poole unmuted his phone. "Is there any salt on or around the body? Around the other blood spots?"

"Salt?"

"On her skin, her clothes...anything at all?"

"Standby."

Jordan came back a moment later. "No visible sign of salt. I don't think she's been dead for very long. She's still warm. Her blood is fresh."

"Any sign of Porter?"

"Lonestar one and two," Grainger said, "any exterior movement?"

"Negative."

"Nothing."

"Gwendle here, again. The walls in this place are covered with pictures of kids. I found one frame on the landing leading upstairs. There's a lot of dust in here, and judging by the smudges on the glass, it's been handled recently."

"Can you send me a photograph?" Poole asked.

"Hang on."

A moment later, Poole's phone chirped. When he looked at the image of the young boy on the screen, he felt the blood drain from his face.

96

Porter

Porter drove as Sarah Werner sat silently in the seat beside him, face forward, hands clasped in her lap. When he tried to speak, nothing came out. He couldn't close his eyes, not even for a second; when he did, he saw Clair beating on that door. He saw Heather looking back at him, a questioning look on her face. Porter had never been able to lie to her, even about the smallest thing—she'd give him that look, and he'd melt. She'd pluck the truth out of him without the need to utter a sound.

"I've never been inside that house, not before tonight," Porter finally managed to say aloud. He said this not only to the image of Heather in his mind, but to himself, to the woman sitting beside him.

"You mean *you don't remember* setting foot inside that house before tonight," Sarah replied, her eyes on the broken yellow line rushing under their SUV. "We both know just how faulty your memory is, Sam. You've got a lifetime locked away up there. You read the file from Dr. Whittenberg."

Porter frowned. "How do you know about that? I didn't tell you."

Sarah smiled. "I know a lot of things."

"Whittenberg's file is bullshit."

"Is it?"

"According to that file, you're not even real. You're some imaginary person my screwed-up brain created. Some kind of ghost in the machine."

Sarah smiled again but said nothing.

Nearly two minutes passed before Porter spoke again. "Are you real?"

Sarah reached over and took Porter's right hand. She placed it over her breast. "Do I feel real?"

He pulled away. "Stop that."

"If I'm not real, it means you killed the real Sarah Werner back in New Orleans. You shot her in the head and left her to rot on her couch. Do you remember doing that, Sam? Maybe to cover more of your past."

"I haven't killed anyone."

"You keep saying that, but that doesn't make it true."

"I'm trying…"

"Trying what?"

"I'm trying to remember, but that part of my life is so cloudy," Porter told her. "It's like trying to remember an old movie that played on the television in the corner of the room while you were also reading a book. Background noise, barely there. When I reach for those thoughts, they pull back, sink a little further in the muck."

"In his file, Dr. Whittenberg said your brain was trying to protect you. Shielding your conscious memory from the horrible events of your past, things you did but you weren't willing to accept. Maybe that's the answer—you need to accept what you did, make peace with your actions, and that cloud will lift." She paused for a second, then added, "You remembered what happened in the alley. The rest is there, too."

Porter hadn't told her that, hadn't mentioned the alley at all. He was sure of that. "I remember…"

But what did he remember?

Porter said, "I remember chasing after that kid. Weasel. I remember parking on Cumberland, cornering him in the alley, running after him. The dealer Hillburn had been trying to collar for months. He…"

"He what?"

"Hurry, they're coming," Porter mumbled, more to himself.

"Why were you in that alley, Sam?"

"I was chasing Weasel."

"Were you?"

Porter reached for the phone sitting in the center console.

"You're not allowed to call anyone," Sarah told him. "You do and your friends will die. You need to remember that. We're watching you, Sam. Don't, even for a second, ever believe you're alone today."

Porter wasn't trying to make a call. He had turned the phone over and was looking at the business card taped to the back. "Where did Anson get this?"

"There's the airport, up there on the left," Sarah said.

97

Clair

The brown paper sack contained a Snickers bar, an orange, and a package of peanut butter crackers. Not exactly the meal of champions but far better than the nothingness that filled Clair's belly earlier. She gobbled the food down, saving the orange for last—washed everything down with about half the water and tried not to eat so fast that the food came back up.

Clair was halfway through the meal before she realized she *had* been hungry, and she knew that was a good sign. A few hours earlier, she had no desire to eat. Her stomach twisted and churned and ached, and the idea of putting any food in there just made her feel sicker. Being hungry was good.

When she finished, Clair went back to the vent. "Are you there?"

At first, there was no reply. She didn't hear anything from the room beside her. When the mayor did speak, his voice was meek. "Yeah."

"Did he give you anything to eat?"

"It's a woman, not a he."

"Describe her for me."

The mayor blew out a breath. "I don't know. She looked young. At first, I thought twenties or thirties, but she may be older than that. Sometimes it's hard to tell. Dark brown hair, shoulder length."

"How tall?"

"About a foot shorter than me."

Clair rolled her eyes. "How tall are you?"

"Six foot."

"So she was only five feet tall?"

"No. Taller than that. Maybe five-foot-four. Five-foot-five."

"Tell me about her breasts."

"Seriously? You swing that way, Detective?"

Clair really wanted to hurt this man. "Does she have breasts? The woman who took you. The one who just gave you food."

"Of course she does. Nice ones. She knew how to show them off in that black slinky dress she was wearing. I like a lady who appreciates her own body."

"Was she wearing a black slinky dress just now?"

"Huh? No. Jeans. Black shirt and that crazy mask."

"Was she five-foot-four or taller?"

The mayor fell silent for a moment. "I know it was her yesterday, even with the mask on. But you're right. This might have been someone different. Maybe a guy. I don't know. They cut off my goddamn ear, cut out my eye. You can't expect me to take detailed notes."

Clair glanced around her room, then leaned back into the vent. "Do you have anything in your room we can use as a weapon? Anything at all?"

"What about you? What do you have?"

"There's nothing in here," she said.

He moved closer.

Through the vent, Clair saw his shadow momentarily block the vent. She heard him slump down against the wall. Softly, he said, "I found a nail."

"Give it to me."

"No way."

"You want to get out of here, right? Pass it over to me, through the vent."

"Find your own nail. Why would I give you mine?" When Clair didn't answer, he added: "I'm using it to pick the lock."

"If your lock is like mine, it's a dead bolt. You'd need at least two nails to get the lock open, and a nail is too thick for lock picking. If you're going to improvise, you'd need something like a paperclip to work the pins and a metal nail file to turn the tumbler."

"Well, I don't have either of those, so I'm using the nail."

"If I had the nail," Clair said, "I'd stab him in the neck with it. Gouge out his fucking face, then I'd walk out of here, unlock your door, and get you out too. Get you some help. But if you'd rather fool around with the lock, you keep on that. Come and get me out when you're done. You'd better hurry, though—if he already took your ear and your eye, he's coming for your tongue next. I can't imagine a politician without a tongue would do too well."

From the vent, Clair heard metal clink. When she looked down, the tip of a rusty nail was sticking through.

"Grab it before I drop it."

Clair did. The nail was long, about four inches. That was good.

She started on her shoelaces then, took both from her shoes and coiled them up in her hand.

98

Porter

Day 6 • 2:18 AM

Located off Charleston Air Force Base, Atlantic Aviation occupied several buildings and had two runways at their disposal. At this hour, most of the facility appeared deserted. Porter was waved through security and ushered toward a waiting Gulfstream. Unlike the previous jet, this one did not have the Talbot Enterprises logo on the tail; aside from an identification number, there were no markings on the plane at all. Running lights were on, the engines were humming, a man in a pilot's uniform stood by the stairs and pointed Porter toward two other parked SUVs.

The co-pilot from his previous flight.

The expression on his face was clearly one of concern.

He opened Porter's door even before he had a chance to shut down the motor. He shouted over the idling jet. "The feds are monitoring all of Talbot's assets. We're borrowing this plane from a friend. I can get you back to Chicago, but I can't guarantee nobody will be waiting for us when we land."

"I don't want to get Emory in any trouble," Porter told him. He still had the phone in his hand, and he shoved it into his pocket.

The pilot grabbed Porter by the shoulder and steered him toward the steps leading up into the plane. "Even if they figure out the shell game, they won't trace it back to Emory. She's clean."

"And you?"

"I'm just a hired hand. Just following orders received via e-mail forwarded through a dozen accounts. They try to trace that back, they'll just get caught up in a sticky web. I'm not worried. I'll just plead ignorance." He nodded up into the plane. "I had those photos developed. They're inside. Get in there and buckle up. We need to move."

"Her too. She's with me," Porter said, turning around on the steps.

The pilot followed his gaze, a puzzled look on his face. "Who?"

Sarah was gone.

99

Nash

"This is where you worked?"

Nash stood in the small office that Klozowski and Clair had used at Stroger Hospital. He was weak but better. The nurse in the ER wasn't thrilled when he pulled the catheter from his arm. She was even less thrilled when he got out of bed and told her he was leaving. She threatened to call security, and Nash told her good, but hurry—tell them to meet me in the cafeteria where they're holding everyone. Nobody leaves, nobody. On the way, Kloz had told him what he could—ran through everything that had happened. They'd stopped in the small office down the hall from the cafeteria. Part of him hoped they'd find Clair in the room, resting, recuperating, or simply passed out, but there was no sign of her.

Nash dialed Espinosa from SWAT for the third time, but the call didn't go through. "Cell service in this place is horrible," he grumbled.

"They're right outside the doors of the hospital. Faster just to walk there," Kloz told him, already pushing out the door.

When they reached the cafeteria, Nash felt his face flush with anger.

The cafeteria was empty.

He picked up a plastic chair and threw it across the room. "Goddamnit!"

Tables were pushed aside, trash littered the floor. It looked like someone had set off a bomb, but the room itself was empty.

"We couldn't hold them, not after the CDC lifted the containment ban."

Nash turned to find a bald black man in his fifties standing near a bank of elevators. "Who the hell are you?"

"Jerome Stout, head of hospital security." Stout walked up and offered his hand, but Nash didn't take it, had turned back to the empty room.

"You let whoever took her walk out of here, do you realize that? You let someone who killed at least two people in *your* hospital, on *your* watch, walk out of here," Nash said. "If something happens to her, if she's hurt in any way, it's on you."

"I had no choice. I'm following orders, same as you. This is a hospital, not a prison, and we came damn close to a riot keeping everyone here as long as we did. We've got names on everyone, contact information."

Nash brushed a hand through his hair. "Oh, I'm glad you took attendance."

An elevator dinged, and three security guards came out.

From another hallway on the opposite side of the cafeteria, someone was shouting.

Anthony Warnick.

There were at least a dozen Metro officers behind him, along with two men in full SWAT gear—Espinosa and Thomas. Espinosa was pale but looked better than the last time Nash had seen him. "We found your two missing officers. Both were in the ER since last night. I spent a few hours there myself, but I'm feeling better now."

Nash said, "Any sign of Clair?"

Espinosa shook his head. "Hurless told us to conduct a room-by-room search. He's coordinating with the feds, and the consensus is whoever is behind this is using the hospital as ground zero. They think the mayor is here too. Unless you want to handle things differently, we'll start on the top floor and work our way down.

I've got people stationed at all the exits. We're confirming IDs on everyone."

"So the people who were in here?"

"We've got records on everyone. Nobody slipped through. You've got my word on that."

Nash squeezed the man's shoulder. "Thank you."

Espinosa nodded and turned toward the large group behind him. "Every room, every closet, under every bed. I want every inch of this building searched. Nothing is off limits. Don't let anyone tell you otherwise. You have any trouble, you touch base with me."

"Comms don't work well," Nash pointed out.

Stout said, "That's always been a problem here. It's all the equipment." He pointed at the wall to his left. "See those red phones? You'll find them throughout the hospital. They're direct lines to my office up in security. Use those, and I'll help coordinate everyone from there. I can patch you in to each other, use the intercom, whatever you need."

"Understood," Espinosa said. He eyed Nash for a moment, then went on with hesitation. "There's one other thing, and this one's tough, no easy way to say it. Recent evidence suggests the person responsible for the deaths here at the hospital, the missing mayor, and our missing detective is working directly with Detective Sam Porter and may be responsible for additional deaths attributed to the 4MK investigation. Keep your guard up and your vigilance high."

Several murmurs passed through the crowd. Everyone here knew Sam.

"Go!" Espinosa shouted. "Fast and organized. Everyone stay sharp!"

The group scrambled. Some went to the elevators, others took the stairs. Within thirty seconds, Kloz and Nash were alone with Warnick.

"I'm under orders to stick with you," Warnick told him. "The mayor remains the priority."

Nash ignored him and turned to Kloz. "Show me exactly where Clair was seen last."

100

Porter

Day 6 • 5:04 AM

Porter turned the last page of Bishop's diary for the third time and swore softly.

He needed to know what happened after they killed Stocks.

None of it made sense. He'd gone back and reread the pages several times during the flight, hoping something there would jog his memory. Nothing had, though.

He looked around the empty cabin.

We're watching you, Sam. Don't, even for a second, ever believe you're alone today.

Fuck you, Sarah. You and your kid.

She ran off. Had to. Unwilling to risk falling into custody. At least that's what Porter told himself a couple hours ago as the jet rolled down the runway and went airborne. He'd stared out the window—she had been down there somewhere, crouching between the vehicles. Maybe still in the BMW. Hiding, waiting for them to leave.

He wasn't willing to accept the alternative.

He wouldn't go there.

"I'm not crazy."

Hearing the words aloud did nothing to make it feel any less true. In fact, the moment the words left his lips, Porter found himself looking around the private cabin to see if anyone had heard him.

He rubbed at both his temples. "I just need to get some sleep."

That aloud didn't sound any less crazy.

From the tray at his side, he ate the last piece of bacon. There had been a full breakfast waiting for him—three poached eggs, two English muffins, bacon, sausage, orange juice, and a carafe of dark roast coffee.

He'd hoped the meal would help, but he still had the worst headache, a grinding pain behind both his eyes as if someone were reaching into his skull and attempting to wring the memories from his brain. His leg bounced, an involuntary nervous tic of some sort. More than once, he'd consciously shut the movement down only to find his leg bouncing again several minutes later.

As the jet began to descend through the clouds, he worked his jaw to minimize the popping in his ears. They'd be on the ground soon; he needed a plan.

The photographs sat atop their envelope on the small table next to him. About three dozen in total. The first few were of several young girls, both posing provocatively, pouting at the camera in one, giggling or laughing in another. Tugging at the edges of their clothing. Most likely, these were Tegan and Kristina, but he had no way to know for sure. He didn't recognize either of them. There was a shot of Anson, too. Young, fourteen or fifteen at most. He stood next to a young girl, the tips of their fingers touching slightly. Her eyes on the camera, his watching something behind. Porter recognized the parlor back at the farmhouse—the furniture, the couch, desk in the corner. Bright sunlight streaming in from an unseen window. No blood.

Not yet.

Soon, though.

This was most likely Libby. Several bruises were visible on her left arm, up near the elbow. Nearly healed but still there.

There was a shot of Paul Upchurch making a silly face for the camera. He was unrecognizable from the man Porter was familiar with. The boy in the photo was young, vibrant, alive. Nothing like the shell of the man back in Chicago. Bald head and ghastly scar.

Porter paused there. That photo still in his hand.

He'd never met Paul Upchurch. Not as a child, not as an adult. How could he know what the man looked like in the end?

He shook it off. Nash had told him, or maybe it was Poole. So much had happened recently. Everything was a blur. Wait, it was Bishop who told him, back in the lobby of the Guyon. Then Porter had called Clair, told him about Upchurch's condition—repeated what Bishop told him, anyway. He'd never actually seen Upchurch, but his mind must have conjured an image based on those conversations.

There was a picture of Finicky. Porter *did* recognize her, but she was younger in the shot. He knew her as the woman pretending to be Bishop's mother. The woman he and Sarah had broken out of prison only to watch Bishop execute in cold blood.

Now, we're even, Bishop had told her.

The next three photographs were of the girls again, Tegan and Kristina. They were nude in the first one, their limbs intertwined in a bed with a green comforter in a room with pale yellow walls. Far too young. They both looked at the camera, and while they attempted to appear enticing, the fear in both was there too, a pleading in their eyes.

Tegan was in the image that followed. This time she was draped over the shoulders of a man. He was naked too. At first, Porter didn't recognize him. His hair was longer, and there was no gray. Far from in shape, he was still at least forty pounds lighter than the man Porter knew. But it was him, he was certain now.

Depending on the year the photo was taken, he was either an alderman or still in private practice—corporate law, from what Porter remembered. He'd never really followed politics.

There was no date stamp on the pictures. These were taken long before the man was sworn into Chicago's highest office, but Porter was sure it was him, their current mayor. He was probably in his thirties here. Tegan and Kristina would have been fifteen, maybe sixteen.

Mayor Barry Milton was with Kristina in the next shot. His

hands were bound together with a leather strap, some kind of gag in his mouth. She was behind him.

Porter put the picture aside. He couldn't look at that.

There were more.

They were worse.

Young boys, young girls—Porter couldn't look at those, either. They made his stomach churn.

He recognized the man in the next photograph as well. Not at first—like the mayor, he was much younger here, with a full head of hair and no glasses. But why would he be in Charleston? Possibly traveling with the mayor? For this? Maybe. How long had they known each other? How far back did they go? Porter had no idea. The man was sitting on the edge of a bed, brushing the hair of a young boy dressed in a black suit. Porter's stomach lurched again. He wanted to put a bullet through the man's skull.

Then he had an idea.

He found a pen on the table at his side, sitting in a slight recess to prevent it from rolling away. Porter uncapped the pen, scribbled a note on the back of the picture, then folded it down the middle before slipping it into his pocket.

The last five photographs were different from the others. These were shot from a lower angle. They weren't in focus. The subjects of the shots weren't necessarily centered or even completely in frame. These felt as if the photographer was holding the camera at his or her side and thumbed the shutter without looking through the viewfinder. Candid shots.

Hillburn.

He was standing next to his van, smoking a cigarette. No denying it was him.

Another of the Carriage House Inn motel. The photographer walking toward the west end.

The next was a shot of the parking lot across the street from the motel. The one Porter had been standing in just hours ago. McDonald's on one side, the auto parts store on the other. A patrol car parked there, on the left side of the image.

The final picture might have been the worst of them all. As Porter held the image in his hand, he found it hard to draw air into his lungs, as if his body no longer wanted to breathe. Blurry, slightly out of focus. This last photograph was one of him staring angrily at the camera.

101

Nash

Day 6 • 5:07 AM

"According to Stout, Clair most likely took these stairs. She went to the cafeteria to deal with something, then he called her and asked her to come up to his office. The CDC had the elevators locked down, so she would have had to take the stairs. These are the closest," Kloz said, his voice echoing in the stairwell.

Nash looked up and down. "What did Stout want?"

Kloz sighed. "I'm sorry, I should have asked that. I didn't think about it."

With the flashlight on his phone, Nash studied the doorframe and the floor, running the beam in a grid pattern over every surface, but didn't find anything.

Warnick paced across the tile behind them. "You're wasting time."

"You're a tool."

"Nice," Warnick chuffed. "With that video of you kicking Bishop in heavy rotation, you're going to need a friend like me. I'm not someone you want to piss on."

"I'm not into that kinky shit, so quit fishing around, asshole." Nash tilted his head up again, then asked Kloz, "What's your read on that Stout guy? Do you think he could be involved?"

"What, like lured her to the stairs so he could hurt her?"

"Yeah."

Kloz bit his lip as he thought this over. "He's former Metro. Seems like he was a good cop, but I guess that doesn't…" His voice trailed off. "I should have checked him out, vetted him, but I just didn't think about it. He obviously knows this hospital. He's someone who could have taken her and got her somewhere unseen for sure. He knew the two hospital victims, but so did half the staff. What's his motive, though? I'm not sure why he'd take her."

"Maybe she saw something. Got a little too close."

This seemed to rattle Kloz. "At this point, I know more about the case than she does. He may come after me."

"We can only hope."

"I need a gun," Kloz said.

"I've seen you shoot. You've got no business with a gun." Nash paused for a moment, then turned to Warnick. "Are you carrying a gun?"

Warnick took several steps back. "He's not taking mine."

"What do you have?"

".380."

"Are you licensed? Show me your license."

"Of course."

The moment Warnick reached for his back pocket, Nash pounced. Leading with his elbow, he slammed into Warnick's stomach, knocking the air out of him. With his free hand, he reached under the man's jacket, got the gun, and pressed the barrel under Warnick's chin. Warnick dropped his wallet and reached for Nash's arm with both hands. Nash dug the barrel deeper into the other man's skin. "Don't."

Warnick's hands fell to his side. He tried to speak, but nothing came out.

Klozowski's eyes were wide. "I don't need a gun, Nash. It's fine. Let him keep it."

Nash leaned in closer to Warnick, twisting the .380. "203. WF15 3k LM. What does that mean to you?"

Warnick said nothing.

Nash thumbed off the safety. "When I asked the woman at Carmine's Pizza about it, she told me to ask you, so I'm asking you. What does it mean?"

Warnick slowly caught his breath. If he was even slightly frightened, he didn't show any outward sign. "What do you think it means?"

"White female, fifteen-years-old, three thousand dollars, with the initials L.M., maybe Libby McInley," Nash told him. "Someone is selling kids."

"How do you know what it means?" Warnick said calmly.

"Because I work in law enforcement, and I've seen this kind of thing far more often than anyone should."

Warnick tried to nod, but the gun under his chin made the movement difficult. "And I know what it means because I work for the mayor's office, and we monitor everything law enforcement does. I see the same reports you do. More, actually. Human trafficking in this city is a problem."

"I think you're part of the problem. I think you're profiting from it."

"Well, you're wrong about that."

"I think the mayor is profiting from it too. That's why Bishop took him and left the photos."

"Bishop didn't leave the photos. The woman working with Porter did. If the mayor was part of something like that, I'd know about it. He's not."

"Why would some two-bit madam running an escort service tell me you were?"

Warnick waved dismissively, sucked in a little more air. "*Because* she's a two-bit madam running an escort service. She knows my name, knows you would know my name, so she threw a bone in your direction to get you off *her* back. This is someone who has spent a lifetime manipulating men. She's good at it. She played you, Detective. She played on your stupidity and misplaced judgement. You just can't see that."

The two men stared at each other for nearly a minute, neither willing to break eye contact. Nash finally lowered the gun. "I'm giving this to Kloz because I don't trust you. I will figure out how you're involved in all this, and I'll take you down. You try something stupid, and I'll shoot you myself. I would absolutely love to shoot you, so please, give me a reason."

Warnick leaned closer and straightened his jacket. "Are you done?"

Nash flicked the safety back on and handed the gun to Kloz.

Kloz pinched it between two fingers. "Seriously?"

"Tuck it in your pants and try not to shoot yourself. You may need it."

Kloz stared at the weapon for a moment, first put it down the front of his pants, shuffled awkwardly, then moved the gun to his back, slipping it under his belt so it stayed in place. "This isn't very comfortable."

Nash ignored him and looked back up the stairwell. "Could Stout have left the hospital and gotten back inside unnoticed? Could anyone?"

Kloz quit fiddling with the gun and attempted to stand up straight. "That was Clair's first thought too. She brought up those old bootlegging tunnels under the city and said Bishop used them to move around undetected for years. She searched the basement but didn't find anything."

"She searched the basement? Alone?"

"Well, no. Stout was with her, two or three security guards, and a maintenance guy she said worked down there. Ernest Skow, I think his name was. They all looked."

"If Stout or one of the security guards is involved, they might have just pretended to look. Maybe even steered her clear of a tunnel until she gave up."

"I suppose."

Nash nodded at Warnick and pointed down the stairs. "You first."

Warnick frowned. "Then give me my gun back."

"You can either walk down or I can push you, your call."

"How do I know you're not working with Porter and planning on killing me down there?"

Nash smiled. "That's an excellent suggestion. I like where your head's at. Or maybe we'll find your mayor. Either way, you're going first. There's no way you're walking behind us."

"Your career is so over," Warnick finally said before turning and starting down the steps.

102

Clair

Day 6 • 5:12 AM

"Goddamn, baby Jesus, son of a whore, come on!"

Clair jumped for the fourth time and missed for the fourth time.

"What are you doing in there?" the mayor said, his voice muffled.

Clair glanced over at the vent, swore under her breath, then turned her attention back to the fluorescent light fixture above her. She jumped again, swung, and missed.

"Fuck me," she grumbled.

She'd taken her shoelaces and tied them together to make one long rope. Holding one end in each hand, she swung the giant looped lace above her head and tried to catch it around the corner of the light fixture. There was only about a half inch of space between the fixture and the ceiling, and the laces kept missing, sliding over the metal, or falling short. The ceilings here were around ten or eleven feet.

She tried again.

Again.

Her strength was far from normal, and she was beginning to feel like she might pass out. She bent over for a moment, rested her hands on her knees, and drew in a deep breath.

Clair closed her eyes, forced her brain to visualize the lace flying through the air just right, catching the light fixture. She pictured this over and over, and when she felt she had it perfect in her head, she counted down from three and tried again.

And missed.

"Dammit!" she shouted.

The mayor must have been watching her through the vent, because he said, "You're swinging too fast. Instead of swinging when you push off, wait a half beat, then try."

"What?"

"I can see it—you're jumping and swinging at the same time, you're swinging too fast and not getting enough height. You're close, but you keep coming up a little short."

Clair sighed, bent at the knees again, coiled the lace—

"Put the lace behind your back, then swing it up over your head, like you're jumping rope."

Clair turned to the vent. "Anything else?"

"Nope, that should do it."

Knees still bent, Clair positioned the long lace behind her back, one end in each hand.

Like jumping rope.

She pushed off the ground, waited, then swung the lace up from behind her back, up over her head. The loop caught the top of the light, in the small space between the fixture and the ceiling, and when she came back down to the ground, she pulled the fixture with her. She felt the screws tear from the drywall, felt the fixture swing down in a heavy arch, and somehow managed to get below it as it swung down and toward the door, cracked against it, and swung back, suspended above the ground on a long coil of wires. One of the fluorescent tubes shattered with the pop of a gunshot. The other flickered momentarily but remained in place, remained lit. Dust rained down from above, and Clair coughed.

"Told you," the mayor said. "Now what?"

Clair reached up and steadied the swinging fixture. She studied the way it was wired. Her father had been an electrician, and when she was younger, he'd drag her to the various side projects he'd pick up on nights and weekends to help make ends meet beyond his work with Carmichael Electric. Typically, little jobs for people around the neighborhood. Fifty dollars here, a hundred dollars there…every bit helped. Clair had hated it; she'd much rather have spent that time with her friends. Growing up on the South Side, the last place her father wanted her was out with friends. He'd put her to work sometimes, taught her the basics, and while she wasn't a fan at the time, she was grateful as she grew older and realized she was perfectly capable of understanding and performing many of the tasks people like her neighbors would hire out to people like her father. Looking down at the backside of the fluorescent light fixture, she found exactly what she expected—the two four-foot bulbs were wired in series, and the electrician who installed the fixture had left a substantial amount of spare wire coiled at the top on the off chance someone would want to reposition the fixture somewhere else in the room at some later date. Splitting the wire would require the installation of a junction box, but this was cleaner and safer. The fixture itself also had nearly eight feet of wiring inside—more than enough.

Clair traced the white wire through the fixture, found the soldered connection, and tore it free. The light went dark, and the room was lit only by light streaming in through the small window in the metal door.

There was a metal hook centered at the top of the door, meant to hold a jacket. Clair squeezed the tip of the wire between the door and hook, then wrapped the long shoelace around both as tight as she could to secure both in place. Because the door opened into the room, there was enough slack in the wire. The hook was above the window, so she was fairly certain her handiwork was not visible from the outside.

She went back to the light fixture and pulled out the black wire. She tugged out as much slack as she could, managed to stretch it to the floor. With the mayor's nail in hand, Clair took off her shoe, knelt down on the ground, and used the shoe to pound the nail into a crack in the floor. Not all the way, just enough so it was standing straight up and immobile, about a foot in front of the door. She then took the black wire from the light and coiled the exposed copper around the nailhead.

Returning to the light fixture, still dangling from the ceiling by several screws and torn drywall, Clair grabbed both sides and yanked it down. She placed it in the corner off to the left of the door, out of sight.

"What exactly are you doing in there? I can't see," the mayor asked.

"Creating a circuit. The black wire is hot and the white wire is neutral. The door's metal, so it should conduct electricity. If this works, when he opens the door and the frame of the door contacts the nail with black wire, the circuit should complete. As long as he's still holding the doorknob, he'll be part of that circuit. This won't be enough to kill him, but it should stun him."

Clair found her water bottle and poured out the contents, forming a puddle at the door where the man had stood earlier. Can't hurt to have a Plan B.

The mayor thought about this for a moment. "What about his gloves, won't they protect him?"

Shit. Maybe. I don't know.

The broken fluorescent bulb was lying at her feet. She scooped that up and studied the jagged glass edge.

A Plan C couldn't hurt, either.

103

Porter

Day 6 • 5:23 AM

Porter put all the photographs back in the envelope. He couldn't look at them anymore.

He grabbed the green duffle bag from the seat across the aisle and stuffed the envelope inside it, buried the photos under the filthy, bloodstained clothes. He recognized the blue shirt, black slacks, loafers, even the tie. He'd been wearing all of it the night he was shot. He didn't know how they ended up in this bag, hidden in Hillburn's van for all these years. He wasn't sure how they got shredded, either, but he suspected they'd cut the clothing from his body at the hospital.

The composition book seemed familiar, too, but that might be because it was the same kind Bishop used for all his diaries. Those diaries had occupied Porter's every waking thought for months. He flipped through the pages, read some of the text—dates, times, observations—most written in some kind of shorthand. His gut told him it was a logbook of some sort—14F, 1k, CH. Paid.

Fourteen-year-old female, one thousand dollars, Carriage House.

The word *paid* was followed by a checkmark on some, the initials DB on others.

Dozens of entries, more of the same.

DB...debit?

Porter had no idea why that popped into his head, but it did.

Some paid when services were rendered, others carried a balance. The good customers, the repeat customers, were permitted the use of credit.

He found the name Tegan on one page.

Porter uncapped the pen again and brought the tip to the page. He wrote the name *Tegan* beside the original.

He didn't have to be an expert to recognize his handwriting was close but not a precise match. He didn't remember writing it.

Not a log. A receipt book. A record of transactions.

My record of transactions?

Porter closed the book and shoved it back into the bag, crammed it under the clothing with the photographs, cash, all of it. He put the diaries in there too.

His file from Camden was gone. Bishop's too.

Dammit, Poole.

The jet lurched as the wheels chirped against the tarmac. Wingflaps extended and the airbrakes screamed.

As instructed, he powered up the phone and it rang immediately.

Unknown.

"What?"

"Welcome to Chicago, Sam. Sorry I had to go."

Sarah.

"Why did you run?"

"You know why."

"I'm sick of this cryptic bullshit."

"That's just the guilt talking," she replied. "Guilt eats at you, devours you from the inside. That's what that pain you're feeling in your stomach is. Admitting your crimes is the first step in healing, moving beyond. Are you ready to do that?"

"I haven't done anything wrong."

"So you still don't remember?"

I remember some.

"No."

"You ran those kids, Sam. You, your partner Hillburn, Stocks, Welderman, all of you. You sold them for sex. Children. Sold them to anyone willing to pay. The Carriage House Inn was your primary location in Charleston. That's where you operated. Stocks and Welderman provided the transportation. Hillburn stayed close to ensure the transaction went smooth, and you watched from a distance as backup. You kept the other cops away, the few good ones who came sniffing around. Once each year, those children were brought to Chicago—the less fortunate ones were sold into the larger trafficking market, the others went back to Finicky's. You brought my boy into that mess—that's your sin. That's why Heather died. That's why you were shot."

Hurry, they're coming.

"You're full of shit."

Sarah sighed. "Is there a television in that fancy plane of yours?"

Porter fought the urge to hang up and glanced around the cabin. A thirty-six inch monitor hung on the wall near the closed cockpit door.

"Turn it on," Sarah said before he even told her there was one.

Velcro held the remote in place on the table. Porter picked it up and pressed the power button.

"Find a news channel."

Porter looked around the cabin. "Can you see me right now?"

"Find a news channel," she repeated, ignoring his question.

Porter flipped through the various networks. It didn't take him long to find what she wanted him to see. He turned up the volume.

Through fluttering snow highlighted by bright lights and the rising sun, a reporter stood in a parking lot crowded with people. The wind caught his dark hair, and he brushed it back. "...started gathering about three hours ago. Although temperatures are hovering in the teens, they seem completely unperturbed. While some are here answering Anson Bishop's call for support, others only want to witness whatever happens, the numbers continue to grow with the size of the crowd becoming problematic. We've seen a large influx of law enforcement personnel as well as federal, local, and state employees all attempting to secure the scene here at the Guyon in anticipation of Bishop's surrender, now less than two hours away. Citizens have torn down fencing and moved barricades aside in an effort to get closer, but the building itself appears to still be sealed. There's been talk of closing off the surrounding streets, but that idea was shot down because those in charge appear to have no idea how Bishop plans to get to the Guyon. They don't want to risk blocking his passage or compromising his surrender."

The plane came to a stop.

The television blinked off as the power in the plane cycled.

Porter looked out the window, expecting to see a dozen law enforcement vehicles and a hundred officers out there waiting for him, but there was no one but an airport employee placing wooden blocks under their tires.

"What did you do with the virus, Sam? Do you remember where you left it?"

Something in his brain clicked. Porter understood what Bishop was doing.

He hung up on her and dialed Poole.

104

Nash

Day 6 • 5:27 AM

Warnick pushed through the steel door at the bottom of the stairwell and stepped into the vast space with trepidation. The air was cold and moist, filled with dust.

Between all the boxes and discarded medical equipment and furniture, Nash couldn't see much of anything beyond where they stood. The bare fluorescent bulbs hanging from the ceiling buzzed softly. "What was the maintenance guy's name?" he asked Kloz.

"Ernest Skow."

Nash cupped his hands around his mouth. "Ernest Skow, are you down here?"

With all the clutter, his voice didn't carry as much as he hoped. He shouted again, louder this time.

"It's late. Maybe he's gone."

"Or maybe he's not," Nash replied, unsnapping the safety strap from the Beretta on his hip. He didn't draw the weapon, not yet, but he wanted to know nothing would slow him down if he needed to.

Klozowski pointed up at the ceiling. "She said they followed those wires back to the outer wall—they're phone lines and Internet. The phone company leases space in the tunnels, so she hoped the lines would lead her right to the tunnels. The outer wall was sealed off, though, cemented over. Apparently, the foundation was rebuilt back in the eighties, and she said it looked like they closed up the tunnel access when they did the work."

From up ahead on the left, several bedpans stacked on an aluminum gurney tumbled over and crashed to the floor. Warnick raised both hands in the air and stepped back from the mess. "Sorry."

Nash recognized the gurneys. They'd wondered where Bishop had gotten them. Nash counted more than twenty of them just where he stood; there might be a hundred of them down here. Bishop easily could have taken a few unnoticed. He might have even returned them when he was through, like this was his own medical storage facility.

"This part of the hospital isn't connected to the old tunnel system," Warnick said. "Never was."

Nash crossed over to him, stepping over the bedpans. "You know what we're talking about?"

A smug look rolled over Warnick's face. "I want my gun back."

"Kloz, go ahead and shoot this man. Just the leg, maybe his knee. Whatever gets him talking."

For a second, Kloz looked like he thought Nash was serious. Then he shook his head and turned back to the wiring on the ceiling.

Nash pushed Warnick's shoulder, nearly knocked him back into the gurneys again. "Spill it."

Warnick brushed some dust from the elbow of his suit jacket. "We're standing in the new Stroger Hospital—this section was built in 2002. If the bootlegging tunnels connect anywhere, it will be in the old part. The section that used to be Cook County General next door."

"You know this how?"

"Developers have had their eye on the old Cook County building for years. It's huge and right in the middle of the city, prime real estate sitting vacant. There's a proposal on the table right now to rehab the entire space—turn it into apartments, a hotel, new parking, office space, shopping, the works." He sighed. "The design was promising, but everything came to a halt when Talbot died."

"Arthur Talbot was behind the project?"

Warnick nodded.

Nash and Klozowski exchanged a glance.

"How do we get there from here?" Nash asked Warnick.

Warnick's brow furrowed, and he turned in a small circle, looking around and over all the discarded equipment. He stopped and pointed toward double doors near the back of the basement. "If I remember correctly from the plans, those doors lead to a hallway connecting both facilities. When this building was finished in 2002, they transported all the patients from Cook through there to this side, then upstairs to the correct department. Took the better part of a day to move everyone. The more critical ones were brought over by ambulance above ground, but most went this way. The Cook building has been locked up ever since."

The three of them made their way across the basement to the double doors. As they neared, Nash pointed his flashlight at the ground. "We've got a lot of foot traffic here."

Several dozen tracks riddled the dust, heading in both directions.

"The door's been jimmied," Klozowski said, pointing at some scratches near the lock.

This time, Nash did draw his gun. "Warnick, get behind me. Kloz you follow behind him. He does anything, you shoot him. This time, I'm not kidding."

Positioning himself on the side of the doorway, Nash pulled open the door and quickly moved through, leading with his gun and flashlight. He found a light switch and flicked it on. Bulbs crackled to life above them, only about half still working.

The hallway was about two hundred yards long, smooth, white tiles on the walls and floor. Another set of double doors on the far end.

He slipped his phone into his pocket and started down the hallway, gun first. Judging by the tracks in the dust, at least three different people had walked through here recently. One far more often than the others. There were also wheel marks, most likely gurney tracks. "Warnick, does the old building have any kind of security?"

"No alarm, if that's what you mean. All the outer doors are either chained or bolted shut, and hospital security checks them regularly as part of their rotation. It's been on the sanctuary list since it closed, though, so we know people can get in and out somehow."

"The sanctuary list?"

Warnick waved a dismissive hand through the air. "We've got buildings all over the city used by the homeless. We let them. Keeps them off the streets. It's one of those unspoken things in city government. People claim they want to help the homeless, but few actually do. At last check, we've got nearly 80,000 in and around the city. We don't have the shelter infrastructure to support that, but we have to put them somewhere. Nobody wants to see them on the streets. Seeing them reminds everyone there is a problem, so we give them places to go where they won't be visible. Like safe spaces. They stay out of view, we leave them alone. There's this unspoken rule."

"Lovely."

They were about halfway down the hallway when the lights went out.

Darkness swallowed them.

A gun went off.

The bullet cracked into the tile a few inches above Nash's head. He dropped to the floor, landing in a crouch. He held his gun out to the dark and fumbled for his phone with his free hand. "Kloz, did you fire?"

"No. Where's Warnick? Can you see him?"

"I can't see shit."

He had his phone halfway out his pocket, when someone kicked him in the gut. The air left his body with a gasping rush and his phone cracked hard against the tile floor somewhere near his feet.

Another shot echoed loudly off all the tile, followed quickly by a pain-filled grunt.

"Kloz? Are you okay?"

For a moment, nobody spoke. There was only heavy breathing as all three men tried to suck in air.

"Yeah," Kloz finally said.

Someone ran. Heavy steps down the hallway toward the old hospital. Nash heard the doors at the far end push open and swing shut again.

"I'm sorry, Nash," Kloz said softly.

The butt of the gun slammed into the side of Nash's head. His head cracked against the wall, then the floor as he fell, and all went dark.

105

Poole

Day 6 • 5:31 AM

When Poole answered his phone, he didn't get a single word in before the other man began to speak, his voice rushed yet low. "Frank, he's working with Kloz. They've got Clair. I don't know where, locked away in some room. I saw a video, but that was a few hours ago. Bishop said he'd kill her if I called you before now. I know what he's doing. You need to get all those people away from the Guyon."

Poole waved a hand at SAIC Hurless, mouthed Porter's name. Hurless was on another line. He tapped the shoulder of a third man sitting at a communications station in the FBI surveillance van, rolled his finger through the air, and pointed back at Poole. The man nodded and began tracing the call.

"We've been looking for Klozowski. Nash and Clair too," Poole told him. "Where are you, Sam? Are you back in Chicago?"

"The virus attack on the hospital, that wasn't real, was it?" Porter asked.

"No. It was a hoax. The needle Clair found *did* contain the actual virus, but the girls were only infected with a potent strain of the flu."

"I think Bishop used the hospital as some kind of trial run—practice to see how fast the first responders would react. You need to get everyone away from the Guyon, now."

SAIC Hurless disconnected his own call, scribbled something down on a sheet of paper, and handed it to Poole. When Poole read the note, he frowned. To Porter, he said, "You think Bishop plans to release the virus here?"

The back door of the van opened, and Captain Dalton climbed inside. He pulled the door shut behind him. Hurless told him who was on the line.

Porter said, "Are you alone right now? Can you talk?"

"SAIC Hurless is here. Your captain, too. Do you want me to put you on speaker?"

Porter fell silent.

Poole read the note again, then handed it to Dalton.

The note said: *Confirmation—Porter rented a room at the Traveler's Best in New Orleans, paid for three nights, stolen vial of virus found in trash—empty.*

Without waiting for a response, Poole put the call on speaker so the others could hear. "Are you still there, Sam?"

"Yeah."

"We found the woman at the farmhouse."

Porter went quiet again.

"Sam, are you here in Chicago?"

"Did she tell you where they're holding Clair?"

Poole glanced at the two men staring at him from across the van. "The woman we found…she's dead, Sam. I think you know that. What happened there? Can you tell me about all the other blood?"

"She's not dead, she just…"

"Sam, you're not well. I think you know that. I read your file from the doctor at Camden. I know what you're going through. Let me help you. Can you do that? Tell me where you are."

"Why not just wait for the trace? I know I'd be tracing this call."

"Things would be better for you if you just turned yourself in."

"They're all in on it," Porter said. "I can't trust anyone."

"It just feels that way. Paranoia is a part of the illness. If you turn yourself in, I'll make sure you get the proper help."

"You can't let Bishop anywhere near that crowd. That's what he wants. Find Clair, get her out of there. Don't trust any of them."

SAIC Hurless leaned over the phone. "We know you have the virus. You need to surrender, now."

Porter hung up.

The man at the communications terminal pointed at a map on his monitor. "He's moving, heading south by southwest."

"Heading toward here," Hurless said, studying the map.

The man nodded.

106

Poole

"I've got snipers in place on four of the surrounding rooftops, uniforms on the ground, and two dozen undercover officers," Dalton told them. "There's no way he's getting in here unseen."

"Porter's been with Metro for how long?" Hurless said. "You don't think he won't recognize his coworkers? He knows your methods, your strategies. I've got twelve agents out there right now and two dozen more en route. Your people will just get in the way."

"I think we can use his familiarity with Metro's personnel and practices against him," Poole said. "Use that to drive him somewhere, maybe funnel him through the crowd to someplace we can safely take him into custody."

Hurless shook his head. "If he's got the virus, we need to take him out the moment we've got eyes on him. We can't let him near this crowd."

"What happens if the virus isn't on him? You kill him and we lose our best shot at finding it. If the hospital was some kind of distraction, how do we know this isn't too?"

"I'm not even sure who we're talking about here." Dalton said. "Who's our focus? Bishop or Porter?"

"Maybe they're both working together and the plan is to consolidate law enforcement here while they release the virus down at a train station, or a school somewhere."

"We need to take them both alive, get them isolated."

A knock at the van door.

Dalton reached over and tugged the latch. A man in a Chicago Metro baseball cap and thick black coat stood there with four cups of coffee balanced precariously in his gloved hands. "Thought you might need some caffeine, sir." With his chin, he pointed at each cup. "This one is heavy with sugar, this one has cream, and these two are black."

Hurless reached past Dalton and plucked one. "Sugar is mine."

The tech said, "Black, please."

Dalton handed a cup to the FBI communications tech, passed the other black coffee to Poole, and took the one with cream for himself.

Several reporters noticed the open door and started toward them.

Dalton quickly thanked the man and pulled the door closed. "We need to keep them both away from the cameras too. We can't let this play out on live television."

Poole set the coffee down on the desk beside him and looked out the window. He could see three satellite dishes on portable towers attached to news vans off to the left. He knew there were at least two more on the opposite end of the parking lot.

Due to the extreme cold, everyone wore heavy coats, gloves, hats, scarfs—many wore ski masks. Nothing but eyes visible on half the people shuffling around out there. He wasn't sure he'd recognize his own mother, let alone Porter or Bishop. "Any luck reestablishing that trace?" he asked the man at the terminal.

The agent shook his head. "He went dark after he hung up with you. Probably took the batteries out."

On the desk at his side, Hurless pressed a microphone button. "Carmichael, are you in position?"

"Affirmative. We found a tunnel access point in the Guyon's basement. I've stationed two men on it. There are obvious signs of recent use but no sign of Bishop or that detective today. Not yet, anyway. I've got six other agents conducting a room-by-room, but the building appears to be deserted."

"Keep me posted."

"Copy."

"I don't think he'll use the tunnels," Poole said. "Bishop wants to keep this public."

"Porter might," Dalton said.

"I don't think he would, either," Hurless said. "He's got to figure we're watching, and he knows it would be near impossible to get out of the building. If he's got the virus, he'll want maximum exposure to all these people."

Another voice crackled over the communications system. "Sir, this is Chen. I've got a body, male, in a room up on the third floor. Ear, eye, and tongue removed, all in white boxes. Somebody carved *I am evil* all over him with a razor blade or something similar. He's been dead—hold on a second."

When he didn't come back right away, Hurless said, "Chen?"

"Sir, we've got two more, same condition. A female and another male. *Father, forgive me* is written on the wall in the second room. I don't think they were killed here—there's not enough blood for that. They're covered in some kind of white powder too. I think it's salt."

Hurless turned to Dalton. "Your people did a complete sweep of this building when Porter was found here, right?"

Dalton nodded. "These were placed recently."

"This is Capshaw, on the fifth floor. I've got one up here too. Male, late sixties, early seventies. Same condition."

"Sir? I've got Porter again." This came from the FBI tech.

"Where?" Poole asked.

"I'm triangulating pings on towers 191390B, 191391A, and 191392B. That's here. He's outside somewhere."

Hurless turned back to the microphone and began barking orders. Dalton was back on his phone, doing the same.

"I'm going out there." Poole pushed out the back door of the van into the crowd before either of them could object. He was halfway to the Guyon's rear entrance when a boy of maybe twelve or thirteen tugged on the corner of his jacket.

"Are you Special Agent Frank Poole?"

"Yes."

The boy shoved something into his hand and vanished in the sea of people before Poole had a chance to say anything else.

A photograph, folded.

Although taken a number of years ago, Poole immediately recognized the man in the picture. His gaze returned to the van, hung there a moment, then returned to the photograph.

On the back, Porter had written, *Not just Kloz—him too*.

Poole started pushing through the crowd toward the building.

He had to find Porter before they did.

107

Nash

Day 6 • 5:37 AM

When Nash woke, pain sliced through his head like a shard of jagged glass. He was on the floor, his arm folded under him. He still had his gun; he could feel it pressing into his gut.

Hallway still?

He couldn't be sure. It was too dark. Felt like it, though.

He didn't know how long he'd been out.

When he tried to sit up, the world spun and his stomach lurched.

His phone wasn't in his pocket. Then he remembered trying to take it out a moment before—

I'm so sorry, Nash.

Kloz?

Kloz hit him?

No, no, no, no. It couldn't be Kloz.

The altered video footage at the prison in New Orleans, Montehugh Labs, Stroger Hospital. The chaos at Metro that allowed for Bishop and Porter to get out. These were all impossible feats for the average person, but they were the kind of thing Klozowski could do with several keystrokes.

Two dead at the hospital.

Clair.

This couldn't be Kloz. He wouldn't hurt Clair, would he?

Nash ran his hand over the floor around him, searching for his phone in the dirt and grime, but he couldn't find it. Either out of reach or taken altogether.

Somebody groaned.

A moan filled with this wet, slurpy sound.

"Warnick?"

Definitely still the hallway. The groan came again, more urgent this time, further down from where Nash lay. Nash reached for the wall at his back and forced himself to stand, fighting the lightheadedness and pain. When he got to his feet, he touched his head with his free hand. His fingers came away wet. He knew he was bleeding, but he wasn't sure how bad.

He could hear Warnick breathing. Quick, ragged breaths.

Nash held himself up with the wall, moved toward the sound, gun drawn.

When he reached Warnick, he nearly tripped over him. The man was slumped on the floor, his shoulders against the wall. His shirt and jacket were soaked in blood, and when Nash found the man's hands, they were over a bullet wound in his chest just above and to the right of his heart. From the sound of it, the bullet pierced his lung. Who knew what else. "Can you talk?"

Warnick said something, but it was far from an intelligible word. Blood spattered from his lips. Nash felt the droplets smack against his own cheek.

Nash leaned in closer. "Do you still have your phone?"

The man nodded, a weak, jerky motion.

Nash patted his pockets and found the phone in his jacket. When the screen lit up, the device indicated no signal. He hadn't expected one, not all the way down here, but still.

Warnick's body spasmed. Grew stiff, then collapsed again.

The hallway grew quiet.

Nash fumbled with the phone, located the flashlight button, and turned it on.

Warnick's dead eyes stared up at him.

There was far more blood than Nash had expected. Along with the lung, the bullet may have nicked the pulmonary artery, maybe even his heart. Pure adrenaline carried him this far. None of that really mattered—he was gone.

Something squeaked at the end of the hallway, and Nash brought up the light.

Standing in the doorway leading to the old hospital was a man in a black mask, his eyes hidden behind dark glasses under the cloth. Some kind of device rested on his forehead, pushed up and out of the way held in place with a strap, maybe night vision goggles. He'd come through the swinging doors with a gurney in tow.

Although his face was covered, Nash recognized his clothing. He brought up his gun. "Don't you fucking move, Kloz!"

108

Porter

Day 6 • 5:39 AM

A heavy wool charcoal overcoat, a gray scarf with matching watch cap, and black leather gloves. Porter had found the clothing in the Cadillac Escalade waiting for him at the airport. The .38 was in his right overcoat pocket. Every time he took his hand out of that pocket, that same hand seemed to find its way back in there out of an unconscious desire to feel the metal of that gun under his touch. The gun brought a grounding familiarity.

In his left hand, Porter held the cell phone. The crowd outside the Guyon was enormous and still growing—he'd parked three blocks over and hustled through the snow, since it was impossible to get closer. The odds of him finding Bishop were slim, but something told him Bishop could find him with that phone.

A helicopter circled overhead.

Law enforcement personnel from various agencies were every-where—uniforms around the perimeter, undercover officers in the crowd. He didn't find them particularly difficult to spot—most of the spectators were talking, making jokes, anxiously checking every approaching car, while the officers tasked with combing the crowd were silent, systematically checking faces.

Looking for him.

He knew they wanted to pick him up as much as they wanted to nab Bishop, so Porter kept the cap pulled low on his head, the scarf covering as much of his face as possible, as he scanned the crowd.

If Bishop planned to release the virus here, he'd need some kind of delivery method. Porter's first thought had been the sprinkler system at the Guyon, particularly after what happened at Metro, but everyone was outside.

The phone vibrated.

Unknown caller.

"Quite the turnout, don't you think?"

Not Sarah, Bishop this time.

Porter looked up a moment, studied the faces of the people around him. He knew the other man was close—his skin tingled with some sort of sixth sense. He didn't see Bishop, though. "Tell me what happened to Libby?"

"You know what happened to Libby."

"I know she's dead now," Porter replied bluntly. "But your diary doesn't say what happened to her after the farmhouse. After you killed Stocks. You eventually found her again, right?"

"Getting sentimental, Sam?"

Porter peered through the crowd—he had to be here. "Connecting dots. Poole found Franklin Kirby's hair hidden in a drawer in that house she was renting here in Chicago. How did she get it? She had the picture of your mother with Mrs. Carter, too. A gun. Fake ID. What happened to her after the farmhouse?"

Bishop sighed. "She and I have a special place in our hearts for Mr. Franklin Kirby."

"You said he ran off with your mother."

"And I *so* wanted to thank him for that myself. Mother was elusive, as you well know. Franklin Kirby, though, he left a bit of a trail in his wake. He wasn't difficult to find. I'd been watching him for years, so imagine my surprise when Libby said she recognized him all those years later." Bishop paused a few seconds. "Why did you kill my friends, Sam? Why couldn't you let us all go? We'd been through so much. Were we really just dollar signs to you? Cattle you needed to get to the meat market?"

Porter saw him then, Bishop—a quick profile, then he turned and faced the other way. About twenty feet away in the crowd, a phone pressed to his ear. Porter pushed his way through and grabbed the back of his coat.

Not Bishop.

"If you get yourself arrested now, Sam, you'll miss all the fun."

Porter gave the man an apologetic look, then turned in a slow circle. "Where the hell are you?"

"Close."

109

Nash

Kloz did move, he moved fast.

Nash squeezed the trigger on his Beretta, and the bullet struck the metal door right where Kloz's leg had been a moment earlier, then ricocheted back into the hallway, cracked the tile in several places along the wall, then finally disappeared with a puff of dust into the ceiling.

Nash forced himself back to his feet, his legs rubbery beneath him. He closed the distance to the doors and pulled the gurney out of the still open doorway. A bullet struck the open door a few inches above his head, and he dropped low. Kloz was deep in the room, near another door, the night vision goggles over his eyes and the gun they'd taken from Warnick pointing back at Nash.

Nash brought up the flashlight. Kloz quickly turned his head to the side, away from the light, then ran out through the door at his back. Crouching low, Nash shuffled after him.

He found himself in another basement surrounded by stagnant air, tomblike, a place sealed away and forgotten a long time ago. The abandoned basement of Cook County General. As the beam of his flashlight worked over the large room, he felt as if he'd stepped into a time capsule. The Cook basement contained much of the same discarded medical equipment as Stroger, but everything was clearly from a different era. Glass IV bottles hung from metal poles. Some of the tubing looked like it was made from cloth or discolored rubber rather than plastic, rotten and degraded. Machinery with large dials and displays, all seemingly impossibly big and heavy, coated in dust. Sheets were draped over some, these things left to die.

Nash caught the movement from the corner of his eye. On the opposite end of the room, another door opened on protesting hinges. Klozowski shouted back at him, "You think you know Sam, but you don't! He's not the man you believe him to be! He's not a good man at all. He's no better than any of the others. Any one of them willing to sacrifice us kids to make a buck. That's all we ever were to them, dollar signs, everybody lining their pockets with our blood. They beat me to within an inch of death just for trying to pass a note, just for fighting for my own freedom and trying to help my friends!"

"Where's Clair?" Nash shouted back. "If you hurt her, I swear the things I'll do to you will be worse than—"

"Worse than what? You can't hurt me," Kloz yelled back. "I'm already dead!"

Nash stood, planted his feet, and fired three quick shots in the direction of Klozowski's voice. He dove back down as another bullet whizzed past his head.

"You kill me, you'll never find her!"

Nash rose just enough to catch Klozowski diving through the open doorway and pulling the heavy metal door shut behind him. He crossed the room as quickly as he could, yanked open the door, and found himself at the base of a staircase, Klozowski's muffled steps above him.

110

Porter

Day 6 • 5:44 AM

"How many years did they sell kids out of this hotel, Sam? Did you ever bring them here, or was it just Hillburn and the others?"

Porter ignored him. "How did Libby get Kirby's hair?"

"I gave it to her."

"Where did you get it?"

"Mother snipped it off the last night she was with him. She cut it off while he was sleeping, held the hair over him when he woke, and told him if he tried to follow her, she'd cut off something else while he slept, something that wouldn't grow back."

"Your mother's a lovely woman."

"She is."

"Have you been in contact with her this entire time?"

"I want to know how you found Libby, Sam. I want to understand why you felt the need to torture her, to kill her; she did nothing to you."

"All these people are waiting on you, Bishop. Where are you?"

"Is the helicopter making you nervous, Sam? You sound jittery. Are you wondering if the FBI can trace your phone in a crowd like this? Are you wondering just how close they are? Maybe watching you from above. I wonder if their IT people are as good as Klozowski. Technology always came so naturally to him, even when we were kids."

III

Nash

Day 6 • 5:46 AM

At least one floor up, Nash heard another door open and close. With his flashlight in one hand and the gun in the other, he followed Klozowski as quickly as he could while still hugging the walls, prepared to dive back if he found him lying in wait, ready to fire.

The next landing was deserted. A small, faded placard beside the door read MENTAL HEALTH. Nash opened the door slowly, ready for another bullet, but none came. Instead, he heard a voice. The Mayor's voice, speaking from down the hall. A woman's voice too. A flickering light.

The Mayor screamed.

The woman laughed.

Nash turned off the phone's flashlight and slipped the device into his pocket before easing through the door, leading with his Beretta. He found himself in the remains of a cafeteria, tables and chairs scattered about. Some broken, others overturned. Several pieces of furniture were draped in heavy white sheets. None of the overhead lights were on; there was only the flickering from the far corner.

The mayor cried out again, a mix of anger and pain. "Talbot funded everything, I was just the middleman—not even that, not really."

"You looked the other way while this was happening in your city," the woman replied, her voice calm, with a slight southern accent. "You profited. You could have stopped them at any time if you wanted to, but you didn't. You turned a blind eye. You're no better than the rest of them."

"I can give you names," the mayor pleaded. "Everyone who was part of it. Or I can pay you—they'll all pay you, you don't have to do this!"

"I want all the names, dear. You're going to write them down for me."

The voices came from a television, an old boxy model mounted near the ceiling in the far corner of the cafeteria. Several others came to life, turning on one at a time in the other three corners, each bringing just a little more light to the room.

Nash spun with his gun, expecting to find Klozowski standing near one of the sets, but he wasn't in the room. On the screen, the mayor lay on a bed, naked, his hands and feet tied to each of the four corners. Nash recognized the room from the Langham—their missing video.

"No! No! No! Don't do that!" the Mayor said.

"Then run through it all, one more time from the beginning," the woman instructed.

"All right, all right." He drew in a breath between clenched teeth. "I don't know all the details. I told you that already. All I did was provide a meeting venue, someplace for them to conduct their business."

"You gave them the Guyon Hotel."

"I didn't give it to them. I just kept it empty, with Talbot. He'd submit plans to revive the place with the building commission. I'd help to tie it up in red tape. When the commission eventually rejected the proposal, his people would come back with another one. As long as he paid the fees to the city, the building remained vacant and locked down, kept the other developers away. If it hadn't been the Guyon, we would have found someplace else."

"And they paid you to meet there?" she said. "To conduct their business?"

The mayor nodded. "This went on before me—you understand that, right? This wasn't my idea, I just stepped into it."

When she didn't respond, he went on. "Every year, they brought the buyers in, then the children...not all kids, sometimes there were adults, too, but mostly kids. Not the good kind; these were the ones nobody wanted."

"Where did the children come from? Those *children nobody wanted*," she said contemptuously.

He shrugged. "Homeless, mostly, that's what they told me. The foster system, I guess. I don't know for sure. I didn't ask. There's a website, the website coordinated everything, that's who you really want, not me. The URL is backpage.com. I bet you take them apart, and you'll have whatever you need. That's who you want. You can bust this wide open, if that's what you're after. I'll help you, and we can go to the feds together, just untie me... just stop."

Her hand lashed out. It looked like she was holding a scalpel, but she moved so fast it was difficult to be sure. The blade flicked across the mayor's cheek, and a line of red appeared. When he tried to turn his head, she cut him on the other side.

"Stop!" he shouted.

She didn't, though. She cut him again on his shoulder.

He grimaced against the pain. "You said they took your son? I can help you find him. I can help you get him back! Is that what you're after? Just give me his name and a phone. You can watch me, I won't try anything, I promise. I'll help you. I know a federal agent, someone we can trust."

She slashed at him again, this time right below his shoulder.

"Just stop!"

The video froze. Then the screen turned to snow.

In the dim light, Klozowski stepped into the cafeteria. He held both his hands up. The gun was gone. Between the fingers of his right hand, he pinched something else.

Nash trained the Baretta on him. "Drop it!"

Klozowski shook his head. "You don't want me to do that."

With his free hand, he pulled back his jacket. An explosive vest was strapped to his chest, a wire trailing from his waist to the trigger in his hand.

112

Porter

Day 6 • 5:51 AM

"The Kid," Porter said softly.

"Yeah, The Kid," Bishop replied with a quiet chuckle. "That day in the War Room, when you ran the case for me, it took every ounce of my willpower not to look at him and burst out laughing. We'd rehearsed, gone over how we wanted it to play out, but there, in the moment…that might have been one of the hardest things I've ever done. Oh, and then later, when he called you in your apartment and told you who I really was! Sam, if you could have seen me in the kitchen when your phone rang."

Porter heard a police siren in the distance, growing closer, coming from the west. He turned in that direction.

On the phone, Bishop continued. "Standing there in your apartment while you talked to The Kid, Klozowski, I thought about everything you did to us—you, Welderman, Stocks, Hillburn—the whole lot of you, and I knew if I slit your throat there in your apartment, you'd get off easy. You needed this, Sam. You needed all of it to fully atone for your sins."

Everything made sense now. Why hadn't Porter seen it earlier? "The hacks that created your identity as Paul Watson, the escape from Metro, all the problems with the security systems and video footage: that was all Kloz?"

"He told all of us how dependent law enforcement was on tech. How you'd blindly follow leads and information from IT as if they held the holy grail, and I didn't think that could possibly be true. He was right, though—through the entire investigation, he'd throw a scrap of meat out on the table, and the rest of you would eat it up like starving dogs. You made this easy, Sam. Today, we clean house. Today, we reset. The virus provides a fresh palate."

Porter thought of the man in the photograph he'd given to Poole. He glanced across the crowd at the FBI communications van.

"What then? You can't possibly expect to walk away from all this."

"You shouldn't have taken Libby away from me, Sam. Not when we were kids, and not in that house. Not ever. All this blood, all on you."

Porter thumbed the business card attached to the phone.

Hurry, they're coming.

"Why did Weasel really run into that alley?"

"You know why, Sam. It's buried in the back of your head. If you want that answer, you need to dig it out."

Porter noticed a shift in the crowd. Everyone seemed to be moving toward the west side of the Guyon parking lot. He moved with them. "Why all the pictures of you and me in the Guyon? Was all that just more misdirection, or did you expect it to trigger some kind of memory?"

Bishop didn't answer.

"Are you still there?"

"I'm still here."

"Who am I to you?"

Bishop hung up then.

At the far corner of the parking lot, voices erupted in screams and cheers, a deafening cacophony.

Porter pushed forward, forcing his way toward the sound.

113

Nash

Day 6 • 5:56 AM

"It's a dead man's switch," Klozowski said calmly. "You shoot me, and we both die. I've got enough explosives on me to take out most of this building."

Nash didn't lower the gun. "Where's Clair? What do you want?"

"I want the truth to finally come out." Klozowski nodded toward a black and white composition book sitting on one of the tables. "Every name you'll need to take down this entire trafficking ring is in that book. I hacked the website the mayor mentioned and found all the principals behind it —they're all in there. The site led me to fourteen more, and I found everyone behind those too." He tossed a videotape across the room. It clattered over the tile and came to a rest at Nash's feet. "That's the mayor's confession. There's much more. She…she was very thorough. I only showed you the highlights."

"Kloz, this isn't you. You're one of us."

"I was one of them first."

"You're not a killer."

"Warnick would tell you otherwise."

"Disable the vest, and let's talk about this."

Klozowski shook his head. "There's no reason to kid each other— we both know this is well beyond the point of talking things out. I crossed that line a long time ago, and I've made peace with that." He nodded at the notebook. "The lives that will be saved when that information surfaces will make it all worthwhile. I don't regret any of the people I killed knowing so many more innocent people will be freed."

"Are you telling me you're 4MK?"

Klozowski's gaze fell to the floor. He kicked an old Pepsi can across the room. "They called me *The Kid* back then. God, that all seems so long ago. I have no idea how Porter tracked all of us down after so many years, but he did. When he killed Libby, I thought for sure he'd come after me next. I covered our tracks well, new identities and all that, but you saw what he did to her, the torture. I figured she must have told him about the rest of us. *Who I really was.* Who could blame her? She was always tough, but nobody could hold out through all that. If he hadn't run off like he did, if he'd come back to Metro, I'm sure I would have been next." His voice dropped off for a second, considering this. "Or maybe he was saving me for last. Probably figured I betrayed him somehow and he wanted me to see the others die, who knows. I can't pretend to understand what's going on in his head." Kloz waved his free hand through the air. "Hell, he hired Paul Upchurch to write up those diaries, and he must have recognized Paul. I don't care what that bullet did to him; nobody goes that blank. Paul said he didn't, though. Paul told me every time he met with Sam, he had no idea who he was." Kloz's eyes narrowed, and he looked at Nash. "I'd love for a psychologist to weigh in on that. I mean, what if his subconscious recognized Paul, and that's what drew him in? I was so young when he first met me. I get he wouldn't recognize me as an adult, but Paul or Anson? Even Vincent, when he saw him in New Orleans. He flat-out talked to him in the warden's office, yet Vincent said there wasn't a spark of recognition. They all should have listened to me, but they didn't—they all wanted to believe he really didn't remember. If they listened to me, they might still be alive."

Nash kept the gun on Klozowski as he slowly shuffled around the room. He wasn't sure what else to do.

"I think he knew who we all were all along and used the amnesia as a cover until he'd gathered enough information and was ready to move, that's what I think. Sam always was patient." Klozowski stopped and turned back to Nash. "He killed Libby first. Tortured her, got what he needed, then killed her. I guess with Paul he figured best to just let nature take its course, but he used Paul to find Tegan and Kristina. Paul and I had been working on updating their identities, preparing everyone in case we had to run again. Sam must have used something he found at Paul's house to track them down. You saw what he did to them. He left Tegan all alone in that cemetery and dropped Kristina on the tracks like yesterday's trash. Oh, man, the anger there. Vincent tried to run, but somehow Sam found him too. He may be focused on Anson now, but I know it's just a matter of time before he gets around to me. He's trying to silence us all. I'm not waiting around for him, no way. I won't end up like the others. If my life is over, it will end on my terms." Klozowski's grip tightened on the switch in his hand.

"I don't believe you," Nash said. "Sam physically couldn't have killed all those people. He was in custody when Tegan and Kristina were found. There's no way he made it all the way down to Simpsonville and back."

Kloz shot him a frustrated look. "He was working with that piece-of-shit from the mayor's office, Warnick. Some fed too. All of these guys are dirty, trying to cover their tracks. Besides, Sam was in custody when they were all *found*, not when they were killed." He nodded toward the window. "They stored the bodies right outside the hospital here in the old salt dome, where they used to house their deicing salt for the parking lot. Right in the center of the city; nobody goes in there anymore. Ask Eisley, the salt screws with time-of-death. I'm sure he did something similar with the body in Simpsonville to confuse things. I'd probably be in that salt right now if not for Anson drawing him away. You'll want to check the salt dome. There might be others in there."

"Disarm the vest. Let's check the building together."

"That's not my job anymore. I've got a bigger purpose."

Someone groaned then, soft, barely audible.

114

Poole

Day 6 • 5:59 AM

The photograph still in his hand, Poole dialed Detective Nash's cell phone again. Straight to voice mail. He didn't know if he could trust any information from Porter, but on the chance the photograph was real and Porter was telling the truth, he needed to get help.

He scrolled through his contacts and located the number for another man.

"Espinosa."

"This is Special Agent Frank Poole. Are you at Stroger?"

"Yes, sir."

Poole looked down at the photo. "I need you to listen to me carefully. I have reason to believe Special Agent in Charge Hurless might be involved in all this. I'm not sure to what extent. He's commanding the team on the ground here at the Guyon. I can't alert anyone on my end without risk of it getting back to him. Do you have anyone here we can trust?"

Espinosa dropped off the line for a moment, probably considering this. "Involved how? Where's Captain Dalton?"

"He's with SAIC Hurless, directing ground assets."

"Is he compromised?"

Poole doubted it but couldn't be sure. "I don't know. They're both in the comm van. I can't risk speaking to him while he's in close quarters with Hurless, and I've got no way to get him out without drawing suspicion."

"Half my team is out with whatever bug we picked up at the Upchurch house. I can send Thomas and maybe two others. Any more than that, and I spread myself too thin on the hospital search."

Poole had reached the back of the Guyon Hotel, where two Metro officers stood guard at the door, when the crowd began to shout near the corner of the parking lot.

Something was happening.

"Send whoever you can, and give them this number. I've got to go."

He hung up, gave the Guyon's back door one more glance, then started through the crowd toward the noise.

115

Nash

Day 6 • 6:00 AM

Nash turned to his right, toward the sound. A white sheet was draped over something large, something tall, near the boarded windows.

Kloz let out a sigh. "That man will not die."

He crossed the room, took hold of the sheet, and tugged it away.

"The statue is called *Protection*," Kloz said. "I thought that was kind of ironic."

The statute was of a woman, towering over the room, clutching a young child tight. The two stood in the center of a shallow pool. The pool no longer contained water. Instead, the scent of gasoline wafted across the room.

The mayor was on his feet, secured to the statue with a thick rope, his hands cuffed behind him, encircling the woman's body. He was naked, barely conscious, and even from this distance, Nash could see the words carved over every inch of exposed skin—*hear no evil, speak no evil, see no evil, do no evil.* On his forehead, carved larger than all others, was, *I am evil.* His left ear was gone. Black blood oozed from his eye socket. There were three white boxes on the edge of the basin—two tied shut with black string, the third empty.

"I left him his tongue. Thought maybe he'd want to make amends. I should have known better," Kloz said. "It's time for you to go, Nash."

When Nash looked back at Klozowski, he was holding the trigger from his vest out in front of his chest.

"You don't want to do that."

Kloz nodded toward the composition book still sitting on one of the tables. "When you combine the information in that book with everything Anson already gave you, you'll have more than enough to get convictions and shut down this entire trafficking ring." He looked down at the videotape still at Nash's feet. "That too—you don't want to forget that. Plus, my computer at the office has information. Give everything to the FBI. Tell them to look in the folder named 'Guyon.'"

"I won't let you do it."

Kloz ignored him and glanced over at a hallway on his right. "Clair is locked in room B18, right down there. You don't need a key from this side. Once you get her, take the stairs at the far end of the hallway back to the main basement. You'll see the opening for the tunnel system on the west wall. You can't miss it." He paused for a second, then went on. "I'm going to count down from one hundred before I set this off. That will give you just enough time, if you run."

"Don't, Kloz. Don't."

"It was a pleasure working with you, Brian. Clair too. Please tell her I'm sorry."

"You can tell her. Just deactivate the bomb." Nash heard the pleading in his own voice, but he didn't care. "Come with me. Testify. Explain everything."

"One hundred. Ninety-nine. Ninety-eight..."

Nash eyed him for another moment, considered tackling him, shooting him, wrestling the remote from his hand...he knew none of that would happen, Kloz would have thought of all that, prepared for it. Instead, he scooped up the videotape from the floor and ran over to the table for the composition book.

From the statue, the mayor's remaining eye opened and he looked down at Nash. "Untie me," he forced out, his voice thick and scratchy.

Nash looked at the rope looped around him, the various knots, the handcuffs. He held up the videotape. "Is this true?"

The mayor licked at the crusty blood on his lips. "Doesn't matter...you have to help me..."

Nash knew he didn't have enough time to both free the mayor and get Clair to safety. Someday, he'd use that to rationalize his actions, not only to others, but to himself. To the mayor, he simply said, "Fuck you."

Kloz smiled at this. *"We're all 4MK,* Brian. Remember that."

Without looking back, Nash ran from the room and down the hallway, as Kloz continued to count. "Ninety-four, ninety-three, ninety-two..."

116

Porter

Day 6 • 6:01 AM

Porter saw him.

This time he was sure.

Bishop.

He wanted to be recognized now.

Anson Bishop. Despite the cold, he wore only a black leather jacket. No gloves, no hat. He had a loose scarf around his neck, and his breath lingered in the air, a pale cloud riding the icy air. He'd arrived in a white van not unlike the one Hillburn had owned, and Porter knew this was no coincidence. The crowd parted, let the van pass, then closed up again behind the vehicle, swallowing the empty space. Voices rose all around as spectators realized who must be inside. There was a patrol car about a hundred feet back, the source of the siren that Porter had heard, but the people wouldn't let it through—not fast enough to close the distance. Only the van was permitted, and only at a snail's pace.

The van had nudged through the crowd and pulled to the curb on the corner of Washington and Pulaski Road. The side door had slid open, and there was Bishop. He surveyed the large crowd, jumped down, and the van drove off again. Porter hadn't seen the driver.

Porter had never seen Bishop look nervous, but he looked nervous now. His shoulders were hunched, and he slumped forward slightly. He straightened up and scanned the area, and when his eyes settled on the Channel Seven news van kitty-corner from where he stood, something resembling relief washed over him. He raised a hand and waved in that direction. Porter caught Lizeth Loudon waving back, no doubt standing on something to see over all the people.

Bishop started toward her.

He had a water bottle in his hand.

Even before Porter saw Bishop's fingers twisting off the cap, Porter knew what that bottle meant, knew what it really contained, and he knew he had to stop him before he could infect this crowd.

His fingers tightened around the .38 in his pocket, and he nearly knocked over an old man as he shoved his way through the tangled mass of people.

117

Clair

Day 6 • 6:02 AM

When she had heard muted footsteps coming down the hallway thirty minutes earlier, barely audible through the heavy door and thick walls, Clair had been ready. She stood just inside the door, pressed into the corner of the room, the six-inch piece of fluorescent bulb in her hand, ready to strike. Her trap (hopefully) ready to electrocute the man the moment he came through that door. Neither of those things happened, though. The footsteps had raced past her door to the next room over. Her captor must have drugged the mayor again, because aside from a quick yelp, there were no sounds of struggle.

Through the small window, she watched the man in the black mask take the mayor away on a gurney in a quick rush with not so much as a glance in her direction.

With a loud pop, much like the one she'd heard earlier, the hallway lights went dark, and without a light in her room, her surroundings plunged into complete darkness. A thick, moist dark that seemed to ooze from the walls, under the door, and wrap around her. She wanted to shake it off, but that only caused the murk to tighten its grip, and as she stood there, alone, pressed into the corner of her room, she wondered if she'd be able to move at all when the moment came, or if that dark would just hold her still for her captor's blade.

As if to test just how strong that hold was, Clair moved her makeshift weapon from her right hand to her left and wiped her sweaty palm on her jeans. Knowing she could still move eased her fears, if only a little. She wondered if this was how Emory Connors had felt, trapped all alone. Larissa Biel, Kati Quigley—all the others who had come before her.

Was 4MK somewhere down the hall, lining up little white boxes and pieces of black string, preparing for her? Maybe testing the sharpness of his blade?

Footsteps again.

Fast.

Louder than earlier, thundering down the hallway.

A flashlight beam swept up and about outside, then was gone.

Clair tightened her grip.

The puddle on the floor had begun to evaporate, but there was still plenty of water there, and she was careful not to step in it.

Flashlight again.

Brighter, closer.

She tightened her grip.

When the light was at her window, shining through into her cell, she hoped to God he couldn't see the missing light fixture, the wires dangling from the ceiling. All of this was such a long shot, but it was the only shot she had.

Unwilling to move before she could strike, Clair sensed a face press to the glass more than saw it, visible only from the corner of her eye.

She squeezed her weapon even tighter and made a conscious effort to not squeeze to the point of shattering the remains of the bulb in her hand.

The doorknob jiggled.

Clair couldn't help but trace the faint lines of the wires, wondering if—

"Clair?"

When she heard her name, she thought she imagined it. For one brief instance, she actually thought she might have passed out again, dreamt the sound, the voice, but then she heard it again. Heard him—a shout this time.

Nash.

The dead bolt twisted with a click.

The door pushed open.

"No! No! Don't!"

The corner of the door reached the nail, and sparks flew with a loud *crack!*

Clair expected Nash to jerk back, maybe convulse as electricity tore through his body, but neither of those things happened—he stood perfectly still, frozen, and she remembered her father's stories of people getting electrocuted, how they were unable to move, forced rigid as the electricity charred their flesh from the inside out. She was ready to rush him, smack into him with all her weight in order to break the circuit when Nash stepped back.

He held a gun in one hand and cell phone with the bright flashlight shining in the other.

He'd pushed the door open with the leather toe of his shoe, he hadn't held the doorknob at all.

Clair tore the white wire from the hook in the door and tossed it aside, pulled the door open, and jumped into Nash's arms with so much force she nearly did knock him over. Her face was nestled in the crook of his shoulder when he grabbed her and pulled her deeper into the hallway.

"Run!"

118

Poole

Poole spotted Bishop. Saw him jump from a white van only to disappear again into the crowd. Not before he caught eye contact with that woman from Channel Seven, though. Poole started that way, but it seemed the thousand people around him had also decided to head for that very same spot, and the crowd became so thick, Poole found it hard to breathe.

A few feet ahead of him and to his left, an older woman lost her footing and went down. The crowd seemed to carry her for a moment, then she vanished somewhere below. Poole elbowed his way over to her, helped her back to her feet. Another moment, and she might have been trampled. He saw a little girl in her mother's arms, clutched against her chest, no more than eight or nine years old. The mother was trying to move in the opposite direction from everyone else, no doubt attempting to escape the mob of people, but like the old woman, the momentum of the many carried her with them. Poole got to her, shouted for her to get behind him, and she did, but then he lost track of her as others moved to fill the little bit of empty space he created.

Up ahead, where Bishop must have been, the shouts were deafening and somehow growing louder. Not just cries for Bishop anymore, but cries to get out. Cries to stop. Cries for help.

When Poole caught sight of Porter, he was at least thirty feet away, also heading toward Bishop. It was a fleeting glance, but Poole was certain it was him, and for one quick instant, their eyes met. For that moment, all else dropped away. It was in that moment that Poole saw Porter's shoulder tense, traced his arm, his hand, down into the pocket of his jacket. It was in that moment that Poole realized Porter had a gun. All of this in under a second. He lost sight of him again as his own hand instinctively went for his weapon and freed the Glock from his shoulder holster.

119

Porter

Lizeth Loudon stood twenty feet to his left.

Anson Bishop was less than a dozen paces away.

Detective Sam Porter took the .38 from his pocket, raised the weapon above his head, and fired three shots into the air.

The crowd froze.

The voices silenced.

With the echo of gunfire, momentum shifted, turned, began to push away from Bishop rather than toward him. When the space between them cleared, Porter trained the weapon on the other man. "Set down the water bottle, now!"

Bishop froze, turned toward Porter. The water bottle, now uncapped, dangled from his fingertips.

Porter leveled the gun, a clean shot at Bishop's chest, if he took it. His finger tightened on the trigger. "I'm not going to ask you again!"

Bishop nodded, slowly crouched, and placed the open water bottle on the cracked asphalt. "It's just water, Sam."

"Drop the gun!"

Poole.

Special Agent Poole pushed through the crowd into the open space, his gun on Porter. "Drop it! Now!"

Porter shook his head and shouted at Bishop, "Step back from the bottle!"

To Poole, he said, "The virus is in that water bottle!"

Bishop shook his head. "It's just water. You brought the virus here, Sam, not me. I wouldn't do something like that."

"He planned to infect everyone," Porter insisted.

Bishop took a step closer. "How was breakfast, Sam?"

As Bishop took another step, Porter shouted, "Don't move!"

Bishop drew closer. "You brought the virus here, not me. If anyone infected all these people, it was you. Everyone around you."

How was breakfast, Sam?

A shot rang out, loud and harsh. Porter heard it a moment after the bullet tore through his chest from the rooftop of one of the surrounding buildings. He didn't remember falling to the ground, but when his brain registered what was happening, that's where he was. Poole was on top of him, wrestling the gun away.

There was an explosion then, a deep rumble, that came from the direction of the hospital.

120

Poole

Day 6 • 6:05 AM

"Hurry, they're coming."

At first, Poole thought he misunderstood him, but Porter repeated the same phrase a moment later, his spittle tainted red with blood.

Poole pressed hard on the wound in Porter's chest, leaned closer. "Who's coming?"

"Weasel…he called me…he said he had evidence…meet him…"

Poole frowned. "Evidence of what? You're not making sense, Sam. Try not to talk—you're losing a lot of blood."

He tore open Porter's jacket.

The bullet, fired by one of the snipers on Washington, struck Porter high in the right side of his chest. Porter's breathing was labored, each breath a quick gasp. "I think the bullet punctured your lung. Just lie still—paramedics are coming."

"I ate the breakfast," Porter said. "Infected. Get…away."

Porter bucked, tried to knock Poole off, but Poole held fast.

"Father, forgive me," a female voice said from somewhere behind Poole. She tossed a black and white composition book onto Porter's bloody chest and disappeared into the crowd before Poole could get a good look at her. Nothing but a wisp of brown hair. He shoved the book aside and applied more pressure to the wound.

About ten feet to Poole's left, four uniformed officers from Metro held Bishop down on the ground while two agents from the Bureau stood over him. His hands were behind his back, secured with plastic zip-tie handcuffs. As they hauled him to his feet, his eyes fixed on Porter, on the gun a few inches from Porter's fallen hand, then met Poole's for an instant before he was turned and dragged through the crowd toward a waiting patrol car.

A large, black cloud of smoke filled the sky deeper into town—near Stroger, if not the hospital itself.

Porter coughed.

Blood sprayed over his shirt.

His eyes rolled up into his head.

A paramedic dropped to the ground next to him, another on his other side.

To the first one, a woman in her late twenties with short red hair, Poole said, "I'm FBI. I think the bullet punctured his lung. He was conscious up until a moment ago."

"His pulse is weak. BP is seventy-three over fifty-five." She had Porter's shirt open, examining the wound. "Step back, please. I've got him."

Poole did as he was told.

The other paramedic handed her a package labeled *QuickClot* and some bandages. He looked up at Poole. "I just came from your communications van—SAIC Hurless has been poisoned. Something in his coffee, we think. You might want to get over there."

Poole looked in the direction of the van. Hurless, Dalton, and the tech who had been tracing Porter's phone, all in there. He turned back to the paramedic. "What about Dalton and the tech?"

He injected Porter with something. "Just Hurless. The others are okay."

A third paramedic arrived, this one with a stretcher. He set it on the ground parallel with Porter.

"Is he breathing?" Poole asked.

None of them answered.

With a practiced movement, two rolled Porter to his side while the third maneuvered the stretcher under him.

"I'm staying with him," Poole said.

"Clear us a path," the female paramedic said. She held an IV bag a few feet above Porter with one hand while pressing a finger first to Porter's wrist, then to his neck. When she noticed Poole watching her, her fingers dropped away, and she wouldn't make eye contact.

Together, they pushed their way through to the ambulance parked at the curb, the bloodstained diary tucked into the waistband of Poole's pants.

121

Diary

Stocks dead.

"Get his gun," Vincent said, looking down at Stocks's lifeless body.

"Stocks? What's happening up there?" Welderman called up from the base of the stairs.

Stocks was dead. Very little blood came from the back of his head where Vincent hit him, but I could see the white of his skull under the matted hair and torn skin. He'd cracked the bone.

"Get the goddamn gun," Vincent repeated. He moved to the side of the doorway and pressed his back against the wall, ready to strike the next person who came into the room.

With a shaking hand, Libby reached down and picked up the gun.

I took the weapon from her. I knew what was coming, and I didn't want her to know what it felt like to take a life. I didn't want her to ever know that feeling.

On his bed, The Kid groaned.

Tegan's face was white. Kristina was pressed up against her, still looking down at Stocks's lifeless body.

"Stocks? I'm coming up!"

"Hurry!" I shouted. "I think he had a heart attack!" I quickly knelt between Stocks and the doorway, blocking any view of his ruined head. My finger on the trigger, I hid the gun behind his body. I didn't know

much about guns, but this was a revolver, so I didn't think it had a safety. I hoped it didn't have a safety.

Vincent pressed so tight against the drywall I thought he might disappear into the wallpaper. He nodded at me quickly, the wrench above his head, ready to swing.

Welderman came up the stairs two at a time. Before I saw him, I saw his shadow on the wall, looming larger with each thud of his feet. When he reached the doorway, time moved so slow. I'm not sure if it was the sight of Stocks on the floor, or the look of fear in Tegan's eyes, or Paul standing in the corner, or me crouched down, but something gave him pause. He froze just outside the doorway.

Vincent had expected him to come into the room, and he had started to swing the wrench when Welderman's footfalls were just outside the door. If Welderman had kept going, the wrench would have hit him square in the jaw. Because he stopped, Vincent hit him high in the forearm instead, just below his shoulder. More of a glancing blow. Welderman staggered backward, fumbling for his gun.

I raised Stocks's revolver and fired, three quick shots. I didn't have a chance to aim, and the first bullet struck the wall a few inches from his head. The gun kicked back for the second and third shots and those went wild—one further up the wall behind him, the other into the ceiling.

Welderman jumped back against the hallway wall, pictures falling around him, then he rolled to the side and disappeared down the steps as I fired a fourth time.

"Give me that!" Vincent snatched the gun from my hand and ran down the hallway after him.

I heard two more shots. Neither had come from Vincent.

122

Diary

I wanted my knife, but I didn't have my knife, Oglesby had my knife. Father would have told me to use the wrench, so I scooped it up, and I followed after Vincent.

I spotted him briefly near the bottom of the stairs. Then he rounded the corner toward the parlor as another shot rang out. The bullet smacked into the plaster near the front door, spraying the air with dust.

Someone yelped at the top of the stairs. I think it was Kristina.

Vincent crouched outside the parlor as another shot came. He quickly pointed at the front door. I understood—there were only two ways in and out of this house, and Welderman was moving toward the back door in the kitchen.

Another shot. This one so close, I heard it whiz by my head.

Vincent fired in the direction of the parlor.

I dropped to the floor, crying out as pain shot up my broken arm. I scrambled for the front door, pulled it open, and rolled across the porch, down the steps to the grass. By the time I stopped moving, the pain was so bad my vision went white. I might have broken my arm again. There was no way to tell with the cast.

I forced myself to stand and ran around the side of the house to the back door.

I found Finicky in the kitchen, a butcher knife in her hand. "You little shit."

She came at me, far faster than I anticipated. She wielded the knife with something between skill and fear—quick swipes back and forth at arm's length, trying to drive me back. Instead, I barreled at her with all my strength. The knife came at me, and I raised my arm with the cast, brought it up hard. I caught the side of the blade, deflected it, and my cast smacked up under her chin. Finicky's head jerked back, cracked against the kitchen counter, then she fell to the floor.

The blow hadn't killed her, but her breathing came in quick, shallow gasps. Her right arm jerked and spasmed.

I dropped the wrench and took up her knife. Not my knife, but a knife, and the blade felt good in my hand.

From the parlor, I heard another shot. Whether from Vincent or Welderman, I couldn't be sure.

Cold sweat trickled down the side of my face. My arm throbbed with my heartbeat, such heavy thumps it felt like they would break the cast from the inside. I tried to ignore the pain, to will it away as Father taught me.

I crossed the kitchen.

The door between the kitchen and parlor was closed. Flimsy and double-hinged, designed to open in either direction. Hardly thick enough to stop a bullet, but with it closed, I had no idea what was happening on the other side.

Another shot.

The report had a deeper sound to it than the one I heard when Vincent fired—this had to be Welderman shooting. Vincent had a revolver. While I had never shot one before tonight, I'd read about them in plenty of comics. Most only held six bullets. I had fired three shots upstairs, and I saw Vincent fire one more. At best, he had two shots left. Maybe less, if any of the others I heard had been him. Father would have searched Stocks for additional ammunition before heading downstairs. I was not my father.

Two more shots.

Definitely Welderman, not Vincent. If Welderman was still shooting, it meant Vincent was still alive. He was probably in the hallway just outside the Parlor.

I kicked the door. It swung open into the room. With the adrenaline, everything moved in slow motion. I took it all in—Vincent barely visible opposite me in the hallway. Welderman was crouched behind the couch, sideways, his gun up. When he saw me, he spun in my direction, squeezing off shots as he came around. Vincent dove into the room, slammed onto the hardwood floor, and fired twice under the couch, maybe an inch off the floor. The first bullet punched through the baseboard to my left, the second bullet caught Welderman in his right foot.

Welderman dropped back onto the couch and was already trying to get back up when I ran toward him and jumped.

He pulled the trigger again, and something hot cut into my thigh.

The butcher knife pierced his neck about an inch below his Adam's apple. I held the knife as Mother had taught me—with my palm pressed against the base of the hilt so my grip wouldn't slide—and I felt pressure as the tip first sliced through skin and muscle, then more resistance when it punctured his windpipe. The blade caught in bone at the back of his throat and blood sprayed out everywhere, hot against my skin.

I dropped to the side of him, rolled off the couch, and found myself on the floor.

I landed on my broken arm, and this time the pain won. I don't re-member passing out. To nobody in particular, I only remember saying, Weasel is still in the van.

123

Diary

Paul slapped me.

When my eyes opened, I saw his hand coming at my face for a second time, and I turned away, barely fast enough to avoid the blow.

"He's awake!" Paul shouted over his shoulder. He was sitting on my chest, holding me down. "Don't move—that prick shot you."

I felt a burn, something horrible in my thigh, and when I tilted my head, I saw Libby pouring peroxide over a tear in my jeans.

"The bullet just grazed you. It could have been much worse." She dabbed at the wound with a dish towel from the kitchen and fished a roll of gauze from a first-aid kit at her side. I had no idea where she found that. She went around my leg several times, pulling the gauze tight.

On the couch, Vincent was going through Welderman's pockets, dumping the contents on a side table. Welderman stared at nothing, a blank, dead gaze. His clothing was soaked in blood, the couch too, the surrounding furniture. I probably hit his jugular; nothing else explained all the blood. The butcher knife was on the floor near his feet.

"Finicky's in the kitchen," I managed to get out, trying to look back that way.

"We found her. Tegan and Kristina are tying her up," Paul told me. "She's still alive. You should have hit her harder."

"Can you get off my chest? I can't breathe."

"Sorry." Paul rolled to the side and got to his feet.

Finished with my leg, Libby wiped the blood from my face. Her expression was filled with a mix of concern, fear, worry, anxiety, yet somehow she managed to smile, and that smile was the most beautiful thing I had ever seen. She hovered over me for a moment, then bent down and kissed me. Her lips soft, warm, perfect. "I think I love you, Anson Bishop."

She said this quietly, only for me. For that brief moment, I forgot about the pain in my leg, my broken arm. There was only her and me, and I told her I loved her too.

Turns out Paul heard us. His face flushed as he looked away.

"Found his keys," Vincent said from the couch. He also had Welderman's gun and at least one extra clip. "I'm going after Weasel."

I tried to sit up. "I'm going too."

"No you're not." Libby frowned.

I forced myself to stand, reigniting the pain in my thigh and arm. "I have to."

"Let Vincent and Paul go."

"We all need to get out of here," Paul said. "We don't know who's coming back and when. His eyes fell on Welderman, all the blood. "Both him and Stocks were cops. There was that other one out there...they're all dirty. We can't let them find us here."

"Don't leave me," Libby pleaded, stroking my cheek.

I went to the desk in the corner of the room and scribbled out my address in Simpsonville. I pressed the paper into her hand and brushed the hair from her eyes. "Help Tegan and Kristina. When they're done with Finicky, get the money from the barn and load up Finicky's car—as much as you can fit. If we're not back in two hours, or you have to leave sooner, meet us at this address—in the trailer behind what's left of the house." I leaned in close and lowered my voice. "We'll get far away from here, just like we planned. I promise."

Vincent had Welderman's gun tucked in his belt. He handed the revolver to Libby. "It's empty, but Stocks might have some more bullets in his pockets."

Libby held the gun with a loose grip, as if it were hot.

"Kristina knows how to use one if you're not comfortable," he told her.

"You may need to take The Kid to the hospital. If you do, don't use real names."

Paul was at the front door. "They've got nearly ten minutes on us. If we're going, we need to leave...now."

I kissed Libby again. "I'll see you soon."

Her eyes glistened with tears. She must have known there was no talking me out of it. She only nodded.

From the floor near the couch, I picked up the knife and wiped the blade on one of the cushions. I felt Libby's eyes on my back, but I couldn't turn around. I knew if I did, I wouldn't have the will to leave, and this was something I had to do.

Vincent, Paul, and I ran out the door to Welderman's Chevy.

With Vincent driving, we shot down the driveway, the farmhouse disappearing into the dark behind.

We knew where they were going.

I tightened my grip on the knife and waited for the lights of Charleston.

124

Diary

"There!" Paul shouted. "There they are!"

Vincent hadn't driven much, and this was clear as he negotiated some of the more narrow roads. He nearly put us in the ditch twice, and when he ran a stop sign on Bulford, a tractor-trailer approaching from the west almost clipped our back end. By the time we reached the highway, he'd improved, if only a little.

He drove far too fast.

We were all covered in blood. We had a gun belonging to a dead police detective in the car, the knife too. There were the bodies back at the farmhouse. Any one of these things would get us in far more trouble than I was willing to consider.

It was on the highway we spotted them—the white van and a Charleston Police cruiser following behind by several car lengths. Vincent fell in behind both of them, keeping several cars between us. He said he knew the route to the motel, so there was no reason to risk getting too close.

Ten minutes later, when we reached the motel, things went wrong.

"Park over there," I told Vincent, pointing at the lot across the street between McDonald's and the auto parts store. I knew we'd be able to watch from there without getting too close. The plan we came up with was a simple one—we'd wait for them to take Weasel into one of the rooms, Paul and I would get him out while Vincent watched Van Man and the *cop. He'd only show himself if necessary. The gun was a last resort, but we'd use it if we needed. Whatever we had to do to get Weasel.*

None of that happened.

The van pulled into the motel parking lot. The police cruiser pulled up beside it and came to a stop.

We were still moving when the back door of the van flew open and Weasel jumped out, running in the opposite direction with the green bag in his hand. Tegan's camera was on a strap around his neck, and it slapped against his back as he bolted through the parking lot and disappeared between two rows of buildings behind the motel.

"Shit!" Vincent cried out, yanking the gearshift back into drive.

He jumped the curb, tires locked up all around us. Somehow he managed to shoot across Crescent as the police cruiser took off down Klondike with the van heading around the block on Boise, no doubt an attempt to box Weasel in.

Vincent's head jerked back and forth, watching both as we rolled through the motel lot. "Which one do I follow?"

I spotted Weasel about a block away, darting between several parked cars, then down the side of a brownstone. "He's running between the buildings. Let us out!"

"You can't catch him on that leg, he's—"

I didn't hear what he said next. I jumped from the car while he was still slowing. Paul came out behind me with a grunt. We both took off running toward the back of the motel, in the direction Weasel had gone. Behind us, tires squealed as Vincent gave the car a little too much gas attempting to turn. He overcompensated, nearly sideswiped a parked station wagon, then righted the Chevy before bouncing back onto Church, going after the van.

Paul was much faster than me. I tried to keep up, but each footfall on my injured leg hurt more than the last, and that was nothing compared to my broken arm rattling around in the cast. Over the past hour, the fingers on that hand had swollen and gone red. They felt hot, and while I couldn't see under the cast, I imagined things there were far worse. In my mind's eye, I pictured both ends of the broken bone scraping against each other, tearing muscle and who knew what else. I imagined the arm continuing to swell and tried not to think about what would happen if it ran out of room to expand in the plaster cast.

I pushed these thoughts out of my head. I willed the pain away, and I chased after Paul as he chased after Weasel, all three of us disappearing into the mess of buildings, side streets, and alleyways behind the motel.

More than once, I lost track of Weasel. At one point, I even lost sight of Paul. He kept glancing back at me, slowing down, and I waved him on, told him to just keep going. I was covered in sweat, and that light-headedness had returned. Breathing became hard, and I had to stop for a moment, bent over with my hand on my knee, sucking in air.

When I stood back up, I caught a glimpse of Paul up ahead. He was halfway down a narrow alley when the Charleston Police cruiser from earlier screeched to a stop on Cumberland. A uniformed officer jumped out and rounded the car before disappearing down a cobblestone alleyway on the opposite side of the street.

Paul was moving so fast he smacked into the front of the police car and nearly went over the hood. He regained his footing and scrambled around the car into the alley.

I was still on the wrong side of Cumberland when the first of three shots cracked through the air. Pop, pop, pop!

125

Diary

By the time I reached the police car, Paul was darting back out of the alley, waving me off with both hands. "Run!" he shouted.

"What happened?"

I was standing near the trunk of the Charleston PD cruiser. The driver-side door was still open, the engine running. Inside, muffled voices rattled from the radio.

Paul didn't answer. He ran past me, down the sidewalk on Cumberland. Didn't even slow down.

I looked back toward the alley, but from where I stood, I couldn't see anything.

I still had the butcher knife, so I went to the open door of the patrol car, leaned inside, and cut the microphone cable. Back outside, I stabbed the left front tire before following after Paul as quickly as I could.

From the mouth of the alley, someone shouted, It sounded like Van Man, but I didn't turn around to check.

Up ahead, Vincent came around the corner from Church and slid to a stop, blocking the intersection. Paul yanked open the back door and dove inside. Horns blared all around. I staggered up, fell onto the seat, and managed to get the door closed behind me as Vincent gunned the engine and we raced back down Cumberland. Van Man was gone when we passed the alley on the way back. I tried to get a look, but it was too dark.

"Where's Weasel?" Vincent said, leaning over the steering wheel. He yanked the wheel hard to the right, and Paul rolled into me as we made a quick turn.

Paul shook all over. His face was horribly pale. He mumbled something, but I couldn't make it out.

I grabbed his shoulder and shook him. "What happened? Where is Weasel?"

Paul looked at me. His mouth fell open, but nothing came out.

"Paul!"

He spoke between gasps. "He's...oh, God...he shot him...he's dead. Weasel's dead."

I tried to get more out of him, but he buried his face in his hands and broke down into heavy sobs.

Lights blaring, another police car shot past us heading in the opposite direction, toward Cumberland.

"We need to get out of here," Vincent said, turning down another side street.

Two more police cars were approaching. Sirens blared everywhere.

I slumped down in the seat, Paul screaming beside me. "Should we go back to the farmhouse?"

Vincent looked at the clock on the radio. "It's been nearly forty minutes, and we're a half hour away."

"I told Libby two hours. Go back."

And we did.

We pulled into the driveway in record time.

Finicky's car was gone.

126
Diary

The drive to Simpsonville was a silent one. Vincent didn't speak, and neither did I. On the backseat beside me, Paul had curled up against the door—his screams became sobs, those becoming whimpers, and finally nothing at all.

In Welderman's glove box, Vincent found a bottle of ibuprofen. I swallowed four of the pills dry, followed by two more thirty minutes later. The pain in my arm and leg reduced to a dull throb, and while the swelling didn't go away completely, it did go down, and I was thankful for that.

I watched the lights of various cities and towns fade behind us until the thick of night engulfed everything. All three of us were in desperate need of sleep but unwilling to rest for even a moment.

"We're almost out of gas," Vincent said.

"It's not much further," I told him.

And it wasn't.

My street, my woods, my house, all as I left it. Waiting for me to return.

"Turn there," I told him.

He was leaning forward again, up over the steering wheel. "Where?"

"At the mailbox, up there on the right."

Vincent whistled as the headlights rolled over the remains of my old house, the burnt out husk of my childhood.

"There's Finicky's car—they made it," Paul said, pointing toward the Carters' place off to the side. This was the first thing he'd said since we left Charleston.

We pulled to a stop next to the remains of Father's car. Weeds had claimed it as their own, and I was glad for that. I didn't want to see it. Vincent killed the motor. The engine noise was replaced with soft clicks as the motor cooled.

The front door to the Carters' place was open. Several backpacks and bags sat in the dirt near Finicky's car.

Vincent was first out. He ran up the steps with Welderman's gun at the ready. "Kristina! Tegan!" he shouted. "Libby!" His voice dimmed as he disappeared inside.

Something was wrong. I think Paul felt it too. As we both got up out of the car, the air was thick with it.

Vincent came back out a moment later, a puzzled look on his face. "They're not here."

I was only half listening to him. I thought I saw someone in the back of Finicky's car, slumped down.

I wanted to believe it was the girls, sleeping maybe—of course they would sleep in the car and wait for us—my mind said. I so wanted that to be true, but as I got closer, I knew that it was not. In the back seat was a man's body.

"That's Welderman," Paul said.

We found Stocks's body in the front. Someone had belted him into the passenger seat.

Vincent cupped his hands around his mouth. "Kristina!"

She didn't answer.

Nobody answered.

Vincent opened the driver-side door and we all saw it—there was blood on the steering wheel. I couldn't tell if it was from Welderman, Stocks, or someone else.

"This is bad," Paul said, stepping back and turning in a slow circle. Looking all around us.

"Open the trunk," I said, moving around to the back.

Neither Paul or Vincent moved.

"Somebody open the trunk."

Vincent found the release switch and pulled.

There was a loud clunk. The trunk rose.

I didn't want to look inside, but I forced myself to do it anyway. My breath catching as I bent forward.

Empty.

For a moment, I felt relief. Then I saw Libby's locket in the dirt near my feet.

"There's a note pinned to Stocks's shirt," Vincent said from inside the car.

"What's it say?"

"You've got an hour to take out the trash before I call the locals. Forget the girls. Don't follow. It's signed Sam Porter.*"*

Six Months Later

127

Porter

Day 198 • 3:18 PM

Porter shifted his weight, and that bought him about thirty seconds of relief before the hard wood of the bench went to work on the opposite side of his ass—happy to have something new to chew on. After nearly three months of trial, he knew better. He should have brought a pillow.

Room 209 of the George N. Leighton Criminal Court building located at 2600 South California Avenue in Chicago was the largest of the building's courts. Able to hold nearly two hundred people in the gallery, there was not a single empty seat today, nor had there been for the duration of the trail.

Early on, there had been motions to hear the case somewhere else in the country—Bishop's lead attorney, a man named Curtis Ruhland, said Bishop would never get a fair shake in Chicago, and while he was probably right about that, his defense team, prosecutors, and the judge were unable to find someplace where he would get a fair shake. Bishop and the 4MK murders had been well known long before February seventeenth of 2015, but the events of that particular day had gone global. Whether newspaper, television, or grandmother's Facebook page, the capture of 4MK was on everyone's lips, the subject of much of the world's Internet traffic.

On February seventeenth, nearly a dozen bodies were found inside the Guyon Hotel, all in varying stages of decomposition. Eye, ear, and tongue removed on each, *I am evil* carved into their flesh, and the words *Father, forgive me* written somewhere nearby. Each of the bodies found matched a name in 4MK's final diary, the one Klozowski had given Nash. Each responsible for some role in the enormous ring of human trafficking laid out in that book. The FBI found three more still buried in the salt dome behind the hospital, right where Klozowski had said they would.

In a video left on his computer at Metro, Edwin Klozowski confessed to all these recent murders. He provided evidence of their crimes, information detailing how he found them, and claimed their deaths would each pay a bit of the toll amassed by their wrongdoing. Klozowski also confessed to the murders of Stanford Pentz and Christie Albee. As "The Kid," after sustaining life threatening injuries at the hands of Welderman and Stocks, he was brought to a back-alley medical practice run by Stanford Pentz. Along with Christie Albee, Pentz stabilized Klozowski before loading him into the back of his car and dropping him at the nearest emergency room.

Klozowski was not one to forget a face.

Mayor Milton was dead.

FBI Special Agent in Charge Foster Hurless was dead. Poisoned. Although Poole was able to offer a detailed description, neither the FBI nor Chicago Metro (who finally found a way to work together) had any leads on the man who delivered coffee that day. He knew enough to offer Hurless sugar. He was also willing to gamble on whether or not one of the others would reach for that cup first.

Both Mayor Milton and SAIC Hurless were linked to the criminal trafficking enterprise in enough ways to justify nearly twenty pages in that little book. They'd wielded their power and influence as both a shield and a weapon to facilitate their crimes. Shortly after the death of his supervisor, Special Agent Frank Poole found an offshore account belonging to Hurless containing nearly three million dollars. Those funds, along with most of the mayor's assets, had been seized.

Edwin Klozowski was dead.

The bomb strapped to his chest had gutted the former Cook County Hospital. The flames left nothing but a charred husk of a building behind. The mayor's partial remains were found, still bound to the statue once called *Protection*.

Nash's report detailed Klozowski's final moments, his confession, his accusations. Nash described Anthony Warnick with a fatal gunshot wound in the tunnel leading from Stroger to the old Cook County Hospital building. A day later, when Warnick's apartment was searched by both the FBI and Chicago Metro, substantial evidence was found that left no doubt as to his actions—on orders from the mayor, Warnick had systematically hunted down Kristina Niven and Tegan Savala, killed them, and left their bodies in the cemetery and the subway station. There were also boxes of information on Vincent Weidner, Paul Upchurch, and Anson Bishop. While there was no proof, it was believed he killed Weidner and placed the body in Porter's apartment. Warnick had been tasked by the principals of BackPage with finding all the children from Finicky's and told to make their murders look as if 4MK were responsible.

When Porter had first woken in the hospital from an induced coma, three surgeries and nearly a week after being shot, Nash had been there. Nash told him Klozowski insisted Porter had been working with Warnick, attempting to track down all the children from Finicky's foster home in an attempt to silence them. Nash told Porter he didn't plan to put that in his report. Porter insisted that he did.

"No more secrets," he had told his partner in a voice barely loud enough to be considered a whisper. "Don't leave anything out."

Nash reluctantly agreed.

Everything was there.

Although Porter had read those reports, he found himself unable to acknowledge or deny the accusations—he simply did not remember. There were flashes, but nothing resembling a complete picture. He had no recollection of ever meeting Warnick.

Hurry, they're coming.

Poole had told him what he said about Weasel moments after being shot, but even that was gone. A fleeting glimpse of his past hidden again behind a closed door.

Poole also told him they found an empty vial of the SARS virus in Porter's hotel room down in New Orleans. Two more were still missing. Porter said he had no idea how it could have gotten there or where the others were.

Porter had not been infected.

Upon arriving at the hospital, he was immediately quarantined. Additional precautions were taken during the surgeries and all care that followed until tests revealed the virus was not in his system. When he was finally well enough for an interview, Porter told the FBI what Bishop had told him—the virus was in the breakfast he ate on the plane. When the plane was searched, there was no trace of the virus, nor did they find any proof Bishop had set foot in the private jet. The food was long gone. Poole had not been there for the interview. The agent who was there simply took his statement stone-faced and left. Porter knew they didn't believe him.

From a doorway at the left front of the courtroom, a bailiff entered and turned toward the large crowd. "All rise for the Honorable Judge Henry Schmitt."

Along with Special Agent Frank Poole on his left and all others in the courtroom, Porter stood, the chains on his wrists and ankles forcing him to hunch a little forward.

128

Porter

Day 198 • 3:21 PM

Along with his attorney, Anson Bishop stood at a table at the front of the room. His hair, now neatly cropped, had been cut for the trial. He wore a dark blue suit. Porter stared at the back of his head from his seat in the third row, willing Bishop to turn around. He did not.

"You may be seated," the bailiff told everyone.

Porter must have remained standing just a little too long. He felt Poole's hand on his arm, tugging him back down onto the bench. The bullet wound in his chest was still tender, and while it no longer hurt all the time, there were the occasional twinges of pain to remind him just how close to death he had come—a little less each day but always there to remind him of February seventeenth.

Throughout the trial, Bishop insisted he was innocent of all crimes. During his testimony, his story never faltered—yes, I changed my name, but I killed no one. Detective Porter told me I was part of an undercover operation to help capture the real 4MK. During closing arguments, Bishop's defense team played Klozowski's confession and ended with one simple thought—he admitted to killing so many people. Was it hard to believe he was actually the one who killed Calli Tremell and the others? All those Anson Bishop stood accused of murdering? After all, Klozowski admitted to tampering with video evidence, directing the investigation, killing others as retribution for their crimes…was it really so hard to believe Edwin Klozowski, not their client, was really responsible?

From the far right corner of the courtroom, the jury filed in. Seven men, five women, ranging in age from early twenties to the oldest at seventy-three. Four black, five white, two Hispanic, and an Asian woman. For the past three months, they had been sequestered in a nearby hotel without access to the Internet or television. Family members were searched prior to meetings to ensure no outside influences found their way into their deliberations. Each day of Bishop's trial, Judge Schmitt reminded them only evidence presented at trial should be considered. Shortly after the start of Bishop's trial, it became abundantly clear that evidence was far more limited than the lead prosecutor had hoped.

From the bench, Porter retrieved his notebook. He'd started the notebook while still in the hospital and had intended to give it to the prosecutor, but the District Attorney's office did not want his notes.

The black and white composition book had *evidence* written across the front.

On the top of the first page, written in large blocky letters, was: *Confession at 314 West Belmont.*

When Porter had found Bishop on the eleventh floor of Talbot's office building, under construction at the time, Arthur Talbot had been near death, secured to an office chair, as Anson Bishop confessed to his crimes. Emory Connors had been far below, at the bottom of an elevator shaft. In the moments leading up to Talbot's murder, Bishop told Porter how he blamed the real estate mogul for destroying his family, how the man had his hands in a multitude of criminal enterprises. Porter tried to stop him as he pushed Talbot across the floor and into an open elevator shaft to his death.

One month into the trial, the *Chicago Examiner* had run a first-page story outlining Porter's actions and memory lapses. Although they refused to divulge their source, they included transcripts of conversations thought to be private, between Porter and his doctors. Damning conversations clearly detailing his missing time. Under subpoena, Bishop's defense team managed to obtain copies of Porter's medical records. As a result, he was ordered to speak to a court-appointed psychologist tasked with determining his current and past mental state.

Ultimately deemed unreliable, Porter had not been permitted to testify. Because only Porter had born witness to Bishop's confession at Talbot's office building, his written report had also been struck from evidence.

In his notebook, Porter drew a line through *Confession at 314 West Belmont.*

Although Porter had also detailed how Bishop stabbed him in his apartment, that event was also stricken from evidence.

Phone calls.

Conversations.

Unreliable.

If there wasn't a third party to corroborate the information, all interactions between Bishop and Porter alone were struck from evidence.

In his notebook, Porter found all the others and drew lines through those too:

Confession at the Guyon

Murder of Jane Doe/Rose Finicky

Every phone call.

The focus of the trial shifted to physical evidence, primarily Bishop's fingerprint found on the railcar used to transport the body of Gunter Herbert in the tunnels beneath the Mulifax Publications building. In his testimony, Bishop insisted he'd never been down there. The fingerprint placed him at the crime scene. The defense team made quick work of it—the fingerprint was collected by Mark Thomas, a member of the SWAT team, and given to Detective Porter. Porter had sole possession of that evidence for how long? Hours. He then gave it to Detective Nash for transport to the lab—*isn't Detective Nash the one on camera kicking my client?*

Porter held little hope for the fingerprint evidence. He drew a line through that too.

Several people in A. Montgomery Ward Park had seen Bishop when Emory Connors was initially taken. None of them were confident enough to identify him in a lineup.

Emory's boyfriend, Tyler Mathers, was unable to ID Bishop.

Emory, held in the bottom of an elevator shaft, had never seen her captor's face.

The origin of all the 4MK diaries came into question, and although Porter insisted he hadn't commissioned Upchurch to create them, *had never even met Upchurch*, he was faced with apprehension and disbelief. And that was by the prosecutors from the district attorney's office. Unwilling to roll the dice, they didn't admit them into evidence.

Hearsay.

Speculation.

Circumstantial.

One by one, the defense tore apart the case. As Porter went through his notebook, drawing lines through this and that, he eventually closed the cover and set it aside.

The jury had deliberated a little over six hours.

Judge Henry Schmitt cracked his gavel. "Order please, order."

Larissa Biel and Katy Quigley were sitting together up in the second row.

Clair and Nash were in Porter's row, on the opposite side of Poole. When Porter glanced over, he noticed the two of them holding hands.

The judge turned his attention to the jury. "Madam Forewoman, has the jury come to a conclusion?"

The Asian woman stood. "We have, your honor."

Turning to Bishop, he said, "Please rise and face the jury."

Anson Bishop stood, buttoning the jacket of his suit, and turned toward the group of twelve.

The judge surveyed those in the gallery with a stern glare. "When the verdict is read, I expect all of you to remain composed and respect the fact that this is a court of law. I will not tolerate outbursts of any kind." He turned back to the woman at the head of the jury box. "And what find you?"

She looked out over the crowd in the gallery, glanced in Bishop's general direction but quickly looked away, unable to make eye contact. Clearing her throat, she read the index card in her hand. "In the case 15-85201008, Cook County vs. Anson Bishop, find the defendant, Anson Bishop, not guilty in violation of Penal Code Section 187(a), a felony upon Calli Tremell, a human being. Not guilty in violation of Penal Code Section 187(a), a felony upon Elle Borton. Not guilty in violation of Penal Code Section 187(a), a felony upon Missy Lumax. Not guilty in violation of Penal Code Section 187(a), a felony upon Barbara…"

Porter didn't hear the rest. The rush of blood in his head, the thumping of his heartbeat in his ears, drowned her out. The gallery erupted with loud gasps, shouts—some cheered while others broke out in tears.

Poole tapped his shoulder and nodded toward the door on the far right of the room. "We need to go."

PORTER'S NOTES

ANSON BISHOP VICTIMS
Calli Tremell
Elle Borton
Missy Lumax
Susan Devoro
Barbara McInley
Allison Crammer
Jodi Blumington
Emory Connors (alive)
Gunther Herbert
Arthur Talbot
Rose Finicky
Detective Freddy Welderman
Detective Ezra Stocks
Dr. Joseph Oglesby

PAUL UPCHURCH VICTIMS
Floyd Reynolds
Ella Reynolds
Randal Davies
Lili Davies
Darlene Biel (alive)
Larissa Biel (alive)
Kati Quigley (alive)
Wesley Hartzler

EDWIN KLOZOWSKI VICTIMS
Mayor Barry Milton
Anthony Warnick
Stanford Pentz – Stroger Hospital
Christie Albee – Stroger Hospital
Dozen + left at the Guyon Hotel

ANTHONY WARNICK (DIRECTED BY BACKPAGE) VICTIMS
(Children from Finicky's)
Libby McInley
Tegan Savala – Rose Hill Cemetery
Kristina Niven – Red Line tracks – Clark Station
Vincent Weidner – Left in Porter's apartment

WELDERMAN, STOCKS, HILLBURN VICTIMS
Weasel

UNKNOWN
Tom Langlin – Simpsonville courthouse steps
Jane Doe – Finicky Farmhouse

129

Porter

Day 199 • 3:18 PM

"I don't want to hear another word about those goddamn diaries!" Captain Henry Dalton slammed his hand down on the table, his face burning red. He glared at Porter. "You and those books. I'm not sure what's worse, the fact that it looks like you had them written or the possibility that you didn't and let the rantings of some madman run this investigation into the ground."

"I didn't—"

Dalton pointed at him, his finger shaking. "Enough."

"Do I need to remind you that my client agreed to attend this meeting today willingly and is under no obligation to be here?"

This came from the man on Porter's left. His union-appointed legal representative: Bob Hessling, late forties, poorly colored thinning dark hair. He turned to the district attorney. "Your office rushed to trial. You let the media pressure you. You tried Bishop for all the murders at once rather than one at a time. He's free because of shortcuts taken by your office, not the actions of my client."

The district attorney's eyes narrowed. "Law enforcement didn't deliver the evidence, and what little they did give us was tainted. We had to group the cases together—they wouldn't have held water individually."

"And now Bishop is off, and with double jeopardy, you can't try him again. Wonderful job."

"If your client would prefer to return to his cell, that's just fine. I think he's done enough here."

"I can help," Porter said softly.

"Shut up," Dalton replied.

From the opposite corner of the table, Special Agent Frank Poole sighed. "You need to tell us about the woman, Sam. The one we found in the farmhouse."

"A farmhouse owned by you, by the way," the District Attorney added.

"That's not my house. I don't own that any more than I own the property in Simpsonville."

"But you don't deny being there with that woman?"

Hessling placed a hand on Porter's arm. "Don't answer that."

Porter shook him off. "I was there with Bishop's mother, the woman I know as Sarah Werner. She and I left together. We've been through this. I don't know who you found."

The D.A. tossed several photographs across the table at him. "That's who they found."

Porter had seen the images before, but they still made his stomach lurch. Using a razor blade or some other sharp implement, someone had repeatedly written *I am evil* over every inch of exposed skin. Her eye, ear, and tongue had been removed and placed in white boxes, like all the other 4MK victims. Her fingerprints weren't in the system, and her face had been so disfigured there was no chance of identification. Nobody held out hope for a DNA match.

Porter looked up from the photos. "*I left with Sarah Werner. I don't know who this is.*"

Poole asked, "Could this be the woman you knew as Sarah Werner?"

Porter shrugged. "Same hair, same build, but it's not her. She was alive when we left."

"Then who is this?" The D.A. pressed.

"I don't know."

The room fell silent for a moment, then Poole turned to the district attorney. "Are you going to tell him?"

The man waved a hand through the air. "Go ahead."

"Tell me what?"

Poole said, "The real Sarah Werner, the one I found murdered in her apartment in New Orleans, she was heavily linked to the people behind www.backpage.com. She represented some, provided legal services to others. Klozowski detailed her crimes in the notes he left behind."

"So she was dirty."

"Yeah."

Porter turned back to the DA. "So if someone manages to ID the woman from the farmhouse, I think you'll find she was dirty, too. The woman I know as Sarah Werner is still out there somewhere." He tapped on the top photograph. "This isn't her."

"You can't be sure."

"I lost her at the airport."

"You lost her at the airport," the DA repeated. "The woman nobody else saw but you."

"That's right."

From his briefcase, Poole took out a thick file, one Porter recognized. His treatment file from Camden. Poole slid it across the table to Porter. "This file says you imagined her."

"That file is bullshit."

Poole looked at the DA, then at Dalton and Hessling, before looking back at Porter. "I know."

Prepared to argue, Porter's mouth opened, but he said nothing.

"I don't think you were ever treated at Camden," Poole said. "We think Upchurch might have created this file, maybe with Klozowski. It's not real. Camden Treatment Center has been closed for nearly three years."

Porter was confused. "I...I met with the doctor. I was there, just last..."

Poole's gaze remained on him. "You met with a man who

claimed to be a doctor named Victor Whittenberg. A man who claimed to have treated you after your gunshot wound. There's no record of a Whittenberg ever on the staff of Camden. When you were there in February, someone went through great lengths to make it appear Camden was still a functioning institution, but it wasn't. They broke in and were gone shortly after you left. They knew you were coming. The blood that was found, the evidence of a crime left behind after your visit, that was all a hoax. The blood wasn't even human. It was feline."

"Feline?"

"A cat."

Bishop's cat.

Poole understood too. "Bishop framed you. I learned that after finding Oglesby."

130

Porter

Day 199 • 10:21 AM

"You found Oglesby?"

"Well, I found a record of Dr. Oglesby," Poole corrected. "He was on staff at Camden for nearly eleven years, but he didn't leave much of a paper trail. Because they're healthcare related, most of Camden's records are confidential. I was able to confirm he signed a number of reports, but I can't get access to the contents. We think he vanished in late '95, but there's no police report. Camden had *job abandonment* listed as their cause of employment termination, but the rest of his employment file is sparse."

"You'll find him in the lake back in Simpsonville," Porter said softly.

"Is that where you put him?" the district attorney asked straight-faced.

"That's where Bishop would have put him after retrieving his knife."

Poole and the district attorney exchanged a glance, then the DA asked, "Did you kill Tom Langlin in Simpsonville?"

Porter's fingers tightened on the edge of the table, but he managed to keep his anger in check. "I didn't kill anyone."

The DA blew out a frustrated breath and nodded at Poole. "Just tell him."

Poole rolled his fingers over the edge of the table, then turned back to Porter. "The woman found at the farmhouse had been dead at least two weeks, maybe longer. Her body had been stored in salt, like the others. We don't think you killed her. We don't believe you killed Langlin or any of the others. I think it was Bishop, Klozowski, maybe others. If we ID her, I'm fairly confident she'll have ties to www.backpage.com and the trafficking ring, like the bodies we found at the Guyon."

"So Bishop's mother is still out there somewhere," Porter said more to himself than to the group.

"If she was ever real." The DA smirked.

Porter's head shot up. "They took her photo at New Orleans prison, when they made our visitor's passes. You need to get that photo."

Poole was already shaking his head. He took a photograph from his briefcase and handed it to Porter. The image was of a middle-aged black woman. "What is this?" Porter frowned.

"That's the photo saved in the prison's central server."

Porter tossed the picture aside. "Klozowski. Had to be."

Dalton, who had remained quiet through most of this, said, "Tom Langlin was responsible for putting the Simpsonville house into your name. Sheriff Banister was able to confirm he had access to change the physical paperwork on file with the county. We think Klozowski might have hacked the electronic property records on the farmhouse. He scrubbed all these databases. They probably killed Langlin as some kind of—"

"Loose end," Porter interrupted in a quiet voice. *Father taught me the importance of picking up after myself.*

"Probably." Dalton nodded. "Looks like he created a wire trail between you and Upchurch, too. We're still piecing that together."

The district attorney took out a yellow postcard, tapped it on the edge of the table several times, then flicked it across the table.

The card was addressed to Porter. "What's that?"

"We found it in your mailbox."

"You went through my mail?"

"You're a suspect in numerous open investigations. Not only have we been going through your mail, we've cataloged it as part of an open warrant."

Porter read the card and frowned. It was an overdue library book notice. "I don't use the library."

Poole had placed four pieces of drywall on the table, each sealed in clear plastic. Porter knew about these, knew Nash had found them inside the chair at his apartment. "Are those the poems cut from the wall at 41st? Where your partner was killed?"

Poole nodded and pointed at the overdue notice. "The book referenced there is called *The Beauty of Death, The Death of Beauty*. A book of poems assembled by a man named Francisco Penafiel. The last person to check that book out was Barbara McInley." He reached across the table and placed his palm over one of the drywall pieces. "We've matched the handwriting here to samples of hers we had on file."

Porter didn't understand. "Barbara McInley, Libby's sister, Bishop's fifth victim, wrote those poems?"

Poole nodded.

"On the wall in the house where Diener was killed?"

Again, Poole nodded.

"When?"

For that, Poole didn't have an answer.

"Are you saying she's still alive?"

The room went quiet again as everyone considered this.

From his briefcase, Poole retrieved the library book. A thin volume, no more than a hundred pages. He slid it across the table to Porter. "We found it in your apartment on the shelf with a few other hardcovers."

Porter pulled the book closer. "Those were Heather's. She loved to read. This, though, I've never seen this one before." He nodded at the pieces of drywall. "Are those poems in here?"

Poole nodded. "All of them. I folded over the pages. Open it."

Porter did. Again, he didn't understand. He turned to the first page with a folded corner, the Emily Dickinson poem entitled "The

Chariot." Someone had drawn a large figure eight on the page with a black marker. As Porter flipped through the book, he realized the same symbol had been drawn on every page. "The infinity symbol," Porter said flatly. "The tattoo." He looked up at Poole. "What does it mean?"

Poole shrugged. "We don't know."

Bishop had tattooed the symbol on Emory Connor's left wrist. They found it on Jacob Kittner, the woman Porter knew as Sarah Werner. Others too.

Nobody spoke for a long time.

"There's more," Poole finally said. He reached back down into his briefcase and took out the cell phone with Porter's old business card still fastened to the back. The one Bishop left for Porter in the old roll-top desk at the farmhouse. Both were in a plastic evidence bag. "This is my phone. Bishop took it from me when he knocked me out." Poole hesitated for a moment, then said, "When I powered it up this morning, there was a text message. A new one. For you."

Porter leaned forward. "Can I see it?"

Poole glanced at the district attorney, who nodded.

Removing the phone from the bag, he handed the device to Porter. Porter's breath caught in his throat.

The message said, *I miss your calls, Sam.*

Porter found it hard to speak. "That's…that's Heather's old cell phone number."

"Your wife?" Dalton asked.

Porter nodded. "After she died, I used to call and listen to her voice mail, listen to her voice. I…I closed the account months ago. I needed to…" Before anyone could stop him, he touched the number on the screen and dialed on speakerphone. The line didn't ring. Instead, the call when straight to voicemail. It wasn't Heather's familiar voice on the other end, though. This time it was Bishop's.

"Hello, Sam. I never did get a chance to say good-bye, and I wanted to apologize for that. It was rude, impolite, and my parents raised me to be anything but rude or impolite. You asked me a question in the Guyon parking lot, something I do feel we need to address now that time permits—I was a bit rushed that morning, but now with all that behind us, the unpleasantness of the trial too, now we're free to talk, and I do so wish to talk to you. You asked who you are to me. I imagine after all we've been through recently you expect a complex answer to that rather basic question, but the truth is, the answer is very simple. *Who are you to me?* You're nothing, Sam. You're a nobody. You are a filthy, faded business card Tegan found on the floor of your partner's van. You're someone who could have helped but didn't. You're someone who looked the other way when you should have had eyes front. You were nothing but a means to an end. Your punishment is to spend the rest of your life knowing what your lack of action brought upon others. Every time you visit Heather's tombstone, I want you to remember one simple thing. You put her there."

Porter felt himself sink a little deeper into his chair, a lump growing in his throat that he was unable to swallow. All eyes in the room were on the phone as Bishop continued.

"It's important you understand loss, Sam. It's important you know loss as I know loss. My parents are gone. Libby McInley, the only person I ever truly cared for, is gone. Weasel, Vincent, Paul, Tegan, Kristina...all gone. The Kid, Klozowski, he gave his own life in their memory—there could be no greater sacrifice. Gone too. You may not believe I feel pain, Sam, but I do. Every time I close my eyes, I still hear Libby crying. I can still taste the salt of her tears on my fingertips. I wake in the middle of the night and feel her hand in mine for that brief moment between slumber and wakefulness. Then she's gone again, and I'm alone. You have been blessed with the ability to forget, but I have no such ability. Your lost time is my darkest memory, and in that, I don't wish to suffer alone. I want you to remember, *need* you to remember. You will do that for me, Sam. You will remember for the sake of all those we have lost. Then we can suffer together.

"I left something for you, Sam. A missing puzzle piece. Your very own white box tied with a black string. I'm honestly surprised it hasn't been found. I suppose it's better to joke about the stink than be the person who has to clean it up. Better to ignore the foul things in life than to face them. Not the first time you've turned your back, and probably not the last. Perhaps next time you'll pause before you walk away."

When Bishop finished speaking, there was a beep. For a moment, they had all forgotten they were listening to a voice mail message.

Porter reached to the phone and clicked the END button. "Take me to Metro, now."

131

Porter

Day 199 • 11:39 AM

The district attorney refused to remove Porter's restraints, and while Porter didn't much care, shuffling through the halls of Chicago Metro drew a number of stares. Most looked away the moment he met their gaze, but others lingered, their eyes filled with contempt. They all looked at him like he was broken.

The press had crucified him—not only had he been blamed for Bishop's initial escape, they doubled down the moment Bishop came out with that undercover op nonsense. When the information Klozowski left behind went public, opinions shifted even further, and Bishop was seen as some kind of hero. These blinders went up around the city, and people landed in one of two camps— those who sided with Bishop and felt Porter was out to frame him, and the lingering few who believed Porter was innocent. The few who had sided with Porter most likely jumped ship with Bishop's not-guilty verdict. Porter was certain the blame would land squarely on his shoulders, and that was where most of his coworkers appeared to be. He blew the case. He lost sight and let Bishop best him. What the press said wasn't relevant, but he dropped the ball as a cop.

Porter clambered inside the elevator with Poole, the district attorney, Dalton, and Hessling.

When the door opened on the basement level, Nash was standing in the hallway.

Porter hadn't seen him since the trial and they hadn't spoken in more than a month. "Brian."

"Hey."

Nash's eyes drifted over Porter—the orange jumpsuit, the handcuffs, and leg restraints. "You'd think someone would spring for one of those Hannibal Lecter masks and a hand truck to complete the look."

The group stepped out of the elevator into the hallway, and the door closed behind them.

Nash looked down at his shoes, shuffled his feet, then back at Porter. "Poole called me last night and filled me in on everything he'd found. I want you to know that Clair and I have always known you were innocent. We wanted to talk to you, but—"

Dalton cleared his throat. "I ordered them not to. Not just them, the entire department. Not until we had all the facts. You've only got three days left on your sentence for the prison break in New Orleans." He glanced at the DA. "In light of this new evidence, I can't imagine there will be additional charges, from anyone. We'll coordinate a joint statement, I'll square away the press…"

Porter ignored him and smiled at Nash. "You and Clair, huh?"

"Yeah, me and Clair."

Something had died in Nash the day Klozowski killed himself. Something died in all of them. Porter was glad the two of them had found some kind of happiness together. In the end, that's what would carry them all through to the other side.

"Is she here?"

Nash nodded down the hall. "She was in the War Room packing up. No more task force, no reason to be down in the basement anymore. We're back at our desks in the bull pen. She went upstairs to meet with a walk-in; someone asking for you. We've gotten a lot of those lately, mainly cranks."

"You'll want to see this," Porter said, starting down the hallway.

"See what?"

Poole had to unlock the door. The feds had changed the lock on their temporary office across the hall from the War Room shortly after Porter stole the McInley file. Although most of the case-related material had been moved to the Bureau's Chicago field office, they hadn't completely vacated the space.

The moment Poole opened the door, the smell hit them. Faint, but there. Hessling wrinkled his nose. Poole stepped into the room and switched on the lights.

Porter shuffled toward the back left corner, his shackles jangling. He nodded at Nash. "Help me move this desk."

"The mystery stain?"

Porter nodded.

Together, they each lifted a corner of the old metal desk and carried it several paces to the right before setting it down again.

The stain in the tan Berber carpet was about a foot in diameter and had been there for years. Certainly not the only stain on the floors of Chicago Metro. Renovation was not high on the city's budget list. The smell had come and gone, at its worst during the summer months. There really wasn't a way to describe it—some kind of cross between skunk, wet wool, and sour milk. Porter had personally sprung for a carpet cleaner at one point, and that seemed to help for a few days, but the smell soon returned. They moved the desk over it, added a few boxes, and went on to other things. When the FBI moved in, they certainly had no reason to deal with it.

On his hands and knees, Porter studied the stain. "The carpet's been pulled up and replaced."

Nash appeared puzzled. "Who would do that?"

"Does anyone have a knife?"

Poole produced a Ranger Buck knife, not unlike the one Bishop used to carry.

Porter opened the blade and used the tip to snag the corner of the carpet and tug it out from under the baseboard. A square had been cut out of the padding. creating a small compartment. Within that space was a white box tied with black string, no bigger than a pen case.

132

Porter

Day 199 • 11:42 AM

Someone muttered something about evidence, but on some level, they all knew they were beyond that. Porter took out the box, removed the string, and opened the cover. Inside were two glass vials, both labeled MONTEHUGH LABS – CORONA VIRUS – SEVERE ACUTE RESPIRATORY SYNDROME.

"Holy shit," Nash said.

"Don't touch it," Poole said. "I'll get someone down here. That's our missing two vials."

Porter stared at the small glass tubes. "Klozowski must have left them here. He was the only one with access. But this means he hid them before he got locked in Stroger. They used one vial to fill that needle Clair found in the hospital locker, left the empty in my New Orleans hotel room, and hid the other two here. They never intended to release the virus."

Poole was on the phone, half listening to Porter.

Nash said, "Could he have used the tunnels to get here from the hospital?"

"No way," Dalton replied. "This building is too new to be part of that network. Besides, someone would have recognized him and said something. All of Metro knew he was stuck in the hospital with the others."

500 • J. D. BARKER

Nobody had heard Clair come into the room. She was standing by the door, her eyes filled with tears. She cleared her throat. "I just met with Robin Hillburn." She looked first to Nash, then to Dalton and Poole, then stepped across the room and knelt down beside Porter, an envelope in her hand. "She...she gave me this, for you. She said Derrick left it under her pillow the day he...died. Left it along with a note for her. She wouldn't share that one, said it was too personal. But she wanted me to give this to you. She said she was sorry she waited so long. She put it away, hid it all these years. Wasn't sure she wanted to share it. She was worried about what it would do to her husband's memory. When Poole visited, with everything in the news, she realized this information wasn't hers to keep, not anymore."

Someone had opened the envelope long ago, the glue no longer tacky. There was a letter inside, several pages, handwritten. Porter scanned the text. "Oh my God."

Clair placed a hand on Porter's shoulder. "I read it, Sam. I know I shouldn't have, but...I'm so sorry." She paused for a second. "Robin thinks Welderman or Stocks forged the note they found with Derrick's body. That scared her, too. She didn't know what they would do to her if this information got out."

By the time Porter finished reading, his hand was shaking. The pages of the letter fluttered to the ground and he found himself sitting, his back against the side of the desk. He looked up at Poole, at Nash, and the others.

Clair put her arms around his neck. "None of this is on you, Sam. You hear me? You need to let it all go. We'll help you, I promise. Forget Bishop, forget what he did, forget all of it."

Sam told her he would. As memories began to flood back, as the holes in his past began to knit together, he swore that he would. He swore this to all of them. Funny, how the littlest of lies begin.

133

Bishop

Day 203 • 9:48 AM

Anson Bishop's attorney notified the press he would be released from custody at noon on Wednesday, September 2, and a press conference would be held in the lobby of the Cook County Courthouse, where Bishop and his attorney would make a joint statement and follow with a question-and-answer period. He was, in fact, released on August 31 at eleven in the evening. He left the courthouse through a loading bay in the back with no one in attendance other than a janitor smoking a cigarette, his foot holding the back door open just enough to prevent the smoke detector six feet away from going off. Bishop climbed into an idling town car, where he found a black leather bag waiting for him on the seat. Within that bag were several forms of identification under various names, credit cards, clothing, toiletries, car keys, and ten thousand dollars in cash. The town car took him directly to the Radisson at Midway Airport, where he darkened his hair, took a three-hour nap, then boarded a red-eye to Boston under the name Daron Metzler.

Without the buzz of paparazzi surrounding him, he went unrecognized both on the plane and as he made his way through Logan International Airport to long-term parking. The keys found in his bag unlocked a silver two-year-old Mercedes C-300 left in space K302 with a full tank of gas.

The drive to New Castle, New Hampshire, should have only taken about an hour, but Bishop stopped for breakfast in Newburyport at a little seaside diner called Mike's. On one of the cable news channels, they played one of the videos Klozowski had left behind on his work computer—in this one he confessed to all the initial 4MK murders. From Calli Tremell right up through the abduction of Emory Connors. When the video finished, several reporters debated whether or not the jury in Bishop's trial had somehow seen the confession, even though it wasn't released until they were in deliberation. Bishop left before hearing whatever they concluded. Here, too, nobody recognized him.

After crossing the bridge from Portsmouth to New Castle Island, he drove slowly through the charming old-world neighborhood, through the center of the island, and followed the signs to the Great Island Common, a quaint park on the shore of the Atlantic. There were only a handful of cars there, most likely belonging to the several joggers or the mothers with their children on the playground.

Bishop got out and walked to one of the benches along the water's edge. He drew in the salty fall air, savored it a moment, then took a seat next to a man reading the morning paper. The headline read: CHICAGO DETECTIVE IN 4MK CASE RELEASED, ON INDEFINITE SUSPENDED LEAVE.

The man beside him turned the page and crossed his legs. He wore the most hideous red and green argyle sweater and glasses that made him appear far older than he probably was. When he looked up from the paper and out at the churning ocean waves, he took them off and let them dangle around his neck on a silver chain. "Beautiful view."

Bishop fought back the urge to smile. "You look ridiculous."

The man shrugged. "I thought you might help me say good-bye to Victor Wittenberg, Ph.D., before I burn the outfit." He raised the glasses and slipped them over the bridge of his nose. "I've grown rather fond of these."

"It's good to see you, Father."

"You too, Anson." He glanced down at his watch. "You're twelve minutes early."

"I'm sorry." Bishop said this before he realized it wasn't a criticism, simply his father pointing out the time.

His father waved a hand dismissively. He folded the newspaper and set it down between them but continued to look out over the water. "I'm proud of you, son. I know that's not something you've heard from me as much as you should have growing up, but I am. I'm proud of the man you've become and all that you've accomplished." He patted the newspaper. "All of this, the people you took down. The world is a better place with you in it."

"The world is a cesspool."

"Less so now."

"Maybe."

Bishop's father tapped the newspaper. "I haven't seen any mentions of the bodies in our lake, not in the press anyway."

Bishop's gaze had found a sailboat about a quarter mile off shore, bobbing in the water near an old lighthouse on a tiny rocky island. "Klozowski said they identified Mr. Carter, Welderman, and Stocks. They suspect Oglesby is another, but they don't have DNA to make a match. The other two are a mystery to them, at least for now."

Father sighed. "You're mother certainly had a temper back then."

They both fell silent for a moment. Then Bishop said, "Have you forgiven her? For running away with Mrs. Carter and Kirby?"

He seemed to consider this for a long time, then nodded softly. "I think we both realized we'd come to an end. We were together for you, not each other, not anymore. The glue holding a relationship needs to be stronger than that. If things hadn't ended when they did, I might have become number seven in that lake." He fidgeted with the corner of the newspaper and grinned. "If you hadn't already killed me in that little book of yours, that is. My clever boy."

"You look terrible in Christmas colors, Gerald."

Bishop and his father both looked to their left. They hadn't heard her walk up.

"Hello, Mother," Bishop said.

She wore a J. Crew sweater over a Loft dress. She'd lightened her hair to a dirty blonde. The color looked good on her.

She smiled out over the water. "This is gorgeous, Gerald. You've been holding out on us."

"I go by Warren now. Warren Cray. I moved here about a year after Simpsonville. I tried a few other places along the way, but something about the sea has always drawn me. I own a small antique store in town now, going on twelve years. A quiet life. I like it."

"I'm looking forward to a quiet life," she said.

Father stood and looked her over. "You look well."

Mother smiled and hugged him. "You too. It's been too long."

Someone honked a horn behind them, three long chirps. Anything but quiet.

A golden retriever running with his owner barked twice.

Bishop knew that horn. "I'm not the only one who's early."

The three of them turned to see a white Ford Mustang with a black racing stripe down the center rolling toward them through the parking lot. The car came to a stop at a short fence a few feet behind the bench. Vincent Weidner got out of the driver's side and stretched. "Had to jump the battery. She's been sitting in storage for so long. Ran like a dream once we got out on the highway, though."

Bishop stood from the bench and walked over. "You look good, for a dead man."

"Not the only one, I see," Vincent said, nodding at Father. He jerked a thumb back at the car. "This guy sang half the trip. I'm never driving with him again. When he wasn't singing, he was screwing with his laptop. Nobody knows how to enjoy a road trip anymore."

"It's not a laptop. It's an Alienware 17 with an eighth-generation processor and GTX video. Don't insult my hardware," a voice called out from the car. "I've got a lot of balls in the air. I need to stay on top of things for a little longer." The passenger door opened. Edwin Klozowski stepped out of the Mustang and nodded. "Hey, Anson."

"Hey, Kid."

134

Bishop

Day 203 • 9:58 AM

"You shaved your head?"

Klozowski ran his hand over his smooth skull, his long hair gone. "This is my *Breaking Bad* look. I'm still working on the goatee."

"Nobody's looking for you. Not anymore. That was a big explosion."

Kloz looked embarrassed. "I may have overestimated the C4. They still haven't found my body in that mess. I went through all that trouble to swap out DNA and fingerprints, and they don't even have a thumb to match."

"They'll find something; give them time."

"Doubt it."

Vincent came up behind him and squeezed Klozowski's shoulders. "I, for one, am a fan of being dead. Student loan debt, gone. Credit card debt, gone. Ex-girlfriends, gone."

Mother had walked up, Father behind her. She was eyeing Klozowski's bald head. "You're sure about this?"

Kloz nodded. "I combed every possible identification database and changed out every bit of information for all of us right down to old driver's license photos on file at the DMV. The bodies we left match the lives we're all leaving behind on every level. As far as the world is concerned, we're all dead. All except for Anson, and he's free and clear on double jeopardy."

"With everyone associated with BackPage either dead or in hiding, nobody is going to miss the few former employees we used here, the ones you swapped for us," Father said. "The police and FBI look so bad at this point, they'll do anything to make all of this go away. Nobody is digging, not anymore."

Reaching into the Mustang, Klozowski removed several leatherbound packages, each tagged with a name. He placed two on the roof of the car and handed the others out. "That's your new identification and credit cards. Bank accounts and credit histories are all established. I set each of us up with multiple banks. Funds are courtesy of the coffers at BackPage. I cleaned them out." He looked at Mother. "When added to the money you and Lisa Carter took from Talbot back in the day, we have nearly four million dollars each."

Somehow, the smile on Vincent's face grew larger.

Father produced a small bottle of Jameson whiskey from a coat pocket. "I'd like to propose a toast."

"I don't drink," Bishop said.

"You do today, son."

Father uncapped the bottle and held it up between them. The edge of his lips curled in a smile as he looked at his son. "You cleaned house, champ. Eye for an eye." He studied the faces of Klozowski, Vincent, and Mother. "All of you. I couldn't be more proud." He raised the bottle to his lips and took a hearty drink, then handed it Bishop.

Bishop looked down at the bottle for a moment, at the whiskey glistening on the lip. He handed the bottle back to his father. "Hold this for a moment."

Reaching into his pocket, he took out a piece of paper and unfolded it, held the drawing up so the others could see. The drawing was of a girl about fourteen wearing a red sweater, a mischievous little smile and a glisten in her eye. "A Paul Upchurch original. Maybelle Markel."

"You know that's Tegan, right?" Vincent said, smiling down at the drawing. "He always had a thing for her."

Bishop nodded. He took out a lighter, and while the others watched, he lit the corner of the page. He held the drawing as long as he could, all of them watching as the flame crawled across the paper, the image slowly turning black and floating away on the wind. He dropped the last bit of it and let it burn on the ground. Nearly a minute passed before he spoke again. He took the bottle from his father and held it close to his chest. "To the ones we lost along the way, Paul Upchurch and Lisa Carter. Their memory will live on in all of us." He took a drink and shared the bottle with the others. For the briefest of moments, he thought Mother might cry at the thought of Mrs. Carter. She didn't, though. She never cried. Instead, she smiled up at him. "What do you plan to do now, Anson? Now that this is all over?"

He considered this a moment. "I think I'll write a book. I've always found it amusing, what people will believe when you slap a colorful cover over some text and tell them it's fiction."

A yellow Volkswagen Bug rolled up behind them and parked near Vincent's Mustang.

Bishop glanced over and smiled. "That's the girls."

135

Bishop

Day 203 • 10:08 AM

Bishop rounded the side of the Volkswagen to the driver side. When the window rolled down, he leaned inside and kissed the driver. "Hey, you."

"Hey, you."

Libby McInley smiled up at him from behind a pair of giant Gucci sunglasses, much too large for her face. Her hair had grown longer since he last saw her, probably halfway down her back now. It had gotten curlier too. Her skin glowed with a healthy tan. She wore white shorts and a red tank top.

Kristina Niven had her door open and bounded out of the passenger seat the moment she saw Vincent Weidner standing off to the side. She jumped up into his arms, wrapped her legs around his back, and kissed him.

Tegan was sound asleep in the back, her legs curled up to her chest.

"How was Florida?" Bishop asked.

"Hot," Libby replied. "Barbara says hello."

Barbara McInley had been the first death he and Klozowski had faked when Anthony Warnick and the others got too close. A trial run, of sorts. The body the authorities believed was Barbara McInley was actually a runaway named Loria Tutson. When

Bishop found Tutson, she had been recruiting other children off the streets for BackPage, luring them in with false promises of money and stability, only to help get them to sale at the Guyon for a 3 percent cut. Bishop had enjoyed ending her.

Libby had his hand in hers and was studying his fingertips. "What did you get into?"

Bishop's fingers were covered in soot.

"I need to wash my hands. Then we should get out of here."

She tilted her head in the direction of a small clapboard building perched on the opposite side of the parking lot. "We passed the bathrooms on the way in."

He leaned back into the car and gave her another kiss. "Wait for me?"

"Always."

As he ran toward the bathroom, he heard the others laughing and joking behind him. There was a time when he thought he'd never hear that sound again. It was nice.

As he pushed through the door into the men's room, a motion sensor turned on the light. The scent of lemons hung in the air, not heavy but present. For a public restroom, he found it immaculate. He washed his hands under the warm water and was busy drying them when he heard the stall door open behind him.

Bishop felt his heart thud as he looked into the mirror, at the face looking back at him. "How did you find me?"

Detective Sam Porter stepped out of the stall, a small black revolver in his gloved hand. "The janitor smoking at the courthouse. He called me with a description of your car. All taxis and town cars in the city are tracked by GPS. My Metro passwords all still work, so that was easy enough. I followed you from the hotel to the airport. Wasn't hard to find out your flight. Fake name didn't really slow things down. Funny how a little money will get whatever information you need, but you know all about that. I took a different flight to Logan, one that landed twelve minutes before yours. I thought for sure you spotted me when you were at the rental car counter, but I guess you didn't. I waited in the parking lot when you went into Mike's and got something to eat. That was tough. I'm still hungry. Then I followed you here." He licked his lips and nodded toward the door. "I knew they were all still alive. I didn't figure it out right away, but I've had some time to think while I was locked up in that little cell you put me in. When we were on the phone back at the Guyon, you told me, 'she and I *have* a special place in our hearts for Mr. Franklin Kirby.' Present tense, not *had*, you said *have*. Your game clicked, then. I realized all of it had been a smokescreen. With Kloz's help, I'm sure you had no trouble making your friends disappear, reinventing them as someone else."

Bishop started to turn around, and Porter brought up the gun. "Don't."

"Okay."

"Put both your palms flat on the counter."

"Sure, Sam."

Porter took a step closer. Bishop noticed he had plastic bags on his shoes. They were taped around his ankles.

"Don't do something you'll regret, Sam."

Porter chuckled softly. "I don't *regret* anymore. I don't really *feel* anymore. You managed to kill that part of me. I would have shot you back at the Guyon if the feds hadn't hit me first. That's what you wanted me to do, right? Shoot you? Just another part of your plan—get the cop to shoot you in public as a final little black bow on your own box, win over those last few people who still thought you might be guilty—Porter tried to shut him down before he could go public, he must be telling the truth—it's the dirty cop, always has been."

Bishop said nothing to this.

The gun twisted in Porter's hand. "Did Warnick actually kill anyone? Or was that all you too? The woman in the cemetery, the one on the tracks, the ones we thought were Tegan and Kristina—I bet those were you. You posed them and copied your own signature. You wanted the world to think your friends were dead, so you pinned those on Warnick, right?"

"Warnick was as dirty as the mayor. As dirty as Talbot and all the others," Bishop said quietly.

"Maybe," Porter interrupted, "but not guilty of killing them."

Again, Bishop said nothing.

Porter nodded toward the door. "I saw your mother drive up. Who was the woman you left at the farmhouse? It wasn't her, so who was it?"

"I don't know what—"

Porter rushed up behind him, dug the barrel of the gun into the back of Bishop's neck. "WHO THE FUCK WAS THE WOMAN AT THE FARMHOUSE?"

"Easy, Sam." Bishop's voice remained calm.

Bishop heard a familiar click—Porter pulling back the hammer on the gun.

"Are you wired? Are you recording this?"

"No," Porter replied.

"She was a nobody, Sam. A low-level runner with BackPage."

"Who happened to look like your mother."

Bishop nodded.

Porter took several steps backwards, toward the stalls. He didn't say anything for nearly a minute. "Poole gave me the rest of the diaries, the ones someone threw at him in the chaos at the Guyon. I didn't leave that note, the one you found pinned to Stocks in Finicky's car."

Bishop went quiet again.

"It wasn't me," Porter insisted.

In the mirror, Bishop looked up at him. "You're as dirty as the rest of them. I saw you there, at the farmhouse. In the alley."

Porter rubbed the back of his neck, stared for several seconds, then took an envelope from the inside pocket of his jacket. He tossed it onto the counter next to Bishop's hand. "Read it."

At first, Bishop didn't move. Then he reached for the envelope and pulled out the pages. "What is this?"

"Hillburn's suicide note," Porter said flatly. "The real one."

In the mirror, Bishop's eyes were locked on Porter. He held his gaze for a moment, then went back to the pages.

"Out loud," Porter instructed.

Bishop nodded, cleared his throat, and began to read, "Dear Sam. I've done some things in my life I don't expect you to understand. I've written this letter about a half dozen times, and every time I start over, I think I'm trying to find an explanation for the things I've done, and it's just not there. I'd hoped for some a-ha moment, something to not only explain my actions to you, my wife, and those who will no doubt ask questions later, but to myself. I've come to the conclusion that those answers don't exist. I don't remember the moment my life went bad—there was never a choice between two doors. Instead, there were a bunch of small missteps, each one leading to another, and before I knew it, when I looked behind me, I'd traveled so far into the woods there was no going back. A couple hands at a poker game didn't go my way, I borrowed a couple bucks from someone I thought was a friend, I tried to win that back with the ponies, had to borrow a little more. Those kinds of people, they're all smiles when they're handing over the cash, not so much when they ask for their money back. Stocks and Welderman, they worked Homicide, not the crew you ran with, so I'd understand if you didn't know them. I met them at the poker games, Welderman's regular Thursday night. Funny to think I almost invited you once, but I knew you weren't into cards. Wonder what would have happened if I had? I bet you would have told me to fold on a two pair of Aces and Kings. If I did, my life would have gone in a very different direction. I didn't invite you, though, and I didn't fold, and a month later, in debt to my eyeballs, I agreed to let those two use my van. The second time, they asked me to drive the van. Little baby steps like that, steps into the mud. You don't realize you're sinking until you're up to your ankles.

"I didn't ask them about the kids. I didn't want to know, and they didn't volunteer much information. They did their thing, and I did mine. I paid down my debt one trip to that motel after another. I'm honestly not sure when you started watching us. I learned later that one of the kids found your business card and called you, told you what was happening, but I didn't know that at the time. The first time I saw you across the street in that parking lot, watching the motel, watching me in my van, I wasn't 100 percent certain it was even you. Tough to see at night. I suppose part of me didn't want to see. It was Stocks who told me it was you. He was the one who told me to handle it. I thought about my debt. Certainly that would knock it down. I didn't want to go there, Sam. You gotta believe me. But I had a wife at home, and we were starting a family. I needed that monkey off my back. They told me to bring you in. I knew you'd never go along, not you, not straight-and-narrow Sam Porter, no way. But I didn't tell them that. I think I saved your life by telling that little fib. Not sure how much time I bought, but I bought you some. Why the hell didn't you back off? Half the cops were on the take—you could have walked away. You didn't, though. I saw you watching me. I saw you following me. When you came out to the farmhouse that night, when you followed me out there. There was no turning back, not for you, not for me...

"There's no easy way to say this, Sam, so I'm just going to come right out with it. We had that farmhouse wired, and we knew that kid Weasel had called you and set up the meet. We also knew it went sideways when you followed me out to the farmhouse. That's why I drove him back to the city. I knew he'd get out, escape the van, *we let him*. I knew he'd try and give you whatever evidence those kids put together. We didn't know where they'd hidden it, though. We needed him to lead us there. Lead you there too. He took the bag with the money, the camera, and led us right to the notebook they'd hidden—the one detailing all the activity at the Carriage House Inn. When I saw the notebook, when I had the notebook, him, and you all together, something inside me closed off. The little bit of good inside me went to sleep, because that's what needed to happen. I knew if I thought about it, I'd never be able to shoot you. I took out the gun Stocks had given me, and so help me, I pulled the trigger on you."

Bishop read the next sentence in his head and paused for a moment. His voice threatened to crack when he read it aloud.

"I finished off the boy too. That's what Stocks and Welderman wanted. I couldn't bring myself to put a second shot in you. I didn't think you'd make it to the hospital, but you did, you tough son-of-a-bitch, you did, and then it was too late for me. The boy's body in my van. Their little bag of evidence in my van. They told me to make it all disappear. I screwed that up too. I kept it. Figured it was some kind of insurance, and best to stash it all away. When you woke from the coma with no memory, I told myself I was in the clear. Nobody knew anything. Here's the thing, though: I knew. No matter what I did to forget, something reminded me, and over the years, those reminders got louder. Guilt has a way of screaming. I could hear that dead kid out in my van, louder every night.

"I didn't start out my life expecting to be a bad cop. A series of small events got me there. Sitting here now, down in my basement, with a rope coiled up on the floor writing a letter to you—guilt got me here. I've got to silence those screams.

"I think those kids blamed you for not acting sooner. For not rushing the farmhouse and arresting everybody. Kids don't understand what it takes to build a case. They don't understand good police work. I suppose, neither do I. You do, Sam. Always did. You're a fine cop. The kind of cop I wish I had been. You do right for the both of us. Take care of my Robin for me. Tell her I was one of the good guys, once."

When Bishop finished, he read the letter a second time to himself, then folded the pages, slipped them back into the envelope, and set it on the counter beside him.

Porter was first to speak. "Tegan called me a few weeks before I came out to the farmhouse. I remember that now. She...she had spoken so fast on that first call. All I got was something about them taking pictures of her at the motel. I didn't know about the prostitution. I didn't even know she was underage. I didn't know how big this all was. I started to piece things together, then I got the call from the boy...Weasel. He told me to meet him, they had evidence for me..."

"And Hillburn shot you when you tried to collect it," Bishop said. "Then he shot Weasel."

Porter nodded.

"I didn't know he called you," Bishop admitted. "Tegan never told me, neither of them did... I...we had no idea..." his voice trailed off as he considered this. How it would have changed so much.

The gun still steady, Porter asked, "What happened to the girls?"

Bishop could have lied, but there was no point. "Tegan and Kristina managed to tie up Finicky back at the farmhouse, but neither of them had a father who taught them the proper knots. Finicky got loose, managed to wrestle the gun from Tegan. Then she made some phone calls. Kirby was part of the crew they sent to clean up. I thought...I thought you were too. They took The Kid to one of their own doctors at first, Stanford Pentz, but his injuries were too severe—he was worthless to them, so they dumped him at a hospital outside Charlotte. I suppose he was lucky they didn't just kill him. The girls were moved to another holding house, this one in Wisconsin. They kept them there until it was time for the sale, time to get to the Guyon. Vincent, Paul, and I didn't learn that until we had a chat with Dr. Oglesby, one final session. He was kind enough to return my knife to me that night, the photo of Mother and Mrs. Carter too. In return, I buried him in my lake with his friends."

Bishop tried to turn, but Porter thrust the gun toward him. "Face the mirror, keep your palms on the counter."

He nodded, did what he was told. "We waited at the Guyon, managed to get them out, and hid in an abandoned brownstone on the west side with some other homeless kids. Stayed there for nearly two years."

Bishop started to turn around again. "Sam, I thought—"

"Don't," Porter said. "Just don't. Face the mirror."

Through the window, near the shoreline, Bishop saw Kristina glued to Vincent's side, a big grin on her face. Tegan was awake, laughing at something Libby must have said. His mother and father were both facing the water, only a few inches apart. Everything as it should be.

Porter didn't say anything for a long while. When he did, there was an edge to his voice. "I need to know the truth about something. Frankly, the only thing I even give a shit about anymore. The *only* thing. Did you really give Harnell Campbell the .38 and drive him to that convenience store?"

Bishop said nothing.

"Or did you just say that to get me to come after you? I've thought a lot about it. You needed me angry. You needed me unstable, running on emotions instead of logic. I understand why you would say something like that, but I need to hear it from you. Was it true or just something you said to get what you needed out of me? I need to know—*are you responsible for Heather's death?*"

In the mirror, Bishop glanced down at the bags on Porter's feet. "Who knows you're here, Sam?"

"Not a damn soul. You're not the only one with access to fake IDs."

Bishop forced his breathing to slow, forced his body to remain calm, as Father had taught him. He nodded toward the window. "If I tell you the truth, will you let them all go? Will you let my Libby go?"

Porter nodded slowly. "You have my word."

"All of them?"

"All of them."

It was Bishop's turn to nod. "I did, Sam. I might as well have killed Heather myself. Harnell Campbell was so hopped up on meth, I could have gotten him to do just about anything that night."

Porter's face went pale. A vein on the side of his head throbbed hard enough to be visible from across the room. It took him a moment to process this. His finger left the guard and wrapped over the trigger.

Porter swallowed, his voice thin. "Calli Tremell, Elle Borton, Missy Lumax, Susan Devoro, Allison Cramer, and Jodi Blumington…did you kill them, did you kidnap Emory…or was it Kloz?"

Bishop looked down at the sink. Some bubbles from the soap were caught on the lip of the drain. He wanted to turn the water on, wash them away. He didn't. Instead, Bishop closed his eyes. "I killed them all, Sam. And it was so fucking sweet."

The single gunshot inside the small cinderblock building was loud enough to echo out over the park. On the rocks near the shoreline, half a dozen seagulls shot up into the air and disappeared into the morning sky before the last of that bang faded away.

*   *   *

May 2019
Pittsburgh, PA

Author's Note

It's hard to say good-bye. I've lived with Sam Porter, Anson Bishop, and the others for several years now, and watching them pack their bags and leave has been difficult for me. I knew this day would come, though, and I prepared as best I could. I like to think they're all in a better place now, moving on with their lives, as I have. Most, anyway.

When I started the series, a particular question weighed heavily on my mind—can a serial killer be made? Is it possible for a good person to be shaped into a sociopath simply because of the environment in which they grew up? Throughout my life, I've met people who were raised under the most horrible of conditions and turned out just fine. To the contrary, I've also known people who, as children, had every possible advantage in life and squandered that opportunity as they grew older. They went sour. I've spoken to countless killers and found they came from every possible background—demographics, social standing, and financial situation may have played a part in the person they would become, but there was always another force at play, one that was stronger—the human spirit. Whether good or bad, that spirit overcame life's obstacles. That killer gene—psychotic or sociopathic—was either there at the get-go or it wasn't. It wasn't a seed that could be planted and nurtured any more than it could be squashed when first noticed in someone thought to be bad.

Anson Bishop believed he was doing the right thing. Was he? I suppose that's up to you to decide.

As with my other books, many of the places described here are real. If you're ever in Chicago, check out the old Cook County Hospital. At last visit, it was still there in the center of town, a padlock on the door, developers unsure what to do. If you happen to get inside, you'll find the statue of Protection right where Kloz left it (although the mayor has been removed).

BackPage.com is real as well, or was, rather. When the site was dismantled, one of the largest human trafficking rings went with it. Child pornography and prostitution as well. What started out as one of the first online answers to printed classified ads shifted focus over time, went bad. I suppose great ideas can go sour too.

Once you've finished reading the FBI page now in place where BackPage.com once thrived, try typing Focused Ultrasound Therapy into your search browser of choice. While still an infant in the medical world, the treatment has shown significant promise, particularly in the treatment of brain tumors. I'd like to thank John Grisham for turning me on to it; fascinating stuff.

Special thanks to Tim Mudie for editing not only this book, but the other two in the series. And thanks to my agents—Kristin Nelson, Jenny Meyer, and Angela Cheng Caplan for helping me find a home for the series around the world both in print and on the screen.

Thanks to the fans everywhere who helped take my little story to the top of various bestseller lists. You're the reason I do this.

Thank you to my incredible wife, Dayna, for putting up with the thousands of Post-it notes around our home necessary to keep this story straight in my head. They can come down now, go in a little white box secured with black string. Maybe one day I'll give them another look.

Until next time—

jd

Lightning Source UK Ltd.
Milton Keynes UK
UKHW012246200120
357305UK00004B/14/J